"Agent [...] [...]g the empty [...] [...]e that should have been occupied by her head.

"Yes, sir," Susan replied through simulated speech across their shared virtual senses. Her current body—a Type-92 combat frame—took the form of a black skeletal humanoid festooned with maneuvering boosters and weaponry. She squared her shoulders and stood at attention within the captain's office aboard Chronoport Defender-Two. "You wished to speak with me?"

"I did." The chronoport captain continued to regard Susan's headless body with barely a tick on his face. "I know I asked to see you immediately after we returned to the True Present, but perhaps our discussion can wait."

"Why's that, sir? Is something wrong?"

"Well . . ." The faintest hint of a grimace leaked through his cool professionalism. "I had assumed you'd switch back into your general purpose synthoid before coming here."

"Oh, right." Susan nodded in understanding. Or rather, tried to. Instead, the severed power and data cables of her neck trunk wiggled back and forth. "I'm sorry to report I'm unable to switch bodies at the moment." She gestured with a thumb over her shoulder. "The operators need to saw me open before they can retrieve my connectome case. I thought you wouldn't want to wait that long, so I came to see you straight away."

"I see. I suppose I can't fault your thought process there, though that still leaves the matter of your head."

"What about it, sir?"

"It appears to have been shot off."

"You should see the other guy."

—from "Doctor Quiet"
by Jacob Holo

BAEN BOOKS edited by HANK DAVIS

The Human Edge by Gordon R. Dickson
The Best of Gordon R. Dickson
We the Underpeople by Cordwainer Smith
When the People Fell by Cordwainer Smith

THE TECHNIC CIVILIZATION SAGA
The Van Rijn Method by Poul Anderson
David Falkayn: Star Trader by Poul Anderson
Rise of the Terran Empire by Poul Anderson
Young Flandry by Poul Anderson
Captain Flandry: Defender of the Terran Empire
by Poul Anderson
Sir Dominic Flandry: The Last Knight of Terra
by Poul Anderson
Flandry's Legacy by Poul Anderson

The Best of the Bolos: Their Finest Hour
created by Keith Laumer

A Cosmic Christmas
A Cosmic Christmas 2 You
In Space No One Can Hear You Scream
The Baen Big Book of Monsters
As Time Goes By
Future Wars…and Other Punchlines
Worst Contact
Things from Outer Space
If This Goes Wrong…

BAEN BOOKS edited by CHRISTOPHER RUOCCHIO

Star Destroyers with Tony Daniel
Space Pioneers with Hank Davis
Overruled with Hank Davis
Cosmic Corsairs with Hank Davis
World Breakers with Tony Daniel
Sword and Planet
Time Troopers with Hank Davis
Worlds Long Lost with Sean CW Korsgaard

To purchase any of these titles in e-book form,
please go to www.baen.com.

TIME TROOPERS

★ ★ ★

edited by HANK DAVIS and CHRISTOPHER RUOCCHIO

Copyright © 2022 by Hank Davis and Christopher Ruocchio

Introduction: "From Here to Eternity . . . and Back Again" © 2022 by Hank Davis; "All You Zombies—" © 1959 by Robert A. Heinlein; "The Archaenaut" © 2022 by Christopher Ruocchio; "The Long Remembered Thunder" © 1963 by Keith Laumer; "Delenda Est" © 1991 by Poul Anderson; "Evading History" © 2022 by Hank Davis; "Recruiting Station" © 1942 by A.E. Van Vogt; "The Oldest Soldier" © 1960 by Fritz Leiber; "House of Bones" © 1988 by Robert Silverberg; "Free Time" © 2022 by Sarah A. Hoyt and Robert A. Hoyt; "Choosers of the Slain" © 2008 by John C. Wright; "Against the Lafayette Escadrille" © 1972 by Gene Wolfe; "Doctor Quiet" © 2022 by Jacob Holo; "Remember the Alamo" © 1961 by T.R. Fehrenbach; "Comrades of Time" © 1939 by Edmond Hamilton; "Time Crime" © 1955 by H. Beam Piper

A Baen Books Original

Baen Publishing Enterprises
P.O. Box 1403
Riverdale, NY 10471
www.baen.com

ISBN: 978-1-9821-9279-2

Cover art by Kieran Yanner

First printing, April 2022
First mass market printing, June 2023

Distributed by Simon & Schuster
1230 Avenue of the Americas
New York, NY 10020

Library of Congress Control Number: 2021060273

Printed in the United States of America

10 9 8 7 6 5 4 3 2 1

Hank has left the dedication of this book to me,
so I'll dedicate it to him.
Thank you for teaching me how to assemble these books,
and for putting up with me always underfoot.
– C.R.

ACKNOWLEDGMENTS

Our thanks to those authors who permitted the use of their stories, and to the estates and their representatives who intervened for those authors unreachable without time travel (we raise a glass to absent friends). Among the very helpful agents deserving thanks are Spectrum Literary Agency, Richard Curtis Associates, the Zeno Literary Agency, and the Virginia Kidd Literary Agency. And thanks for help and advice from others I'm unforgivably forgetting. Gratitude is also due to the Internet Speculative Fiction Database (ISFDB.org) for existing and being a handy source of raw data, and to the devoted volunteers who maintain that very useful site.

CONTENTS

CONTENTS

TIME
TROOPERS

★ ★ ★

INTRODUCTION: FROM HERE TO ETERNITY... AND BACK AGAIN

by Hank Davis

Suppose time travel is possible. And, as long as you're up, suppose the past can be changed.

Read any good horror stories lately?

Here's one: if time travel is possible and the past can be changed, then everything in your life, everyone you know, everything you've accomplished, is subject not just to change without notice, but to complete obliteration. And you may not even still exist to notice it, may never have existed at all—which might be a kindness, of sorts. While plain old global thermonuclear war could bring everything in your life, including yourself, to a permanent stop, an attack through time would not really bring a stop. Because the past had changed and there never was a *start*.

No doubt governments would try to suppress it, so maybe we can all breathe a sigh of relief. We all know what a good job governments have done in suppressing booze, gambling, guns in the hands of criminals, pot, heroin, cocaine, ecstasy, and other such examples of better living through chemistry. And they've done such a great job of handling pandemics.

Besides, governments have their own interests to look after. Lost that election? Hmmm, maybe if we sent a few thousand voters back in time...(Could *that* be why elections take so long to decide lately?)

From that, it's a natural step into military matters. Lost that battle? Hmm, maybe if we sent a division (or two, or three, or ...) back in time...If no battle plan survives contact with the enemy, then different plans can be brought on board until the brass has one that works.

But then, if the enemy also has time travel, a lot more plans would be required...on both sides, which might lead to a diverging series.

It might be simpler, not to mention less messy, instead of sending battalions, or even just platoons, backwards or forwards in time, to use tweezers instead of battering rams. Algis Budrys's short story "The Skirmisher" (1957) has one man eliminating people, sometimes with a faked phone call, sometimes less subtly, to prevent their having descendants. The story did not spell out whether the agent of change was an agent sent back in time, a lone operator with the power of precognition, or something else. (It's one story I wish were in this book, but at least you can find it in the highly recommended 1963 Budrys collection, *The Furious Future*.)

A lone sniper, sent back in time to a crucial moment, might make a profound change by eliminating an indispensable individual; or a time-traveling thief might swipe the plans for the battle to the other side, in time to thwart a surprise attack. If the Germans had known the plans for the invasion of Normandy, D-Day might have come off very differently. If the right people in the U.S. government had known about the plans to attack Pearl Harbor,[1] that episode might have happened with different headlines (instead of "Infamy," maybe "Better Luck Next Time"), many tons of Asian steel underwater, and possibly a cascade effect. Would the U.S. still have declared war on Japan? If not, would Japan's ally Germany have had a reason to declare war on the U.S., bringing the Yanks into the war, with the results seen in the history books?

But then, with time-traveling meddlers, the history books are only works in progress. Think of our present, seemingly inevitable reality as a multitude of inverted pyramids, all delicately balanced on their apexes, needing just the slight push of a finger to be toppled. Or maybe the mere weight of a pigeon (doves would not be appropriate here) landing on top, near the edge, would lower the boom.

On the other hand, it might be that the reality we know has its own inertia, and is not so sensitive to tiny pushes, but still can be changed if enough force is brought to bear. That brings us back to sending battalions through time. But then, if both sides have time travel, the popular (if misattributed) quip about "getting there firstest with the mostest" might change to *everybody* getting there simultaneously with everything they've got. That would

---

[1] I am not going to get involved in the endless controversy as to whether or not Roosevelt knew in advance about the Japanese plans and did nothing for what he thought was the greater good. I already have too many hobbies.

be a mess and I think neither General von Clausewitz nor Doctor Who would approve.

Fortunately, time travel (into the past, at least) so far doesn't seem to exist (guards, please eject that quantum mechanic over there). Or maybe those aforementioned governments are doing something right for a change. But it's a fun concept to kick around in science fiction, with no more than on-paper characters ceasing to be, along with their equally evanescent but fictional ancestors, and only ink or printer toner being spilled, at worst, rather than blood.

There is very little that is new in science fiction, and time travel with a military aspect has a long lineage. Almost as far back as fictional time travel itself. I won't try to be exhaustive (and hope the reader's patience won't be exhausted) and point out that Mark Twain's *A Connecticut Yankee in King Arthur's Court* (1889) is both one of the earliest time travel stories, and also has a military aspect, with a war near the novel's end, fomented by the Catholic clergy to put a stop to the title character's innovations from the future (for some reason, that part never gets into the movie and TV versions). Since it's an early piece, the time-traveling troublemaker is sent back through the centuries by a knock on the head and returns to his own time by a spell cast by Merlin, who seemed to be a charlatan up to that point.

Probably Twain had no idea how to get his hero back in time, or back home without resorting to magic, but H. G. Wells used a more modern form of magic, calling it a time machine. As the industrial revolution thundered on, machines were remaking the world, and invoking a device which could move freely in time was more believable than a clout on the noggin, or a wizard's spell, even if no one, Wells included, had any idea how such a thing could work. He introduced the idea in an unfinished serial titled "The Chronic Argonauts" (1888) in an obscure publication, then, six years after *A Connecticut Yankee*, redid it in one of his most popular works, the novella, *The Time Machine* (1895). That enduring classic has no military aspect (in the 1960 movie version, the Time Traveler passes through three world wars, the last nuclear, but they were added by the screenwriter, David Duncan), but Mr. Wells, who later prophetically extended combat into the third dimension in *The War in the Air*, didn't neglect the possibility of carrying it into the fourth dimension, and I'll get back to him shortly.

First, I want to briefly lay some groundwork. With time travel, obviously, you can hop in your trusty time machine and go forward or backward. And with the right sort of time machine, you can go sideways, or as Murray Leinster put it in the title of his classic story, "Sidewise in Time" (1934). That is, travel to parallel time tracks where history came out differently. I think I can get away without explaining that in detail, since parallel universes have been made familiar to many through *Star Trek*, *Red Dwarf*, *Superboy*, and other TV shows; such movies as *Parallel* and *Sliding Doors* and *Everything Everywhere All at Once*; and comic books such as DC's Justice Society and Justice League both existing (with some overlapping characters) in two adjacent parallel universes, plus a third with only super-powered villains.

(Ironically, while accelerated travel into the future is

possible according to special relativity, and parallel
universes may exist according to some versions of quantum
mechanics, such as the many-worlds interpretation—
though whether anyone could travel from one to another
is another matter—going back in time has no possible
basis that I know about and the butterflies in Bradbury's
"A Sound of Thunder" can keep on flitting peacefully
among the lumbering dinosaurs. Of course, I'm way
behind in my reading of *New Scientist* and possibly should
be more cautious in my dogmatism . . .)

Given those three types (or directions) of time travel,
what has science fiction done with the idea?

There's the realistic approach. Travel near the speed of
light and arrive scarcely aged in the future. This might
figure in certain long-range types of military action, and
my intrepid co-editor has one such in the pages which
follow. An earlier example is a novel which should be
better known, L. Ron Hubbard's *Return to Tomorrow*
(1954), originally serialized in *Astounding* as *To the Stars*
(1950). Though Hubbard makes some howlers about
relativity, the story is very effective, particularly when the
starship returns to a militarized Earth and must fight its
way in to be resupplied. (I think the novel is not as well-
known as it should be, but for all I know, hordes of
Scientologists may have memorized the text. If so, good
for them.) That allows only a one-way trip in time, with
no hope of returning to the time the viewpoint character
knew, and Hubbard effectively treats the tragic aspect of
the situation.

And one of Kenneth Bulmer's novels made effective
use of a military strategy using long-range planning and

slower-than-light travel, but I can't describe the story or even give the title, without possibly spoiling it for future readers.

Another one-way road to the future is the possibility of suspended animation, where life and aging are somehow slowed or even arrested, then resumed in the future. H. G. Wells got there early on, once again, in *When the Sleeper Wakes* (1899), also known as *The Sleeper Awakes* (1910 revision), though no machine is involved this time, and the title character, after a protracted inability to sleep, simply takes drugs which bring about a *long* snooze and wakes up in the far future where, through investments made in his name while he was stacking Z's, he owns most of the world. A revolutionary war ensues. (Also another war precedes the opening of the story, since in some editions, the characters mention the Martian invasion of *The War of the Worlds* as something in their recent past.)

But a time machine, or medical condition, that can only go forward in time, with no way of returning, is of much less interest than the younger Wells's more versatile time machine, impossible or not.

Maybe impossible, but great fun are such devices being used and misused in Poul Anderson's Time Patrol series, collected in one volume by Baen as *Time Patrol* (2006), plus a novel, *The Shield of Time* (1990). The function of the Patrol is to be time cops, making sure that time travelers, accidently or purposefully, do not change the past, consequently changing the future. Still they sometimes must mount genuine military operations to achieve that end, as in "Delenda Est" in these pages.

In the absence of some such sort of time cops,

opposing sides might tinker with the past to achieve a desirable future, with the opposed sides altering and unaltering, and realtering the past as the "changewar" goes on (or goes back) across the centuries. That's the situation in Fritz Leiber's Changewar series. In that fluctuating universe, the opposed sides are the Snakes and Spiders, identified by either a serpentine mark or an asterisk on their foreheads. And in some cases, different versions of the same individual may be fighting on both sides. Considering this aspect, and that the future the two sides are competing to establish is not described, this may be a comment by Leiber, who was a committed pacifist, on the nature of war.

There are not as many Changewar stories as I would wish, just the Hugo-winning novel *The Big Time* (1958), and a handful of shorter tales, and maybe a Snake or Spider agent could go back to ask Leiber to write additional yarns. Also, the various collections of the stories, such as *Changewar* (1983), include a couple of tales, "A Deskful of Girls" (1958) and "When the Change-Winds Blow" (1964), which are barely connected to the series, only mentioning the opposed sides briefly. Perhaps the connection was stronger before a time-jaunting agent went back and changed our literary past.

A more recent tale of such a changewar, "This Is How You Lose the Time War" (2019) by Amal El-Mohtar and Max Gladstone, won the Hugo, Nebula, and BSFA awards in the novella category. As with Leiber's series, two opposed sides are trying to change the past to achieve an undefined victory in the future, or futures, since parallel universes seem to be involved. As with Leiber, the reader is not moved to root for either side, about which little is shown. Instead, the focus is on Red and Blue, women agents on opposite sides, who begin by exchanging taunting letters, inventively using unorthodox media of transmission, then begin to respect each other, and finally fall in love. The authors have filled the story with striking images wittily described, such as, "Blue approaches the temple in pilgrim's guise: hair shorn to show the shine of circuitry curling around the ears and up to scalp, eyes goggled, mouth a smear of chrome sheen, eyelids chrome hooded. She wears antique typewriter keys on her fingers in veneration of the great god Hack..." and chuckle-worthy lines from their cross-time correspondence, such as "How many boards would the Mongols hoard if the Mongol horde got bored?" If more recent Hugo-winners were this good, I might stop thinking of that once notable literary prize as instead, lately, a burnt-out exercise in triviality.

Turning to a past war which, though tragic, was certainly about something and is still reverberating in this timeline, including recent displays of self-righteous fanaticism (hey, didn't there used to be a statue over there?), the American Civil War has not lacked for time twisters. One from outside the SF field is James Thurber's "If Grant Had Been Drinking at Appomattox" (1935). While Thurber's classic did not involve time travel, General Grant's beverage of choice also figures in another hilarious yarn, Jack Finney's "Quit Zoomin' Those Hands Through the Air" (1951), in which, on the eve of a battle, a Union soldier invents a time machine, goes forward with the narrator to borrow the Wright Brothers' biplane from the Smithsonian (he returns it later), and, with the first-person narrator at the controls, goes off to spy from the air on the disposition of the Confederate forces. Unfortunately, the narrator and pilot had imbibed some of General Grant's refreshments (actually, make that a *lot* of said refreshments) and the results are not as planned. Mark this as another story I wish were in these pages.

Of course, the Union won the war with no help from time travelers (unless that's what they *want* us to think), but in Charles L. Harness's short story "Quarks at Appomattox" (1983), a time traveler goes back to offer Robert E. Lee automatic weapons which could turn the tide of battle, but Lee declines the offer for reasons I will not give here. Harry Turtledove posed a similar situation in his 1992 novel *The Guns of the South*, and while the rebels win the war, things do not go quite as the meddlers from the future had hoped.

Ward Moore, in his 1953 novel *Bring the Jubilee*, approached the situation from the other side, showing in inventive detail a world where the rebel states were victorious, until a time traveler goes back to observe history in the making and inadvertently remakes it.

Another subcategory (perhaps needing a couple more "subs" thrown in) of time-traveling military SF has accidental time travelers, who walk around a team of horses, say, and are never more seen in their own world. (Reference both to a line from Charles Fort and an H. Beam Piper story.) Stumbling backwards in time, the involuntary traveler might either change the past, or just happen to cause the past as it was "supposed" to unfold. As for going in the opposite direction, let the future beware! In Philip K. Dick's novella "The Variable Man" (1953), the title character, an itinerant mender, is plucked from the early twentieth century into a war between Earth and its colonies and throws all their plans out of whack. One of the best stories from the first season of TV's *The Twilight Zone* had a First World War ace landing his plane at a future (late 1950s, in his case) military air base and having to fly back into a strange cloud and return to his time and save the fellow pilot he had given up for dead when they were surrounded by enemy planes. The title of that episode was "The Last Flight" (1960), scripted by SF and fantasy master Richard Matheson. According to Wikipedia (which is far from infallible) the script was based on a Matheson short story titled "Flight," and I would have considered that story for inclusion in this book, except that I was unable to find any other mention of a story by Matheson with that title. Oh, well. I recommend that the reader see the *TZ* episode online or on video.

Flying through time in the other direction, Dean McLaughlin's "Hawk Among the Sparrows" (1968) has a modern jet pilot hurled back into that same first aerial war with his powerful jet fighter and finds that his superbly engineered modern craft is not really appropriate for jousting with the fragile biplanes of the past.

Harlan Ellison sent a future soldier back to the present day across millennia from a bleak time of perpetual war in his story "Soldier from Tomorrow" (1957, reprinted as "Soldier"). The story is early Ellison and minor, but seven years later the author freely adapted it for TV's *The Outer Limits*, one of the high points of that frequently disappointing program. Both the original story and the script are included in Ellison's story collection *From the*

Land of Fear (1967). There is a slight resemblance to the situation in the first two Terminator movies, but, in my opinion, much too slight for Ellison to have received financial compensation and a belated screen credit after he sued their makers. I'm not a lawyer, but I'm aware of stories similar to "Soldier" and "I Have No Mouth and I Must Scream" published earlier than those two stories.

Two final examples of accidental time displacement involve very large ships. In 1959, Jack Sharkey's "Ship Ahoy" sent an entire aircraft carrier from 1944 back to the Trojan War. Since Sharkey was the most notable writer of humorous SF and fantasy since Robert Sheckley, the situation is played for laughs, as when that early war correspondent, Homer, turns up and the crew are surprised that he is not blind. Turns out he is a heavy drinker and should actually have been known as blind *drunk* Homer. This is yet another story whose absence from this book I regret, but you can find it in the e-book *The Essential Jack Sharkey* (2020). The other example is the movie *The Final Countdown* (1980) involving another aircraft carrier being sent back from, presumably, the late 1970s to 1941, shortly before the Japanese attack on Pearl Harbor. The movie is well worth seeing, though I can't help wondering if its makers ever read "Ship Ahoy."

Getting back to time travel done for military reasons and on purpose, the very prolific and very excellent Andre Norton did a four-novel series beginning with *The Time Traders* (1958), and continuing with *Galactic Derelict* (1959, combining time travel and space travel), *The Defiant Agents* (1962), and *Key Out of Time* (1963). Book reviewers in the fifties and sixties frequently dismissed Norton for writing juvenile category novels for teenagers (what would now be called "young adult") but that was their loss. More recently, three more novels in the series have appeared, written with collaborators, which I have not read and cannot comment on, but that may be *my* loss.

So far, I've scarcely touched on the third type of time travel—into alternate worlds, or parallel universes. The previously mentioned novel, Ward Moore's *Bring the Jubilee*, posited a world in which the South had won the American Civil War (until an unwary time traveler went back and changed it), but the parallel universe concept could have a world in which the Confederacy won the war, and another, existing simultaneously, in which the Union won. No reason to stop there. Suppose Mexico saw an opportunity and made it a three-cornered fracas. Or maybe the Aztecs were still around and had developed gunpowder and joined the party. Or the British saw a chance to take back the rebellious colonies. Or H. G. Wells's Martians invaded three decades earlier and landed in a larger landmass than the British Isles. Or, or, or . . .

Speaking (once more) of H. G. Wells, a little historical perspective brings us back to that extraordinary SF pioneer. His *A Modern Utopia* (1905) begins with a duplicate Earth, like ours and complete with duplicated people, but the duplicate Earth is in this universe, though light-years away, so parallel universes are not involved (but don't give up on the limey yet), and the "novel" is really a lecture and slideshow on how a utopia would work. I understand that at the end, the narrator wakes as if from a dream, but I'm taking the word of others for that, since I've never been able to get very far into the book. Besides, utopias don't have wars (unlike workers' paradises), so it's a bit off our theme.

Closer is Wells's 1923 novel *Men Like Gods*, and this one is actually a novel, with fewer lectures, in which a bunch of contemporary Londoners are transported to another Earth with a utopian anarchistic society, this one in a different universe. Eventually, the Londoners, one of whom is apparently a caricature of young Winston Churchill (!), decide that the wimpy utopia needs to be set right, and sort of start a sort of war. But one of them, who writes for a "liberal" weekly (read: "socialist," though the novel includes a critique of Marxism) helps thwart the plan, not that it had much chance in the first place, and the duplicate Earth's scientists send the upstarts back to their own dismal world.

Men Like Gods gets closer to this anthology's theme, though the military aspect is slight, if not downright ineffectual, and the two Earths are separated by a fourth *spatial* dimension, rather than by a time separation. I'll note that while the novel has sometimes been cited as the first parallel worlds story, it was preceded by Frances Steven's novel *The Heads of Cerberus*, serialized in *The Thrill Book* in 1919. While Ms. Stevens's story has the transition between worlds accomplished by magical means, her novel has considerably more plot than Wells thought necessary and is much more entertaining.

As I keep returning to Wells, now I'll return to the almost as prolific Andre Norton. Her 1956 novel *The Crossroads of Time* has opposing sides scuffling behind the scenes in parallel worlds, and was followed by a YA sequel, *Quest Crosstime* (1965), which has the agents of the Crosstime Corps jumping through parallel worlds to thwart a would-be dictator's grand design. The two novels have been combined in *Crosstime* (Baen, 2008).

Keith Laumer, whose "The Long Remembered Thunder" is included herein, wrote a series of novels with battling parallel worlds, beginning with *Worlds of the Imperium* (1961), followed by *The Other Side of Time* (1964), and *Assignment in Nowhere* (1968). The second in the series is one of Laumer's best, which is saying something. Much later, after a debilitating stroke, he wrote a fourth Imperium novel, *Zone Yellow* (1990), which I can't recommend. Baen Books combined the first three novels in the omnibus *Imperium* (2005), which included the first book appearance of the complete *Worlds of the Imperium*. Previous book editions had been abridged from the magazine serial in *Fantastic*, regrettably omitting a striking scene of what one would see crossing changing parallel worlds, all similar, but each slightly different from the other.

Probably the author most noted for parallel world adventures was H. Beam Piper, whose Paratime series assumes that one Earth (not our own) has developed the technology for traveling between the parallel worlds and is secretly exploiting those other Earths (including our own). It has established the Paratime Police to ensure that the exploitation is done benignly and secretly, so that the paratime travel secret remains a monopoly. Paratime cop Verkan Vall figures in most of the stories, as well as the novel *Lord Kalvan of Otherwhen* (1965), and his duties are usually those of a policeman, but sometimes a serious military operation is in order, and "Time Crime," included in these pages, demonstrates Vall's (and Piper's) talent for that sort of operation.

Piper's story has a larger canvas than most of the stories in *Time Troopers*, but then, it is a novella, with more room for razzle-dazzle, and combining military action with time travel yields a wide-ranging concept that benefits from room enough to explore its implications.

That's certainly true of another novella included here, A. E. Van Vogt's classic *Recruiting Station*. Also known as *Masters of Time* and *Earth's Last Fortress*, it originally appeared in *Astounding Science Fiction* in 1942 and in the decades since, it has lost none of its fascinating pyrotechnics, but then I've been a Van Vogt fan since the second grade and including one of his stories in an anthology brings out the fanboy in me (speaking of time travel . . .), so the readers should plunge in and see for themselves. Imagination was Van Vogt's middle name, even if his name wasn't written as A. I. Van Vogt.

Another highly imaginative story uses novel length to explore its concept, combining swashbuckling action with quantum theory. Jack Williamson's *The Legion of Time* (1938) assumes that, like Schrödinger's celebrated cat, sort of dead and alive until you open the box and look, there exist two possible futures, seemingly mutually exclusive, each trying to influence the past so that it will become the actual future after the wave function collapses. Did I write "trying?" Make that *battling*, one side fighting to kill the present-day man who is pivotal to the struggle, the other intervening to protect him. It gets more complicated, and did I mention that both sides are led by very, ah, attractive ladies? I won't say more, referring the reader instead to

John C. Wright (who has a story in this book, if you haven't noticed) and his excellent essay on the novel, pointing out that many of the critics who have written about the story are very sloppy readers, who even get the hair colors of the opposing heroine and villainess wrong. Mr. Wright's essay can be found at: https://www.scifiwright.com/fancies/reviews/the-legion-of-time-by-jack-williamson.

The essay includes a link to where Williamson's novel can be found online, which is fortunate, since there was no possibility of including it here.

I can't ignore two stories which defy categorization, "Time War" and "Time War: Second Front" (2010 and 2011) by Stephen D. Sullivan, both available as e-stories. The second is not a sequel to the first, since they are unfolding simultaneously, showing the same battle seen from two different characters' perspectives, but then it is a *big* battle involving character types from SF, fantasy, and history. For an example of the last, there are Nazis involved, along with the line, "You can't have a time war without Nazis." The whole thing is like an explosion in a comic bookstore, or maybe in a comic-con. One of the narrators is an immortal redheaded woman, which strikes me as an excellent idea, since there are never enough of those to fill the demand. Mr. Sullivan is planning a third story in the setting. Count me in.

If the stories in *Time Troopers* have stirred your appetite for more such tales, there are a number of novels of military adventures in time in addition to those already mentioned, such as *The Corridors of Time* (1965) and *There Will Be Time* (1972), both by Poul Anderson, and John Brunner's novel *Threshold of Eternity* (1959), the last showing a strong Van Vogt influence. And if you'll pardon a plug for the home team, David Weber and Jacob Holo have collaborated on two best-selling novels for Baen in their Gordian Division series, *The Gordian Protocol* (2019) and *The Valkyrie Protocol* (2020). Jacob Holo has also contributed a short story set in that series, "Doctor Quiet," to this book.

Also worth seeking out are the stories which I would have liked to have had between these covers, but which, for various reasons, were not available. I've already mentioned the out-of-reach stories by Algis Budrys, Jack Finney, Jack Sharkey, and particularly regrettable was my not being able to include Connie Willis's "Fire Watch" (1982), dealing with a historian sent back through time to London during the Blitz. He is supposed to only observe, then report upon his return, but when he thinks he has discovered a saboteur, he may have difficulty sticking to that rule. The story won the Hugo and Nebula Awards, and is part of a series, including the novels *Doomsday Book* (1992), *To Say Nothing of the Dog* (1997), and *Blackout/All Clear* (2010). The reader who has missed "Fire Watch" up 'til now can find it in Ms. Willis's highly recommended collection, *The Best of Connie Willis* (2013).

I think the intersection of military science fiction and time travel (in whichever direction) still has untapped potential, but in the meantime a number of gems have been produced, and I hope Christopher Ruocchio and I have captured some of the brightest in this book and given enjoyment to the reader.

—Hank Davis
August 2021

"ALL YOU ZOMBIES—"
by Robert A. Heinlein

Back in the 1950s the sophisticated editors of that sophisticated magazine Playboy *asked Robert A. Heinlein for a story, an adult story, of course, and Heinlein sent along this eye-opening mind-bender. Turned out the editors of the bunny mag weren't sophisticated enough to wrap their brains around "—All You Zombies—" and rejected the story, after which it saw publication in* The Magazine of Fantasy and Science Fiction, *which may have lacked a foldout but was sophisticated enough to see the story's merits. So did Michael Spierig and Peter Spierig, who in 2014 made the story, with small changes, into a very effective movie,* Predestination, *well worth checking out.*

2217 Time Zone V (EST) 7 Nov 1970 NYC–"Pop's Place": I was polishing a brandy snifter when the Unmarried Mother came in. I noted the time—10.17 P.M. zone five or eastern time November 7th, 1970. Temporal agents always notice time & date; we must.

The Unmarried Mother was a man twenty-five years old, no taller than I am, immature features and a touchy temper. I didn't like his looks—I never had—but he was a lad I was here to recruit, he was my boy. I gave him my best barkeep's smile.

Maybe I'm too critical. He wasn't swish; his nickname came from what he always said when some nosy type asked him his line: "I'm an unmarried mother." If he felt less than murderous he would add: "—at four cents a word. I write confession stories."

If he felt nasty, he would wait for somebody to make something of it. He had a lethal style of in-fighting, like a female cop—one reason I wanted him. Not the only one.

He had a load on and his face showed that he despised people more than usual. Silently I poured a double shot of Old Underwear and left the bottle. He drank, poured another.

I wiped the bar top. "How's the 'Unmarried Mother' racket?"

His fingers tightened on the glass and he seemed about to throw it at me; I felt for the sap under the bar. In temporal manipulation you try to figure everything, but there are so many factors that you never take needless risks.

I saw him relax that tiny amount they teach you to watch for in the Bureau's training school. "Sorry," I said. "Just asking, 'How's business?' Make it 'How's the weather?'"

He looked sour. "Business is okay. I write 'em, they print 'em, I eat."

I poured myself one, leaned toward him. "Matter of

fact," I said, "you write a nice stick—I've sampled a few. You have an amazingly sure touch with the woman's angle."

It was a slip I had to risk; he never admitted what pen names he used. But he was boiled enough to pick up only the last. "'Woman's angle!'" he repeated with a snort. "Yeah, I know the woman's angle. I should."

"So?" I said doubtfully. "Sisters?"

"No. You wouldn't believe me if I told you."

"Now, now," I answered mildly, "bartenders and psychiatrists learn that nothing is stranger than the truth. Why, son, if you heard the stories I do—well, you'd make yourself rich. Incredible."

"You don't know what 'incredible' means!"

"So? Nothing astonishes me. I've always heard worse."

He snorted again. "Want to bet the rest of the bottle?"

"I'll bet a full bottle." I placed one on the bar.

"Well—" I signaled my other bartender to handle the trade. We were at the far end, a single-stool space that I kept private by loading the bar top by it with jars of pickled eggs and other clutter. A few were at the other end watching the fights and somebody was playing the jukebox—private as a bed where we were. "Okay," he began, "to start with, I'm a bastard."

"No distinction around here," I said.

"I mean it," he snapped. "My parents weren't married."

"Still no distinction," I insisted. "Neither were mine."

"When—" He stopped, gave me the first warm look I ever saw on him. "You mean that?"

"I do. A one-hundred-percent bastard. In fact," I added, "no one in my family ever marries. All bastards."

"Don't try to top me—*you're* married." He pointed at my ring.

"Oh, that." I showed it to him. "It just looks like a wedding ring; I wear it to keep women off." That ring is an antique I bought in 1985 from a fellow operative—he had fetched it from pre-Christian Crete. "The Worm Ouroboros...the World Snake that eats its own tail, forever without end. A symbol of the Great Paradox."

He barely glanced at it. "If you're really a bastard, you know how it feels. When I was a little girl—"

"Wups!" I said. "Did I hear correctly?"

"Who's telling this story? When I was a little girl— Look, ever hear of Christine Jorgenson? Or Roberta Cowell?"

"Uh, sex change cases? You're trying to tell me—"

"Don't interrupt or swelp me, I won't talk. I was a foundling, left at an orphanage in Cleveland in 1945 when I was a month old. When I was a little girl, I envied kids with parents. Then, when I learned about sex—and, believe me, Pop, you learn fast in an orphanage—"

"I know."

"—I made a solemn vow that any kid of mine would have both a pop and a mom. It kept me 'pure,' quite a feat in that vicinity—I had to learn to fight to manage it. Then I got older and realized I stood darned little chance of getting married—for the same reason I hadn't been adopted." He scowled. "I was horse-faced and buck-toothed, flat-chested and straight-haired."

"You don't look any worse than I do."

"Who cares how a barkeep looks? Or a writer? But people wanting to adopt pick little blue-eyed golden-haired morons. Later on, the boys want bulging breasts, a cute face, and an Oh-you-wonderful-male manner." He shrugged. "I couldn't compete. So I decided to join the W.E.N.C.H.E.S."

"Eh?"

"Women's Emergency National Corps, Hospitality & Entertainment Section, what they now call 'Space Angels'—Auxiliary Nursing Group, Extraterrestrial Legions."

I knew both terms, once I had them chronized. Although we now use still a third name; it's that elite military service corps: Women's Hospitality Order Refortifying & Encouraging Spacemen. Vocabulary shift is the worst hurdle in time-jumps—did you know that "service station" once meant a dispensary for petroleum fractions? Once on an assignment in the Churchill Era a woman said to me, "Meet me at the service station next door"—which is *not* what it sounds; a "service station" (then) wouldn't have a bed in it.

He went on: "It was when they first admitted you can't send men into space for months and years and not relieve the tension. You remember how the wowsers screamed?—that improved my chances, volunteers were scarce. A gal had to be respectable, preferably virgin (they liked to train them from scratch), above average mentally, and stable emotionally. But most volunteers were old hookers, or neurotics who would crack up ten days off Earth. So I didn't need looks; if they accepted me, they would fix my buck teeth, put a wave in my hair, teach me to walk and dance and how to listen to a man pleasingly, and everything else—plus training for the prime duties.

They would even use plastic surgery if it would help—nothing too good for Our Boys.

"Best yet, they made sure you didn't get pregnant during your enlistment—and you were almost certain to marry at the end of your hitch. Same way today, A.N.G.E.L.S. marry spacers—they talk the language.

"When I was eighteen I was placed as a 'mother's helper.' This family simply wanted a cheap servant but I didn't mind as I couldn't enlist till I was twenty-one. I did housework and went to night school—pretending to continue my high school typing and shorthand but going to a charm class instead, to better my chances for enlistment.

"Then I met this city slicker with his hundred dollar bills." He scowled. "The no-good actually did have a wad of hundred dollar bills. He showed me one night, told me to help myself.

"But I didn't. I liked him. He was the first man I ever met who was nice to me without trying to take my pants off. I quit night school to see him oftener. It was the happiest time of my life.

"Then one night in the park my pants did come off."

He stopped. I said, "And then?"

"And then *nothing*! I never saw him again. He walked me home and told me he loved me—and kissed me goodnight and never came back." He looked grim. "If I could find him, I'd kill him!"

"Well," I sympathized, "I know how you feel. But killing him—just for doing what comes naturally—hmm ... Did you struggle?"

"Huh? What's that got to do with it?"

"Quite a bit. Maybe he deserves a couple of broken arms for running out on you, but—"

"He deserves worse than that! Wait till you hear. Somehow I kept anyone from suspecting and decided it was all for the best. I hadn't really loved him and probably would never love anybody—and I was more eager to join the W.E.N.C.H.E.S. than ever. I wasn't disqualified, they didn't insist on virgins. I cheered up.

"It wasn't until my skirts got tight that I realized."

"Pregnant?"

"The bastard had me higher 'n a kite! Those skinflints I lived with ignored it as long as I could work—then kicked me out and the orphanage wouldn't take me back. I landed in a charity ward surrounded by other big bellies and trotted bedpans until my time came.

"One night I found myself on an operating table, with a nurse saying, 'Relax. Now breathe deeply.'

"I woke up in bed, numb from the chest down. My surgeon came in. 'How do you feel?' he says cheerfully.

"'Like a mummy.'

"'Naturally. You're wrapped like one and full of dope to keep you numb. You'll get well-but a Caesarian isn't a hangnail.'

"'Caesarian?' I said. 'Doc—*did I lose the baby?*'

"'Oh, no. Your baby's fine.'

"'Oh. Boy or girl?'

"'A healthy little girl. Five pounds, three ounces.'

"I relaxed. It's something, to have made a baby. I told myself I would go somewhere and tack 'Mrs.' on my name and let the kid think her papa was dead—no orphanage for *my* kid!

"But the surgeon was talking. 'Tell me, uh—' He avoided my name. '—did you ever think your glandular setup was odd?'

"I said, 'Huh? Of course not. What are you driving at?'

"He hesitated. 'I'll give you this in one dose, then a hypo to let you sleep off your jitters. You'll have 'em.'

"'Why?' I demanded.

"'Ever hear of that Scottish physician who was female until she was thirty-five?—then had surgery and became legally and medically a man? Got married. All okay.'

"'What's that got to do with me?'

"'That's what I'm saying. You're a man.'

"'I tried to sit up. '*What?*'

"'Take it easy. When I opened you, I found a mess. I sent for the Chief of Surgery while I got the baby out, then we held a consultation with you on the table— and worked for hours to salvage what we could. You had two full sets of organs, both immature, but with the female set well enough developed that you had a baby. They could never be any use to you again, so we took them out and rearranged things so that you can develop properly as a man.' He put a hand on me. 'Don't worry. You're young, your bones will readjust, we'll watch your glandular balance—and make a fine young man out of you.'

"I started to cry. 'What about my *baby*?'

"'Well, you can't nurse her, you haven't milk enough for a kitten. If I were you, I wouldn't see her—put her up for adoption.'

"'*No!*'

"He shrugged. 'The choice is yours; you're her

mother—well, her parent. But don't worry now; we'll get you well first.'

"Next day they let me see the kid and I saw her daily—trying to get used to her. I had never seen a brand-new baby and had no idea how awful they look—my daughter looked like an orange monkey. My feeling changed to cold determination to do right by her. But four weeks later that didn't mean anything."

"Eh?"

"She was snatched."

"'Snatched?'"

The Unmarried Mother almost knocked over the bottle we had bet. "Kidnapped—stolen from the hospital nursery!" He breathed hard. "How's that for taking the last thing a man's got to live for?"

"A bad deal," I agreed. "Let's pour you another. No clues?"

"Nothing the police could trace. Somebody came to see her, claimed to be her uncle. While the nurse had her back turned, he walked out with her."

"Description?"

"Just a man, with a face-shaped face, like yours or mine." He frowned. "I think it was the baby's father. The nurse swore it was an older man but he probably used makeup. Who else would swipe my baby? Childless women pull such stunts—but whoever heard of a man doing it?"

"What happened to you then?"

"Eleven more months of that grim place and three operations. In four months I started to grow a beard; before I was out I was shaving regularly . . . and no longer doubted that I was male." He grinned wryly. "I was staring down nurses' necklines."

"Well," I said, "seems to me you came through okay. Here you are, a normal man, making good money, no real troubles. And the life of a female is not an easy one."

He glared at me. "A lot you know about it!"

"So?"

"Ever hear the expression 'a ruined woman'?"

"Mmm, years ago. Doesn't mean much today."

"I was as ruined as a woman can be; that bastard *really* ruined me—I was no longer a woman...and I didn't know *how* to be a man."

"Takes getting used to, I suppose."

"You have no idea. I don't mean learning how to dress, or not walking into the wrong rest room; I learned those in the hospital. But how could I *live*? What job could I get? Hell, I couldn't even drive a car. I didn't know a trade; I couldn't do manual labor—too much scar tissue, too tender.

"I hated him for having ruined me for the W.E.N.C.H.E.S., too, but I didn't know how much until I tried to join the Space Corps instead. One look at my belly and I was marked unfit for military service. The medical officer spent time on me just from curiosity; he had read about my case.

"So I changed my name and came to New York. I got by as a fry cook, then rented a typewriter and set myself up as a public stenographer—what a laugh! In four months I typed four letters and one manuscript. The manuscript was for *Real Life Tales* and a waste of paper, but the goof who wrote it, sold it. Which gave me an idea; I bought a stack of confession magazines and studied them." He looked cynical. "Now you know how I get the authentic woman's angle on an unmarried-mother story . . . through the only version I haven't sold—the true one. Do I win the bottle?"

I pushed it toward him. I was upset myself, but there was work to do. I said, "Son, you still want to lay hands on that so-and-so?"

His eyes lighted up—a feral gleam.

"Hold it!" I said. "You wouldn't kill him?"

He chuckled nastily. "Try me."

"Take it easy. I know more about it than you think I do. I can help you. I know where he is."

He reached across the bar. "*Where is he?*"

I said softly, "Let go my shirt, sonny—or you'll land in the alley and we'll tell the cops you fainted." I showed him the sap.

He let go. "Sorry. But where is he?" He looked at me. "And how do you know so much?"

"All in good time. There are records—hospital records, orphanage records, medical records. The matron of your orphanage was Mrs. Fetherage—right? She was followed by Mrs. Gruenstein—right? Your name, as a girl, was 'Jane'—right? And you didn't tell me any of this—right?"

I had him baffled and a bit scared. "What's this? You trying to make trouble for me?"

"No indeed. I've your welfare at heart. I can put this character in your lap. You do to him as you see fit—and I guarantee that you'll get away with it. But I don't think you'll kill him. You'd be nuts to—and you aren't nuts. Not quite."

He brushed it aside. "Cut the noise. *Where is he?*"

I poured him a short one; he was drunk but anger was offsetting it. "Not so fast. I do something for you—you do something for me."

"Uh . . . what?"

"You don't like your work. What would you say to high pay, steady work, unlimited expense account, your own boss on the job, and lots of variety and adventure?"

He stared. "I'd say, 'Get those goddam reindeer off my roof!' Shove it, Pop—there's no such job."

"Okay, put it this way: I hand him to you, you settle with him, then try my job. If it's not all I claim—well, I can't hold you."

He was wavering; the last drink did it. "When d'yuh d'liver 'im?" he said thickly.

"If it's a deal—*right now!*"

He shoved out his hand. "It's a deal!"

I nodded to my assistant to watch both ends, noted the time—2300—started to duck through the gate under the bar—when the juke box blared out: *"I'm My Own Granpaw!"* The service man had orders to load it with old Americana and classics because I couldn't stomach the "music" of 1970, but I hadn't known that tape was in it. I called out, "Shut that off! Give the customer his money back." I added, "Storeroom, back in a moment," and headed there with my Unmarried Mother following.

It was down the passage across from the johns, a steel door to which no one but my day manager and myself had a key; inside was a door to an inner room to which only I had a key. We went there.

He looked blearily around at windowless walls. "Where is 'e?"

"Right away." I opened a case, the only thing in the room; it was a U.S.F.F. Coordinates Transformer Field Kit, series 1992, Mod. II—a beauty, no moving parts, weight twenty-three kilos fully charged, and shaped to pass as a suitcase. I had adjusted it precisely earlier that day; all I had to do was to shake out the metal net which limits the transformation field.

Which I did. "Wha's that?" he demanded.

"Time machine," I said and tossed the net over us.

"Hey!" he yelled and stepped back. There is a technique to this; the net has to be thrown so that the subject will instinctively step back *onto* the metal mesh, then you close the net with both of you inside completely—else you might leave shoe soles behind or a piece of foot, or scoop up a slice of floor. But that's all the skill it takes. Some agents con a subject into the net; I tell the truth and use that instant of utter astonishment to flip the switch. Which I did.

1030-V-3 April 1963–Cleveland, Ohio–Apex Bldg.: "Hey!" he repeated. "Take this damn thing off!"

"Sorry," I apologized and did so, stuffed the net into the case, closed it. "You said you wanted to find him."

"But—You said that was a time machine!"

I pointed out a window. "Does that look like November? Or New York?" While he was gawking at new buds and spring weather, I reopened the case, took out a packet of hundred dollar bills, checked that the numbers and signatures were compatible with 1963. The Temporal Bureau doesn't care how much you spend (it costs nothing) but they don't like unnecessary anachronisms.

Too many mistakes and a general court martial will exile
you for a year in a nasty period, say 1974 with its strict
rationing and forced labor. I never make such mistakes,
the money was okay. He turned around and said, "What
happened?"

"He's here. Go outside and take him. Here's expense
money." I shoved it at him and added, "Settle him, then
I'll pick you up."

Hundred dollar bills have a hypnotic effect on a person
not used to them. He was thumbing them unbelievingly
as I eased him into the hall, locked him out. The next
jump was easy, a small shift in era.

1700-V-10 March 1964–Cleveland–Apex Bldg.: There
was a notice under the door saying that my lease expired
next week; otherwise the room looked as it had a moment
before. Outside, trees were bare and snow threatened; I
hurried, stopping only for contemporary money and a
coat, hat and topcoat I had left there when I leased the
room. I hired a car, went to the hospital. It took twenty
minutes to bore the nursery attendant to the point where
I could swipe the baby without being noticed; we went
back to the Apex Building. This dial setting was more
involved as the building did not yet exist in 1945. But I
had precalculated it.

0100-V-20 Sept 1945–Cleveland–Skyview Motel: Field
kit, baby, and I arrived in a motel outside town. Earlier I
had registered as "Gregory Johnson, Warren, Ohio," so we
arrived in a room with curtains closed, windows locked,
and doors bolted, and the floor cleared to allow for waver

as the machine hunts. You can get a nasty bruise from a chair where it shouldn't be—not the chair of course, but backlash from the field.

No trouble. Jane was sleeping soundly; I carried her out, put her in a grocery box on the seat of a car I had provided earlier, drove to the orphanage, put her on the steps, drove two blocks to a "service station" (the petroleum products sort) and phoned the orphanage, drove back in time to see them taking the box inside, kept going and abandoned the car near the motel—walked to it and jumped forward to the Apex Building in 1963.

2200-V-24 April 1963–Cleveland–Apex Bldg.: I had cut the time rather fine—temporal accuracy depends on span, except on return to zero. If I had it right, Jane was discovering, out in the park this balmy spring night, that she wasn't quite as "nice" a girl as she had thought. I grabbed a taxi to the home of those skinflints, had the hackie wait around a corner while I lurked in shadows.

Presently I spotted them down the street, arms around each other. He took her up on the porch and made a long job of kissing her good-night—longer than I had thought. Then she went in and he came down the walk, turned away. I slid into step and hooked an arm in his. "That's all, son," I announced quietly. "I'm back to pick you up."

"*You!*" He gasped and caught his breath.

"Me. Now you know who *he* is—and after you think it over you'll know who *you* are . . . and if you think hard enough, you'll figure out who the baby is . . . and who *I* am."

He didn't answer, he was badly shaken. It's a shock to have it proved to you that you can't resist seducing yourself. I took him to the Apex Building and we jumped again.

2300-Vll-12 Aug 1985–Sub Rockies Base: I woke the duty sergeant, showed my I.D., told the sergeant to bed him down with a happy pill and recruit him in the morning. The sergeant looked sour but rank is rank, regardless of era; he did what I said—thinking, no doubt, that the next time we met he might be the colonel and I the sergeant. Which can happen in our corps. "What name?" he asked.

I wrote it out. He raised his eyebrows. "Like so, eh? *Hmm—*"

"You just do your job, Sergeant." I turned to my companion. "Son, your troubles are over. You're about to start the best job a man ever held—and you'll do well. I *know.*"

"But—"

"'But' nothing. Get a night's sleep, then look over the proposition. You'll like it."

"That you will!" agreed the sergeant. "Look at me— born in 1917—still around, still young, still enjoying life." I went back to the jump room, set everything on preselected zero.

2301-V-7 Nov 1970–NYC–"Pop's Place": I came out of the storeroom carrying a fifth of Drambuie to account for the minute I had been gone. My assistant was arguing with the customer who had been playing "I'm My Own Granpaw!" I said, "Oh, let him play it, then unplug it." I was very tired.

It's rough, but somebody must do it and it's very hard
to recruit anyone in the later years, since the Mistake of
1972. Can you think of a better source than to pick people
all fouled up where they are and give them well-paid,
interesting (even though dangerous) work in a necessary
cause? Everybody knows now why the Fizzle War of 1963
fizzled. The bomb with New York's number on it didn't
go off, a hundred other things didn't go as planned—all
arranged by the likes of me.

But not the Mistake of '72; that one is not our fault—
and can't be undone; there's no paradox to resolve. A thing
either is, or it isn't, now and forever amen. But there won't
be another like it; an order dated "1992" takes precedence
any year.

I closed five minutes early, leaving a letter in the cash
register telling my day manager that I was accepting his
offer, so see my lawyer as I was leaving on a long vacation.
The Bureau might or might not pick up his payments, but
they want things left tidy. I went to the room back of the
storeroom and forward to 1993.

*2200-VIJ-12 Jan 1993–Sub Rockies Annex–HQ
Temporal DOL:* I checked in with the duty officer and
went to my quarters, intending to sleep for a week. I had
fetched the bottle we bet (after all, I won it) and took a
drink before I wrote my report. It tasted foul and I
wondered why I had ever liked Old Underwear. But it was
better than nothing; I don't like to be cold sober, I think
too much. But I don't really hit the bottle either; other
people have snakes—*I* have people.

I dictated my report: forty recruitments all okayed by

the Psych Bureau—counting my own, which I knew would be okayed. I was here, wasn't I? Then I taped a request for assignment to operations; I was sick of recruiting. I dropped both in the slot and headed for bed.

My eye fell on "The By-Laws of Time," over my bed:

Never Do Yesterday What Should Be Done Tomorrow.
If At Last You Do Succeed, Never Try Again.
A Stitch in Time Saves Nine Billion.
A Paradox May Be Paradoctored.
It Is Earlier When You Think.
Ancestors Are Just People.
Even Jove Nods.

They didn't inspire me the way they had when I was a recruit; thirty subjective-years of time-jumping wears you down. I undressed and when I got down to the hide, I looked at my belly. A Caesarian leaves a big scar but I'm so hairy now that I don't notice it unless I look for it.

Then I glanced at the ring on my finger.

The Snake That Eats Its Own Tail, Forever and Ever . . . I *know* where I came from—but *where did all you zombies come from?*

I felt a headache coming on, but a headache powder is one thing I do not take. I did once—and you all went away.

So I crawled into bed and whistled out the light.

You aren't really there at all. There isn't anybody but me—Jane—here alone in the dark.

I miss you dreadfully!

THE ARCHAENAUT
by Christopher Ruocchio

There's time travel, and then there's time travel. While some may jump in a telephone booth and be whisked off to God-knows-when, there are those who take the long way round. There are no telephone booths in Ruocchio's Sun Eater universe, leaving those seeking to ply the oceans of time with only the more... conventional option.

"It should have been torn apart," said Lieutenant Phanu from the navigator's seat. "Sensor grid clocked it running thirty-nine percent *c* when it hit the edge of the system. There shouldn't be anything left after an impact at that speed."

"It could have been a glancing blow," said Captain Misra, pulling herself forward so that she hung in freefall behind Phanu's chair.

"Some glancing blow, ma'am!" Phanu replied, unable to keep the incredulity from his voice. He thumbed a couple controls, threw switches in sequence, relayed a comment to the helmsman at his side.

"Do we have a visual yet?" the captain asked.

Phanu shook his head. "Too far out. Won't see anything for half an hour, I wager. Assuming we can catch it at all."

From her place back and to port, the comms officer chimed in, "Do you think it's a ship, Captain?"

"Command thinks it is," Misra replied, peering intently out the alumglass canopy, as if expecting the answer to be written out there somewhere in the ink-dark of space. If it was so written, it was written in ink itself, and was thus invisible.

The *object* had first registered on the edge of the Aglovale system three days prior, when it struck an asteroid in deep orbit. The collision had cost the interloper nearly all its tremendous speed, and had set it on a new trajectory—not skirting the heliopause—but tumbling down the gravity well in-system toward Aglovale's twin suns. It had taken the better part of the first day for news to reach command on the home planet, and just as long for orders to bounce to Fort Caspian, where Misra and the crew of the *ISV Defiant* had their berth orbiting Lot, the system's farthest, coldest little world.

"It could as easily be an asteroid," said Edevane, the science chief.

"At forty percent c?" Phanu said. "Pretty damned unlikely."

"More likely than a ship," Edevane replied. "There's no distress beacon. No heat signature."

"Doesn't mean anything," Phanu said. "Might be busted up pretty bad. Riding momentum."

"Let's not leap to conclusions, Michael," Edevane said. "We don't know anything yet."

"I'm not leaping anywhere, Doctor," the navigator said. "Just thinking ahead."

Edevane grunted, prompting the captain to clear her throat. "Lysander, Michael, enough."

"Aye, ma'am," they both said in unison.

Captain Cassia Misra shut her eyes. It was bad enough dealing with the two men's posturing back on the station with nothing to do. Far worse to deal with it in the heat of the moment. Edevane and Phanu were both good officers, but prickly and too similar to ever truly cooperate. They needed different ships, but Aglovale's System Defense had too few, and so far from the home planet, there simply wasn't much opportunity for reassignment.

Patrolling their borders with infinity had not been quite as romantic as she'd imagined when she enlisted in the Baron's fleet. Not once in her seven years as captain of the *Defiant* had the system been attacked by outworld barbarians, and but for once in the six years prior—when an *exonaut* cruiser had sailed into the system in hope of finding fuel and a place to sell their wares—had anything happened outside the routine. The *exonauts* had been given fuel, but denied the right to make planetfall by the Baron's fleet. They'd too much of the stink of machines about them, or so old Captain Blinn had said. Misra had missed the *exonaut* affair. She'd been stationed on the ground then, chained to a flight control console in the old capital, but Blinn told her the *exonaut* captain had been eight feet tall and wore an exoskeleton to protect himself from Aglovale's crushing gravity. It had been a *part* of him, or so old Blinn said.

Misra shuddered.

For just about three thousand years, the Sollan Empire had been expanding, growing out from the ashes of ruined Earth, carried farther and farther on faster and faster ships. It seemed like every other year they were launching new peregrinations, new seed ships and new families for new worlds. Aglovale was a minor demesne, a system of little consequence on the borders of Imperial space. There were times Misra thought about changing her commission, signing on with the Emperor's own, leaving her home system for a post that really mattered...

But that was all a dream, and she knew it. Aglovale was home, had been home all her life.

And there was a mission, at any rate.

"We should be in position now," Phanu said, leaning back in his seat. Glancing over his shoulder, he said, "You may wish to strap in, Captain. If we need to move suddenly..."

She didn't need for him to finish the thought, but found her place in the command seat behind and to center. They'd set an intercept course to catch the object as it fell in-system, and all they had to do was wait. Assuming Phanu had done his calculations properly, they lay directly in the path of...whatever it was. Their mission was simple: identify it. If it was only an asteroid, as Edevane speculated, they would vaporize it rather than let it pass and pose a threat to the inner system. If it was anything else, well...

Safely strapped in her chair, Misra said, "Are we ready to launch probe buoys?"

"Aye, ma'am," said the helmsman to Phanu's right. "On your mark."

"Fire."

The *Defiant* juddered slightly, and two points like flares shot past the bow of the ship, glittering in the dark ahead. They diverged, forming a triangle with the *Defiant* at the vertex, each shooting off smaller flares as they went, each flare a smaller sensor buoy, forming a net in space between them and the target. "I want eyes on as soon as possible!" she said. "Let's get a look at this thing."

"We've got it!" Phanu's voice cracked the tense silence.

"Put it on monitor," Misra said.

The holograph display in the bridge's center glowed to life, and a series of confused, reddish images displayed themselves. Each was not perfectly three-dimensional, but a kind of bas-relief snapshot where the probes' long-range scanners took snapshots of the *thing* as it tumbled toward them. It was hard to get a precise look. The radar scans betrayed contours, could guess at size and scope, but the material and color of the object was still a mystery.

"It's not that big," said the comms officer.

"It's bigger than we are," Edevane interjected. "Two-point-one kilometers."

That was nearly three times the length of the *Defiant*. Misra frowned. "Can you composite the images? I want a sense of what we're looking at, Lysander."

"Already on it," the science officer replied. Each radar ping had captured a different profile of the thing falling into their system, a different snapshot, like photographs taken of a sculpture from all sides. Edevane bent over his terminal, fingers tapping as he attempted to align one image with the next.

On the holograph before the captain, the image of the *thing* took form.

"That isn't an asteroid," Phanu said, peering round his seat to look at it on the monitor tube.

"So it would seem," Edevane said in answer.

The vessel had the look of some metal mushroom, or of the hilt of a gladiator's sword. A huge, round shield plate stood at one end, badly chipped along one edge, a perfect circle no more. In its shadow, stretching from the center like a stem, lay the main axis and chassis of the ship itself, a broad ring rotated not far behind the shield plate, and behind that a great mast protruded up and down from the core shaft, and from each extremity a tangle of confused geometry fluttered. At the far end, opposite the shield, the stem swelled until it was twice its original size. There must be clustered the drive core and the mighty engines that had carried her across the stars.

In hushed tones, the comms officer voiced the thought Misra knew she at least had been having. "I've never seen a ship like that."

Misra had seen ships with shield plates once or twice; the older bulk-freighters that plied the spaceways sometimes used them to guard their delicate hulls against micrometeor impacts and so on. Modern ships relied on hypercarbons, like the Adamant patented and produced by Hopper Industries, to create hulls impervious to that kind of damage. But she'd never seen one attached to so narrow a chassis before, and those masts, the confused tangles on the holograph . . . were they solar sails?

"Could be *exos*," Phanu said. "They use spinships, don't they? See the ring?"

"They're not under thrust," the helmsman said.

"Try hailing," Misra ordered the comms officer. "All frequencies. Go."

"Unidentified ship, this is the *Defiant*. You are entering Sollan Imperial space. This system is under the protection of Baron Constantine Martel. Identify yourself." Nothing. "Unidentified ship, this is the *Defiant*. Identify yourself."

The comms officer looked round at Misra, who made a gesture for quiet.

"They're dead in the water, ma'am," said the helmsman. "We're picking up what might be an emergency reactor. Life support may be intact, but they're not under thrust. Primary systems are all down. They were coasting on their way in-system. They're dead as dead, I'm sure."

Less sure herself, Misra ordered the comms officer to patch her through. Taking an instant to catch her breath, the captain keyed her microphone. "Unidentified ship, this is Captain Cassia Misra of the *ISV Defiant*. We are in position to render assistance should you require. Please reply."

Silence. Total and absolute.

"Michael," Misra addressed Lieutenant Phanu, "how long until they're on us?"

"Nine minutes, twenty seconds," he said, checking his readout. "They're closing fast."

Misra swore under her breath. "Scramble the lighters. I want grapnels on that ship. We need to stabilize their orbit and figure out where in Earth's black face they came from."

* * *

It took hours to rein the wild vessel in. The *Defiant* launched its full complement of lighter craft, and the smaller ships—using magnetic grapnels—caught and tethered the strange ship. Working in tandem, the flight crews—two men to a lighter—used their attitudinal jets to stabilize the broken vessel's wild tumble. Firing retros, they bled much of what remained of the ship's velocity and slid her smoothly into orbit around Aglovale's twin suns. Misra watched those suns through the canopy that fronted the *Defiant's* bridge. So far away they were that they almost seemed lost among the other stars, the bright white one with its duller, red companion, like mismatched eyes.

Tearing her eyes away, Misra studied the images on the comm console to her left, where a bank of monitors showed visions the lighter craft had taken of the derelict. Its hull glowed white as snow, as the streaks of cloud that mottled Aglovale's green surface, with here and there the shadow of a scratch or pockmark from some long-ago collision. Misra floated free of her seat and pulled herself over the console, black hair floating off her left shoulder in its braid.

"Are we sure it's one of ours?" she asked.

"Human, do you mean?" asked Lieutenant Edevane. "It looks the part."

"But are there any markings? Words?"

"Not that we've seen," the comms officer replied.

Phanu interjected as was his custom. "If they've been out in the black long enough, radiation's probably done in the paint job."

Edevane grumbled something. Misra caught the word *obviously*, but said nothing.

"If it's *exos*, it could be . . ." The comms officer's voice trailed off in horror. "Machines."

Misra and a couple of the others made warding gestures. Phanu cursed. The *exonauts* and other outworld barbarians did not cleave to the Imperium's laws forbidding the use and manufacture of artificial intelligence. For so many, the specter of the Foundation War and the Mericanii Totality still loomed large, and though it was written in the *Chant of Earth* that the first Emperor had smashed the machines forever, there were many who believed it was only a matter of time before hubris and human sin brought the horrors of the homeworld screaming back to blacken the stars. The *exonauts* flirted with such horrors, it was said, and if what Blinn had told her of the refugees who'd come to Aglovale was true, Misra was ready to believe even the darkest rumors.

"From the dominion of steel, O Mother, deliver us," she prayed, and traced a circle on her forehead. She was far from the most pious observer of the faith, but was it not said that even the most ardent skeptic cries out to Mother Earth and Emperor in the face of the unknown? She exhaled sharply through her nose. "If it is *exos*, we needn't fear. You know the protocol. If anyone's alive, detain them. Question them. Turn them back. If not, we strip the ship and launch it into one of the suns."

Her words—or the sharp reminder of protocol they carried—seemed to comfort the bridge crew. Misra studied the images another minute then in silence. The ship *looked* human enough. The silver foil of the solar sails, crumpled and twisted where they hung torn from their masts, had the look of many a satellite or orbital yacht she'd seen plying the spaceways above the skies of Aglovale, but surely mankind could not be the only creatures to have developed such things in the galaxy. There *were* other peoples, other races—primitive by comparison, to be sure, less developed than man. But they needn't all be so. As a girl, Misra had watched holos about the tree-dwelling Niawangu who—six-limbed—dwelt amid the bottomless jungles of Marakand, never touching the ground. They were savages, little better than the forefathers of man who had carved rude symbols into the mouths of caves, but surely not all that dwelt among the stars were so backwards.

What if it's . . . aliens?

The thought had chewed at the corners of her mind since the call came in, since they'd been dispatched from Fort Caspian. It wasn't likely, that much she knew, but it was possible that she, Cassia Alexandra Misra, daughter of a civil servant, granddaughter of an urban farmer, would be the first human being in history to make contact with another race capable of sailing the dark between the stars.

"We need to prepare a boarding party," she said. "Edevane, I want you with me, and twenty of the men."

"You're going yourself?" The science officer turned in his seat, bright eyes widening. "Captain, this is very irregular! Protocol dictates—"

Misra made a slashing gesture with one hand. "Don't cite the regs to me, Lysander. I'm going." She did her best to float imposingly in the center of the bridge, eyes narrow. No one else challenged her, and after a brief pause, she said, "Mister Phanu, you have the bridge."

★ ★ ★

The captain had a brief glimpse of her armored frame in the window of the hatch before it opened. Her armor, like that of her men, had been purchased from the Imperial Legions and repainted in the Baron's red and gold. Their faces all lay hid behind close-fitting plates of black glass, their necks protected by Romanesque neck-flanges. The suits themselves were bulky, but fit well, heavy though the ceramic plating was over the environment suit with its thick layer of sintered armorgel. They looked larger than any human ought to be, like squat statues of red-painted marble with fields of onyx for faces.

Chessmen.

The door opened on vastness and silence, and for a beat all Misra could hear was the rasp of her own breathing. She hated space—strange as that was for the captain of a starship to admit—and focused on the deck of the white ship beneath her feet to ground her universe. She could not see the *Defiant* when she looked up, though she knew it was there, black against that greater blackness. They'd ridden a shuttle across to the other ship, parked it on the main column of the vessel not far from where the masts rose and fell from that central spine. Still looking up through the tatters of the silver sails in search of her own ship, Cassia knew a moment of vertigo, fearing to fall into that bottomless night. She shook herself. The electromagnets in her boots were working fine. She would not fall.

"Find a hatch!" she ordered via the common band, stepping down from the ramp to the gently curving surface of the craft. The main shaft could not have been more than two hundred feet in diameter, and its surface curved away to either side. The base of the mast lay dead ahead, canted at a slight angle where they had not landed directly in line. Her men swarmed out after her, moving in pairs. They hurried right and left, following the curve of the hull, moving in the strange, hotfooted way men must wearing the iron boots that kept them clamped to the hull, high-stepping and awkward.

"See anything, Captain?" Phanu's voice sounded in her ear.

"Nothing yet," she answered. "Don't you have eyes on?"

"We do. Just asking."

Keeping a hand on her sidearm, Captain Misra stomped forward along the curving hull. The surface was far from smooth. Conduits ran bracketed to the hull, coated in places with ice, and raised panels rose as much as a foot, giving the place the appearance of some horribly paved road. And there were hooks and hard points where workers might tether a line, or bits of more delicate machinery hid under grates. It was an ugly, rough vessel, and ahead, beyond the masts, Misra saw the fat end of the engine cluster rising like white hills. Looking back and over the squat, beetle shape of their shuttle, she could see the ring section still spinning, and the gray shadow of the shield plate a thousand feet high.

"Found it, ma'am!" came the call. "Far side. Base of the mast!"

Misra acknowledged receipt and pointed for the four men of her guard to head right and counterclockwise around the shaft of the ruined vessel. The door was lozenge-shaped and built at an angle into the structure where the solar sail mast rose from a turret two thirds of the length of the spine from the forward plate. A manual lever stood vertical on the right side of the sealed portal, clamped in place and covered in peeled flecks of paint that once might have been yellow and black, but were so sun-bleached and faded they recalled old bones.

Seeing it, Lieutenant Edevane said, "Human or no, they're right-handed."

"I'm sorry?" Misra asked as Lysander brushed past her to the door. Behind him, the captain signaled her men to take up positions at either side of the airlock.

Edevane didn't answer, but fiddled with the clamps that secured the lever in place.

"Do we need a breaching charge?" Misra asked.

"No no!" came Edevane's reply. He'd freed the clamps already and gripped the lever. "Black planet!" he cursed. "Thing's corroded. You, man!" He pointed to the soldier at his right, and gesturing to the lever, said, "You push. I pull. Savvy?"

The other man tapped his helmet twice to signal he understood and joined Lysander in torquing the handle. It ground an inch, and Misra swore she could feel the faint squeal of metal on metal through her boots as they did so. Edevane swore again, but an instant later the corrosion gave way, and the lever slammed down.

It took three men pulling to get the airlock hatch open, but open it they did. The bulkhead was nearly a hand's span thick and slightly curved, and the glass in the window was just as thick. True glass, then, not the aluminum ceramic that passed for glass in most starships. That wasn't all; there were markings stenciled on the inside of the hatch, letters Misra didn't recognize. Judging by the red arrows, they were instructions for operating the manual release on the inside, but they were in no alphabet Misra had ever learned to read.

Edevane frowned at it. "Human after all," he said.

"Can *you* read it?" Misra asked.

The lieutenant peered up at her. "It's English. Old-style English. You see it on *exo* ships."

"*Exos*?" Misra repeated the word, unable to stop the welter of disappointment bubbling from her depths. She had dared to hope—if only for a passing moment—that it was inhumans. Too much to hope for, she guessed. She shook her head to clear it. No sense getting lost in childish dreams when there was work to do. It may not have been aliens, but it *was* the *exonauts*, and that was dangerous enough. There was no telling what might lay in wait behind that inner door.

Edevane nodded, let two of the armed men file in. "Some of their clans still speak the old tongue. Never picked up the standard. Too isolated."

Misra accepted this explanation with a tight nod and the double tap that signified she'd heard him. "Can we get the inner door open?"

"It *is* open, Captain!" called one of the others. "Internal environment's well compromised!"

Captain Misra shouldered her way past Lieutenant Edevane and into the airlock, triggering her suit's low-beams as she went. Their light illuminated padded white walls and silver panels with glass buttons and dead readouts, controls—she guessed—for the defunct airlock. A ladder exited through a hole in the floor, descending the mast turret toward the central column of the vessel itself. One of her men had already reached it, and—diving through it headfirst—pulled himself down. It was a strange, disorienting experience, even after all her years aboard the *Defiant*, a stark reminder that they were far from the warm embrace of Aglovale's gravity well.

A moment later, sconce lights embedded in the wall of the antechamber flickered to life, reacting, perhaps, to the opening of the outer door or the movement of men within the room. Following her over the threshold, Lysander Edevane said, "Something's still working, at least. Emergency power?"

"We'll have to find out," Misra said. "We need to find the bridge. See if we can't access their computers."

"There may be survivors," Edevane said, prodding one of the dead displays in the hopes of coaxing some life out of it.

"With the main cabin compromised?" Misra asked.

"Could be on ice, or—if they're *exonauts*—who knows?" His voiced darkened. "They might be playing dead."

Misra took his point well enough. They'd both heard enough horror stories about bodies being pulled in from the black of space, only to be reanimated by machines impregnating the sacred flesh to wreak havoc upon the men who'd salvaged the apparently dead sailor. Misra keyed all comms, spoke to her team. "Stay alert. Keep an eye out for any bodies, or any signs of a fugue pod. Don't take any chances. Assume any dead you find are hostile."

"Ma'am?" came the confusion over the line.

"Just play it safe, Ginherroc."

"Yes, ma'am."

The captain turned to her science officer, trying to see his face through the tinted black visor. "Forward, then," she said, and followed her men to the ladder, imitating the awkward diving motion that uncoupled her feet from the deck so that she climbed *up* the down ladder and into the central shaft. More lights had flickered on ahead of her, following those of her men who'd taken the lead. Here and there one refused to light, or sputtered and died. How long had it been adrift, riding its momentum across the stars at a respectable fraction of the speed of light? How many years or decades had flowed by that hull and leeched the color from it? And whence had it come? From what dark station between the stars and far from the light of the Empire had it been launched? And to what purpose?

Misra hauled herself forward, following her men along the core shaft, which she guessed ran the entire length of the vessel from forward plate to engine cluster, though bulkheads were shut to fore and aft. Misra propelled herself after her men, Edevane close behind. More lights pulsed on as her people glided by, using rungs bracketed on all sides of the tubular shaft to press forward or slow themselves as their momentum became too great. Concave doors matching the curvature of the tunnel stood open or closed at intervals along the hall and at ninety-degree angles to one another. At one of these she halted, peered inside with her suit lamps.

It was a storage room, and within small crates floated behind the netting that held them in their niche, and the contents of one opened locker drifted like detritus in the bottom of a long-neglected well. Ration packs in silver foil, spoiled long ago, shimmered in the light of her torch beam, and what looked like a pair of brass dice on a thin chain.

Human, after all.

The next open door seemed a kind of primitive lavatory. She recognized the waste elimination systems for what they were at once—some things never changed— but the shower stalls, if such they could be called, were not the sonic booths she was used to, but simple alcoves equipped with sanitary-napkin dispensers and privacy screens. She'd seen such things in history lessons at the academy, and tried to imagine the animal stink of the place when it had had air, nose wrinkling.

"They didn't design this place with boots in mind, did they?" groused one of the men.

He was right. Though ladder rungs ran along the sides of the shaft, there was no sense of *decks* at all. The chambers opening on four sides had all been built such that their floors were all aligned with the engine cluster beneath them, so that the ship might impart some imitation of gravity while under thrust. It was primitive, but ingenious in its way, that the crew might inhabit the spire while under the thrust, and the spin section ahead while not.

Ships like the *Defiant* took into account magnetized boots such as those they all wore, and so patterned their design more after the fashion of oceangoing vessels, with decks perpendicular to the axis of thrust. The warp drives used for faster-than-light travel imparted no inertia at all, and so ships like the *Defiant* spent most of their flight time not under what any ancient physicist would have recognized as *thrust*.

"Help me with this!" The words of the soldier ahead shook Misra from her reflection on the strangeness of the vessel, and looking forward she saw four men attempting to slide back the double doors of the bulkhead. The inner door had partly failed, had been open a couple inches. Wide enough to let any air there had been out, but not wide enough to admit any one of them.

The men groaned over the common band as they braced themselves against opposing walls—no easy task in free fall. But the door ground open, and when it had traveled a few inches, some long-dormant system kicked in and rolled the portal back.

"What's all this?" Edevane asked, casting his suit lamp over the room beyond. The walls were honeycombed with little round apertures—each perhaps five centimeters wide. The section continued for perhaps five meters before giving way to a ring of controls that girdled the entire passage. He drifted to one wall, seized handles between banks of the silver-capped apertures. Misra imagined she could hear the man squinting as he tapped one of the circles, wiped a thin caul of frost from the end. "Cold storage," he mused aloud, and leaned in to read some label on the end cap. Reacting to his touch, the little disc slid outward, outgassing as it went, revealing a narrow cylinder three times longer than it was wide, with glass sides revealing the blue fluid within.

"Lysander, leave it!" Misra ordered.

But the science chief leaned further in, focusing his suit light on the glass sides to better peer within. "Earth and Emperor!" he exclaimed.

"What is it?" Misra asked, unable to help herself.

"A child!" he said, holding up thumb and forefinger about two centimeters apart. "An embryo! About this big!"

Misra felt her heat tighten in her chest. "Human?"

"Well, I'm no biologist, but I'd say so," Edevane said, and tapped the tube again. It slid neatly back into place. He pushed back from the walls, caught hold of a rung near what passed for the ceiling, given Misra's vantage point. "There could be . . . ten thousand of them here! Maybe more. It's hard to say!" He turned to look down at his captain where she clung to the wall opposite. "Cassia, I think this is a colony seed ship."

"Never heard of the *exos* trying to launch a colony before," she said.

"Aglovale's pretty far out," said one of the men. "Maybe they thought it was uninhabited."

"You think?" asked the man called Ginherroc.

"Anything's possible," the first man said.

"What about the crew?" asked another.

"Maybe they had to evacuate?" Ginherroc said.

"Keep moving," Misra said. "We haven't found the bridge yet. It's good that these systems are still working. We'll find our answers ahead." But she was unable to shake the sense that something was very wrong about all this. The ship had no warp drive, of that she was certain. They would have seen the engines on their approach. She had never heard of a colony seed ship without warp drive.

How long were they in coming here?

"Captain, Lieutenant Edevane. Door's open!" said one of the soldiers. He'd gone on ahead to the round door at the extreme end of the core shaft, and found it functional.

Misra and Edevane broke off their conversation, and

both kicked off the walls to reach the door. The room beyond the door revolved slowly, a great wheel turning floor to wall to ceiling in a steady clockwise motion. They had reached the ring section, Misra realized, and the two doors that faced each other across the vestibule turned with the great spokes that connected that ring to the central spire. A third door lay dead ahead, in the center of the far wall, but it was locked. One of the soldiers was prodding a control panel as she entered, but nothing changed.

"We may need to cut our way in," he said.

"Hold that thought," Edevane interjected. "There might be atmo on the far side still." He turned back through the door whence they had come, then back to Misra. "Could be an airlock."

Misra chewed her lip. "We won't all fit in here."

"We can leave the lads to search downship. Might be something in engineering anyhow."

The captain nodded. If Edevane was right, it was better not to force the door, and if he was wrong, well, they'd be separated for a long time.

As the lieutenant floated to the door to shout his orders, Misra radioed the ship. "Mr. Phanu, can you run a scan of the forward sections? There's power coming from somewhere. I'd like to know where that is."

"On it," the gruff lieutenant replied. "Any idea whose ship it is?"

Misra hesitated only a moment. "Lysander thinks it's *exos*. All the signs are in Old English."

"English?" Phanu's scowl crackled over the comm. "Talking pre-war English? Could be Mericanii."

"That's enough, Michael," Misra snapped. "The Mericanii are three thousand years gone."

"I'm just kidding, Captain." She could hear the laughter in the navigator's voice. "Watch out for robots!"

"I said that's enough!" the captain snapped, but smiled beneath her visor. "Anything on scan?"

"Still going."

Edevane had returned by then and cycled the rear door, sealing the two officers and five men in the low-lit vestibule. "Try the door!" he said, pointing to the man nearest the panel. Misra pressed herself nearer the rotating wall, grabbed a handle to pull herself away from the others clustered near the center. Her lower body thudded against the wall as she turned, was lifted above her compatriots to better see the door as Edevane's fellow tapped again at the controls.

Again. Nothing.

"Is it dead?" she asked.

"I don't know!"

"This is interesting," came Phanu's voice on the comms. "On a lark I spectrographed the light coming from the windows on the forward section. There's air in there. Good air, but cold."

Edevane spoke up. "Explains the door."

"Can we cycle this room?" Misra asked. "Use it like an airlock?"

"I don't see any controls like that," said the man at the door.

"Michael?" Misra asked. "Any ideas?"

As if in answer, a green light filled the vestibule, and a moment later the door just above where Misra clung to the rotating perimeter of the room opened, and a cold, white light flickered to life. A dry rasp of air—thin as the last breath of a dying man—rushed from the tunnel into the vestibule, making Misra think of the tombs of the desert kings of old her father had talked about when she was just a girl. The men all moved with well-oiled reflexes, drawing reactionless phase disruptors and taking aim. But there was no intruder, only an empty stretch of corridor of ladder descending to the ring section above.

Below?

"Was that you, Damien?" Edevane asked the fellow on the controls.

Damien shrugged. "Might have been?"

"Captain, let me go first!" called one of the others, but Misra had already hauled herself through the opening, her own disruptor in her hands. They were right behind her, pulling themselves over the lip and into the spoke that descended toward the ring. The captain caught hold of the ladder built into one side and pushed herself down. The ring section below was not spinning enough to create the full effects of simulated gravity; it had slowed over who knew how many years, but still she felt a phantom weight as she descended, and when her feet were on the lip above the lower door she did not float away, light though she was.

The lower door opened to admit her, and a rush of frigid air filled the shaft above, blowing her armor's gold-fringed tunic up like the skirt of some silly little girl. Edevane and the others were just above her, so she leaped down through the aperture to the deck of the ring below. She landed catfooted, gun raised, in the center of what looked for all the world just like one of the rec rooms back on Fort Caspian. Low couches—black against the white walls a floor—carved out their square sitting areas around low tables, all built into the floor. But the walls were bare of any decoration, and a thin layer of frost lay on almost everything.

Edevane swung off the bottom of the ladder at her side—not one to leap as she had done—and the others came clambering down. "Living quarters?" he asked, looking round.

"Looks like."

"Still no sign of the crew. Fugue, do you reckon?"

Misra shook her head. "I didn't see any crèches, did you?"

"Maybe down by the engines?"

A distant sound broke the sepulchral quiet of the place, and all seven of them jumped, pointing disruptors. What looked like a screwdriver rolled into sight from around a counter up ahead, and hurrying toward it, Misra saw a metal toolbox smashed open on the ground. She could see where it had rested on the counter—a clear spot stood dark against the glimmering frost. She stooped to pick it up. It *was* a screwdriver, a common screwdriver. She held it up for Edevane and the others to see.

Then a huge, white shape burst from over the counter and hurled itself at her. Edevane shouted. Too late! Whatever it was, it tackled Misra to the ground, knocked the disruptor from fingers suddenly nerveless. Cassia Misra reacted fast as she could, cuffed her assailant in what she guessed was the side of its head.

"Don't shoot!" Edevane shouted. "You'll hit the captain!"

Man-shaped it was and huge, hulking and padded beneath layers of what felt like rubber and Kevlar. A hand seized Misra by the jaw, forcing her head back. Her gun could not have gone far. She felt for it, hand slapping at the deck beneath her. Where were the others?

There!

The creature's huge hand closed on hers and the gun in it, and before she could retaliate, before she could react—it was gone. Rolled off her and onto one knee.

"Stɑp!" it shouted, pointing the gun at her, at them. "ðæts fɑr mʌf!" His words were strange, not wholly unfamiliar, but *wrong*. Misra slid backward where she lay, shamed to have been caught off guard so easily. Seeing her movement, her assailant snapped the weapon toward her. "hu ɑɹ ju? aɪdɛntəfaɪ jɔɹsɛlvz!"

Guns glared at each other across the space between the demon in white and Misra's men.

She didn't understand.

"dɪd ju ətæk maɪ ʃɪp?"

Now that she had gained the space to breathe, Misra understood what it was that had attacked her. It *was* a man, or nearly one, clad in a heavy environment suit of heavy white cloth over layers of padded material. The helmet was not close-fitting at all, but a white dome with a bronzed visor that hid his face—for *he* he certainly was. The voice was deeply masculine, but human as anything in the cosmos.

"hu ɑɹ ju?" he roared once more, and pointing the disruptor at the ground he fired. The energy bolt flashed white in the dimness. "ɹɛbəlz? ɪz ðæt ɪt?"

"Put the gun down!" Misra said, returning to her knees.

The man thrust the gun back in her face. His hand wavered. "ju doʊnt əndəstænd mi..." His words trailed away to nothing. No one moved for a long moment.

"Who are you?" Misra asked, taking advantage of the man's faltering to stand. He turned to look at her, perhaps recognizing the feminine in her voice. How long had it been since he'd heard a woman's voice? Or any man's? Misra tapped her chest. "Misra," she said. "Misra."

"Misra?" the man echoed the word in his curious accent. Then with one bulky gauntlet he lifted his bronze visor with the air of a knight long afield.

The captain gasped, and sensed the same thrill of horror run through the others.

It was a man, indeed, but a man like and yet unlike any she had ever seen. He wore his blond hair in a short burr flat on top and nearly absent on the sides. His face was broad and clean-shaven, strong-jawed and pale of skin, and Misra could tell that even were his padded suit removed he would be a big man, broad-shouldered and strong. But it was his eyes that drew hers, and drew those of all the others in the room.

They were solid silver, like twin pools of mercury in his otherwise unremarkable but handsome face. Like mirrors, they reflected all they saw, and seemed to glow with an inner light. And what was more, the left side of his head from his temple to behind his ear shone just as silver and gleamed with faint, blue light.

"Mother Earth!" swore one of the men. "He's *exonaut*, all right."

The stranger cocked his head, as confused by the strange *wrongness* of their words as they were by his, as though he could *almost* understand them. Lowering his stolen weapon, he said, "ɜθ?" And again, "Earth?"

"Earth?" Edevane asked.

"juɹ fɹɹəm ɜθ?" His jaw went slack, and it was only slowly that he lifted a hand to his own chest, jostling the air and water hoses fastened to the pack there. "hwiłɝ. Aɪm kə'mænɗɝ æłən hwiłɝ."

"Wheeler?" Edevane echoed the man's word. "Your name is Wheeler?"

The man nodded. Misra's gun still wavered in his hands, half raised.

"Edevane?" Misra asked.

"He's speaking English, ma'am. *Old* English."

"You understand him?"

"Not well," said the lieutenant. "Never thought I'd have to *speak* it." He lowered his own gun and advanced a step, his empty hands raised. Pointing at his black-visored face, he said, "Aɪm idvem, łutɛnənt łaɪsænɗɝ idvem."

"Lieutenant?"

Wheeler took a step back, raising his guns. "łutɛnənt fɔɹ hu? Hu du ju wɜk fɔɹ?"

Edevane glanced sidelong at his captain. "He wants to know who we work for, Captain."

"Tell him, Lysander!"

"We're soldiers of the Sollan Empire," Edevane said, words muddy as he stumbled through the *exonaut's* unfamiliar tongue. "This system is ours. Who are you?"

"jɔɹz?" Wheeler said, shining eyes narrowing. "Yours? This system's uninhabited. No one's been out here. What's the Sollan Empire?"

"What does he mean 'what's the Sollan Empire'?"

Misra echoed when Edevane had repeated the strange sailor's words. The Sollan Empire ruled over thousands of star systems—more than ten thousand, or so it was said! The Empire ruled over the ruins of Earth itself, safeguarded the homeworld in trust against the day the radiation faded and mankind was free to return and plant her hills anew. How could anyone—even one of the *exonauts*—not know of the Empire? "It doesn't make sense."

Edevane turned to the man called Wheeler, and again speaking the fellow's arcane tongue, he said, "Who are you, exactly? What is this ship? What is your purpose here?"

"maɪ pɜˑpəs?" Wheeler echoed. "My purpose? We're a colony mission! Or we were."

He continued on in that vein for a long moment, and when he was done, Edevane translated, saying: "He says their life support failed in transit."

"What happened to the rest of the crew?" Misra asked.

Edevane repeated the question in halting, broken English.

"Dead," the *exonaut* replied. That word, at least, had not changed as Old English and the Galactic Standard drifted further and further apart. Misra felt a twinge of sympathy for the lone sailor then. She could not imagine how long he had been alone, surviving off what ambient air remained in the vast ship, off the rebreather and the oxygen tanks left in storage.

Wheeler kept speaking then, continued for a long moment. Edevane hesitated for just a moment when he was done, asked a question in the *exo*'s aged tongue. "He says there were twelve of them."

"Only twelve?" Misra was unable to keep the shock

from her voice. There were three hundred on the *Defiant*, and it was less than half the volume. "What happened to them?"

Edevane asked.

"əpłoʊdɪd," Wheeler said.

The lieutenant didn't answer at once, so Misra asked, "What did he say?"

Edevane shook his head. "'Uploaded'?" he said, repeating the *exonaut's* word sound-for-sound.

The captain shook her head as well. The word was English, and what it might mean she couldn't begin to guess. "We need to radio Fort Caspian," she said, "get up with command. Tell them it's another *exo* incursion." She studied Wheeler's face, the mirrored eyes and implant on his temple. The mingling of flesh and machine was strictly forbidden. That was why the *exonauts* existed in the first place. They had chosen to flee, chosen exile rather than rejoin the human family after the war, after the Advent and annihilation of Earth and her machines.

The last *exonaut* ship had simply needed fuel and had been sent on its way, but Wheeler's ship was in no state to sail, and so he would have no choice but to submit to Imperial rule. His eyes would have to be removed, and the *thing* in his head with them. If new eyes could not be found or grown for him, he would live blind but *human* as a guest of the Baron's. It was the law.

Something of the interloper's earlier behavior clicked in Misra then, and she turned her gaze back to Edevane. "Lysander, ask him where he came from."

The lieutenant did as he was ordered, repeating her words in the stumbling, archaic way.

Wheeler's silver eyes blinked, and he frowned at them as if this was the most foolish question in all the galaxy.

"hwɛɹ dɪd wi kəm fɹəm?" he asked, repeating Edevane's question. Misra's gun wavered in his confused hand. "aɪ . . . ɜ̃θ. Wiɹ fɹeɪm ɜ̃θ."

Lysander Edevane might have been transmuted to stone. He stood there, utterly still, a suit of armor on display in some museum.

"What is it?" Misra asked, marking the unease that rippled through the other men to see their lieutenant's reaction. But she already knew, could sense the answer in the way Wheeler had reacted to one of the soldier's oaths.

Earth.

"He's from Earth," Edevane said.

"What?" one of the others interjected.

"Impossible!" Misra replied. "Earth was destroyed three thousand years ago!"

Picking up on the fear and anger in the voice of Misra and her men, Wheeler took a step back, raised his gun. "hwət aɹ ðeɪ seɪɪŋ?" His voice had sharpened, and clearly Misra heard the fear in it.

Edevane didn't answer him. "It's not impossible," he said, turning to face her. "This ship is old. Pre-warp. If she could push light speed. Get right up against c . . . ."

Misra could only stare at her lieutenant. He was talking about relativity. Special relativity. That hadn't been relevant to space travel—not really—since Mann and Ibson created the warp drive. Modern ships like her *Defiant* were not even capable of achieving near-light speeds, relying instead on fusion engines for short, hard burns and ion drives and even solar sails to boost

momentum over long distances. Warp drives sidestepped
the issues of relativity, kept sailors from slipping away
thousands of years into the future.

From traveling through time.

"Three thousand years ..." Misra's voice was shaking.
"That would mean ... that would make him ..."

Edevane was well ahead of her. "Mericanii. This is a
Mericanii ship!" His hand snapped back up, disruptor
pointed at Wheeler's chest. The other men stiffened,
retrained their weapons on the target.

It wasn't possible. Couldn't be possible. Beneath her
helmet, Cassia Misra's mouth hung open. The Mericanii
were gone. William the Great had stamped them out, tore
up their iron colonies by the roots and hounded them
back to the green hills of Earth where they and their
machines had made their final stand. She looked at
Wheeler. He was no *exonaut*, but an *archaenaut*, an
ancient sailor borne by the winds of light from some half-
remembered history. Her mouth worked, but no sound
came out. Never in all her wildest dreams had she thought
such a thing might be possible, might happen *to her.*

History did not come to life, did not sail out of the dark
between the stars and menace her sleeping world. History
was for books, for holographs and children. Not for the
light of day.

But history had come to Aglovale, and to her.

"hwəts goʊɪn ɑn?" Wheeler asked, pointing his stolen
gun now at Edevane.

How many billions had the Mericanii and their
machine masters killed, and on how many worlds? How
many people had died in the name of their *progress*, their

giant leap forward? The machines would not tolerate any man or woman to live free of their network. All were to be incorporated, that the machines might set them *free*. Of suffering, of pain, of the iniquities of ordinary life. Of rank and difference itself. Such equity demanded the machines to enforce it, and enforce it they had. Every blade of grass that stood tall was cut down, and every crawling weed was straightened, and all who would not kneel were destroyed less they threaten to Totality.

There were worlds besides Earth where still no life grew, and it was said that when the war was done, only the smallest portion of mankind yet stood free.

"They're dead!" Misra objected, looking at Wheeler. "The Mericanii are dead."

"Looks like this one was a long time coming here," Edevane said. "What should we do? You know the Protocols. If there's a *machine* on board..."

Misra knew the rules as well as any officer. Three thousand years later, and every man and woman on every ship from every world in the Imperium was still made to memorize the Avalon Protocols.

"This ship has to be destroyed." She looked to Wheeler. *And every man on it.*

"hwəts goʊm ɑn?" Wheeler asked again, clearly not guessing his danger. And how could he? He had come from a different world. A different universe. A universe forever changed by the actions of the power he had served—*if* he had served them.

"Ask him!" Misra said. "Name. Rank. Serial number. Ask him, Lysander!"

Lysander did as he was ordered.

The man called Wheeler did not lower his gun. "aɪ toʊɫd ju!" he said, still perhaps not understanding. "aɪ æm kəmændɚ æɫən hwiɫɚ, ju ɛs ɛs æməzɑn, əv ðə pipəɫz junaɪtɪd steɪts əv əmɛɹəkə."

Captain Misra did not need Edevane to translate the *archaenaut's* words. Strange though his accent was, his last words needed no translation.

A Merican.

THE LONG REMEMBERED THUNDER

by Keith Laumer

Sent from his top-secret government project to investigate signals indicating that someone else also had the secret, Tremaine returned to the town where he had grown up to find a mysterious man who repeatedly fought a strange battle against an implacable alien menace. Getting personal, I (Hank) greatly enjoyed this story when in 1963 I read it in the first issue of Worlds of Tomorrow, *and it remains one of this Laumer fan's all-time favorites.*

I

In his room at the Elsby Commercial Hotel, Tremaine opened his luggage and took out a small tool kit, used a screwdriver to remove the bottom cover plate from the telephone. He inserted a tiny aluminum cylinder, crimped wires and replaced the cover. Then he dialed a long-distance Washington number and waited half a minute for the connection.

"Fred, Tremaine here. Put the buzzer on." A thin hum sounded on the wire as the scrambler went into operation.

"Okay, can you read me all right? I'm set up in Elsby. Grammond's boys are supposed to keep me informed. Meantime, I'm not sitting in this damned room crouched over a dial. I'll be out and around for the rest of the afternoon."

"I want to see results," the thin voice came back over the filtered hum of the jamming device. "You spent a week with Grammond—I can't wait another. I don't mind telling you certain quarters are pressing me."

"Fred, when will you learn to sit on your news breaks until you've got some answers to go with the questions?"

"I'm an appointive official," Fred said sharply. "But never mind that. This fellow Margrave—General Margrave. Project Officer for the hyperwave program— he's been on my neck day and night. I can't say I blame him. An unauthorized transmitter interfering with a Top Secret project, progress slowing to a halt, and this Bureau—"

"Look, Fred. I was happy in the lab. Headaches, nightmares and all. Hyperwave is my baby, remember? You elected me to be a leg-man: now let me do it my way."

"I felt a technical man might succeed where a trained investigator could be misled. And since it seems to be pinpointed in your home area—"

"You don't have to justify yourself. Just don't hold out on me. I sometimes wonder if I've seen the complete files on this—"

"You've seen all the files! Now I want answers, not

questions! I'm warning you, Tremaine. Get that
transmitter. I need someone to hang!"

Tremaine left the hotel, walked two blocks west along
Commerce Street and turned in at a yellow brick building
with the words ELSBY MUNICIPAL POLICE cut in the
stone lintel above the door. Inside, a heavy man with a
creased face and thick gray hair looked up from behind
an ancient Underwood. He studied Tremaine, shifted a
toothpick to the opposite corner of his mouth.

"Don't I know you, mister?" he said. His soft voice
carried a note of authority.

Tremaine took off his hat. "Sure you do, Jess. It's been
a while, though."

The policeman got to his feet. "Jimmy," he said,
"Jimmy Tremaine." He came to the counter and put out
his hand. "How are you, Jimmy? What brings you back to
the boondocks?"

"Let's go somewhere and sit down, Jess."

In a back room Tremaine said, "To everybody but you
this is just a visit to the old home town. Between us, there's
more."

Jess nodded. "I heard you were with the guv'ment."

"It won't take long to tell; we don't know much yet."
Tremaine covered the discovery of the powerful
unidentified interference on the high-security hyperwave
band, the discovery that each transmission produced not
one but a pattern of "fixes" on the point of origin. He passed
a sheet of paper across the table. It showed a set of
concentric circles, overlapped by a similar group of rings.

"I think what we're getting is an echo effect from each

of these points of intersection. The rings themselves represent the diffraction pattern—"

"Hold it, Jimmy. To me it just looks like a beer ad. I'll take your word for it."

"The point is this, Jess: we think we've got it narrowed down to this section. I'm not sure of a damn thing, but I think that transmitter's near here. Now, have you got any ideas?"

"That's a tough one, Jimmy. This is where I should come up with the news that Old Man Whatchamacallit's got an attic full of gear he says is a time machine. Trouble is, folks around here haven't even taken to TV. They figure we should be content with radio, like the Lord intended."

"I didn't expect any easy answers, Jess. But I was hoping maybe you had something . . ."

"Course," said Jess, "there's always Mr. Bram . . ."

"Mr. Bram," repeated Tremaine. "Is he still around? I remember him as a hundred years old when I was a kid."

"Still just the same, Jimmy. Comes in town maybe once a week, buys his groceries and hikes back out to his place by the river."

"Well, what about him?"

"Nothing. But he's the town's mystery man. You know that. A little touched in the head."

"There were a lot of funny stories about him, I remember," Tremaine said. "I always liked him. One time he tried to teach me something I've forgotten. Wanted me to come out to his place and he'd teach me. I never did go. We kids used to play in the caves near his place, and sometimes he gave us apples."

★★★

"I've never seen any harm in Bram," said Jess. "But you know how this town is about foreigners, especially when they're a mite addled. Bram has blue eyes and blond hair—or did before it turned white—and he talks just like everybody else. From a distance he seems just like an ordinary American. But up close, you feel it. He's foreign, all right. But we never did know where he came from."

"How long's he lived here in Elsby?"

"Beats me, Jimmy. You remember old Aunt Tress, used to know all about ancestors and such as that? She couldn't remember about Mr. Bram. She was kind of senile, I guess. She used to say he'd lived in that same old place out on the Concord road when she was a girl. Well, she died five years ago . . . in her seventies. He still walks in town every Wednesday . . . or he did up till yesterday anyway."

"Oh?" Tremaine stubbed out his cigarette, lit another. "What happened then?"

"You remember Soup Gaskin? He's got a boy, name of Hull. He's Soup all over again."

"I remember Soup," Tremaine said. "He and his bunch used to come in the drug store where I worked and perch on the stools and kid around with me, and Mr. Hempleman would watch them from over back of the prescription counter and look nervous. They used to raise cain in the other drug store. . . ."

"Soup's been in the pen since then. His boy Hull's the same kind. Him and a bunch of his pals went out to Bram's place one night and set it on fire."

"What was the idea of that?"

"Dunno. Just meanness, I reckon. Not much damage done. A car was passing by and called it in. I had the whole caboodle locked up here for six hours. Then the sob sisters went to work: poor little tyke routine, high spirits, you know the line. All of 'em but Hull are back in the streets playin' with matches by now. I'm waiting for the day they'll make jail age."

"Why Bram?" Tremaine persisted. "As far as I know, he never had any dealings to speak of with anybody here in town."

"Oh hoh, you're a little young, Jimmy," Jess chuckled. "You never knew about Mr. Bram—the young Mr. Bram—and Linda Carroll."

Tremaine shook his head.

"Old Miss Carroll. School teacher here for years; guess she was retired by the time you were playing hookey. But her dad had money, and in her day she was a beauty. Too good for the fellers in these parts. I remember her ridin by in a high-wheeled shay, when I was just a nipper. Sitting up proud and tall, with that red hair piled up high. I used to think she was some kind of princess...."

"What about her and Bram? A romance?"

Jess rocked his chair back on two legs, looked at the ceiling, frowning. "This would ha' been about nineteen-oh-one. I was no more'n eight years old. Miss Linda was maybe in her twenties—and that made her an old maid, in those times. The word got out she was setting her cap for Bram. He was a good-looking young feller then, over six foot, of course, broad backed, curly yellow hair—and a stranger to boot. Like I said, Linda Carroll wanted nothin to do with the local bucks. There was a big shindy planned. Now, you know Bram was funny about any kind of socializing; never would go any place at night. But this was a Sunday afternoon and someways or other they got Bram down there; and Miss Linda made her play, right there in front of the town, practically. Just before sundown they went off together in that fancy shay. And the next day, she was home again—alone. That finished off her reputation, as far as the biddies in Elsby was concerned. It was ten years 'fore she even landed the teaching job. By that time, she was already old. And nobody was ever fool enough to mention the name Bram in front of her."

Tremaine got to his feet. "I'd appreciate it if you'd keep your ears and eyes open for anything that might build into a lead on this, Jess. Meantime, I'm just a tourist, seeing the sights."

"What about that gear of yours? Didn't you say you had some kind of detector you were going to set up?"

"I've got an oversized suitcase," Tremaine said. "I'll be setting it up in my room over at the hotel."

"When's this bootleg station supposed to broadcast again?"

"After dark. I'm working on a few ideas. It might be an infinitely repeating logarithmic sequence, based on—"

"Hold it, Jimmy. You're over my head." Jess got to his feet. "Let me know if you want anything. And by the way—" he winked broadly—"I always did know who busted Soup Gaskin's nose and took out his front teeth."

II

Back in the street, Tremaine headed south toward the Elsby Town Hall, a squat structure of brownish-red brick, crouched under yellow autumn trees at the end of Sheridan Street. Tremaine went up the steps and past heavy double doors. Ten yards along the dim corridor, a hand-lettered cardboard sign over a black-varnished door said "MUNICIPAL OFFICE OF RECORD." Tremaine opened the door and went in.

A thin man with garters above the elbow looked over his shoulder at Tremaine.

"We're closed," he said.

"I won't be a minute," Tremaine said. "Just want to check on when the Bram property changed hands last."

The man turned to Tremaine, pushing a drawer shut with his hip. "Bram? He dead?"

"Nothing like that. I just want to know when he bought the place."

The man came over to the counter, eyeing Tremaine. "He ain't going to sell, mister, if that's what you want to know."

"I want to know when he bought."

The man hesitated, closed his jaw hard. "Come back tomorrow," he said.

Tremaine put a hand on the counter, looked thoughtful. "I was hoping to save a trip." He lifted his hand and scratched the side of his jaw. A folded bill opened on the counter. The thin man's eyes darted toward it. His hand eased out, covered the bill. He grinned quickly.

"See what I can do," he said.

It was ten minutes before he beckoned Tremaine over to the table where a two-foot-square book lay open. An untrimmed fingernail indicated a line written in faded ink:

"May 19. Acreage sold, One Dollar and other G&V consid. NW Quarter Section 24, Township Elsby. Bram. (see Vol. 9 & cet.)"

"Translated, what does that mean?" said Tremaine.

"That's the ledger for 1901; means Bram bought a quarter section on the nineteenth of May. You want me to look up the deed?"

"No, thanks," Tremaine said. "That's all I needed." He turned back to the door.

"What's up, mister?" the clerk called after him. "Bram in some kind of trouble?"

"No. No trouble."

The man was looking at the book with pursed lips. "Nineteen-oh-one," he said. "I never thought of it before, but you know, old Bram must be dern near to ninety years old. Spry for that age."

"I guess you're right."

The clerk looked sideways at Tremaine. "Lots of funny stories about old Bram. Useta say his place was haunted. You know; funny noises and lights. And they used to say there was money buried out at his place."

"I've heard those stories. Just superstition, wouldn't you say?"

"Maybe so." The clerk leaned on the counter, assumed a knowing look. "There's one story that's not superstition. . . ."

Tremaine waited.

"You—uh—paying anything for information?"

"Now why would I do that?" Tremaine reached for the door knob.

The clerk shrugged. "Thought I'd ask. Anyway—I can

swear to this. Nobody in this town's ever seen Bram between sundown and sunup."

Untrimmed sumacs threw late-afternoon shadows on the discolored stucco facade of the Elsby Public Library. Inside, Tremaine followed a paper-dry woman of indeterminate age to a rack of yellowed newsprint.

"You'll find back to nineteen-forty here," the librarian said. "The older are there in the shelves."

"I want nineteen-oh-one, if they go back that far."

The woman darted a suspicious look at Tremaine. "You have to handle these old papers carefully."

"I'll be extremely careful." The woman sniffed, opened a drawer, leafed through it, muttering.

"What date was it you wanted?"

"Nineteen-oh-one; the week of May nineteenth."

The librarian pulled out a folded paper, placed it on the table, adjusted her glasses, squinted at the front page. "That's it," she said. "These papers keep pretty well, provided they're stored in the dark. But they're still flimsy, mind you."

"I'll remember." The woman stood by as Tremaine looked over the front page. The lead article concerned the opening of the Pan-American Exposition at Buffalo. Vice President Roosevelt had made a speech. Tremaine leafed over, reading slowly.

On page four, under a column headed *County Notes* he saw the name Bram:

Mr. Bram has purchased a quarter section of fine grazing land, north of town, together with a sturdy house,

from J.P. Spivey of Elsby. Mr. Bram will occupy the home
and will continue to graze a few head of stock. Mr. Bram,
who is a newcomer to the county, has been a resident of
Mrs. Stoate's Guest Home in Elsby for the past months.

"May I see some earlier issues; from about the first of
the year?"

The librarian produced the papers. Tremaine turned
the pages, read the heads, skimmed an article here and
there. The librarian went back to her desk. An hour later,
in the issue for July 7, 1900, an item caught his eye:

A Severe Thunderstorm. Citizens of Elsby and the
country were much alarmed by a violent cloudburst,
accompanied by lightning and thunder, during the night
of the fifth. A fire set in the pine woods north of Spivey's
farm destroyed a considerable amount of timber and
threatened the house before burning itself out along the
river.

The librarian was at Tremaine's side. "I have to close
the library now. You'll have to come back tomorrow."

Outside, the sky was sallow in the west: lights were
coming on in windows along the side streets. Tremaine
turned up his collar against a cold wind that had risen,
started along the street toward the hotel.

A block away a black late-model sedan rounded a
corner with a faint squeal of tires and gunned past him, a
heavy antenna mounted forward of the left rear tail fin
whipping in the slipstream. Tremaine stopped short,
stared after the car.

"Damn!" he said aloud. An elderly man veered, eyeing
him sharply. Tremaine set off at a run, covered the two

blocks to the hotel, yanked open the door to his car, slid into the seat, made a U-turn, and headed north after the police car.

Two miles into the dark hills north of the Elsby city limits, Tremaine rounded a curve. The police car was parked on the shoulder beside the highway just ahead. He pulled off the road ahead of it and walked back. The door opened. A tall figure stepped out.

"What's your problem, mister?" a harsh voice drawled.

"What's the matter? Run out of signal?"

"What's it to you, mister?"

"Are you boys in touch with Grammond on the car set?"

"We could be."

"Mind if I have a word with him? My name's Tremaine."

"Oh," said the cop, "you're the big shot from Washington." He shifted chewing tobacco to the other side of his jaw. "Sure, you can talk to him." He turned and spoke to the other cop, who muttered into the mike before handing it to Tremaine.

The heavy voice of the State Police chief crackled. "What's your beef, Tremaine?"

"I thought you were going to keep your men away from Elsby until I gave the word, Grammond."

"That was before I knew your Washington stuffed shirts were holding out on me."

"It's nothing we can go to court with, Grammond. And the job you were doing might have been influenced if I'd told you about the Elsby angle."

Grammond cursed. "I could have put my men in the town and taken it apart brick by brick in the time—"

"That's just what I don't want. If our bird sees cops cruising, he'll go underground."

"You've got it all figured, I see. I'm just the dumb hick you boys use for the spade work, that it?"

"Pull your lip back in. You've given me the confirmation I needed."

"Confirmation, hell! All I know is that somebody somewhere is punching out a signal. For all I know, it's forty midgets on bicycles, pedalling all over the damned state. I've got fixes in every county—"

"The smallest hyperwave transmitter Uncle Sam knows how to build weighs three tons," said Tremaine. "Bicycles are out."

Grammond snorted. "Okay, Tremaine," he said. "You're the boy with all the answers. But if you get in trouble, don't call me; call Washington."

Back in his room, Tremaine put through a call.

"It looks like Grammond's not willing to be left out in the cold, Fred. Tell him if he queers this—"

"I don't know but what he might have something," the voice came back over the filtered hum. "Suppose he smokes them out—"

"Don't go dumb on me, Fred. We're not dealing with West Virginia moonshiners."

"Don't tell me my job, Tremaine!" the voice snapped. "And don't try out your famous temper on me. I'm still in charge of this investigation."

"Sure. Just don't get stuck in some senator's hip

pocket." Tremaine hung up the telephone, went to the dresser and poured two fingers of Scotch into a water glass. He tossed it down, then pulled on his coat and left the hotel.

He walked south two blocks, turned left down a twilit side street. He walked slowly, looking at the weathered frame houses. Number 89 was a once-stately three-storied mansion overgrown with untrimmed vines, its windows squares of sad yellow light. He pushed through the gate in the ancient picket fence, mounted the porch steps and pushed the button beside the door, a dark panel of cracked varnish. It was a long minute before the door opened. A tall woman with white hair and a fine-boned face looked at him coolly.

"Miss Carroll," Tremaine said. "You won't remember me, but I—"

"There is nothing whatever wrong with my faculties, James," Miss Carroll said calmly. Her voice was still resonant, a deep contralto. Only a faint quaver reflected her age—close to eighty, Tremaine thought, startled.

"I'm flattered you remember me, Miss Carroll," he said.

"Come in." She led the way to a pleasant parlor set out with the furnishings of another era. She motioned Tremaine to a seat and took a straight chair across the room from him.

"You look very well, James," she said, nodding. "I'm pleased to see that you've amounted to something."

"Just another bureaucrat, I'm afraid."

"You were wise to leave Elsby. There is no future here for a young man."

"I often wondered why you didn't leave, Miss Carroll. I thought, even as a boy, that you were a woman of great ability."

"Why did you come today, James?" asked Miss Carroll.

"I . . ." Tremaine started. He looked at the old lady. "I want some information. This is an important matter. May I rely on your discretion?"

"Of course."

"How long has Mr. Bram lived in Elsby?"

Miss Carroll looked at him for a long moment. "Will what I tell you be used against him?"

"There'll be nothing done against him, Miss Carroll . . . unless it needs to be in the national interest."

"I'm not at all sure I know what the term 'national interest' means, James. I distrust these glib phrases."

"I always liked Mr. Bram," said Tremaine. "I'm not out to hurt him."

"Mr. Bram came here when I was a young woman. I'm not certain of the year."

"What does he do for a living?"

"I have no idea."

"Why did a healthy young fellow like Bram settle out in that isolated piece of country? What's his story?"

"I'm . . . not sure that anyone truly knows Bram's story."

"You called him 'Bram,' Miss Carroll. Is that his first name . . . or his last?"

"That is his only name. Just . . . Bram."

"You knew him well once, Miss Carroll. Is there anything—"

A tear rolled down Miss Carroll's faded cheek. She wiped it away impatiently.

"I'm an unfulfilled old maid, James," she said. "You must forgive me."

Tremaine stood up. "I'm sorry. Really sorry. I didn't mean to grill you. Miss Carroll. You've been very kind. I had no right. . . ."

Miss Carroll shook her head. "I knew you as a boy, James. I have complete confidence in you. If anything I can tell you about Bram will be helpful to you, it is my duty to oblige you; and it may help him." She paused. Tremaine waited.

"Many years ago I was courted by Bram. One day he asked me to go with him to his house. On the way he told me a terrible and pathetic tale. He said that each night he fought a battle with evil beings, alone, in a cave beneath his house."

Miss Carroll drew a deep breath and went on. "I was torn between pity and horror. I begged him to take me back. He refused." Miss Carroll twisted her fingers together, her eyes fixed on the long past. "When we reached the house, he ran to the kitchen. He lit a lamp and threw open a concealed panel. There were stairs. He went down . . . and left me there alone.

"I waited all that night in the carriage. At dawn he emerged. He tried to speak to me but I would not listen.

"He took a locket from his neck and put it into my hand. He told me to keep it and, if ever I should need him, to press it between my fingers in a secret way . . . and he would come. I told him that until he would consent to see a doctor, I did not wish him to call. He drove me home. He never called again."

"This locket," said Tremaine, "do you still have it?"

Miss Carroll hesitated, then put her hand to her throat, lifted a silver disc on a fine golden chain. "You see what a foolish old woman I am, James."

"May I see it?"

She handed the locket to him. It was heavy, smooth. "I'd like to examine this more closely," he said. "May I take it with me?"

Miss Carroll nodded.

"There is one other thing," she said, "perhaps quite meaningless . . ."

"I'd be grateful for any lead."

"Bram fears the thunder."

III

As Tremaine walked slowly toward the lighted main street of Elsby a car pulled to a stop beside him. Jess leaned out, peered at Tremaine and asked:

"Any luck, Jimmy?"

Tremaine shook his head. "I'm getting nowhere fast. The Bram idea's a dud, I'm afraid."

"Funny thing about Bram. You know, he hasn't showed up yet. I'm getting a little worried. Want to run out there with me and take a look around?"

"Sure. Just so I'm back by full dark."

As they pulled away from the curb Jess said, "Jimmy, what's this about State Police nosing around here? I thought you were playing a lone hand from what you were saying to me."

"I thought so too, Jess. But it looks like Grammond's a

jump ahead of me. He smells headlines in this; he doesn't want to be left out."

"Well, the State cops could be mighty handy to have around. I'm wondering why you don't want 'em in. If there's some kind of spy ring working—"

"We're up against an unknown quantity. I don't know what's behind this and neither does anybody else. Maybe it's a ring of Bolsheviks...and maybe it's something bigger. I have the feeling we've made enough mistakes in the last few years; I don't want to see this botched."

The last pink light of sunset was fading from the clouds to the west as Jess swung the car through the open gate, pulled up under the old trees before the square-built house. The windows were dark. The two men got out, circled the house once, then mounted the steps and rapped on the door. There was a black patch of charred flooring under the window, and the paint on the wall above it was bubbled. Somewhere a cricket set up a strident chirrup, suddenly cut off. Jess leaned down, picked up an empty shotgun shell. He looked at Tremaine. "This don't look good," he said. "You suppose those fool boys...?"

He tried the door. It opened. A broken hasp dangled. He turned to Tremaine. "Maybe this is more than kid stuff," he said. "You carry a gun?"

"In the car."

"Better get it."

Tremaine went to the car, dropped the pistol in his coat pocket, rejoined Jess inside the house. It was silent, deserted. In the kitchen Jess flicked the beam of his flashlight around the room. An empty plate lay on the oilcloth-covered table.

"This place is empty," he said. "Anybody'd think he'd been gone a week."

"Not a very cozy—" Tremaine broke off. A thin yelp sounded in the distance.

"I'm getting jumpy," said Jess. "Dern hound dog, I guess."

A low growl seemed to rumble distantly. "What the devil's that?" Tremaine said.

Jess shone the light on the floor. "Look here," he said. The ring of light showed a spatter of dark droplets all across the plank floor.

"That's blood, Jess...." Tremaine scanned the floor. It was of broad slabs, closely laid, scrubbed clean but for the dark stains.

"Maybe he cleaned a chicken. This is the kitchen."

"It's a trail." Tremaine followed the line of drops across the floor. It ended suddenly near the wall.

"What do you make of it. Jimmy?"

A wail sounded, a thin forlorn cry, trailing off into silence. Jess stared at Tremaine. "I'm too damned old to start believing in spooks," he said. "You suppose those damn-fool boys are hiding here, playing tricks?"

"I think." Tremaine said, "that we'd better go ask Hull Gaskin a few questions."

At the station Jess led Tremaine to a cell where a lanky teen-age boy lounged on a steel-framed cot, blinking up at the visitor under a mop of greased hair.

"Hull, this is Mr. Tremaine," said Jess. He took out a heavy key, swung the cell door open. "He wants to talk to you."

"I ain't done nothin," Hull said sullenly. "There ain't nothin wrong with burnin out a Commie, is there?"

"Bram's a Commie, is he?" Tremaine said softly. "How'd you find that out, Hull?"

"He's a foreigner, ain't he?" the youth shot back. "Besides, we heard . . ."

"What did you hear?"

"They're lookin for the spies."

"Who's looking for spies?"

"Cops."

"Who says so?"

The boy looked directly at Tremaine for an instant, flicked his eyes to the corner of the cell. "Cops was talkin about 'em," he said.

"Spill it, Hull," the policeman said. "Mr. Tremaine hasn't got all night."

"They parked out east of town, on 302, back of the woodlot. They called me over and asked me a bunch of questions. Said I could help 'em get them spies. Wanted to know all about any funny-actin people around here."

"And you mentioned Bram?"

The boy darted another look at Tremaine. "They said they figured the spies was out north of town. Well, Bram's a foreigner, and he's out that way, ain't he?"

"Anything else?"

The boy looked at his feet.

"What did you shoot at, Hull?" Tremaine said. The boy looked at him sullenly.

"You know anything about the blood on the kitchen floor?"

"I don't know what you're talkin about," Hull said. "We was out squirrel-huntin."

"Hull, is Mr. Bram dead?"

"What you mean?" Hull blurted. "He was—"

"He was what?"

"Nothin."

"The Chief won't like it if you hold out on him, Hull," Tremaine said. "He's bound to find out."

Jess looked at the boy. "Hull's a pretty dumb boy," he said. "But he's not that dumb. Let's have it, Hull."

The boy licked his lips. "I had Pa's .30-30, and Bovey Lay had a twelve-gauge...."

"What time was this?"

"Just after sunset."

"About seven-thirty, that'd be," said Jess. "That was half an hour before the fire was spotted."

"I didn't do no shootin. It was Bovey. Old Bram jumped out at him, and he just fired off the hip. But he didn't kill him. He seen him run off...."

"You were on the porch when this happened. Which way did Bram go?"

"He ... run inside."

"So then you set fire to the place. Whose bright idea was that?"

Hull sat silent. After a moment Tremaine and Jess left the cell.

"He must have gotten clear, Jimmy," said Jess. "Maybe he got scared and left town."

"Bram doesn't strike me as the kind to panic." Tremaine looked at his watch. "I've got to get on my way, Jess. I'll check with you in the morning."

Tremaine crossed the street to the Paradise Bar and Grill, pushed into the jukebox-lit interior, took a stool and ordered a Scotch and water. He sipped the drink, then sat staring into the dark reflection in the glass. The idea of a careful reconnoitre of the Elsby area was gone, now, with police swarming everywhere. It was too bad about Bram. It would be interesting to know where the old man was . . . and if he was still alive. He'd always seemed normal enough in the old days: a big solid-looking man, middle-aged, always pleasant enough, though he didn't say much. He'd tried hard, that time, to interest Tremaine in learning whatever it was. . . .

Tremaine put a hand in his jacket pocket, took out Miss Carroll's locket. It was smooth, the size and shape of a wrist-watch chassis. He was fingering it meditatively when a rough hand slammed against his shoulder, half knocking him from the stool. Tremaine caught his balance, turned, looked into the scarred face of a heavy-shouldered man in a leather jacket.

"I heard you was back in town, Tremaine," the man said.

The bartender moved up. "Looky here, Gaskin, I don't want no trouble—"

"Shove it!" Gaskin squinted at Tremaine, his upper lip curled back to expose the gap in his teeth. "You tryin to make more trouble for my boy, I hear. Been over to the jail, stickin your nose in."

Tremaine dropped the locket in his pocket and stood up. Gaskin hitched up his pants, glanced around the room. Half a dozen early drinkers stared, wide-eyed. Gaskin squinted at Tremaine. He smelled of unwashed flannel.

"Sicked the cops onto him. The boy was out with his friends, havin a little fun. Now there he sets in jail."

Tremaine moved aside from the stool, started past the man. Soup Gaskin grabbed his arm.

"Not so fast! I figger you owe me damages. I—"

"Damage is what you'll get," said Tremaine. He slammed a stiff left to Gaskin's ribs, drove a hard right to the jaw. Gaskin jack-knifed backwards, tripped over a bar stool, fell on his back. He rolled over, got to hands and knees, shook his head.

"Git up, Soup!" someone called. "Hot dog!" offered another.

"I'm calling the police!" the bartender yelled.

"Never mind," a voice said from the door. A blue-jacketed State Trooper strolled into the room, fingers hooked into his pistol belt, the steel caps on his boot heels clicking with each step. He faced Tremaine, feet apart.

"Looks like you're disturbin the peace, Mr. Tremaine," he said.

"You wouldn't know who put him up to it, would you?" Tremaine said.

"That's a dirty allegation," the cop grinned. "I'll have to get off a hot letter to my congressman."

Gaskin got to his feet, wiped a smear of blood across his cheek, then lunged past the cop and swung a wild right. Tremaine stepped aside, landed a solid punch on Gaskin's ear. The cop stepped back against the bar. Soup whirled, slammed out with lefts and rights. Tremaine lashed back with a straight left; Gaskin slammed against the bar, rebounded, threw a knockout right . . . and Tremaine ducked, landed a right uppercut that sent

Gaskin reeling back, bowled over a table, sent glasses flying. Tremaine stood over him.

"On your feet, jailbird," he said. "A workout is exactly what I needed."

"Okay, you've had your fun," the State cop said. "I'm taking you in, Tremaine."

Tremaine looked at him. "Sorry, copper," he said. "I don't have time right now." The cop looked startled, reached for his revolver.

"What's going on here, Jimmy?" Jess stood in the door, a huge .44 in his hand. He turned his eyes on the trooper.

"You're a little out of your jurisdiction," he said. "I think you better move on 'fore somebody steals your bicycle."

The cop eyed Jess for a long moment, then holstered his pistol and stalked out of the bar. Jess tucked his revolver into his belt, looked at Gaskin sitting on the floor, dabbing at his bleeding mouth. "What got into you, Soup?"

"I think the State boys put him up to it," Tremaine said. "They're looking for an excuse to take me out of the picture."

Jess motioned to Gaskin. "Get up, Soup. I'm lockin you up alongside that boy of yours."

Outside, Jess said, "You got some bad enemies there, Jimmy. That's a tough break. You ought to hold onto your temper with those boys. I think maybe you ought to think about getting over the state line. I can run you to the bus station, and send your car along. . . ."

"I can't leave now, Jess. I haven't even started."

IV

In his room, Tremaine doctored the cut on his jaw, then opened his trunk, checked over the detector gear. The telephone rang.

"Tremaine? I've been on the telephone with Grammond. Are you out of your mind? I'm—"

"Fred," Tremaine cut in, "I thought you were going to get those state cops off my neck."

"Listen to me, Tremaine. You're called off this job as of now. Don't touch anything! You'd better stay right there in that room. In fact, that's an order!"

"Don't pick now to come apart at the seams, Fred," Tremaine snapped.

"I've ordered you off! That's all!" The phone clicked and the dial tone sounded. Tremaine dropped the receiver in its cradle, then walked to the window absently, his hand in his pocket.

He felt broken pieces and pulled out Miss Carroll's locket. It was smashed, split down the center. It must have gotten hit in the tussle with Soup, Tremaine thought. It looked—

He squinted at the shattered ornament. A maze of fine wires was exposed, tiny condensers, bits of glass.

In the street below, tires screeched. Tremaine looked down. A black car was at the curb, doors sprung. Four uniformed men jumped out, headed for the door. Tremaine whirled to the phone. The desk clerk came on.

"Get me Jess—fast!"

The police chief answered.

"Jess, the word's out I'm poison. An earful of State law

is at the front door. I'm going out the back. Get in their way all you can." Tremaine dropped the phone, grabbed up the suitcase and let himself out into the hall. The back stairs were dark. He stumbled, cursed, made it to the service entry. Outside, the alley was deserted.

He went to the corner, crossed the street, thrust the suitcase into the back seat of his car and slid into the driver's seat. He started up and eased away from the curb. He glanced in the mirror. There was no alarm.

It was a four-block drive to Miss Carroll's house. The housekeeper let Tremaine in.

"Oh, yes, Miss Carroll is still up," she said. "She never retires until nine. I'll tell her you're here, Mr. Tremaine."

Tremaine paced the room. On his third circuit Miss Carroll came in.

"I wouldn't have bothered you if it wasn't important," Tremaine said. "I can't explain it all now. You said once you had confidence in me. Will you come with me now? It concerns Bram...and maybe a lot more than just Bram."

Miss Carroll looked at him steadily. "I'll get my wrap."

On the highway Tremaine said, "Miss Carroll, we're headed for Bram's house. I take it you've heard of what happened out there?"

"No, James. I haven't stirred out of the house. What is it?"

"A gang of teen-age toughs went out last night. They had guns. One of them took a shot at Bram. And Bram's disappeared. But I don't think he's dead."

Miss Carroll gasped. "Why? Why did they do it?"

"I don't think they know themselves."

"You say . . . you believe he still lives. . . ."

"He must be alive. It dawned on me a little while ago . . . a little late, I'll admit. The locket he gave you. Did you ever try it?"

"Try it? Why . . . no. I don't believe in magic, James."

"Not magic. Electronics. Years ago Bram talked to me about radio. He wanted to teach me. Now I'm here looking for a transmitter. That transmitter was busy last night. I think Bram was operating it."

There was a long silence.

"James," Miss Carroll said at last, "I don't understand."

"Neither do I, Miss Carroll. I'm still working on finding the pieces. But let me ask you: that night that Bram brought you out to his place. You say he ran to the kitchen and opened a trapdoor in the floor—"

"Did I say floor? That was an error: the panel was in the wall."

"I guess I jumped to the conclusion. Which wall?"

"He crossed the room. There was a table, with a candlestick. He went around it and pressed his hand against the wall, beside the wood-box. The panel slid aside. It was very dark within. He ducked his head, because the opening was not large, and stepped inside. . . ."

"That would be the east wall . . . to the left of the back door?"

"Yes."

"Now, Miss Carroll, can you remember exactly what Bram said to you that night? Something about fighting something, wasn't it?"

"I've tried for sixty years to put it out of my mind,

James. But I remember every word, I think." She was silent for a moment.

"I was beside him on the buggy seat. It was a warm evening, late in spring. I had told him that I loved him, and . . . he had responded. He said that he would have spoken long before, but that he had not dared. Now there was that which I must know.

"His life was not his own, he said. He was not . . . native to this world. He was an agent of a mighty power, and he had trailed a band of criminals. . . ." She broke off. "I could not truly understand that part, James. I fear it was too incoherent. He raved of evil beings who lurked in the shadows of a cave. It was his duty to wage each night an unceasing battle with occult forces."

"What kind of battle? Were these ghosts, or demons, or what?"

"I don't know. Evil powers which would be unloosed on the world, unless he met them at the portal as the darkness fell and opposed them."

"Why didn't he get help?"

"Only he could stand against them. I knew little of abnormal psychology, but I understood the classic evidence of paranoia. I shrank from him. He sat, leaning forward, his eyes intent. I wept and begged him to take me back. He turned his face to me, and I saw the pain and anguish in his eyes. I loved him . . . and feared him. And he would not turn back. Night was falling, and the enemy awaited him."

"Then, when you got to the house . . . ?"

"He had whipped up the horses, and I remember how I clung to the top braces, weeping. Then we were at the house. Without a word he jumped down and ran to the door. I followed. He lit a lamp and turned to me. From somewhere there was a wailing call, like an injured animal. He shouted something—an unintelligible cry—and ran toward the back of the house. I took up the lamp and followed. In the kitchen he went to the wall, pressed against it. The panel opened. He looked at me. His face was white.

"'In the name of the High God. Linda Carroll, I entreat you...'

"I screamed. And he hardened his face, and went down...and I screamed and screamed again...." Miss Carroll closed her eyes, drew a shuddering breath.

"I'm sorry to have put you through this, Miss Carroll," Tremaine said. "But I had to know."

Faintly in the distance a siren sounded. In the mirror, headlights twinkled half a mile behind. Tremaine stepped on the gas. The powerful car leaped ahead.

"Are you expecting trouble on the road, James?"

"The State police are unhappy with me, Miss Carroll. And I imagine they're not too pleased with Jess. Now they're out for blood. But I think I can outrun them."

"James." Miss Carroll said, sitting up and looking behind. "If those are police officers, shouldn't you stop?"

"I can't, Miss Carroll. I don't have time for them now. If my idea means anything, we've got to get there fast...."

Bram's house loomed gaunt and dark as the car whirled through the gate, ground to a stop before the porch. Tremaine jumped out, went around the car and helped Miss Carroll out. He was surprised at the firmness of her step. For a moment, in the fading light of dusk, he glimpsed her profile. *How beautiful she must have been....*

He reached into the glove compartment for a flashlight.

"We haven't got a second to waste," he said. "That other car's not more than a minute behind us." He reached into the back of the car, hauled out the heavy suitcase. "I hope you remember how Bram worked that panel."

On the porch Tremaine's flashlight illuminated the broken hasp. Inside, he led the way along a dark hall, pushed into the kitchen.

"It was there," Miss Carroll said, pointing. Outside, an engine sounded on the highway, slowing, turning in. Headlights pushed a square of cold light across the kitchen wall. Tremaine jumped to the spot Miss Carroll had indicated, put the suitcase down, felt over the wall.

"Give me the light, James," Miss Carroll said calmly. "Press there." She put the spot on the wall. Tremaine leaned against it. Nothing happened. Outside, there was the thump of car doors; a muffled voice barked orders.

"Are you sure ... ?"

"Yes. Try again, James."

Tremaine threw himself against the wall, slapped at it, searching for a hidden latch.

"A bit higher; Bram was a tall man. The panel opened below...."

Tremaine reached higher, pounded, pushed up, sideways—

With a click a three-by-four-foot section of wall rolled

silently aside. Tremaine saw greased metal slides and, beyond, steps leading down.

"They are on the porch now, James," said Miss Carroll.

"The light!" Tremaine reached for it, threw a leg over the sill. He reached back, pulled the suitcase after him. "Tell them I kidnapped you, Miss Carroll. And thanks."

Miss Carroll held out her hand. "Help me, James. I hung back once before. I'll not repeat my folly."

Tremaine hesitated for an instant, then reached out, handed Miss Carroll in. Footsteps sounded in the hall. The flashlight showed Tremaine a black pushbutton bolted to a two by four stud. He pressed it. The panel slid back in place.

Tremaine flashed the light on the stairs.

"Okay, Miss Carroll," he said softly. "Let's go down."

There were fifteen steps, and at the bottom, a corridor, with curved walls of black glass, and a floor of rough boards. It went straight for twenty feet and ended at an old-fashioned five-panel wooden door. Tremaine tried the brass knob. The door opened on a room shaped from a natural cave, with waterworn walls of yellow stone, a low uneven ceiling, and a packed-earth floor. On a squat tripod in the center of the chamber rested an apparatus of black metal and glass, vaguely gunlike, aimed at the blank wall. Beside it, in an ancient wooden rocker, a man lay slumped, his shirt blood-caked, a black puddle on the floor beneath him.

"Bram!" Miss Carroll gasped. She went to him, took his hand, staring into his face.

"Is he dead?" Tremaine said tightly.

"His hands are cold . . . but there is a pulse."

A kerosene lantern stood by the door. Tremaine lit it, brought it to the chair. He took out a pocketknife, cut the coat and shirt back from Bram's wound. A shotgun blast had struck him in the side; there was a lacerated area as big as Tremaine's hand.

"It's stopped bleeding," he said. "It was just a graze at close range, I'd say." He explored further. "It got his arm too, but not as deep. And I think there are a couple of ribs broken. If he hasn't lost too much blood..." Tremaine pulled off his coat, spread it on the floor.

"Let's lay him out here and try to bring him around."

Lying on his back on the floor, Bram looked bigger than his six-foot-four, younger than his near-century, Tremaine thought. Miss Carroll knelt at the old man's side, chafing his hands, murmuring to him.

Abruptly a thin cry cut the air.

Tremaine whirled, startled. Miss Carroll stared, eyes wide. A low rumble sounded, swelled louder, broke into a screech, cut off.

"Those are the sounds I heard that night," Miss Carroll breathed. "I thought afterwards I had imagined them, but I remember... James, what does it mean?"

"Maybe it means Bram wasn't as crazy as you thought," Tremaine said.

Miss Carroll gasped sharply. "James! Look at the wall—"

Tremaine turned. Vague shadows moved across the stone, flickering, wavering.

"What the devil...!"

Bram moaned, stirred. Tremaine went to him. "Bram!" he said. "Wake up!"

Bram's eyes opened. For a moment he looked dazedly at Tremaine, then at Miss Carroll. Awkwardly he pushed himself to a sitting position.

"Bram . . . you must lie down," Miss Carroll said.

"Linda Carroll," Bram said. His voice was deep, husky.

"Bram, you're hurt . . ."

A mewling wail started up. Bram went rigid "What hour is this?" he grated.

"The sun has just gone down; it's after seven—"

Bram tried to get to his feet. "Help me up," he ordered. "Curse the weakness. . . ."

Tremaine got a hand under the old man's arm. "Careful, Bram," he said. "Don't start your wound bleeding again."

"To the Repellor," Bram muttered. Tremaine guided him to the rocking chair, eased him down. Bram seized the two black pistol-grips, squeezed them.

"You, young man," Bram said. "Take the circlet there; place it about my neck."

The flat-metal ring hung from a wire loop. Tremaine fitted it over Bram's head. It settled snugly over his shoulders, a flange at the back against his neck.

"Bram," Tremaine said. "What's this all about?"

"Watch the wall there. My sight grows dim. Tell me what you see."

"It looks like shadows: but what's casting them?"

"Can you discern details?"

"No. It's like somebody waggling their fingers in front of a slide projector."

"The radiation from the star is yet too harsh," Bram muttered. "But now the node draws close. May the High Gods guide my hand!"

A howl rang out, a raw blast of sound. Bram tensed. "What do you see?" he demanded.

"The outlines are sharper. There seem to be other shapes behind the moving ones. It's like looking through a steamy window. . . ." Beyond the misty surface Tremaine seemed to see a high narrow chamber, bathed in white light. In the foreground creatures like shadowy caricatures of men paced to and fro. "They're like something stamped out of alligator hide," Tremaine whispered. "When they turn and I see them edge-on, they're thin. . . ."

"An effect of dimensional attenuation. They strive now to match matrices with this plane. If they succeed, this earth you know will lie at their feet."

"What are they? Where are they? That's solid rock—"

"What you see is the Niss Command Center. It lies in another world than this, but here is the multihedron of intersection. They bring their harmonic generators to bear here in the hope of establishing an aperture of focus."

"I don't understand half of what you're saying, Bram. And the rest I don't believe. But with this staring me in the face, I'll have to act as though I did."

Suddenly the wall cleared. Like a surface of moulded glass the stone threw back ghostly highlights. Beyond it, the Niss technicians, seen now in sharp detail, worked busily, silently, their faces like masks of ridged red-brown leather. Directly opposite Bram's Repellor, an apparatus like an immense camera with a foot-wide silvered lens stood aimed, a black-clad Niss perched in a saddle atop it. The white light flooded the cave, threw black shadows across the floor. Bram hunched over the Repellor, face tensed in strain. A glow built in the air around the Niss machine. The alien technicians stood now, staring with tiny bright-red eyes. Long seconds passed. The black-clad Niss gestured suddenly. Another turned to a red-marked knife-switch, pulled. As suddenly as it had cleared, the wall went milky, then dulled to opacity. Bram slumped back, eyes shut, breathing hoarsely.

"Near were they then," he muttered, "I grow weak...."

"Let me take over," Tremaine said. "Tell me how."

"How can I tell you? You will not understand."

"Maybe I'll understand enough to get us through the night."

Bram seemed to gather himself. "Very well. This must you know...

"I am an agent in the service of the Great World. For centuries we have waged war against the Niss, evil beings who loot the continua. They established an Aperture here, on your Earth. We detected it and found that a Portal could be set up here briefly. I was dispatched with a crew to counter their move—"

"You're talking gibberish," Tremaine said. "I'll pass the Great World and the continua ... but what's an Aperture?"

"A point of material contact between the Niss world and this plane of space-time. Through it they can pump this rich planet dry of oxygen, killing it—then emerge to feed on the corpse."

"What's a Portal?"

"The Great World lies in a different harmonic series than do Earth and the Niss World. Only at vast intervals can we set up a Portal of temporary identity as the cycles mesh. We monitor the Niss emanations, and forestall them when we can, now in this plane, now in that."

"I see: denial to the enemy."

"But we were late. Already the multihedron was far advanced. A blinding squall lashed outside the river cave where the Niss had focused the Aperture, and the thunder rolled as the ionization effect was propagated in the atmosphere. I threw my force against the Niss Aperture but could not destroy it . . . but neither could they force their entry."

"And this was sixty years ago? And they're still at it?"

"You must throw off the illusion of time! To the Niss only a few days have passed. But here—where I spend only minutes from each night in the engagement, as the patterns coincide—it has been long years."

"Why don't you bring in help? Why do you have to work alone?"

"The power required to hold the Portal in focus against the stresses of space-time is tremendous. Even then the cycle is brief. It gave us first a fleeting contact of a few seconds; it was through that that we detected the Niss activity here. The next contact was four days later and lasted twenty-four minutes—long enough to set up the Repellor. I fought them then . . . and saw that victory was in doubt. Still, it was a fair world; I could not let it go without a struggle. A third identity was possible twenty days later; I elected to remain here until then, attempt to repel the Niss, then return home at the next contact. The Portal closed, and my crew and I settled down to the engagement.

"The next night showed us in full the hopelessness of the contest. By day, we emerged from where the Niss had focussed the Aperture, and explored this land, and came to love its small warm sun, its strange blue sky, its mantle of green . . . and the small humble grass-blades. To us of an ancient world it seemed a paradise of young life. And then I ventured into the town . . . and there I saw such a maiden as the Cosmos has forgotten, such was her beauty. . . .

"The twenty days passed. The Niss held their foothold—yet I had kept them back.

"The Portal reopened. I ordered my crew back. It closed. Since then, have I been alone. . . ."

"Bram," Miss Carroll said. "Bram . . . you stayed when you could have escaped—and I—"

"I would that I could give you back those lost years, Linda Carroll," Bram said. "I would that we could have been together under a brighter sun than this."

"You gave up your world, to give this one a little time," Tremaine said. "And we rewarded you with a shotgun blast."

"Bram . . . when will the Portal open again?"

"Not in my life, Linda Carroll. Not for ten thousand years."

"Why didn't you recruit help?" Tremaine said. "You could have trained someone. . . ."

"I tried, at first. But what can one do with frightened rustics? They spoke of witchcraft, and fled."

"But you can't hold out forever. Tell me how this thing works. It's time somebody gave you a break!"

V

Bram talked for half an hour, while Tremaine listened. "If I should fail," he concluded, "take my place at the

Repellor. Place the circlet on your neck. When the wall clears, grip the handles and pit your mind against the Niss. Will that they do not come through. When the thunder rolls, you will know that you have failed."

"All right. I'll be ready. But let me get one thing straight: this Repellor of yours responds to thoughts, is that right? It amplifies them—"

"It serves to focus the power of the mind. But now let us make haste. Soon, I fear, will they renew the attack."

"It will be twenty minutes or so, I think," said Tremaine. "Stay where you are and get some rest."

Bram looked at him, his blue eyes grim under white brows. "What do you know of this matter, young man?"

"I think I've doped out the pattern; I've been monitoring these transmissions for weeks. My ideas seemed to prove out okay the last few nights."

"No one but I in all this world knew of the Niss attack. How could you have analyzed that which you knew not of?"

"Maybe you don't know it, Bram, but this Repellor of yours has been playing hell with our communications. Recently we developed what we thought was a Top-Secret project—and you're blasting us off the air."

"This is only a small portable unit, poorly screened," Bram said. "The resonance effects are unpredictable. When one seeks to channel the power of thought—"

"Wait a minute!" Tremaine burst out.

"What is it?" Miss Carroll said, alarmed.

"Hyperwave," Tremaine said. "Instantaneous transmission. And thought. No wonder people had headaches—and nightmares! We've been broadcasting on the same band as the human mind!"

"This 'hyperwave,'" Bram said. "You say it is instantaneous?"

"That's supposed to be classified information."

"Such a device is new in the cosmos," Bram said. "Only a protoplasmic brain is known to produce a null-lag excitation state."

Tremaine frowned. "Bram, this Repellor focuses what I'll call thought waves for want of a better term. It uses an interference effect to damp out the Niss harmonic generator. What if we poured more power to the Repellor?"

"No. The power of the mind cannot be amplified—"

"I don't mean amplification; I mean an additional source. I have a hyperwave receiver here. With a little rewiring, it'll act as a transmitter. Can we tie it in?"

Bram shook his head. "Would that I were a technician," he said. "I know only what is required to operate the device."

"Let me take a look," Tremaine said. "Maybe I can figure it out."

"Take care. Without it, we fall before the Niss."

"I'll be careful." Tremaine went to the machine, examined it, tracing leads, identifying components.

"This seems clear enough," he said. "These would be powerful magnets here; they give a sort of pinch effect. And these are refracting-field coils. Simple, and brilliant. With this idea, we could beam hyperwave—"

"First let us deal with the Niss!"

"Sure." Tremaine looked at Bram. "I think I can link my apparatus to this," he said. "Okay if I try?"

"How long?"

"It shouldn't take more than fifteen minutes."

"That leaves little time."

"The cycle is tightening," Tremaine said. "I figure the next transmissions . . . or attacks . . . will come at intervals of under five minutes for several hours now; this may be the last chance."

"Then try," said Bram.

Tremaine nodded, went to the suitcase, took out tools and a heavy black box, set to work. Linda Carroll sat by Bram's side, speaking softly to him. The minutes passed.

"Okay," Tremaine said. "This unit is ready." He went to the Repellor, hesitated a moment, then turned two nuts and removed a cover.

"We're off the air," he said. "I hope my formula holds."

Bram and Miss Carroll watched silently as Tremaine worked. He strung wires, taped junctions, then flipped a switch on the hyperwave set and tuned it, his eyes on the dials of a smaller unit.

"Nineteen minutes have passed since the last attack," Bram said. "Make haste."

"I'm almost done," Tremaine said.

A sharp cry came from the wall. Tremaine jumped. "What the hell makes those sounds?"

"They are nothing—mere static. But they warn that the harmonic generators are warming." Bram struggled to his feet. "Now comes the assault."

"The shadows!" Miss Carroll cried.

Bram sank into the chair, leaned back, his face pale as wax in the faint glow from the wall. The glow grew brighter; the shadows swam into focus.

"Hurry, James," Miss Carroll said. "It comes quickly."

Bram watched through half-closed eyes. "I must

man the Repellor. I . . ." He fell back in the chair, his
head lolling.

"Bram!" Miss Carroll cried. Tremaine snapped the
cover in place, whirled to the chair, dragged it and its
occupant away from the machine, then turned, seized the
grips. On the wall the Niss moved in silence, readying the
attack. The black-clad figure was visible, climbing to his
place. The wall cleared. Tremaine stared across at the
narrow room, the gray-clad Niss. They stood now, eyes on
him. One pointed. Others erected leathery crests.

Stay out, you ugly devils, Tremaine thought. *Go back,
retreat, give up. . . .*

Now the blue glow built in a flickering arc across the
Niss machine. The technicians stood, staring across the
narrow gap, tiny red eyes glittering in the narrow alien
faces. Tremaine squinted against the brilliant white light
from the high-vaulted Niss Command Center. The last
suggestion of the sloping surface of the limestone wall was
gone. Tremaine felt a draft stir; dust whirled up, clouded
the air. There was an odor of iodine.

Back, Tremaine thought. *Stay back. . . .*

There was a restless stir among the waiting rank of
Niss. Tremaine heard the dry shuffle of horny feet against
the floor, the whine of the harmonic generator. His eyes
burned. As a hot gust swept around him he choked and
coughed.

NO! he thought, hurling negation like a weightless
bomb. *FAIL! RETREAT!*

Now the Niss moved, readying a wheeled machine,
rolling it into place. Tremaine coughed rackingly, fought

to draw a breath, blinking back blindness. A deep thrumming started up; grit particles stung his cheek, the backs of his hands. The Niss worked rapidly, their throat gills visibly dilated now in the unaccustomed flood of oxygen....

Our oxygen, Tremaine thought. *The looting has started already, and I've failed, and the people of Earth will choke and die....*

From what seemed an immense distance, a roll of thunder trembled at the brink of audibility, swelling.

The black-clad Niss on the alien machine half rose, erecting a black-scaled crest, exulting. Then, shockingly, his eyes fixed on Tremaine's, his trap-like mouth gaped, exposing a tongue like a scarlet snake, a cavernous pink throat set with a row of needle-like snow-white teeth. The tongue flicked out, a gesture of utter contempt.

And suddenly Tremaine was cold with deadly rage. *We have a treatment for snakes in this world*, he thought with savage intensity. *We crush 'em under our heels....* He pictured a writhing rattler, broken-backed, a club descending; a darting red coral snake, its venom ready, slashed in the blades of a power mower; a cottonmouth, smashed into red ruin by a shotgun blast....

BACK, SNAKE, he thought. *DIE! DIE!*

The thunder faded.

And atop the Niss Generator, the black-clad Niss snapped his mouth shut, crouched.

"DIE!" Tremaine shouted. "Die!"

The Niss seemed to shrink in on himself, shivering. His crest went flaccid, twitched twice. The red eyes winked out and the Niss toppled from the machine. Tremaine coughed, gripped the handles, turned his eyes to a gray-uniformed Niss who scrambled up to replace the operator.

I SAID DIE, SNAKE!

The Niss faltered, tumbled back among his fellows, who darted about now like ants in a broached anthill. One turned red eyes on Tremaine, then scrambled for the red cut-out switch.

NO, YOU DON'T, Tremaine thought. *IT'S NOT THAT EASY, SNAKE. DIE!*

The Niss collapsed. Tremaine drew a rasping breath, blinked back tears of pain, took in a group of Niss in a glance.

Die!

They fell. The others turned to flee then, but like a scythe Tremaine's mind cut them down, left them in windrows. Hate walked naked among the Niss and left none living.

Now the machines. Tremaine thought. He fixed his eyes on the harmonic generator. It melted into slag. Behind it, the high panels set with jewel-like lights blackened, crumpled into wreckage. Suddenly the air was clean again. Tremaine breathed deep. Before him the surface of the rock swam into view.

NO! Tremaine thought thunderously. *HOLD THAT APERTURE OPEN!*

The rock-face shimmered, faded. Tremaine looked into the white-lit room, at the blackened walls, the huddled dead. *No pity,* he thought. *You would have sunk those white teeth into soft human throats, sleeping in the dark... as you've done on a hundred worlds. You're a cancer in the cosmos. And I have the cure.*

WALLS, he thought, *COLLAPSE!*

The roof before him sagged, fell in. Debris rained down from above, the walls tottered, went down. A cloud of roiled dust swirled, cleared to show a sky blazing with stars.

Dust, stay clear, Tremaine thought. *I want good air to breathe for the work ahead.* He looked out across a landscape of rock, ghostly white in the starlight.

LET THE ROCKS MELT AND FLOW LIKE WATER!

An upreared slab glowed, slumped, ran off in yellow rivulets that were lost in the radiance of the crust as it bubbled, belching released gasses. A wave of heat struck Tremaine. *Let it be cool here*, he thought. *Now, Niss world....*

"No!" Bram's voice shouted. "Stop, stop!"

Tremaine hesitated. He stared at the vista of volcanic fury before him.

I could destroy it all, he thought. *And the stars in the Niss sky....*

"Great is the power of your hate, man of Earth," Bram cried. "But curb it now, before you destroy us all!"

"Why?" Tremaine shouted. "I can wipe out the Niss and their whole diseased universe with them, with a thought!"

"Master yourself," Bram said hoarsely. "Your rage destroys you! One of the suns you see in the Niss sky is your Sol!"

"Sol?" Tremaine said. "Then it's the Sol of a thousand years ago. Light takes time to cross a galaxy. And the earth is still here ... so it wasn't destroyed!"

"Wise are you," Bram said. "Your race is a wonder in

the Cosmos, and deadly is your hate. But you know nothing of the forces you unloose now. Past time is as mutable as the steel and rock you melted but now."

"Listen to him, James," Miss Carroll pleaded. "Please listen."

Tremaine twisted to look at her, still holding the twin grips. She looked back steadily, her head held high. Beside her, Bram's eyes were sunken deep in his lined face.

"Jess said you looked like a princess once, Miss Carroll," Tremaine said, "when you drove past with your red hair piled up high. And Bram: you were young, and you loved her. The Niss took your youth from you. You've spent your life here, fighting them, alone. And Linda Carroll waited through the years, because she loved you . . . and feared you. The Niss did that. And you want me to spare them?"

"You have mastered them," said Bram. "And you are drunk with the power in you. But the power of love is greater than the power of hate. Our love sustained us; your hate can only destroy."

Tremaine locked eyes with the old man. He drew a deep breath at last, let it out shudderingly. "All right," he said, "I guess the God complex got me." He looked back once more at the devastated landscape. "The Niss will remember this encounter, I think. They won't try Earth again."

"You've fought valiantly, James, and won," Miss Carroll said. "Now let the power go."

Tremaine turned again to look at her. "You deserve better than this, Miss Carroll," he said. "Bram, you said time is mutable. Suppose—"

"Let well enough alone," Bram said. "Let it go!"

"Once, long ago, you tried to explain this to Linda Carroll. But there was too much against it; she couldn't understand. She was afraid. And you've suffered for sixty years. Suppose those years had never been. Suppose I had come that night . . . instead of now—"

"It could never be!"

"It can if I will it!" Tremaine gripped the handles tighter. *Let this be THAT night,* he thought fiercely. *The night in 1901, when Bram's last contact failed. Let it be that night, five minutes before the portal closed. Only this machine and I remain as we are now; outside there are gas lights in the farm houses along the dirt road to Elsby, and in the town horses stand in the stables along the cinder alleys behind the houses; and President McKinley is having dinner in the White House. . . .*

There was a sound behind Tremaine. He whirled. The ravaged scene was gone. A great disc mirror stood across the cave, intersecting the limestone wall. A man stepped through it, froze at the sight of Tremaine. He was tall, with curly blond hair, fine-chiseled features, broad shoulders.

"Fdazh ha?" he said. Then his eyes slid past Tremaine, opened still wider in astonishment. Tremaine followed the stranger's glance. A young woman, dressed in a negligee of pale silk, stood in the door, a hair-brush in her hand, her red hair flowing free to her waist. She stood rigid in shock.

Then . . .

"Mr. Bram . . . !" she gasped. "What—"

Tremaine found his voice. "Miss Carroll, don't be afraid," he said. "I'm your friend, you must believe me."

Linda Carroll turned wide eyes to him. "Who are you?" she breathed. "I was in my bedroom—"

"I can't explain. A miracle has been worked here tonight...on your behalf." Tremaine turned to Bram. "Look—" he started.

"What man are you?" Bram cut in in heavily accented English. "How do you come to this place?"

"Listen to me, Bram!" Tremaine snapped. "Time is mutable. You stayed here, to protect Linda Carroll—and Linda Carroll's world. You've just made that decision, right?" Tremaine went on, not waiting for a reply. "You were stuck here...for sixty years. Earth technology developed fast. One day a man stumbled in here, tracing down the signal from your Repellor; that was me. You showed me how to use the device...and with it I wiped out the Niss. And then I set the clock back for you and Linda Carroll. The Portal closes in two minutes. Don't waste time...."

"Mutable time?" Bram said. He went past Tremaine to Linda. "Fair lady of Earth," he said. "Do not fear...."

"Sir, I hardly know you," Miss Carroll said. "How did I come here, hardly clothed—"

"Take her, Bram!" Tremaine shouted. "Take her and get back through that Portal—fast." He looked at Linda Carroll. "Don't be afraid," he said. "You know you love him; go with him now, or regret it all your days."

"Will you come?" asked Bram. He held out his hand to her. Linda hesitated, then put her hand in his. Bram went with her to the mirror surface, handed her through. He looked back at Tremaine.

"I do not understand, man of Earth," he said "But I thank you." Then he was gone.

★★★

Alone in the dim-lit grotto Tremaine let his hands fall from the grips, staggered to the rocker and sank down. He felt weak, drained of strength. His hands ached from the strain of the ordeal. How long had it lasted? Five minutes? An hour? Or had it happened at all . . . ?

But Bram and Linda Carroll were gone. He hadn't imagined that. And the Niss were defeated.

But there was still his own world to contend with. The police would be waiting, combing through the house. They would want to know what he had done with Miss Carroll. Maybe there would be a murder charge. There'd be no support from Fred and the Bureau. As for Jess, he was probably in a cell now, looking a stiff sentence in the face for obstructing justice. . . .

Tremaine got to his feet, cast a last glimpse at the empty room, the outlandish shape of the Repellor, the mirrored portal. It was a temptation to step through it. But this was his world, with all its faults. Perhaps later, when his strength returned, he could try the machine again. . . .

The thought appalled him. *The ashes of hate are worse than the ashes of love*, he thought. He went to the stairs, climbed them, pressed the button. Nothing happened. He pushed the panel aside by hand and stepped into the kitchen. He circled the heavy table with the candlestick, went along the hall and out onto the porch. It was almost the dawn of a fresh spring day. There was no sign of the police. He looked at the grassy lawn, the row of new-set saplings.

Strange, he thought. *I don't remember any saplings. I thought I drove in under a row of trees.* . . . He squinted into the misty early morning gloom. His car was gone. That wasn't too surprising; the cops had impounded it, no doubt. He stepped down, glanced at the ground ahead. It was smooth, with a faint footpath cut through the grass. There was no mud, no sign of tire tracks—

The horizon seemed to spin suddenly. *My God!!* Tremaine thought *I've left myself in the year 1901 . . . !*

He whirled, leaped up on the porch, slammed through the door and along the hall, scrambled through the still-open panel, bounded down the stairs and into the cave—

The Repellor was gone. Tremaine leaped forward with a cry—and under his eyes, the great mirror twinkled, winked out. The black box of the hyperwave receiver lay alone on the floor, beside the empty rocker. The light of the kerosene lamp reflected from the featureless wall.

Tremaine turned, stumbled up the steps, out into the air. The sun showed a crimson edge just peeping above distant hills.

1901, Tremaine thought. *The century has just turned. Somewhere a young fellow named Ford is getting ready to put the nation on wheels, and two boys named Wright are about to give it wings. No one ever heard of a World War, or the roaring Twenties, or Prohibition, or FDR, or the Dust Bowl, or Pearl Harbor. And Hiroshima and Nagasaki are just two cities in distant floral Japan. . . .*

He walked down the path, stood by the rutted dirt road. Placid cows nuzzled damp grass in the meadow beyond it. In the distance a train hooted.

There are railroads, Tremaine thought. *But no jet planes, no radio, no movies, no automatic dish-washers. But then there's no TV, either. That makes up for a lot. And there are no police waiting to grill me, and no murder charge, and no neurotic nest of bureaucrats waiting to welcome me back....*

He drew a deep breath. The air was sweet. *I'm here,* he thought. *I feel the breeze on my face and the firm sod underfoot. It's real, and it's all there is now, so I might as well take it calmly. After all, a man with my education ought to be able to do well in this day and age!*

Whistling, Tremaine started the ten-mile walk into town.

DELENDA EST
by Poul Anderson

Poul Anderson was renowned as much for his several series as for his innumerable stand-alone novels and stories, and his annals of the Time Patrol was a stunning achievement, with many stories, novelettes, novellas and one novel, The Shield of Time. *While the agents of the Patrol are more like police than soldiers, working to keep the past from being changed by unscrupulous time travelers, sometimes a desperate situation calls for a military operation. And this situation was very desperate . . .*

1

The hunting is good in Europe twenty thousand years ago, and the winter sports are unexcelled anywhen. So the Time Patrol, always solicitous for its highly trained personnel, maintains a lodge in the Pleistocene Pyrenees.

Manse Everard stood on a glassed-in verandah and looked across ice-blue distances toward the northern slopes where the mountains fell off into woodland, marsh, and tundra. His big body was clad in loose green trousers and tunic of twenty-third century insulsynth, boots handmade by a nineteenth-century French-Canadian; he smoked a foul old briar of indeterminate origin. There was a vague restlessness about him, and he ignored the noise from within, where half a dozen agents were drinking and talking and playing the piano.

A Crô-Magnon guide went by across the snow-covered yard, a tall handsome fellow dressed rather like an Eskimo (why had romance never credited paleolithic man with enough sense to wear jacket, pants, and footgear in a glacial period?), his face painted, one of the steel knives he had earned at his belt. The Patrol could act quite freely, this far back in time; there was no danger of upsetting the past, for the metal would rust away and the strangers be forgotten in a few centuries. The main nuisance was that female agents from the more libertine periods upstairs were always having affairs with the native hunters.

Piet Van Sarawak (Dutch-Indonesian-Venusian, early twenty-fourth A.D.), a slim, dark young man whose looks and technique gave the guides some stiff competition, joined Everard. They stood for a moment in companionable silence. He was also Unattached, on call to help out in any milieu, and had worked with the American before. They had taken their first vacation together.

He spoke first, in Temporal. "I hear they've spotted a few mammoths near Toulouse." The city would not be built for a long while yet, but habit was powerful.

"I've bagged one," said Everard impatiently. "I've also

been skiing and mountain-climbing and watched the native dances."

Van Sarawak nodded, took out a cigarette, and puffed it into lighting. The bones stood out in his lean brown face as he sucked the smoke inward. "A pleasant loafing spell, this," he agreed, "but after a bit the outdoor life begins to pall."

There were still two weeks left of their furlough. In theory, since he could return almost to the moment of departure, an agent could take indefinite vacations; but actually he was supposed to devote a certain percentage of his probable lifetime to the job. (They never told you when you were scheduled to die, and you had better sense than to try finding out for yourself. It wouldn't have been certain anyhow, time being mutable. One perquisite of an agent's office was the Danellian longevity treatment.)

"What I would enjoy," continued Van Sarawak, "is some bright lights, music, girls who've never heard of time travel—"

"Done!" said Everard.

"Augustan Rome?" asked the other eagerly. "I've never been there. I could get a hypno on language and customs here."

Everard shook his head. "It's overrated. Unless we want to go way upstairs, the most glorious decadence available is right in my own milieu. New York, say.... If you know the right phone numbers, and I do."

Van Sarawak chuckled. "I know a few places in my own sector," he replied, "but by and large, a pioneer society has little use for the finer arts of amusement. Very good, let's be off to New York, in—when?"

"Make it 1960. That was the last time I was there, in my public *persona*, before coming here-now."

They grinned at each other and went off to pack. Everard had foresightedly brought along some midtwentieth garments in his friend's size.

Throwing clothes and razor into a small suitcase, the American wondered if he could keep up with Van Sarawak. He had never been a high-powered roisterer, and wouldn't have known how to buckle a swash anywhere in space-time. A good book, a bull session, a case of beer—that was about his speed. But even the soberest men must kick over the traces occasionally.

Or a little more than that, if he was an Unattached agent of the Time Patrol; if his job with the Engineering Studies Company was only a blind for his wanderings and warrings through all history; if he had seen that history rewritten in minor things—not by God, which would have been endurable, but by mortal and fallible men—for even the Danellians were somewhat less than God; if he was forever haunted by the possibility of a major change, such that he and his entire world would never have existed at all.... Everard's battered, homely face screwed into a grimace. He ran a hand through his stiff brown hair, as if to brush the idea away. Useless to think about. Language and logic broke down in the face of the paradox. Better to relax at such moments as he could.

He picked up the suitcase and went to join Piet Van Sarawak.

Their little two-place antigravity scooter waited on its skids in the garage. You wouldn't believe, to look at it, that the controls could be set for any place on Earth and any moment of time. But an airplane is wonderful too, or a ship, or a fire.

Auprés de ma blonde
Qu'il fait bon, fait bon, fait bon,
Auprés de ma blonde
Qu'il fait bon dormir!

Van Sarawak sang it aloud, his breath steaming from him in the frosty air as he hopped onto the rear saddle. He'd picked up the song once when accompanying the army of Louis XIV. Everard laughed. "Down, boy!"

"Oh, come, now," warbled the younger man. "It is a beautiful continuum, a merry and gorgeous cosmos. Hurry up this machine."

Everard was not so sure; he had seen enough human misery in all the ages. You got case-hardened after a while, but down underneath, when a peasant stared at you with sick brutalized eyes, or a soldier screamed with a pike through him, or a city went up in radioactive flame, something wept. He could understand the fanatics who had tried to change events. It was only that their work was so unlikely to make anything better. . . .

He set the controls for the Engineering Studies warehouse, a good confidential place to emerge. Thereafter they'd go to his apartment, and then the fun could start.

"I trust you've said good-bye to all your lady friends here," Everard remarked.

"Oh, most gallantly, I assure you. Come along there. You're as slow as molasses on Pluto. For your information, this vehicle does not have to be rowed home."

Everard shrugged and threw the main switch. The garage blinked out of sight.

2

For a moment, shock held them unstirring.

The scene registered in bits and pieces. They had materialized a few inches above ground level—the scooter was designed never to come out inside a solid object—and since that was unexpected, they hit the pavement with a teeth-rattling bump. They were in some kind of square. Nearby a fountain jetted, its stone basin carved with intertwining vines. Around the plaza, streets led off between squarish buildings six to ten stories high, of brick or concrete, wildly painted and ornamented. There were automobiles, big clumsy-looking things of no recognizable type, and a crowd of people.

"Jumping gods!" Everard glared at the meters. The scooter had landed them in lower Manhattan, 23 October 1960, at 11:30 A.M. and the spatial coordinates of the warehouse. But there was a blustery wind throwing dust and soot in his face, the smell of chimneys, and...

Van Sarawak's sonic stunner jumped into his fist. The crowd was milling away from them, shouting in some babble they couldn't understand. It was a mixed lot: tall, fair roundheads, with a great deal of red hair; a number of Amerinds; half-breeds in all combinations. The men wore loose colorful blouses, tartan kilts, a sort of Scotch bonnet, shoes and knee-length stockings. Their hair was long and many favored drooping mustaches. The women had full skirts reaching to the ankles and tresses coiled under hooded cloaks. Both sexes went in for massive bracelets and necklaces.

"What happened?" whispered the Venusian. "Where are we?"

Everard sat rigid. His mind clicked over, whirling through all the eras he had known or read about. Industrial culture—those looked like steam cars, but why the sharp prows and figurehead?—coal-burning— postnuclear Reconstruction? No, they hadn't worn kilts then, and they had spoken English. . . .

It didn't fit. There was no such milieu recorded.

"We're getting out of here!"

His hands were on the controls when the large man jumped him. They went over on the pavement in a rage of fists and feet. Van Sarawak fired and sent someone else down unconscious; then he was seized from behind. The mob piled on top of them both, and things became hazy.

Everard had a confused impression of men in shining coppery breastplates and helmets, who shoved a billy- swinging way through the riot. He was fished out and supported in his grogginess while handcuffs were snapped on his wrists. Then he and Van Sarawak were searched and hustled off to a big enclosed vehicle. The Black Maria is much the same in all times.

He didn't come back to full consciousness until they were in a damp and chilly cell with an iron-barred door.

"Name of a flame!" The Venusian slumped on a wooden cot and put his face in his hands.

Everard stood at the door, looking out. All he could see

was a narrow concrete hall and the cell across it. The map of Ireland stared cheerfully through those bars and called something unintelligible.

"What's going on?" Van Sarawak's slim body shuddered.

"I don't know," said Everard very slowly. "I just don't know. That machine was supposed to be foolproof, but maybe we're bigger fools than they allowed for."

"There's no such place as this," said Van Sarawak desperately. "A dream?" He pinched himself and managed a rueful smile. His lip was cut and swelling, and he had the start of a gorgeous shiner. "Logically, my friend, a pinch is no test of reality, but it has a certain reassuring effect."

"I wish it didn't," said Everard.

He grabbed the bars so hard they rattled. "Could the controls have been askew, in spite of everything? Is there any city, anywhen on Earth—because I'm damned sure this is Earth, at least—any city, however obscure, which was ever like this?"

"Not to my knowledge."

Everard hung on to his sanity and rallied all the mental training the Patrol had ever given him. That included total recall; and he had studied history, even the history of ages he had never seen, with a thoroughness that should have earned him several Ph.D.'s.

"No," he said at last. "Kilted brachycephalic whites, mixed up with Indians and using steam-driven automobiles, haven't happened."

"Coordinator Stantel V," said Van Sarawak faintly. "In the thirty-eighth century. The Great Experimenter— colonies reproducing past societies—"

"Not any like this," said Everard.

The truth was growing in him, and he would have traded his soul for things to be otherwise. It took all the strength he had to keep from screaming and bashing his brains out against the wall.

"We'll have to see," he said in a flat tone.

A policeman (Everard assumed they were in the hands of the law) brought them a meal and tried to talk to them. Van Sarawak said the language sounded Celtic, but he couldn't make out more than a few words. The meal wasn't bad.

Toward evening, they were led off to a washroom and got cleaned up under official guns. Everard studied the weapons: eight-shot revolvers and long-barreled rifles. There were gas lights, whose brackets repeated the motif of wreathing vines and snakes. The facilities and firearms, as well as the smell, suggested a technology roughly equivalent to the earlier nineteenth century.

On the way back he spied a couple of signs on the walls. The script was obviously Semitic, but though Van Sarawak had some knowledge of Hebrew through dealing with the Israeli colonies on Venus, he couldn't read it.

Locked in again, they saw the other prisoners led off to do their own washing: a surprisingly merry crowd of bums, toughs, and drunks. "Seems we get special treatment," remarked Van Sarawak.

"Hardly astonishing," said Everard. "What would you do with total strangers who appeared out of nowhere and had unheard-of weapons?"

Van Sarawak's face turned to him with an unwonted grimness. "Are you thinking what I'm thinking?" he asked.

"Probably."

The Venusian's mouth twisted, and horror rode his voice: "Another time line. Somebody *has* managed to change history."

Everard nodded.

They spent an unhappy night. It would have been a boon to sleep, but the other cells were too noisy. Discipline seemed to be lax here. Also, there were bedbugs.

After a bleary breakfast, Everard and Van Sarawak were allowed to wash again and shave with safety razors not unlike the familiar type. Then a ten-man guard marched them into an office and planted itself around the walls.

They sat down before a desk and waited. The furniture was as disquietingly half-homelike, half-alien, as everything else. It was some time before the big wheels showed up. They were two: a white-haired, ruddy-cheeked man in cuirass and green tunic, presumably the chief of police, and a lean, hard-faced half-breed, gray-haired but black-mustached, wearing a blue tunic, a tam-o'-shanter, and on his left breast a golden bull's head which seemed an insigne of rank. He would have had a certain aquiline dignity had it not been for the thin hairy legs beneath his kilt. He was followed by two younger men, armed and uniformed much like himself, who took up their places behind him as he sat down.

Everard leaned over and whispered: "The military, I'll bet. We seem to be of interest."

Van Sarawak nodded sickly.

The police chief cleared his throat with conscious importance and said something to the—general? The latter answered impatiently, and addressed himself to the prisoners. He barked his words out with a clarity that helped Everard get the phonemes, but with a manner that was not exactly reassuring.

Somewhere along the line, communication would have to be established. Everard pointed to himself. "Manse Everard," he said. Van Sarawak followed the lead and introduced himself similarly.

The general started and went into a huddle with the chief. Turning back, he snapped, "*Yrn Cimberland?*"

Then: "Gothland? Svea? Nairoin Teutonach?"

"Those names—if they are names—they sound Germanic, don't they?" muttered Van Sarawak.

"So do our names, come to think of it," answered Everard tautly. "Maybe they think we're Germans." To the general: "*Sprechen sie Deutsch?*" Blankness rewarded him. "*Taler ni svensk? Niederlands? Dönsk tunga? Parlez-vous français?* Goddammit, *¿habla usted español?*"

The police chief cleared his throat again and pointed to himself. "Cadwallader Mac Barca," he said. The general hight Cynyth ap Ceorn. Or so, at least, Everard's Anglo-Saxon mind interpreted the noises picked up by his ears.

"Celtic, all right," he said. Sweat prickled under his arms. "But just to make sure..." He pointed inquiringly at a few other men, being rewarded with monikers like Hamilcar ap Angus, Asshur yr Cathlan, and Finn O'Carthia. "No...there's a distinct Semitic element here too. That fits in with their alphabet."

Van Sarawak wet his lips. "Try classical languages," he urged harshly. "Maybe we can find out where this history went insane."

"Loquerisne latine?" That drew a blank. "'Ελλενίζεις'?"

General ap Ceorn jerked, blew out his mustache, and narrowed his eyes. *"Hellenach?"* he demanded. *"Yrn Parthia?"*

Everard shook his head. "They've at least heard of Greek," he said slowly. He tried a few more words, but no one knew the tongue.

Ap Ceorn growled something to one of his men, who bowed and went out. There was a long silence.

Everard found himself losing personal fear. He was in a bad spot, yes, and might not live very long; but whatever happened to him was ludicrously unimportant compared to what had been done to the entire world.

God in Heaven! To the universe!

He couldn't grasp it. Sharp in his mind rose the land he knew, broad plains and tall mountains and prideful cities. There was the grave image of his father, and yet he remembered being a small child and lifted up skyward while his father laughed beneath him. And his mother . . . they had a good life together, those two.

There had been a girl he knew in college, the sweetest little wench a man would ever have been privileged to walk in the rain with; and Bernie Aaronson, the nights of beer and smoke and talk; Phil Brackney, who had picked him out of the mud in France when machine guns were raking a ruined field; Charlie and Mary Whitcomb, high tea and a low cannel fire in Victoria's London; Keith and Cynthia Denison in their chrome-plated eyrie above New York; Jack Sandoval among tawny Arizona crags; a dog he had once had; the austere cantos of Dante and the ringing thunder of Shakespeare; the glory which was York Minster and the Golden Gate Bridge—Christ, a man's life, and the lives of who knew how many billions of human creatures, toiling and enduring and laughing and going down into dust to make room for their sons . . . It had never been.

He shook his head, dazed with grief, and sat devoid of real understanding.

The soldier came back with a map and spread it out on the desk. Ap Ceorn gestured curtly, and Everard and Van Sarawak bent over it.

Yes, Earth, a Mercator projection, though eidetic memory showed that the mapping was rather crude. The continents and islands were there in bright colors, but the nations were something else.

"Can you read those names, Van?"

"I can make a guess, on the basis of the Hebraic alphabet," said the Venusian. He began to read out the words. Ap Ceorn grunted and corrected him.

North America down to about Columbia was Ynys yr Afallon, seemingly one country divided into states. South America was a big realm, Huy Braseal, and some smaller countries whose names looked Indian. Australasia, Indonesia, Borneo, Burma, eastern India, and a good deal of the Pacific belonged to Hinduraj. Afghanistan and the rest of India were Punjab. Han included China, Korea, Japan, and eastern Siberia. Littorn owned the rest of Russia and reached well into Europe. The British Isles were Britrys, France and the Low Countries were Gallis, the Iberian peninsula was Celtan. Central Europe and the Balkans were divided into many small nations, some of which had Hunnish-looking names. Switzerland and Austria made up Helveti; Italy was Cimberland; the

Scandinavian peninsula was split down the middle, Svea in the north and Gothland in the south. North Africa looked like a confederacy, reaching from Senegal to Suez and nearly to the equator under the name of Carthagalann; the southern part of the continent was partitioned among minor sovereignties, many of which had purely African titles. The Near East held Parthia and Arabia.

Van Sarawak looked up. He had tears in his eyes.

Ap Ceorn snarled a question and waved his finger about. He wanted to know where they were from.

Everard shrugged and pointed skyward. The one thing he could not admit was the truth. He and Van Sarawak had agreed to claim they were from another planet, since this world hardly had space travel.

Ap Ceorn spoke to the chief, who nodded and replied. The prisoners were returned to their cell.

3

"And now what?" Van Sarawak slumped on his cot and stared at the floor.

"We play along," said Everard grayly. "We do anything to get at our scooter and escape. Once we're free, we can take stock."

"But what happened?"

"I don't know, I tell you! Offhand, it looks as if something upset the Graeco-Romans and the Celts took over, but I couldn't say what it was." Everard prowled the room. A bitter determination was growing in him.

"Remember your basic theory," he said. "Events are the result of a complex. There are no single causes. That's why it's so hard to change history. If I went back to, say, the Middle Ages, and shot one of FDR's Dutch forebears, he'd still be born in the late nineteenth century—because he and his genes resulted from the entire world of his ancestors, and there'd have been compensation. But every so often, a really key event does occur. Some one happening is a nexus of so many world lines that its outcome is decisive for the whole future.

"Somehow, for some reason, somebody has ripped up one of those events, back in the past."

"No more Hesperus City," mumbled Van Sarawak. "No more sitting by the canals in the blue twilight, no more Aphrodite vintages, no more—did you know I had a sister on Venus?"

"Shut up!" Everard almost shouted it. "I know. To hell with that. What counts is what we can do.

"Look," he went on after a moment, "the Patrol and the Danellians are wiped out. (Don't ask me why they weren't 'always' wiped out; why this is the first time we came back from the far past to find a changed future. I don't understand the mutable-time paradoxes. We just did, that's all.) But anyhow, such of the Patrol offices and resorts as antedate the switch point won't have been affected. There must be a few hundred agents we can rally."

"If we can get back to them."

"We can then find that key event and stop whatever interference there was with it. We've got to!"

"A pleasant thought. But . . ."

Feet tramped outside. A key clicked in the lock. The prisoners backed away. Then, all at once, Van Sarawak was bowing and beaming and spilling gallantries. Even Everard had to gape.

The girl who entered in front of three soldiers was a knockout. She was tall, with a sweep of rusty-red hair past her shoulders to the slim waist; her eyes were green and alight, her face came from all the Irish colleens who had ever lived; the long white dress was snug around a figure meant to stand on the walls of Troy. Everard noticed vaguely that this time-line used cosmetics, but she had small need of them. He paid no attention to the gold and amber of her jewelry, or to the guns behind her.

She smiled, a little timidly, and spoke: "Can you understand me? It was thought you might know Greek."

Her language was Classical rather than modern. Everard, who had once had a job in Alexandrine times, could follow it through her accent if he paid close heed—which was inevitable anyway.

"Indeed I do," he replied, his words stumbling over each other in their haste to get out.

"What are you snakkering?" demanded Van Sarawak.

"Ancient Greek," said Everard.

"It would be," mourned the Venusian. His despair seemed to have vanished, and his eyes bugged.

Everard introduced himself and his companion. The girl said her name was Deirdre Mac Morn. "Oh, no," groaned Van Sarawak. "This is too much. Manse, teach me Greek. Fast."

"Shut up," said Everard. "This is serious business."

"Well, but can't I have some of the business?"

Everard ignored him and invited the girl to sit down. He joined her on a cot, while the other Patrolman hovered unhappily by. The guards kept their weapons ready.

"Is Greek still a living language?" asked Everard.

"Only in Parthia, and there it is most corrupt," said Deirdre. "I am a Classical scholar, among other things. *Saorann* ap Ceorn is my uncle, so he asked me to see if I could talk with you. Not many in Afallon know the Attic tongue."

"Well"—Everard suppressed a silly grin—"I am most grateful to your uncle."

Her eyes rested gravely on him. "Where are you from? And how does it happen that you speak only Greek, of all known languages?"

"I speak Latin, too."

"Latin?" She frowned in thought. "Oh, the Roman speech, was it not? I am afraid you will find no one who knows much about it."

"Greek will do," said Everard firmly.

"But you have not told me whence you came," she insisted.

Everard shrugged. "We've not been treated very politely," he hinted.

"I'm sorry." It seemed genuine. "But our people are so excitable. Especially now, with the international situation what it is. And when you two appeared out of thin air . . ."

That had an unpleasantly familiar ring. "What do you mean?" he inquired.

"Surely you know. With Huy Braseal and Hinduraj about to go to war, and all of us wondering what will happen . . . It is not easy to be a small power."

"A small power? But I saw a map. Afallon looked big enough to me."

"We wore ourselves out two hundred years ago, in the great war with Littorn. Now none of our confederated states can agree on a single policy." Deirdre looked directly into his eyes. "What is this ignorance of yours?"

Everard swallowed and said, "We're from another world."

"What?"

"Yes. A planet (no, that means 'wanderer')... an orb encircling Sirius. That's our name for a certain star."

"But—what do you mean? A world attendant on a star? I cannot understand you."

"Don't you know? A star is a sun like..."

Deirdre shrank back and made a sign with her finger. "The Great Baal aid us," she whispered. "Either you are mad or... The stars are mounted in a crystal sphere."

Oh, no!

"What of the wandering stars you can see?" asked Everard slowly. "Mars and Venus and—"

"I know not those names. If you mean Moloch, Ashtoreth, and the rest, of course they are worlds like ours, attendant on the sun like our own. One holds the spirits of the dead, one is the home of witches, one..."

All this and steam cars too. Everard smiled shakily. "If you'll not believe me, then what do you think I am?"

Deirdre regarded him with large eyes. "I think you must be sorcerers," she said.

There was no answer to that. Everard asked a few weak questions, but learned little more than that this city was

Catuvellaunan, a trading and manufacturing center. Deirdre estimated its population at two million, and that of all Afallon at fifty million, but wasn't sure. They didn't take censuses here.

The Patrolmen's fate was equally undetermined. Their scooter and other possessions had been sequestrated by the military, but no one dared monkey with the stuff, and treatment of the owners was being hotly debated. Everard got the impression that all government, including the leadership of the armed forces, was rather a sloppy process of individualistic wrangling. Afallon itself was the loosest of confederacies, built out of former nations—Brittic colonies and Indians who had adopted European culture—all jealous of their rights. The old Mayan Empire, destroyed in a war with Texas (Tehannach) and annexed, had not forgotten its time of glory, and sent the most rambunctious delegates of all to the Council of Suffetes.

The Mayans wanted to make an alliance with Huy Braseal, perhaps out of friendship for fellow Indians. The West Coast states, fearful of Hinduraj, were toadies of the Southeast Asian empire. The Middle West (of course) was isolationist; the Eastern States were torn every which way, but inclined to follow the lead of Brittys.

When he gathered that slavery existed here, though not on racial lines, Everard wondered briefly and wildly if the time changers might not have been Dixiecrats.

Enough! He had his own neck, and Van's, to think about. "We are from Sirius," he declared loftily. "Your ideas about the stars are mistaken. We came as peaceful explorers, and if we are molested, there will be others of our kind to take vengeance."

Deirdre looked so unhappy that he felt conscience-stricken. "Will they spare the children?" she begged. "The children had nothing to do with it." Everard could imagine the vision in her head, small crying captives led off to the slave markets of a world of witches.

"There need be no trouble at all if we are released and our property returned," he said.

"I shall speak to my uncle," she promised, "but even if I can sway him, he is only one man on the Council. The thought of what your weapons could mean if we had them has driven men mad."

She rose. Everard clasped both her hands—they lay warm and soft in his—and smiled crookedly at her. "Buck up, kid," he said in English. She shivered, pulled free of him, and made the hex sign again.

"Well," demanded Van Sarawak when they were alone, "what did you find out?" After being told, he stroked his chin and murmured. "That was one glorious little collection of sinusoids. There could be worse worlds than this."

"Or better," said Everard roughly. "They don't have atomic bombs, but neither do they have penicillin, I'll bet. Our job is not to play God."

"No. No, I suppose not." The Venusian sighed.

4

They spent a restless day. Night had fallen when lanterns glimmered in the corridor and a military guard unlocked the cell. The prisoners were led silently to a rear exit where two automobiles waited; they were put into one, and the whole troop drove off.

Catuvellaunan did not have outdoor lighting, and there wasn't much night traffic. Somehow that made the sprawling city unreal in the dark. Everard paid attention to the mechanics of his car. Steam-powered, as he had guessed, burning powdered coal; rubber-tired wheels; a sleek body with a sharp nose and serpent figurehead; the whole simple to operate and honestly built, but not too well designed. Apparently this world had gradually developed a rule-of-thumb engineering, but no systematic science worth talking about.

They crossed a clumsy iron bridge to Long Island, here also a residential section for the well-to-do. Despite the dimness of oil-lamp headlights, their speed was high. Twice they came near having an accident: no traffic signals, and seemingly no drivers who did not hold caution in contempt.

Government and traffic . . . hm. It all looked French, somehow, ignoring those rare interludes when France got a Henry of Navarre or a Charles de Gaulle. And even in Everard's own twentieth century, France was largely Celtic. He was no respecter of windy theories about inborn racial traits, but there was something to be said for traditions so ancient as to be unconscious and ineradicable. A Western world in which the Celts had become dominant, the Germanic peoples reduced to a few small outposts. . . . Yes, look at the Ireland of home; or recall how tribal politics had queered Vercingetorix's revolt. . . . But what about Littorn? Wait a minute! In *his* early Middle Ages, Lithuania had been a powerful state;

it had held off Germans, Poles, and Russians alike for a
long time, and hadn't even taken Christianity till the
fifteenth century. Without German competition,
Lithuania might very well have advanced eastward. . . .

In spite of the Celtic political instability, this was a
world of large states, fewer separate nations than
Everard's. That argued an older society. If his own
Western civilization had developed out of the decaying
Roman Empire about, say, A.D. 600, the Celts in this
world must have taken over earlier than that.

Everard was beginning to realize what had happened
to Rome, but reserved his conclusions for the time
being.

The cars drew up before an ornamental gate set in a
long stone wall. The drivers talked with two armed guards
wearing the livery of a private estate and the thin steel
collars of slaves. The gate was opened and the cars went
along a graveled driveway between lawns and trees. At the
far end, almost on the beach, stood a house. Everard and
Van Sarawak were gestured out and led toward it.

It was a rambling wooden structure. Gas lamps on the
porch showed it painted in gaudy stripes; the gables and
beam ends were carved into dragon heads. Close by he
heard the sea, and there was enough light from a sinking
crescent moon for Everard to make out a ship standing in
close: presumably a freighter, with a tall smokestack and
a figurehead.

The windows glowed yellow. A slave butler admitted
the party. The interior was paneled in dark wood, also
carved, the floors thickly carpeted. At the end of the hall
was a living room with overstuffed furniture, several

paintings in a stiff conventionalized style, and a merry
blaze in an enormous stone fireplace.

Saorann ap Ceorn sat in one chair, Deirdre in another.
She laid aside a book as they entered and rose, smiling.
The officer puffed a cigar and glowered. Some words
were swapped, and the guards disappeared. The butler
fetched in wine on a tray, and Deirdre invited the
Patrolmen to sit down.

Everard sipped from his glass—the wine was an
excellent burgundy—and asked bluntly, "Why are we
here?"

Deirdre dazzled him with a smile. "Surely you find it
more pleasant than the jail."

"Of course. As well as more ornamental. But I still want
to know. Are we being released?"

"You are . . ." She hunted for a diplomatic answer, but
there seemed to be too much frankness in her. "You are
welcome here, but may not leave the estate. We hope you
can be persuaded to help us. You would be richly
rewarded."

"Help? How?"

"By showing our artisans and druids how to make more
weapons and magical carts like your own."

Everard sighed. It was no use trying to explain. They
didn't have the tools to make the tools to make what was
needed, but how could he get that across to a folk who
believed in witchcraft?

"Is this your uncle's home?" he asked.

"No, my own," said Deirdre. "I am the only child of my
parents, who were wealthy nobles. They died last year."

Ap Ceorn clipped out several words. Deirdre

translated with a worried frown: "The tale of your advent is known to all Catuvellaunan by now; and that includes the foreign spies. We hope you can remain hidden from them here."

Everard, remembering the pranks Axis and Allies had played in little neutral nations like Portugal, shivered. Men made desperate by approaching war would not likely be as courteous as the Afallonians.

"What is this conflict going to be about?" he inquired.

"The control of the Icenian Ocean, of course. In particular, certain rich islands we call Ynys yr Lyonnach." Deirdre got up in a single flowing movement and pointed out Hawaii on a globe. "You see," she went on earnestly, "as I told you, Littorn and the western alliance—including us—wore each other out fighting. The great powers today, expanding, quarreling, are Huy Braseal and Hinduraj. Their conflict sucks in the lesser nations, for the clash is not only between ambitions, but between systems: the monarchy of Hinduraj against the sun-worshipping theocracy of Huy Braseal."

"What is your religion, if I may ask?"

Deirdre blinked. The question seemed almost meaningless to her. "The more educated people think that there is a Great Baal who made all the lesser gods," she answered at last, slowly. "But naturally, we maintain the ancient cults, and pay respect to the more powerful foreign gods too, such as Littorn's Perkunas and Czernebog, Wotan Ammon of Cimberland, Brahma, the Sun ... Best not to chance their anger."

"I see."

Ap Ceorn offered cigars and matches. Van Sarawak

inhaled and said querulously, "Damn it, this would have to be a time line where they don't speak any language I know." He brightened. "But I'm pretty quick to learn, even without hypno. I'll get Deirdre to teach me."

"You and me both," said Everard in haste. "But listen, Van." He reported what he had learned.

"Hm." The younger man rubbed his chin. "Not so good, eh? Of course, if they'd just let us aboard our scooter, we could make an easy getaway. Why not play along with them?"

"They're not such fools," answered Everard. "They may believe in magic, but not in undiluted altruism."

"Funny they should be so backward intellectually, and still have combustion engines."

"No. It's quite understandable. That's why I asked about their religion. It's always been purely pagan; even Judaism seems to have disappeared, and Buddhism hasn't been very influential. As Whitehead pointed out, the medieval idea of one almighty God was important to the growth of science, by inculcating the notion of lawfulness in nature. And Lewis Mumford added that the early monasteries were probably responsible for the mechanical clock—a very basic invention—because of having regular hours for prayer. Clocks seem to have come late in this world." Everard smiled wryly, a shield against the sadness within. "Odd to talk like this. Whitehead and Mumford never lived."

"Nevertheless—"

"Just a minute." Everard turned to Deirdre. "When was Afallon discovered?"

"By white men? In the year 4827."

"Um . . . when does your reckoning start from?"

Deirdre seemed immune to further startlement. "The creation of the world. At least, the date some philosophers have given. That is 5964 years ago."

Which agreed with Bishop Ussher's famous 4004 B.C., perhaps by sheer coincidence—but still, there was definitely a Semitic element in this culture. The creation story in Genesis was of Babylonian origin too.

"And when was steam *(pneuma)* first used to drive engines?" he asked.

"About a thousand years ago. The great druid Boroihme O'Fiona—"

"Never mind." Everard smoked his cigar and mulled his thoughts for a while before looking back at Van Sarawak.

"I'm beginning to get the picture," he said. "The Gauls were anything but the barbarians most people think. They'd learned a lot from Phoenician traders and Greek colonists, as well as from the Etruscans in Cisalpine Gaul. A very energetic and enterprising race. The Romans, on the other hand, were a stolid lot, with few intellectual interests. There was little technological progress in our world till the Dark Ages, when the Empire had been swept out of the way.

"In *this* history, the Romans vanished early. So, I'm pretty sure, did the Jews. My guess is, without the balance-of-power effect of Rome, the Syrians did suppress the Maccabees; it was a near thing even in our history. Judaism disappeared and therefore Christianity never came into existence. But anyhow, with Rome removed, the Gauls got the supremacy. They started exploring, building better ships, discovering America in the ninth century. But they weren't so far ahead of the Indians that those couldn't catch up . . . could even be stimulated to build empires of their own, like Huy Braseal today. In the eleventh century, the Celts began tinkering with steam engines. They seem to have gotten gunpowder too, maybe from China, and to have made several other inventions. But it's all been cut-and-try, with no basis of real science."

Van Sarawak nodded. "I suppose you're right. But what did happen to Rome?"

"I don't know. Yet. But our key point is back there somewhere."

Everard returned his attention to Deirdre. "This may surprise you," he said smoothly. "Our people visited this world about twenty-five hundred years ago. That's why I speak Greek but don't know what has occurred since. I would like to find out from you; I take it you're quite a scholar."

She flushed and lowered long dark lashes such as few redheads possess. "I will be glad to help as much as I can." With a sudden appeal: "But will you help us in return?"

"I don't know," said Everard heavily. "I'd like to. But I don't know if we can."

Because after all, my job is to condemn you and your entire world to death.

5

When Everard was shown to his room, he discovered that local hospitality was more than generous. He was too tired and depressed to take advantage of it...but at least, he thought on the edge of sleep, Van's slave girl wouldn't be disappointed.

They got up early here. From his upstairs window, Everard saw guards pacing the beach, but they didn't detract from the morning's freshness. He came down with Van Sarawak to breakfast, where bacon and eggs, toast and coffee added the last touch of dream. Ap Ceorn had gone back to town to confer, said Deirdre; she herself had put wistfulness aside and chattered gaily of trivia. Everard learned that she belonged to an amateur dramatic group which sometimes gave Classical Greek plays in the original: hence her fluency. She liked to ride, hunt, sail, swim—"And shall we?" she asked.

"Huh?"

"Swim, of course." Deirdre sprang from her chair on the lawn, where they had been sitting under flame-colored leaves, and whirled innocently out of her clothes. Everard thought he heard a dull clunk as Van Sarawak's jaw hit the ground.

"Come!" she laughed. "Last one in is a Sassenach!"

She was already tumbling in the gray surf when Everard and Van Sarawak shuddered their way down to the beach. The Venusian groaned. "I come from a warm planet. My ancestors were Indonesians. Tropical birds."

"There were some Dutchmen too, weren't there?" Everard grinned.

"They had the sense to move to Indonesia."

"All right, stay ashore."

"Hell! If she can do it, I can!" Van Sarawak put a toe in the water and groaned again.

Everard summoned up all the control he had ever learned and ran in. Deirdre threw water at him. He plunged, got hold of a slender leg, and pulled her under. They frolicked about for several minutes before running back to the house for a hot shower. Van Sarawak followed in a blue haze.

"Speak about Tantalus," he mumbled. "The most beautiful girl in the whole continuum, and I can't talk to her and she's half polar bear."

Toweled dry and dressed in the local garb by slaves, Everard returned to stand before the living-room fire. "What pattern is this?" he asked, pointing to the tartan of his kilt.

Deirdre lifted her ruddy head. "My own clan's," she answered. "An honored guest is always taken as a clan member during his stay, even if a blood feud is going on." She smiled shyly. "And there is none between us, Manslach."

It cast him back into bleakness. He remembered what his purpose was.

"I'd like to ask you about history," he said. "It is a special interest of mine."

She nodded, adjusted a gold fillet on her hair, and got a book from a crowded shelf. "This is the best world history, I think. I can look up any details you might wish to know."

And tell me what I must do to destroy you.

Everard sat down with her on a couch. The butler wheeled in lunch. He ate moodily, untasting.

To follow up his hunch—"Did Rome and Carthage ever fight a war?"

"Yes. Two, in fact. They were allied at first, against Epirus, but fell out. Rome won the first war and tried to restrict Carthaginian enterprise." Her clean profile bent over the pages, like a studious child's. "The second war broke out twenty-three years later, and lasted . . . hmm . . . eleven years all told, though the last three were only a mopping up after Hannibal had taken and burned Rome."

Ah-hah! Somehow, Everard did not feel happy at his success.

The Second Punic War (they called it the Roman War here)—or, rather, some crucial incident thereof—was the turning point. But partly out of curiosity, partly because he feared to tip his hand, Everard did not at once try to identify the deviation. He'd first have to get straight in his mind what had actually happened, anyway. (No . . . what had *not* happened. The reality was here, warm and breathing beside him; he was the ghost.)

"So what came next?" he asked tonelessly.

"The Carthaginian empire came to include Hispania, southern Gaul, and the toe of Italy," she said. "The rest of Italy was impotent and chaotic, after the Roman confederacy had been broken up. But the Carthaginian government was too venal to remain strong. Hannibal himself was assassinated by men who thought his honesty stood in their way. Meanwhile, Syria and Parthia fought for the eastern Mediterranean, with Parthia winning and thus coming under still greater Hellenic influence than before.

"About a hundred years after the Roman Wars, some Germanic tribes overran Italy." (That would be the Cimbri, with their allies the Teutones and Ambrones, whom

Marius had stopped in Everard's world.) "Their destructive path through Gaul had set the Celts moving too, eventually into Hispania and North Africa as Carthage declined. And from Carthage the Gauls learned much.

"A long period of wars followed, during which Parthia waned and the Celtic states grew. The Huns broke the Germans in middle Europe, but were in turn defeated by Parthia; so the Gauls moved in and the only Germans left were in Italy and Hyperborea." (That must be the Scandinavian peninsula.) "As ships improved, trade grew up with the Far East, both from Arabia and directly around Africa." (In Everard's history, Julius Caesar had been astonished to find the Veneti building better vessels than any in the Mediterranean.) "The Celtanians discovered southern Afallon, which they thought was an island—hence the 'Ynys'—but they were thrown out by the Mayans. The Brittic colonies farther north did survive, though, and eventually won their independence.

"Meanwhile Littorn was growing apace. It swallowed up most of Europe for a while. The western end of the continent only regained its freedom as part of the peace settlement after the Hundred Years' War I've told you about. The Asian countries have shaken off their exhausted European masters and modernized themselves, while the Western nations have declined in their turn." Deirdre looked up from the book, which she had been skimming as she talked. "But this is only the barest outline, Manslach. Shall I go on?"

Everard shook his head. "No, thanks." After a moment: "You are very honest about the situation of your own country."

Deirdre said roughly, "Most of us won't admit it, but I think it best to look truth in the eyes."

With a surge of eagerness: "But tell me of your own world. This is a marvel past belief."

Everard sighed, switched off his conscience, and began lying.

The raid took place that afternoon.

Van Sarawak had recovered his poise and was busily learning the Afallonian language from Deirdre. They walked through the garden hand in hand, stopping to name objects and act out verbs. Everard followed, wondering vaguely if he was a third wheel or not, most of him bent to the problem of how to get at the scooter.

Bright sunlight spilled from a pale cloudless sky. A maple was a shout of scarlet, a drift of yellow leaves scudded across the grass. An elderly slave was raking the yard in a leisurely fashion, a young-looking guard of Indian race lounged with his rifle slung on one shoulder, a pair of wolfhounds dozed under a hedge. It was a peaceful scene; hard to believe that men prepared murder beyond these walls.

But man was man, in any history. This culture might not have the ruthless will and sophisticated cruelty of Western civilization; in fact, in some ways it looked strangely innocent. Still, that wasn't for lack of trying. And in this world, a genuine science might never emerge, man might endlessly repeat the cycle of war, empire, collapse, and war. In Everard's future, the race had finally broken out of it.

For what? He could not honestly say that this

continuum was worse or better than his own. It was different, that was all. And didn't these people have as much right to their existence as—as his own, who were damned to nullity if he failed?

He knotted his fists. The issue was too big. No man should have to decide something like this.

At the showdown, he knew, no abstract sense of duty would compel him, but the little things and the little folk he remembered.

They rounded the house and Deirdre pointed to the sea. "*Awarkinn,*" she said. Her loose hair burned in the wind.

"Now does that mean 'ocean' or 'Atlantic' or 'water'?" laughed Van Sarawak. "Let's go see." He led her toward the beach.

Everard trailed. A kind of steam launch, long and fast, was skipping over the waves, a mile or two offshore. Gulls trailed it in a snowstorm of wings. He thought that if he'd been in charge, a Navy ship would have been on picket out there.

Did he even have to decide anything? There were other Patrolmen in the pre-Roman past. They'd return to their respective eras and...

Everard stiffened. A chill ran down his back and congealed in his belly.

They'd return, and see what had happened, and try to correct the trouble. If any of them succeeded, this world would blink out of spacetime, and he would go with it.

Deirdre paused. Everard, standing in a sweat, hardly noticed what she was staring at, till she cried out and pointed. Then he joined her and squinted across the sea.

The launch was standing in close, its high stack fuming smoke and sparks, the gilt snake figurehead agleam. He could see the forms of men aboard, and something white, with wings.... It rose from the poop deck and trailed at the end of a rope, mounting. A glider! Celtic aeronautics had gotten that far, at least.

"Pretty," said Van Sarawak. "I suppose they have balloons, too."

The glider cast its tow and swooped inward. One of the guards on the beach shouted. The rest pelted from behind the house. Sunlight flashed off their guns. The launch headed straight for the shore. The glider landed, plowing a furrow in the beach.

An officer yelled and waved the Patrolmen back. Everard had a glimpse of Deirdre's face, white and uncomprehending. Then a turret on the glider swiveled— a detached part of his mind guessed it was manually operated—and a light cannon spoke.

Everard hit the dirt. Van Sarawak followed, dragging the girl with him. Grapeshot plowed hideously through the Afallonian soldiers.

There followed a spiteful crack of guns. Men sprang from the aircraft, dark-faced men in turbans and sarongs. *Hinduraj!* thought Everard. They traded shots with the surviving guards, who rallied about their captain.

The officer roared and led a charge. Everard looked up from the sand to see him almost upon the glider's crew. Van Sarawak leaped to his feet. Everard rolled over, caught him by the ankle, and pulled him down before he could join the fight.

"Let me *go!*" The Venusian writhed, sobbing. The dead

and wounded left by the cannon sprawled nightmare red. The racket of battle seemed to fill the sky.

"No, you bloody fool! It's us they're after, and that wild Irishman's done the worst thing he could have—" A fresh outburst yanked Everard's attention elsewhere.

The launch, shallow-draft and screw-propelled, had run up into the shallows and was retching armed men. Too late the Afallonians realized that they had discharged their weapons and were now being attacked from the rear.

"Come on!" Everard hauled Deirdre and Van Sarawak to their feet. "We've got to get out of here—get to the neighbors . . ."

A detachment from the boat saw him and veered. He felt rather than heard the flat smack of a bullet into soil, as he reached the lawn. Slaves screamed hysterically inside the house. The two wolfhounds attacked the invaders and were gunned down.

Crouched, zigzag, that was the way: over the wall and out onto the road! Everard might have made it, but Deirdre stumbled and fell. Van Sarawak halted to guard her. Everard stopped also, and then it was too late. They were covered.

The leader of the dark men snapped something at the girl. She sat up, giving him a defiant answer. He laughed shortly and jerked his thumb at the launch.

"What do they want?" asked Everard in Greek.

"You." She looked at him with horror. "You two—" The officer spoke again. "And me to translate. . . . No!"

She twisted in the hands that had closed on her arms, got partly free and clawed at a face. Everard's fist traveled in a short arc that ended in a squashing of nose. It was too

good to last. A clubbed rifle descended on his head, and
he was only dimly aware of being frog-marched off to the
launch.

6

The crew left the glider behind, shoved their boat into
deeper water, and revved it up. They left all the
guardsmen slain or disabled, but took their own casualties
along.

Everard sat on a bench on the plunging deck and
stared with slowly clearing eyes as the shoreline dwindled.
Deirdre wept on Van Sarawak's shoulder, and the
Venusian tried to console her. A chill noisy wind flung
spindrift in their faces.

When two white men emerged from the deckhouse,
Everard's mind was jarred back into motion. Not Asians
after all. Europeans! And now when he looked closely, he
saw the rest of the crew also had Caucasian features. The
brown complexions were merely greasepaint.

He stood up and regarded his new owners warily. One
was a portly, middle-aged man of average height, in a red
silk blouse and baggy white trousers and a sort of
astrakhan hat; he was clean-shaven and his dark hair was
twisted into a queue. The other was somewhat younger, a
shaggy blond giant in a tunic sewn with copper links,
legginged breeches, a leather cloak, and a purely
ornamental horned helmet. Both wore revolvers at their
belts and were treated deferentially by the sailors.

"What the devil?" Everard looked around once more.

They were already out of sight of land, and bending north. The hull quivered with the haste of the engine, spray sheeted when the bows hit a wave.

The older man spoke first in Afallonian. Everard shrugged. Then the bearded Nordic tried, first in a completely unrecognizable dialect but afterward: *"Taelan thu Cimbric?"*

Everard, who knew several Germanic languages, took a chance, while Van Sarawak pricked up his Dutch ears. Deirdre huddled back, wide-eyed, too bewildered to move.

"Ja," said Everard, *"ein wenig."* When Goldilocks looked uncertain, he amended it: "A little."

"Ah, aen litt. Gode!" The big man rubbed his hands. *"Ik hait Boierik Wulfilasson ok main gefreond heer erran Boleslav Arkonsky."*

It was no language Everard had ever heard of—couldn't even be the original Cimbric, after all these centuries—but the Patrolman could follow it reasonably well. The trouble came in speaking; he couldn't predict how it had evolved.

"What the hell erran thu maching, anyway?" he blustered. "Ik bin aen man auf Sirius—the stern Sirius, mil planeten ok all. Set uns gebach or willen be der Teufel to pay!"

Boierik Wulfilasson looked pained and suggested that the discussion be continued inside, with the young lady for interpreter. He led the way back into the deckhouse, which turned out to include a small but comfortably furnished saloon. The door remained open, with an armed guard looking in and more on call.

Boleslav Arkonsky said something in Afallonian to Deirdre. She nodded, and he gave her a glass of wine. It seemed to steady her, but she spoke to Everard in a thin voice.

"We've been captured, Manslach. Their spies found out where you were kept. Another group is supposed to steal your traveling machine. They know where that is, too."

"So I imagined," replied Everard. "But who in Baal's name are they?"

Boierik guffawed at the question and expounded lengthily on his own cleverness. The idea was to make the Suffetes of Afallon think Hinduraj was responsible. Actually, the secret alliance of Littorn and Cimberland had built up quite an effective spy service. They were now bound for the Littornian embassy's summer retreat on Ynys Llangollen (Nantucket), where the wizards would be induced to explain their spells and a surprise prepared for the great powers.

"And if we don't do this?"

Deirdre translated Arkonsky's answer word for word: "I regret the consequences to you. We are civilized men, and will pay well in gold and honor for your free cooperation. If that is withheld, we will get your forced cooperation. The existence of our countries is at stake."

Everard looked closely at them. Boierik seemed embarrassed and unhappy, the boastful glee evaporated from him. Boleslav Arkonsky drummed on the tabletop, his lips compressed but a certain appeal in his eyes. *Don't make us do this. We have to live with ourselves.*

They were probably husbands and fathers, they must enjoy a mug of beer and a friendly game of dice as well as the next man, maybe Boierik bred horses in Italy and Arkonsky was a rose fancier on the Baltic shores. But none of this would do their captives a bit of good, when the almighty Nation locked horns with its kin.

Everard paused to admire the sheer artistry of this operation, and then began wondering what to do. The launch was fast, but would need something like twenty hours to reach Nantucket, as he remembered the trip. There was that much time, at least.

"We are weary," he said in English. "May we not rest awhile?"

"*Ja deedly,*" said Boierik with a clumsy graciousness. "*Ok wir skallen gode gefreonds bin, ni?*"

Sunset smoldered in the west. Deirdre and Van Sarawak stood at the rail, looking across a gray waste of waters. Three crewmen, their makeup and costumes removed, poised alert and weaponed on the poop; a man steered by compass; Boierik and Everard paced the quarterdeck. All wore heavy clothes against the wind.

Everard was getting some proficiency in the Cimbrian language; his tongue still limped, but he could make himself understood. Mostly, though, he let Boierik do the talking.

"So you are from the stars? These matters I do not understand. I am a simple man. Had I my way, I would manage my Tuscan estate in peace and let the world rave as it will. But we of the Folk have our obligations." The Teutonics seemed to have replaced the Latins altogether in Italy, as the English had done the Britons in Everard's world.

"I know how you feel," said the Patrolman. "Strange that so many should fight when so few want to."

"Oh, but this is necessary." A near whine. "Carthagalann stole Egypt, our rightful possession."

"Italia irredenta," murmured Everard.

"Hunh?"

"Never mind. So you Cimbri are allied with Littorn, and hope to grab off Europe and Africa while the big powers are fighting in the East."

"Not at all!" said Boierik indignantly. "We are merely asserting our rightful and historic territorial claims. Why, the king himself said . . . ." And so on and so on.

Everard braced himself against the roll of the deck. "Seems to me you treat us wizards rather hard," he remarked. "Beware lest we get really angered at you."

"All of us are protected against curses and shapings."

"Well—"

"I wish you would help us freely. I will be happy to demonstrate to you the justice of our cause, if you have a few hours to spare."

Everard shook his head, walked off and stopped by Deirdre. Her face was a blur in the thickening dusk, but he caught a forlorn fury in her voice: "I hope you told him what to do with his plans, Manslach."

"No," said Everard heavily. "We are going to help them."

She stood as if struck.

"What are you saying, Manse?" asked Van Sarawak. Everard told him.

"No!" said the Venusian.

"Yes," said Everard.

"By God, no! I'll—"

Everard grabbed his arm and said coldly: "Be quiet. I know what I'm doing. We can't take sides in this world; we're against everybody, and you'd better realize it. The only thing to do is play along with these fellows for a while. And don't tell that to Deirdre."

Van Sarawak bent his head and stood for a moment, thinking. "All right," he said dully.

7

The Littornian resort was on the southern shore of Nantucket, near a fishing village but walled off from it. The embassy had built in the style of its homeland: long, timber houses with roofs arched like a cat's back, a main hall and its outbuildings enclosing a flagged courtyard. Everard finished a night's sleep and a breakfast which Deirdre's eyes had made miserable by standing on deck as they came in to the private pier. Another, bigger launch was already there, and the grounds swarmed with hard-looking men. Arkonsky's excitement flared up as he said in Afallonian: "I see the magic engine has been brought. We can go right to work."

When Boierik interpreted, Everard felt his heart slam.

The guests, as the Cimbrian insisted on calling them, were led into an outsize room where Arkonsky bowed the knee to an idol with four faces, that Svantevit which the Danes had chopped up for firewood in the other history. A fire burned on the hearth against the autumn chill, and guards were posted around the walls. Everard had eyes only for the scooter, where it stood gleaming on the door.

"I hear the fight was hard in Catuvellaunan to gain this thing," remarked Boierik. "Many were killed; but our gang got away without being followed." He touched a handlebar gingerly. "And this wain can truly appear anywhere its rider wishes, out of thin air?"

"Yes," said Everard.

Deirdre gave him a look of scorn such as he had rarely known. She stood haughtily away from him and Van Sarawak.

Arkonsky spoke to her, something he wanted translated. She spat at his feet. Boierik sighed and gave the word to Everard:

"We wish the engine demonstrated. You and I will go for a ride on it. I warn you, I will have a revolver at your back. You will tell me in advance everything you mean to do, and if aught untoward happens, I will shoot. Your friends will remain here as hostages, also to be shot on the first suspicion. But I'm sure," he added, "that we will all be good friends."

Everard nodded. Tautness thrummed in him; his palms felt cold and wet. "First I must say a spell," he answered.

His eyes flickered. One glance memorized the spatial reading of the position meters and the time reading of the clock on the scooter. Another look showed Van Sarawak seated on a bench, under Arkonsky's drawn pistol and the rifles of the guards. Deirdre sat down too, stiffly, as far from him as she could get. Everard made a close estimate of the bench's position relative to the scooter's, lifted his arms, and chanted in Temporal:

"Van, I'm going to try to pull you out of here. Stay exactly where you are now, repeat, exactly. I'll pick you up on the fly. If all goes well, that'll happen about one minute after I blink off with our hairy comrade."

The Venusian sat wooden-faced, but a thin beading of sweat sprang out on his forehead.

"Very good," said Everard in his pidgin Cimbric. "Mount on the rear saddle, Boierik, and we'll put this magic horse through her paces."

The blond man nodded and obeyed. As Everard took the front seat, he felt a gun muzzle held shakily against his back. "Tell Arkonsky we'll be back in half an hour," he instructed. They had approximately the same time units here as in his world, both descended from the Babylonian. When that had been taken care of, Everard said, "The first thing we will do is appear in midair over the ocean and hover."

"F-f-fine," said Boierik. He didn't sound very convinced.

Everard set the space controls for ten miles east and a thousand feet up, and threw the main switch.

They sat like witches astride a broom, looking down on greenish-gray immensity and the distant blur which was land. The wind was high, it caught at them and Everard gripped tight with his knees. He heard Boierik's oath and smiled stiffly.

"Well," he asked, "how do you like this?"

"Why . . . it's wonderful." As he grew accustomed to the idea, the Cimbrian gathered enthusiasm. "Balloons are as nothing beside it. With machines like this, we can soar above enemy cities and rain fire down on them."

Somehow, that made Everard feel better about what he was going to do.

"Now we will fly ahead," he announced, and sent the

scooter gliding through the air. Boierik whooped exultantly. "And now we will make the instantaneous jump to your homeland."

Everard threw the maneuver switch. The scooter looped the loop and dropped at a three-gee acceleration.

Forewarned, the Patrolman could still barely hang on. He never knew whether the curve or the dive had thrown Boierik. He only got a moment's glimpse of the man, plunging down through windy spaces to the sea, and wished he hadn't.

For a little while, then, Everard hung above the waves. His first reaction was a shudder. Suppose Boierik had had time to shoot? His second was a thick guilt. Both he dismissed, and concentrated on the problem of rescuing Van Sarawak.

He set the space verniers for one foot in front of the prisoners' bench, the time unit for one minute after he had departed. His right hand he kept by the controls— he'd have to work fast—and his left free.

Hang on to your hats, fellas. Here we go again.

The machine flashed into existence almost in front of Van Sarawak. Everard clutched the Venusian's tunic and hauled him close, inside the spatiotemporal drive field, even as his right hand spun the time dial back and snapped down the main switch.

A bullet caromed off metal. Everard had a moment's glimpse of Arkonsky shouting. And then it was all gone and they were on a grassy hill sloping down to the beach. It was two thousand years ago.

He collapsed shivering over the handlebars.

A cry brought him back to awareness. He twisted

around to look at Van Sarawak where the Venusian sprawled on the hillside. One arm was still around Deirdre's waist.

The wind lulled, and the sea rolled in to a broad white strand, and clouds walked high in heaven.

"Can't say I blame you, Van." Everard paced before the scooter and looked at the ground, "But it does complicate matters."

"What was I supposed to do?" the other man asked on a raw note. "Leave her there for those bastards to kill— or to be snuffed out with her entire universe?"

"Remember, we're conditioned. Without authorization, we couldn't tell her the truth even if we wanted to. And I, for one, don't want to."

Everard glanced at the girl. She stood breathing heavily, but with a dawn in her eyes. The wind ruffled her hair and the long thin dress.

She shook her head, as if to clear it of nightmare, ran over and clasped their hands. "Forgive me, Manslach," she breathed. "I should have known you'd not betray us."

She kissed them both. Van Sarawak responded as eagerly as expected, but Everard couldn't bring himself to. He would have remembered Judas.

"Where are we?" she continued. "It looks almost like Llangollen, but no dwellers. Have you taken us to the Happy Isles?" She spun on one foot and danced among summer flowers. "Can we rest here a while before returning home?"

Everard drew a long breath. "I've bad news for you, Deirdre," he said.

She grew silent. He saw her gather herself.

"We can't go back."

She waited mutely.

"The . . . the spells I had to use, to save our lives—I had no choice. But those spells debar us from returning home."

"There is no hope?" He could barely hear her.

His eyes stung. "No," he said.

She turned and walked away. Van Sarawak moved to follow her, but thought better of it and sat down beside Everard. "What'd you tell her?" he asked.

Everard repeated his words. "It seems the best compromise," he finished. "I can't send her back to what's waiting for this world."

"No." Van Sarawak sat quiet for a while, staring across the sea. Then: "What year is this? About the time of Christ? Then we're still upstairs of the turning point."

"Yeh. And we still have to find out what it was."

"Let's go back to some Patrol office in the farther past. We can recruit help there."

"Maybe." Everard lay down in the grass and regarded the sky. Reaction overwhelmed him. "I think I can locate the key event right here, though, with Deirdre's help. Wake me when she comes back."

She returned dry-eyed, though one could see she had wept. When Everard asked if she would assist in his own mission, she nodded, "Of course. My life is yours who saved it."

After getting you into the mess in the first place. Everard said carefully: "All I want from you is some information. Do you know about . . . about putting people to sleep, a sleep in which they may believe anything they're told?"

She nodded doubtfully. "I've seen medical druids do that."

"It won't harm you. I only wish to make you sleep so you can remember everything you know, things you believe forgotten. It won't take long."

Her trustfulness was hard for him to endure. Using Patrol techniques, he put her in a hypnotic state of total recall and dredged out all she had ever heard or read about the Second Punic War. That added up to enough for his purposes.

Roman interferences with Carthaginian enterprise south of the Ebro, in direct violation of treaty, had been the final goading. In 219 B.C. Hannibal Barca, governor of Carthaginian Spain, laid siege to Saguntum. After eight months he took it, and thus provoked his long-planned war with Rome. At the beginning of May, 218, he crossed the Pyrenees with 90,000 infantry, 12,000 cavalry, and 37 elephants, marched through Gaul, and went over the Alps. His losses en route were gruesome: only 20,000 foot and 6,000 horse reached Italy late in the year. Nevertheless, near the Ticinus River he met and broke a superior Roman force. In the course of the following year, he fought several bloodily victorious battles and advanced into Apulia and Campania.

The Apulians, Lucanians, Bruttians, and Samnites went over to his side. Quintus Fabius Maximus fought a grim guerrilla war, which laid Italy waste and decided nothing. But meanwhile Hasdrubal Barca was organizing Spain, and in 211 he arrived with reinforcements. In 210

Hannibal took and burned Rome, and by 207 the last cities of the confederacy had surrendered to him.

"That's it," said Everard. He stroked the coppery mane of the girl lying beside him. "Go to sleep now. Sleep well and wake up glad of heart."

"What'd she tell you?" asked Van Sarawak.

"A lot of detail," said Everard. The whole story had required more than an hour. "The important thing is this: her knowledge of those times is good, but she never mentioned the Scipios."

"The whos?"

"Publius Cornelius Scipio commanded the Roman army at Ticinus. He was beaten there all right, in our world. But later he had the intelligence to turn westward and gnaw away the Carthaginian base in Spain. It ended with Hannibal being effectively cut off in Italy, and what little Iberian help could be sent him was annihilated. Scipio's son of the same name also held a high command, and was the man who finally whipped Hannibal at Zama; that's Scipio Africanus the Elder.

"Father and son were by far the best leaders Rome had. But Deirdre never heard of them."

"So . . ." Van Sarawak stared eastward across the sea, where Gauls and Cimbri and Parthians were ramping through the shattered Classical world. "What happened to them in this time line?"

"My own total recall tells me that both the Scipios were at Ticinus, and very nearly killed. The son saved his father's life during the retreat, which I imagine was more like a stampede. One gets you ten that in *this* history the Scipios died there."

"Somebody must have knocked them off," said Van Sarawak. His voice tightened. "Some time traveler. It could only have been that."

"Well, it seems probable, anyhow. We'll see." Everard looked away from Deirdre's slumbrous face. "We'll see."

8

At the Pleistocene resort—half an hour after having left it for New York—the Patrolmen put the girl in charge of a sympathetic Greek-speaking matron and summoned their colleagues. Then the message capsules began jumping through spacetime.

All offices prior to 218 B.C.—the closest was Alexandria, 250–230—were "still" there, with two hundred or so agents altogether. Written contact with the future was confirmed to be impossible, and a few short jaunts upstairs clinched the proof. A worried conference met at the Academy, back in the Oligocene Period. Unattached agents ranked those with steady assignments, but not each other; on the basis of his own experience, Everard found himself the chairman of a committee of top-bracket officers.

That was a frustrating job. These men and women had leaped centuries and wielded the weapons of gods. But they were still human, with all the ingrained orneriness of their race.

Everyone agreed that the damage would have to be repaired. But there was fear for those agents who had gone ahead into time before being warned, as Everard himself had done. If they weren't back when history was realtered, they would never be seen again. Everard deputized parties to attempt rescue, but doubted there'd be much success. He warned them sternly to return within a day, local time, or face the consequences.

A man from the Scientific Renaissance had another point to make. Granted, the survivors' plain duty was to restore the "original" time track. But they had a duty to knowledge as well. Here was a unique chance to study a whole new phase of humankind. Several years' anthropological work should be done before—Everard slapped him down with difficulty. There weren't so many Patrolmen left that they could take the risk.

Study groups had to determine the exact moment and circumstances of the change. The wrangling over methods went on interminably. Everard glared out the window, into the prehuman night, and wondered if the sabertooths weren't doing a better job after all than their simian successors.

When he had finally gotten his various gangs dispatched, he broke out a bottle and got drunk with Van Sarawak.

Reconvening next day, the steering committee heard from its deputies, who had run up a total of years in the future. A dozen Patrolmen had been rescued from more or less ignominious situations; another score would simply have to be written off. The spy group's report was more interesting. It seemed that two Helvetian mercenaries had joined Hannibal in the Alps and won his confidence. After the war, they had risen to high positions in Carthage. Under the names of Phrontes and Himilco, they had practically run the government, engineered Hannibal's murder, and set new records for luxurious living. One of the Patrolmen had seen their homes and the men themselves. "A lot of improvements that hadn't been thought of in Classical times. The fellows looked to me like Neldorians, two-hundred-fifth millennium."

Everard nodded. That was an age of bandits who had "already" given the Patrol a lot of work. "I think we've settled the matter," he said. "It makes no difference whether they were with Hannibal before Ticinus or not. We'd have hell's own time arresting them in the Alps without such a fuss that we'd change the future ourselves. What counts is that they seem to have rubbed out the Scipios, and that's the point we'll have to strike at."

A nineteenth-century Britisher, competent but with elements of Colonel Blimp, unrolled a map and discoursed on his aerial observations of the battle. He'd used an infrared telescope to look through low clouds. "And here the Romans stood—"

"I know," said Everard. "A thin red line. The moment when they took flight is the critical one, but the confusion then also gives us our chance. Okay, we'll want to surround the battlefield unobtrusively, but I don't think we can get away with more than two agents actually on the scene. The baddies are going to be alert, you know, looking for possible counterinterference. The Alexandria office can supply Van and me with costumes."

"I say," exclaimed the Englishman, "I thought I'd have the privilege."

"No. Sorry." Everard smiled with one corner of his mouth. "No privilege, anyway. Just risking your neck, in order to negate a world full of people like yourself."

"But dash it all—"

Everard rose. "I've got to go," he said flatly. "I don't know why, but I've got to."

Van Sarawak nodded.

They left their scooter in a clump of trees and started across the field.

Around the horizon and up in the sky waited a hundred armed Patrolmen, but that was small consolation here among spears and arrows. Lowering clouds hurried before a cold whistling wind, there was a spatter of rain; sunny Italy was enjoying its late fall.

The cuirass was heavy on Everard's shoulders as he trotted across blood-slippery mud. He had helmet, greaves, a Roman shield on his left arm and a sword at his waist; but his right hand gripped a stunner. Van Sarawak loped behind, similarly equipped, eyes shifting under the wind-ruffled officer's plume.

Trumpets howled and drums stuttered. It was all but lost among the yells of men and tramp of feet, screaming riderless horses and whining arrows. Only a few captains and scouts were still mounted; as often before stirrups were invented, what started to be a cavalry battle had become entirely a fight on foot after the lancers fell off their mounts. The Carthaginians were pressing in, hammering edged metal against the buckling Roman lines. Here and there the struggle was already breaking up into small knots, where men cursed and cut at strangers.

The combat had passed over this area already. Death lay around Everard. He hurried behind the Roman force, toward the distant gleam of the eagles. Across helmets and corpses, he made out a banner that fluttered triumphant red and purple. And there, looming monstrous against the gray sky, lifting their trunks and bawling, came a squad of elephants.

War was always the same: not a neat affair of lines across maps, nor a hallooing gallantry, but men who gasped and sweated and bled in bewilderment.

A slight, dark-faced youth squirmed nearby, trying feebly to pull out the javelin which had pierced his stomach. He was a slinger from Carthage, but the burly Italian peasant who sat next to him, staring without belief at the stump of an arm, paid no attention.

A flight of crows hovered overhead, riding the wind and waiting.

"This way," muttered Everard. "Hurry up, for God's sake! That line's going to break any minute."

The breath was raw in his throat as he jogged toward the standards of the Republic. It came to him that he'd always rather wished Hannibal had won. There was something repellent about the frigid, unimaginative greed of Rome. And here he was, trying to save the city. Well-a-day, life was often an odd business.

It was some consolation that Scipio Africanus was one of the few decent men left after the war.

Screaming and clangor lifted, and the Italians reeled back. Everard saw something like a wave smashed against a rock. But it was the rock which advanced, crying out and stabbing, stabbing.

He began to run. A legionary went past, howling his panic. A grizzled Roman veteran spat on the ground, braced his feet, and stood where he was till they cut him down. Hannibal's elephants squealed and blundered about. The ranks of Carthage held firm, advancing to an inhuman pulse of drums.

Up ahead, now! Everard saw men on horseback, Roman officers. They held the eagles aloft and shouted, but nobody could hear them above the din.

A small group of legionaries trotted past. Their leader hailed the Patrolmen: "Over here! We'll give 'em a fight, by the belly of Venus!"

Everard shook his head and continued. The Roman snarled and sprang at him. "Come here, you cowardly..." A stun beam cut off his words. He crashed into the muck. His men shuddered, someone wailed, and the party broke into flight.

The Carthaginians were very near, shield to shield and swords running red. Everard could see a scar livid on the cheek of one man, the great hook nose of another. A hurled spear clanged off his helmet. He lowered his head and ran.

A combat loomed before him. He tried to go around, and tripped on a gashed corpse. A Roman stumbled over him in turn. Van Sarawak cursed and dragged him clear. A sword furrowed the Venusian's arm.

Beyond, Scipio's men were surrounded and battling without hope. Everard halted, sucked air into starved lungs, and looked into the thin rain. Armor gleamed wetly as a troop of Roman horsemen galloped closer, with mud up to their mounts' noses. That must be the son, Scipio Africanus to be, hastening to rescue his father. The hoofbeats made thunder in the earth.

"Over there!"

Van Sarawak cried out and pointed. Everard crouched where he was, rain dripping off his helmet and down his face. From another direction, a Carthaginian party was riding toward the battle around the eagles. And at their head were two men with the height and craggy features of Neldor. They wore G.I. armor, but each of them held a slim-barreled gun.

"This way!" Everard spun on his heel and dashed toward them. The leather in his cuirass creaked as he ran.

The Patrolmen were close to the Carthaginians before they were seen. Then a horseman called the warning. Two crazy Romans! Everard saw how he grinned in his beard. One of the Neldorians raised his blast rifle.

Everard flopped on his stomach. The vicious blue-white beam sizzled where he had been. He snapped a shot, and one of the African horses went over in a roar of metal. Van Sarawak stood his ground and fired steadily. Two, three, four—and there went a Neldorian, down in the mud!

Men hewed at each other around the Scipios. The Neldorians' escort yelled with terror. They must have had the blaster demonstrated beforehand, but these invisible blows were something else. They bolted. The second of the bandits got his horse under control and turned to follow.

"Take care of the one you potted, Van," gasped Everard. "Drag him off the battlefield—we'll want to question—" He himself scrambled to his feet and made for a riderless horse. He was in the saddle and after the Neldorian before he was fully aware of it.

Behind him, Publius Cornelius Scipio and his son fought clear and joined their retreating army.

Everard fled through chaos. He urged speed from his mount, but was content to pursue. Once they had gotten out of sight, a scooter could swoop down and make short work of his quarry.

The same thought must have occurred to the time rover. He reined in and took aim. Everard saw the blinding flash and felt his cheek sting with a near miss. He set his pistol to wide beam and rode in shooting.

Another firebolt took his horse full in the breast. The animal toppled and Everard went out of the saddle. Trained reflexes softened the fall. He bounced to his feet and lurched toward his enemy. The stunner was gone, fallen into the mud, no time to look for it. Never mind, it could be salvaged later, if he lived. The widened beam had found its mark; it wasn't strong enough at such dilution to knock a man out, but the Neldorian had dropped his blaster and the horse stood swaying with closed eyes.

Rain beat in Everard's face. He slogged up to the mount. The Neldorian jumped to earth and drew a sword. Everard's own blade rasped forth.

"As you will," he said in Latin. "One of us will not leave this field."

9

The moon rose over mountains and turned the snow to a sudden wan glitter. Far in the north, a glacier threw back the light, and a wolf howled. The Crô-Magnons chanted in their cave, the noise drifted faintly through to the verandah.

Deirdre stood in darkness, looking out. Moonlight dappled her face and caught a gleam of tears. She started as Everard and Van Sarawak came up behind her.

"Are you back so soon?" she asked. "You only came here and left me this morning."

"It didn't take long," said Van Sarawak. He had gotten a hypno in Attic Greek.

"I hope—" she tried to smile—"I hope you have finished your task and can rest from your labors."

"Yes," said Everard, "we finished it."

They stood side by side for a while, looking out on a world of winter.

"Is it true what you said, that I can never go home?" Deirdre spoke gently.

"I'm afraid so. The spells . . ." Everard swapped a glance with Van Sarawak.

They had official permission to tell the girl as much as they wished and take her wherever they thought she could live best. Van Sarawak maintained that would be Venus in his century, and Everard was too tired to argue.

Deirdre drew a long breath. "So be it," she said. "I'll not waste of life lamenting. But the Baal grant that they have it well, my people at home."

"I'm sure they will," said Everard.

Suddenly he could do no more. He only wanted to sleep. Let Van Sarawak say what had to be said, and reap whatever rewards there might be.

He nodded at his companion. "I'm turning in," he declared. "Carry on, Van."

The Venusian took the girl's arm. Everard went slowly back to his room.

EVADING HISTORY
by Hank Davis

*Being able to travel back in time wouldn't necessarily rule
out also being able to travel sideways to parallel Earths.
And if one were used as a weapon, the other might be able
to counter the attack.*

* * *

Mulling over her impending speech, the President walked
down the hallway toward the door leading to the big room
where the press awaited, likely with hostilities simmering.
Her high heels clicked on the polished hallway floor in
counterpoint to the steps of the three Secret Service
agents, one on either side, and the third walking behind.
Their concealed weapons were loaded, naturally, but
holstered, not immediately at hand.

The Commander in Chief expected trouble, but that
would come after she had given her speech, and then only
the political sort, with words as the weapons; and that
would be from the opposition and from the media, who
were much the same thing.

So, when a slender figure in an odd face-covering

helmet and what looked like some sort of body armor stepped forward on one side, as if through a door, a door that wasn't there, said, "I'm sorry, guys," and raised what turned out to be a weapon and began firing, the guards never had a chance.

The President froze, though not in fear. She had seen military service two decades earlier and was thinking rapidly, evaluating the situation . . . which looked hopeless.

"Madam President," the intruder said, "you are in danger but not from me. We only have minutes—" The intruder stopped talking as a second figure appeared, again stepping forward into the hall as if from a door that wasn't there. The first intruder fired with a different weapon, this one causing a glowing hole to appear in the midsection of the second arrival, who dropped something that looked like some futuristic movie's idea of a rifle, then collapsed to the polished floor.

The President fought off shock as her old battle habits awoke, and tried to catch up with what had just happened. Even so, an idiot part of her mind was still running on autopilot, still going over the speech she had been about to give. At the same time, still seeing no escape from this impossible assassin, she caught up with the moment enough to think that the second intruder had been larger, stockier, dressed oddly, but still seeming to be in a uniform, while the first intruder was shorter, more slender, and—seconds after she had heard that one speak, the President realized that the assassin had spoken with a woman's voice, a *familiar* woman's voice . . .

"Madam President," that familiar voice was saying, "you have to believe me that I'm not here to harm you—"

She paused as two more armed uniformed figures stepped from nowhere into the hall and attacked the first arrival. She dropped them both, but one had managed a grazing shot that made their target's shin glow dull red and sent a curling wisp of smoke into the air.

With a growing feeling of being disconnected from reality, the President wondered if the rising smoke would mar the paintings sprawling across the ceiling. And she noticed that the stranger didn't seem to be in pain from the shot that had grazed her leg, nor was she having any trouble standing on that leg. And that the part of the wall which had received most of the weapon's fire was blackened with flames licking about that part's edges.

The part of her mind that had written, then edited, then rewritten and reedited the speech during the past week was still running it through her consciousness, like a mindless playback machine. *My fellow Americans, as President Lincoln once reminded his countrymen, "We cannot escape history . . ."*

"Madam President—Jaybird—you *must* escape history. Right now," the first unauthorized arrival said.

Hearing a variation on the quotation in her speech brought her into focus. She realized that only a few seconds had elapsed, still long enough for her world to collapse into violent death and chaos, and that the stranger's voice was as familiar as her own. She had heard that voice speaking from innumerable soundbites, campaign ad clips, from interview playbacks. It was . . .

The intruder removed the helmet as she stepped forward, showing the familiar Roman nose, the green eyes, the red hair with the familiar invasions of gray . . .

... her own voice. Her own face.

"Jaybird," her own voice said, using the stranger's mouth, "I'm finished, but you've got to get out of here. You have to make that speech."

President Rachel Jaye Carlyle had stopped running over the speech in her head, and now the stranger had started the recording running again, bizarrely, insanely, with the stranger—her twin?—addressing her by the nickname her father had given her. Her father was long dead and nobody else had ever called her that, not even her late husband...

... until now.

Stepping forward, the intruder was now standing only a meter away from her, and the President stepped backwards, only now becoming conscious that her guards, not just guards but each a friend, all friends outside of duty, were lying dead on the floor. But she couldn't look down, couldn't look away from this insane woman's face, from her own face, her own green-eyed gaze.

Then she saw motion, barely visible at the bottom of her field of vision, and did look down. One of the Secret Service agents—Trevor—was stirring slightly, moving an arm aimlessly.

"They're not dead; or at least they shouldn't be," the strange woman said. "But snooze darts don't always work as advertised." She grimaced, then returned those mirrorlike green eyes to the President's face. "They're my friends, too, in another, uh, location, and I'm sorry to steal their last few moments of consciousness, but they would have been dead in a few minutes anyway, just as you will be, if you don't listen to me. So snap out of it, Jaybird!"

Then the intruder fired her gun over the President's shoulder. The sound of something or someone falling to the floor came from behind the President, who did not turn around.

"Listen! If we were characters in a story, here's what they call the expository lump. I remember that from English 101, so you remember it, too. I've come from a parallel universe, like in that Murray Leinster story we both read in Dad's old book, and I'm the President there, in that universe, as you are in this one. I have to give that speech—"

"*My* speech? But—"

"No time! If you start asking questions, we're both dead. That speech is going to have unintended and unexpected consequences, an avalanche of them. It will go around the world and be repeated by multitudes—"

"It's only a routine speech about our commitment to—"

"No time, Jaybird. Nobody expected the impact, but that speech changed the world. So people who didn't like those changes sent agents back in time to kill me before I could deliver it."

"They failed? Then why—?"

"No, they succeeded. I'll be dead in a few minutes. My world's technology is over a century ahead of yours, but it can't save me, so I've used our knowledge of time to cross the universes to get you to deliver the speech. You're a parallel version of me. And you have nothing to lose."

"Why did those men only shoot at you, then? Why not me?"

"They would have, if I hadn't gotten them first. But

they weren't trying to kill me, just stop me. I'm already dead and if they take me down, the game's over and you're harmless. You're the secondary target. If I go down while we're both here, you can't take my place. But you have to leave right now, before it's too late."

"Too late? Why do you keep saying that? And what do you mean that you're already dead?"

The alternate President Carlyle grimaced, as if from a sudden internal pain. "They got to me somehow, maybe in my meals, maybe in my drinks. You know how much social drinking we have to do. Maybe even in the air I inhaled. Over a period of weeks or months, I took in nanotech devices. They lived in me, off me, invisible to X-rays, growing, separate pieces coming together, assembling inside me. By the time we found out, it was too late. The device couldn't be removed, and it's counting down. When it goes off, it'll incinerate me. New meaning for 'ashes to ashes.' So I can't give the speech in my world—you'll have to go there and do it."

"I can't just leave, even if I believe you—and I think I do. Abandon my responsibilities. And my Vice President isn't up to—"

"Neither is mine," the other President said, grinning, but with a hint of pain behind it. "We both were stuck with the same bozo from the northeast. But your version doesn't matter, either, since he's over in the Senate right now."

"What does that have to do with it? And why do you keep saying I have nothing to lose?"

In a few hard, ruthless words, the dying President told the living one, who took a deep breath, then forgot about breathing.

The alternate President added, "I could show you tomorrow's headlines, but we don't have time for more than a glance." The offer received a headshake, and the visitor glanced down at the three fallen Secret Service agents. And said, "They have nothing to lose, either. But their counterparts are still alive in that other universe."

This universe's President was just starting to breathe again, when her counterpart added, "And Alfred is still alive where I come from."

Rachel's breathing stopped again, and she couldn't understand why her heart hadn't done the same. The words *Alf alive* were thundering in her brain, drowning out everything else for a moment.

"And he still hates to be called 'Alfred.' Thinks it's a name for a butler."

The world came into focus again, though not the same world she had known a few minutes ago. No, not even a few seconds ago. *He's alive!*

"I believe you. I'll go. But if more of those assassins come after me—?"

"We had tracked down all but four of them with our cross-temporal tech, and that's the number decorating the floor over there. As for travelers back from the future, we've set up a counter-entropic shield around Washington to stop them for now. And after you give the speech, they won't matter."

"We must be almost out of time—"

"We are. If we can't escape history, maybe we can evade it. Thank you, Jaybird."

The President from elsewhen took a thick metallic belt from around her waist and clicked it in place around the

President from this timeline, who said, "No, thank *you*," as the visiting head of state pressed a recessed button on the buckle.

She had time to say, "Kiss him for me . . ." before the other President Carlyle seemed to shrink, with openings etched in nothingness shaped like her silhouette, increasing in number as she grew smaller, surrounding her like the concentric rings of a freshly sawn tree stump.

". . . in all his favorite places," the dying woman finished her sentence. She glanced at the four dead would-be assassins. Their crosstime equipment hadn't run out of juice yet, or they would have disappeared back when they had come. It took considerable power to go into a parallel universe, and more to remain there. Unless you changed places with a copy of yourself, as she had done. She glanced next at the three still unconscious Secret Service agents and again said, "I'm sorry, guys," this time in a whisper.

She heard the door behind her open, turned and saw the press secretary, Ashley, a duplicate of her own, holding one of the double doors open and looking into the hall, probably to see what the delay and noise was. She could see the floor-to-ceiling windows behind him, and closed her eyes, snapping her face away from the sight barely in time, as the windows filled with a light brighter than any eyes could handle which had evolved at the bottom of a protective atmosphere.

Squinting carefully, Rachel looked back and saw the expanding incandescent fireball of plasma rushing toward those windows, outpacing the shock wave that otherwise would have sent thousands of glass daggers into the room and the hallway and through her.

Nice try, you little bastard, she thought at the humming killer inside her, *but you've been beaten to the punch*. In her last fraction of a second of existence, she realized that she had seen films and videos of the familiar mushroom clouds of nuclear explosions but never one with her own eyes. Nor would she see this one.

But she would be part of it. A tiny invisible part of inescapable history.

This one is for A.E. Van Vogt.

RECRUITING STATION
by A.E. Van Vogt

Before the United States had entered the war raging in Europe and the Pacific (and which, it might be argued, was not yet a second World War), Americans who felt strongly that the fight was everyone's fight might enlist in foreign military services to join the struggle. This novella, published in 1942, but written before the attack on Pearl Harbor, was obviously conceived thinking of such recruiting stations, but with A.E. Van Vogt's incandescent imagination in the driver's seat, we are thrust into a war raging through time, and a man and woman can count on nothing, except each other.

She didn't dare! Suddenly, the night was a cold, enveloping thing. The edge of the broad, black river gurgled evilly at her feet as if, now that she had changed her mind—it hungered for her.

Her foot slipped on the wet, sloping ground; and her mind grew blurred with the terrible senseless fear that *things* were reaching out of the night, trying to drown her now against her will.

She fought up the bank—and slumped breathless onto the nearest park bench, coldly furious with her fear. Dully, she watched the gaunt man come along the pathway past the light standard. So sluggish was her brain that she was not aware of surprise when she realized he was coming straight toward her.

The purulent yellowish light made a crazy patch of his shadow across her where she sat. His voice, when he spoke, was vaguely foreign in tone, yet modulated, cultured. He said:

"Are you interested in the Calonian cause?"

Norma stared. There was no quickening in her brain, but suddenly she began to laugh. It was funny, horribly, hysterically *funny* funny. To be sitting here, trying to get up the nerve for another attempt at those deadly waters, and then to have some crackbrain come along and—

"You're deluding yourself, Miss Matheson," the man went on coolly. "You're not the suicide type."

"Nor the pickup type!" she answered automatically. "Beat it before—"

Abruptly, it penetrated that the man had called her by name. She looked up sharply at the dark blank that was his face. His head against the background of distant light nodded as if in reply to the question that quivered in her thought.

"Yes, I know your name. I also know your history and your *fear!*"

"What do you mean?"

"I mean that a young scientist named Garson arrived

in the city tonight to deliver a series of lectures. Ten years ago, when you and he graduated from the same university, he asked you to marry him, but it was a career you wanted—and now you've been terrified that, in your extremity, you would go to him for assistance and—"

"Stop!"

The man seemed to watch her as she sat there breathing heavily. He said at last, quietly:

"I think I have proved that I am not simply a casual philanderer."

"What other kind of philanderer is there?" Norma asked, sluggish again. But she made no objection as he sank down on the far end of the bench. His back was still to the light, his features night-developed.

"Ah," he said, "you joke; you are bitter. But that *is* an improvement. You feel now, perhaps, that if somebody has taken an interest in you, all is not lost."

Norma said dully: "People who are acquainted with the basic laws of psychology are cursed with the memory of them even when disaster strikes into their lives. All I've done the last ten years is—"

She stopped; then: "You're very clever. Without more than arousing my instinctive suspicions, you've insinuated yourself into the company of an hysterical woman. What's your purpose?"

"I intend to offer you a job."

Norma's laugh sounded so harsh in her own ears that she thought, startled: "I am hysterical!"

Aloud, she said: "An apartment, jewels, a car of my own, I suppose?"

His reply was cool: "No! To put it frankly, you're not pretty enough. Too angular, mentally and physically. That's been one of your troubles the last ten years; a developing introversion of the mind which has influenced the shape of your body unfavorably."

The words shivered through the suddenly stiffened muscles of her body. With an enormous effort, she forced herself to relax. She said: "I had that coming to me. Insults are good for hysteria; so now what?"

"Are you interested in the Calonian cause?"

"There you go again," she complained. "But yes, I'm for it. Birds of a feather, you know."

"I know very well indeed. In fact, in those words you named the reason why I am here tonight, hiring a young woman who is up against it. Calonia, too, is up against it and—" He stopped; in the darkness, he spread his shadow-like hands. "You see: good publicity for our recruiting centers."

Norma nodded. She did see, and, suddenly, she didn't trust herself to speak; her hand trembled as she took the key he held out.

"This key," he said, "will fit the lock of the front door of the recruiting station; it will also fit the lock of the door leading to the apartment above it. The apartment is yours while you have the job. You can go there tonight if you wish, or wait until morning if you fear this is merely a device—now, I must give you a warning."

"Warning?"

"Yes. The work we are doing is illegal. Actually, only the American government can enlist American citizens and operate recruiting stations. We exist on sufferance and sympathy, but at any time someone may lay a charge; and the police will have to act."

Norma nodded rapidly. "That's no risk," she said. "No judge would ever—"

"The address is 322 Carlton Street," he cut in smoothly. "And for your information, my name is Dr. Lell."

Norma had the distinct sense of being pushed along too swiftly for caution. She hesitated, her mind on the street address. "Is that near Bessemer?"

It was his turn to hesitate. "I'm afraid," he confessed, "I don't know this city very well, at least not in its twentieth century...that is," he finished suavely. "I was here many years ago, before the turn of the century."

Norma wondered vaguely why he bothered to explain; she said, half-accusingly: "You're not a Calonian. You sound—French, maybe."

"You're not a Calonian, either!" he said, and stood up abruptly. She watched him walk off into the night, a great gloom-wrapped figure that vanished almost immediately.

She stopped short in the deserted night street. The sound that came was like a whisper touching her brain; a machine whirring somewhere with almost infinite softness. For the barest moment, her mind concentrated on the shadow vibrations; and then, somehow, they seemed to fade like figments of her imagination. Suddenly, there was only the street and the silent night.

The street was dimly lighted; and that brought doubt, sharp and tinged with a faint fear. She strained her eyes and traced the numbers in the shadow of the door: 322! That was it!

The place was dark. She peered at the signs that made up the window display:

> "FIGHT FOR THE BRAVE CALONIANS"
> "THE CALONIANS ARE FIGHTING FREEDOM'S FIGHT—
> YOUR FIGHT!"
> "IF YOU CAN PAY YOUR OWN WAY,
> IT WOULD BE APPRECIATED;
> OTHERWISE WE'LL GET YOU OVER!"

There were other signs, but they were essentially the same, all terribly honest and appealing, if you really thought about the desperate things that made up their grim background.

Illegal, of course. But the man had admitted that, too. With sudden end of doubt, she took the key from her purse.

There were two doorways, one on either side of the window. The one to the right led into the recruiting room. The one on the left—

The stairs were dimly lighted, and the apartment at the top was quite empty of human beings. The door had a bolt; she clicked it home, and then, wearily, headed for the bedroom.

And it was as she lay in the bed that she grew aware again of the incredibly faint whirring of a machine. The shadow of a shadow sound; and, queerly, it seemed to reach into her brain: the very last second before she drifted into sleep, the pulse of the vibration, remote as the park bench, was a steady beat inside her.

All through the night that indescribably faint whirring

was there. Only occasionally did it seem to be in her head; she was aware of turning, twisting, curling, straightening and, in the fractional awakedness that accompanied each move, the tiniest vibrational tremors would sweep down along her nerves like infinitesimal currents of energy.

Spears of sunlight piercing brilliantly through the window brought her awake at last. She lay taut and strained for a moment, then relaxed, puzzled. There was not a sound from the maddening machine, only the noises of the raucous, awakening street.

There was food in the refrigerator and in the little pantry. The weariness of the night vanished swiftly before the revivifying power of breakfast. She thought in gathering interest: what did he look like, this strange-voiced man of night?

Relieved surprise flooded her when the key unlocked the door to the recruiting room, for there had been in her mind a little edged fear that this was all quite mad.

She shuddered the queer darkness out of her system. What was the matter with her, anyway? The world was sunlit and cheerful, not the black and gloomy abode of people with angular introversion of the mind.

She flushed at the memory of the words. There was no pleasure in knowing that the man's enormously clever analysis of her was true. Still stinging, she examined the little room. There were four chairs, a bench, a long wooden counter and newspaper clipping of the Calonian War on the otherwise bare walls.

There was a back door to the place. Dimly curious, she tried the knob—once! It was locked, but there was something about the feel of it—

A tingling shock of surprise went through her. The door, in spite of its wooden appearance, was solid metal!

Momentarily, she felt chilled; finally she thought: "None of my business!"

And then, before she could turn away, the door opened, and a gaunt man loomed on the threshold. He snapped harshly, almost into her face, "Oh, yes, it is your business."

It was not fear that made her back away. The deeps of her mind registered the cold hardness of his voice, so different from the previous night. Vaguely she was aware of the ugly sneer on his face. But there was no real emotion in her brain, nothing but a blurred blankness.

It was not fear; it couldn't be fear because all she had to do was run a few yards, and she'd be out on a busy street. And besides she had never been afraid of Negroes, and she wasn't now.

The first impression was so sharp, so immensely surprising that the fast-following second impression seemed like a trick of her eyes. For the man wasn't actually a Negro; he was—

She shook her head, trying to shake that trickiness out of her vision. But the picture wouldn't change. He wasn't a Negro, he wasn't white, he wasn't—anything!

Slowly her brain adjusted itself to his alienness. She saw that he had slant eyes like a Chinaman, his skin, though dark in texture, was dry with a white man's dryness. The nose was sheer chiseled beauty, the most handsome, most normal part of his face; his mouth was thin-lipped, commanding; his chin bold and giving strength and power to the insolence of his steel-gray eyes. His sneer deepened as her eyes grew wider and wider.

"Oh, no," he said softly, "you're not afraid of me, are you? Let me inform you that my purpose is to *make* you afraid. Last night I had the purpose of bringing you here. That required tact, understanding. My new purpose requires, among other things, the realization on your part that you are in my power beyond the control of your will or wish.

"I could have allowed you to discover gradually that this is not a Calonian recruiting station. But I prefer to get these early squirmings of the slaves over as soon as possible. The reaction to the power of the machine is always so similar and unutterably boring."

"I—don't—understand!"

He answered coldly: "Let me be brief. You have been vaguely aware of a machine. That machine has attuned the rhythm of your body to itself, and through its actions I can control you against your desire. Naturally, I don't expect you to believe me. Like the other women, you will test its mind-destroying power. Notice that I said *women!* We always hire women; for purely psychological reasons they are safer than men. You will discover what I mean if you should attempt to warn any applicant on the basis of what I have told you."

He finished swiftly: "Your duties are simple. There is a pad on the table made up of sheets with simple questions printed on them. Ask those questions, note the answers, then direct the applicants to me in the back room. I have—er—a medical examination to give them."

Out of all the things he had said, the one that briefly,

searingly, dominated her whole mind had no connection with her personal fate: "But," she gasped, "if these men are not being sent to Calonia, where—"

He hissed her words short: "Here comes a man. Now, remember!"

He stepped back, to one side out of sight in the dimness of the back room. Behind her, there was the dismaying sound of the front door opening. A man's baritone voice blurred a greeting into her ears.

Her fingers shook as she wrote down the man's answers to the dozen questions. Name, address, next of kin— His face was a ruddy-cheeked blur against the shapeless shifting pattern of her racing thoughts.

"You can see," she heard herself mumbling, "that these questions are only a matter of identification. Now, if you'll go into that back room—"

The sentence shattered into silence. She'd said it! The uncertainty in her mind, the unwillingness to take a definite stand until she had thought of some way out, had made her say the very thing she had intended to avoid saying. The man said:

"What do I go in there for?"

She stared at him numbly. Her mind felt thick, useless. She needed time, calm. She said: "It's a simple medical exam, entirely for your own protection."

Sickly, Norma watched his stocky form head briskly toward the rear door. He knocked; and the door opened. Surprisingly, it stayed open—surprisingly, because it was then, as the man disappeared from her line of vision, that she saw the machine.

The end of it that she could see reared up immense

and darkly gleaming halfway to the ceiling, partially hiding a door that seemed to be a rear exit from the building.

She forgot the door, forgot the men. Her mind fastened on the great engine with abrupt intensity as swift memory came that *this* was the machine—

Unconsciously her body, her ears, her mind, strained for the whirring sound that she had heard in the night. But there was nothing, not the tiniest of tiny noises, not the vaguest stir of vibration, not a rustle, not a whisper The machine crouched there, hugging the floor with its solidness, its clinging metal strength; and it was utterly dead, utterly motionless.

The doctor's smooth, persuasive voice came to her: "I hope you don't mind going out the back door, Mr. Baron. We ask applicants to use it because—well, our recruiting station here is illegal. As you probably know, we exist on sufferance and sympathy, but we don't want to be too blatant about the success we're having in getting young men to fight for our cause."

Norma waited. As soon as the man was gone, she would force a showdown on this whole fantastic affair. If this was some distorted scheme of Calonia's enemies, she would go to the police and—

The thought twisted into a curious swirling chaos of wonder. The machine—

Incredibly, the machine was coming alive, a monstrous, gorgeous, swift aliveness. It glowed with a soft, swelling white light; and then burst into enormous flame. A breaker of writhing tongues of fire, blue and red and green and yellow, stormed over that first glow, blotting it from view instantaneously. The fire sprayed and flashed like an intricately designed fountain, with a wild and violent beauty, a glittering blaze of unearthly glory.

And then—just like that—the flame faded. Briefly, grimly stubborn in its fight for life, the swarming, sparkling energy clung to the metal.

It was gone. The machine lay there, a dull, gleaming mass of metallic deadness, inert, motionless. The doctor appeared in the doorway.

"Sound chap!" he said, satisfaction in his tone. "Heart requires a bit of glandular adjustment to eradicate the effects of bad diet. Lungs will react swiftly to gas-immunization injections, and our surgeons should be able to patch that body up from almost anything except an atomic storm."

Norma licked dry lips. "What are you talking about?" she asked wildly. "W-what happened to that man?"

She was aware of him staring at her blandly. His voice was cool, faintly amused: "Why—he went out the back door."

"He did not. He—"

She realized the uselessness of words. Cold with the confusion of her thought, she emerged from behind the counter. She brushed past him, and then, as she reached the threshold of the door leading into the rear room, her knees wobbled. She grabbed at the door jamb for support and knew that she didn't dare go near that machine. With an effort, she said:

"Will you go over there and open it?"

He did so, smiling. The door squealed slightly as it opened. When he closed it, it creaked audibly, and the automatic lock clicked loudly.

There had been no such sound. Norma felt the deepening whiteness in her cheeks. She asked, chilled:

"What is this machine?"

"Owned by the local electric company, I believe," he answered suavely, and his voice mocked her. "We just have permission to use the room, of course."

"That's not possible," she said thickly. "Electric companies don't have machines in the back rooms of shabby buildings."

He shrugged. "Really," he said indifferently, "this is beginning to bore me. I have already told you that this is a very special machine. You have seen some of its powers, yet your mind persists in being practical after a twentieth century fashion. I will repeat merely that you are a slave of the machine, and that it will do you no good to go to the police, entirely aside from the fact that I saved you from drowning yourself, and gratitude alone should make you realize that you owe everything to me; nothing to the world you were prepared to desert. However, that is too much to expect. You will learn by experience."

Quite calmly, Norma walked across the room. She opened the door, and then, startled that he had made no move to stop her, turned to stare at him. He was still standing where she had left him. He was smiling.

"You must be quite mad," she said after a moment. "Perhaps you had some idea that your little trick, whatever it was, would put the fear of the unknown into me. Let me dispel that right now. I'm going to the police—this very minute."

The picture that remained in her mind as she climbed aboard the bus was of him standing there, tall and casual and terrible in his contemptuous derision. The chill of that memory slowly mutilated the steady tenor of her forced calm.

The sense of nightmare vanished as she climbed off the streetcar in front of the imposing police building. Sunshine splashed vigorously on the pavement, cars honked; the life of the city swirled lustily around her, and brought wave on wave of returning confidence.

The answer, now that she thought of it, was simplicity itself. Hypnotism! That was what had made her see a great, black, unused engine burst into mysterious flames. And no hypnotist could force his will on a determined, definitely opposed mind.

Burning inwardly with abrupt anger at the way she had been tricked, she lifted her foot to step on the curb—and amazed shock stung into her brain.

The foot, instead of lifting springily, dragged; her muscles almost refused to carry the weight. She grew aware of a man less than a dozen feet from her, staring at her with popping eyes.

"Good heavens!" he gasped audibly. "I must be seeing things."

He walked off rapidly; and the part of her thoughts that registered his odd actions simply tucked them away. She felt too dulled, mentally and physically, even for curiosity.

With faltering steps she moved across the sidewalk. It was as if something was tearing at her strength, holding her with invisible but immense forces. The machine!— she thought—and panic blazed through her.

Will power kept her going. She reached the top of the steps and approached the big doors. It was then the first sick fear came that she couldn't make it; and as she strained feebly against the stone-wall-like resistance of the door, a very fever of dismay grew hot and terrible inside her. What had happened to her? How could a machine reach over a distance, and strike unerringly at one particular individual with such enormous, vitality-draining power?

A shadow leaned over her. The booming voice of a policeman who had just come up the steps was the most glorious sound she had ever heard.

"Too much for you, eh, madam? Here, I'll push that door for you."

"Thank you," she said; and her voice sounded so harsh and dry and weak and unnatural in her own ears that a new terror flared: in a few minutes she wouldn't be able to speak above a whisper.

"A *slave of the machine*," he had said; and she knew with a clear and burning logic that if she was ever to conquer, it was now. She must get into this building. She must see someone in authority, and she must tell him— must—must— Somehow, she pumped strength into her brain and courage into her heart and forced her legs to carry her across the threshold into the big modern building with its mirrored anteroom and its fine marble corridors. Inside, she knew suddenly that she had reached her limit.

She stood there on the hard floor and felt her whole body shaking from the enormous effort it took simply to stay erect. Her knees felt dissolved and cold, like ice turning to strengthless liquid. She grew aware that the big policeman was hovering uncertainly beside her.

"Anything I can do, mother?" he asked heartily.

"Mother!" she echoed mentally with a queer sense of insanity. Her mind skittered off after the word. Did he really say that, or had she dreamed it? Why, she wasn't a mother. She wasn't even married. She—

She fought the thought off. She'd have to pull herself together, or there was madness here. No chance now of getting to an inspector or an officer. This big constable must be her confidant, her hope to defeat the mighty power whose ultimate purpose she could not begin to imagine. She—

There it was again, her mind pushing off into obscure, action-destroying defeating thoughts! She turned to the policeman, started to part her lips in speech; and it was then she saw the mirror.

She saw a tall, thin, old, old woman standing beside the fresh-cheeked bulk of a blue-garbed policeman. It was such an abnormal trick of vision that it fascinated her. In some way, the mirror was missing her image, and reflecting instead the form of an old woman who must be close behind and slightly to one side of her. Queerest thing she had ever seen.

She half-lifted her red-gloved hand toward the policeman, to draw his attention to the distortion. Simultaneously, the red-gloved hand of the old woman in the mirror reached toward the policeman. Her own raised hand stiffened in mid-air; so did the old woman's. Funny.

Puzzled, she drew her gaze from the mirror, and stared with briefly blank vision at that rigidly uplifted hand. A tiny, uneven bit of her wrist was visible between the end of the glove and the end of the sleeve of her serge suit. Her skin wasn't really as dark as—that!

Two things happened then. A tall man came softly through the door—Dr. Lell—and the big policeman's hand touched her shoulder.

"Really, madam, at your age, you shouldn't come here. A phone call would serve—"

And Dr. Lell was saying: "My poor old grandmother—"

Their voices went on, but the sense of them jangled in her brain as she jerked frantically to pull the glove off a hand wrinkled and shriveled by incredible age— Blackness pierced with agonized splinters of light reached mercifully into her brain. Her very last thought was that it must have happened just before she stepped onto the curb, when the man had stared at her pop-eyed and thought himself crazy. He must have seen the change taking place.

The pain faded; the blackness turned gray, then white. She was conscious of a car engine purring, and of forward movement. She opened her eyes—and her brain reeled from a surge of awful memory.

"Don't be afraid!" said Dr. Lell, and his voice was as soothing and gentle as it had been hard and satirical at the recruiting station. "You are again yourself; in fact, approximately ten years younger."

He removed one hand from the steering wheel and flashed a mirror before her eyes. The brief glimpse she had of her image made her grab at the silvered glass as if it were the most precious thing in all the world.

One long, hungry look she took; and then her arm, holding the mirror, collapsed from sheer, stupendous relief. She lay back against the cushions, tears sticky on her cheeks, weak and sick from dreadful reaction. At last she said steadily:

"Thanks for telling me right away. Otherwise I should have gone mad."

"That, of course, was why I told you," he said; and his voice was still soft, still calm. And she felt soothed, in spite of the dark terror just past, in spite of the intellectual realization that this diabolical man used words and tones and human emotions as coldly as Pan himself piping his reed, sounding what stop he pleased. That quiet, deep voice went on:

"You see, you are now a valuable member of our twentieth-century staff, with a vested interest in the success of our purpose. You thoroughly understand the system of rewards and punishments for good or bad service. You will have food, a roof over your head, money to spend—and eternal youth! Woman, look at your face again, look hard, and rejoice for your good fortune! Weep for those who have nothing but old age and death as their future! Look hard, I say!"

It was like gazing at a marvelous photograph out of the past, except that she had been somewhat prettier in the actuality, her face more rounded, not so sharp, more girlish. She was twenty again, but different, more mature, leaner. She heard his voice go on dispassionately, a distant background to her own thoughts, feeding, feeding at the image in the mirror. He said:

"As you can see, you are not truly yourself as you were at twenty. This is because we could only manipulate the time tensions which influenced your thirty-year-old body according to the rigid mathematical laws governing the energies and forces involved. We could not undo the harm wrought these last rather prim, introvert years of your life because you have already lived them, and nothing can change that."

It came to her that he was talking to give her time to recover from the deadliest shock that had ever stabbed into a human brain. And for the first time she thought not of herself, but of the incredible things implied by every action that had occurred, every word spoken.

"Who . . . are . . . you?"

He was silent; the car twisted in and out of the clamorous traffic; and she watched his face not, that lean, strange, dark, finely chiseled, *evil* face with its glittering dark eyes. For the moment she felt no repulsion, only a gathering storm of fascination at the way that strong chin tilted unconsciously as he said in a cold, proud, ringing voice:

"We are masters of time. We live at the farthest frontier of time itself, and all the ages belong to us. No words could begin to describe the vastness of our empire or the futility of opposing us. We—"

He stopped. Some of the fire faded from his dark eyes. His brows knit, his chin dropped, his lips clamped into a thin line, then parted as he snapped:

"I hope that any vague ideas you have had for further opposition will yield to the logic of events and of fact. Now you know why we hire women who have no friends."

"You—devil!" She half sobbed the words.

"Ah," he said softly, "I can see you understand a woman's psychology. Two final points should clinch the argument I am trying to make: First, I can read your mind, every thought that comes into it, every vaguest emotion that moves it. And second, before establishing the machine in that particular building, we explored the years to come; and during all the time investigated, found the machine unharmed, its presence unsuspected by those in authority. Therefore, the future record is that you did—nothing! I think you will agree with me that this is convincing."

Norma nodded dully, her mirror forgotten. "Yes," she said, "yes, I suppose it is."

Miss Norma Matheson,
Calonian Recruiting Station,
322 Carolton Street,

Dear Norma:
I made a point of addressing the envelope of this letter to you c/o General Delivery, instead of the above address. I would not care to put you in any danger, however imaginary. I use the word imaginary deliberately, for I cannot even begin to describe how grieved and astounded I was to receive such a letter from the girl I once loved— it's eleven years since I proposed on graduation day, isn't it?—and how amazed I was by your questions and statements re time travel.

I might say that if you are not already mentally unbalanced, you will be shortly unless you take hold of yourself. The very fact that you were nerving yourself to commit suicide when this man—Dr. Lell—hired you from a park bench to be clerk in the recruiting station at the foregoing address, is evidence of hysteria. You could have gone on city relief.

I see that you have lost none of your powers of expression in various mediums. Your letter, mad though it is in subject matter, is eminently coherent and well thought out. Your drawing of the face of Dr. Lell is quite a remarkable piece of work.

If it is a true resemblance, then I agree that he is definitely not—shall I say—Western. His eyes are distinctly slanting, Chinese-style. His skin you say is, and shown as, dark in texture, indicating a faint Negro strain. His nose is very fine and sensitive, strong in character.

This effect is incremented by his firm mouth, though those thin lips are much too arrogant—the whole effect is of an extraordinarily intelligent-looking man, a super-mongrel in appearance. Such bodies could very easily be produced in the far-Eastern provinces of Asia.

I pass without comment over your description of the machine which swallows up the unsuspecting recruits. The superman has apparently not objected to answering your questions since the police station episode; and so we have a new theory of time and space:

Time—he states—is the all, the only reality. Every unfolding instant the Earth and its life, the universe and all its galaxies are re-created by the titanic energy that is time—and always it is essentially the same pattern that is re-formed, because that is the easiest course.

He makes a comparison. According to Einstein, and in this he is correct, the Earth goes around the Sun, not because there is such a force as gravitation, but because it is easier for it to go around the Sun in exactly the way it does than to hurtle off into space.

It is easier for time to re-form the same pattern of rock, the same man, the same tree, the same earth. That is all, that is the law.

The rate of reproduction is approximately ten billion a second. During the past minute, therefore, six hundred billion replicas of myself have been created; and all of them are still there, each a separate body occupying its own space, completely unaware of the others. Not one has been destroyed. There is no purpose; it is simply easier to let them stay there, than to destroy them.

If those bodies ever met in the same space, that is if I should go back to shake hands with my twenty-year-old self, there would be a clash of similar patterns, and the interloper would be distorted out of memory and shape.

I have no criticism to make of this theory other than that it is utterly fantastic. However, it is very interesting in the vivid picture it draws of an eternity of human beings, breeding and living and dying in the quiet eddies of the time stream, while the great current flares on ahead in a fury of incredible creation.

I am puzzled by the detailed information you are seeking—you make it almost real—but I give the answers for what they are worth:

1. Time travel would naturally be based on the most rigid mechanical laws.

2. It seems plausible that they would be able to investigate your future actions.

3. Dr. Lell used phrases such as "atomic storm" and "gas immunization injections." The implication is that they are recruiting for an unimaginably great war.

4. I cannot see how the machine could act on you over a

distance—unless there was some sort of radio-
controlled intermediate. In your position, I would ask
myself one question: Was there anything, any metal,
anything, upon my person that might have been placed
there by the enemy?

5. Some thoughts are so dimly held that they could not
possibly be transmitted. Presumably, sharp, clear
thoughts might be receivable. If you could keep your
mind calm, as you say you did while deciding to write
the letter—the letter itself is proof that you succeeded.

6. It is unwise to assume that here is greater basic
intelligence, but rather greater development of the
potential forces of the mind. If men ever learn to read
minds, it will be because they train their innate
capacity for mind reading; they will be cleverer only
when new knowledge adds new techniques of training.

To become personal, I regret immeasurably having
heard from you. I had a memory of a rather brave spirit,
rejecting my proposal of marriage, determined to remain
independent, ambitious for advancement in the important
field of social services. Instead, I find a sorry ending, a
soul disintegrated, a mind feeding on fantasia and a sense
of incredible persecution. My advice is: go to a psychiatrist
before it is too late, and to that end I enclose a money
order for $200.00 and extend you my best wishes.

Yours in memory,
Jack Garson

At least there was no interference with her private life.
No footsteps but her own ever mounted the dark, narrow

flight of stairs that led to her tiny apartment. At night, after the recruiting shop closed, she walked the crowded streets; sometimes, there was a movie that seemed to promise surcease from the deadly strain of living; sometimes a new book on her old love, the social sciences, held her for a brief hour.

But there was nothing, nothing, absolutely nothing, that could relax the burning pressure of the reality of the machine. It was there always like a steel band drawn tautly around her mind.

It was crazy funny to read about the war, and the victories and the defeats—when out there, somewhere, in the future another greater war was being fought; a war so vast that all the ages were being ransacked for manpower.

And men came! Dark men, blond men, young men, grim men, hard men, and veterans of other wars—the stream of them made a steady flow into that dimly lighted back room. And one day she looked up from an intent, mindless study of the pattern of the stained, old counter— and there was Jack Garson!

It was as simple as that. There he stood, not much older-looking after ten years, a little leaner of face perhaps, and there were tired lines all around his dark-brown eyes. While she stared in dumb paralysis, he said:

"I had to come, of course. You were the first emotional tie I had, and also the last; when I wrote the letter, I didn't realize how strong that emotion still was. What's all this about?"

She thought with a flaming intensity: Often, in the past, Dr. Lell had vanished for brief periods during the day hours; once she had seen him disappear into the flamboyant embrace of the light shed by the machine. Twice, she had opened the door to speak to him, and found him gone!

All accidental observations! It meant he had stepped scores of times into his own world when she hadn't seen him and—

Please let this be one of the times when he was away!

A second thought came, so fierce, so sharply focused that it made a stabbing pain inside her head: She must be calm. She must hold her mind away from give-away thoughts, if it was not already ages too late.

Her voice came into the silence like a wounded, fluttering bird, briefly stricken by shock, then galvanized by agony:

"Quick! You must go—till after six! Hurry! Hurry!"

Her trembling hands struck at his chest, as if by those blows she would set him running for the door. But the thrust of her strength was lost on the muscles of his breast, defeated by the way he was leaning forward. His body did not even stagger.

Through a blur, she saw he was staring down at her with a grim, set smile. His voice was hard as chipped steel as he said:

"Somebody's certainly thrown a devil of a scare into you. But don't worry! I've got a revolver in my pocket. And don't think I'm alone in this. I wired the Calonian embassy at Washington, then notified the police here of their answer: no knowledge of this place. The police will arrive in minutes. I came in first to see that you didn't get hurt in the shuffle. Come on—outside with you, because—"

It was Norma's eyes that must have warned him, her

eyes glaring past him. She was aware of him whirling to face the dozen men who were trooping out of the back room. The men came stolidly, and she had time to see that they were short, squat, ugly creatures, more roughly built than the lean, finely molded Dr. Lell; and their faces were not so much evil as half dead with unintelligence.

A dozen pair of eyes lighted with brief, animal-like curiosity, as they stared at the scene outside the window; then they glanced indifferently at herself and Jack Garson and the revolver he was holding so steadily; finally, their interest fading visibly, their gazes reverted expectantly to Dr. Lell, who stood smiling laconically on the threshold of the doorway.

"Ah, yes, Professor Garson, you have a gun, haven't you? And the police are coming. Fortunately, I have something here that may convince you of the uselessness of your puny plans."

His right hand came from behind his back, where he had been half hiding it. A gasp escaped from Norma as she saw that in it he held a blazing ball, a globe of furious flame, a veritable ball of fire.

The thing burned there in his palm, crude and terrible in the illusion of incredible, destroying incandescence. The mockery in Dr. Lell's voice was utterly convincing, as he said in measured tones *at her:*

"My dear Miss Matheson, I think you will agree that you will not offer further obstacles to our purpose now that we have enlisted this valuable young man into the invincible armies of the Glorious—and, as for you, Garson, I suggest you drop that gun before it burns off your hand. It—"

His words were lost in the faint cry that came from Jack Garson. Amazed, Norma saw the gun fall to the floor and lie there, burning with a white-hot, an abnormal violence.

"Good heaven!" said Jack Garson; and Norma saw him stare at the weapon enthralled, mindless of danger as it shrank visibly in that intense fire.

In seconds there was no weapon, no metal; the fire blinked out—and where it had been the floor was not even singed.

From Dr. Lell came a barked command, oddly twisted, foreignish words that nevertheless sounded like: "Grab him!"

She looked up, abruptly sick; but there was no fight. Jack Garson did not even resist, as the wave of beast men flowed around him. Dr. Lell said:

"So far, professor, you haven't made a very good showing as a gallant rescuer. But I'm glad to see that you have already recognized the hopelessness of opposing us. It is possible that, if you remain reasonable, we will not have to destroy your personality. But now—"

Urgency sharpened his tone. "I had intended to wait and capture your burly policemen, but as they have not arrived at the proper moment—a tradition with them, I believe—I think we shall have to go without them. It's just as well, I suppose."

He waved the hand that held the ball of fire, and the men carrying Jack Garson literally ran into the back room. Almost instantly, they were out of sight. Norma had a brief glimpse of the machine blazing into wondrous life; and then there was only Dr. Lell striding forward, leaning over the bench, his eyes glaring pools of menace.

"Go upstairs instantly! I don't think the police will recognize you—but if you make one false move, *he* will pay. Go—quickly!"

As she hurried past the window on semiliquid legs, she saw his tall figure vanish through the door into the back room. Then she was climbing the stairs.

Halfway up, her movements slowed as if she had been struck. Her mirror told the story of her punishment. The lean face of a woman of fifty-five met her stunned gaze.

The disaster was complete. Cold, stiff, tearless, she waited for the police.

For Garson, the world of the future began as a long, dim corridor that kept blurring before his unsteady vision. Heavy hands held him erect as he walked and—a wave of blur blotted the uncertain picture—

When he could see again, the pressure of unpleasant hands was gone from him, and he was in a small room, sitting down. His first dim impression was that he was alone, yet when he shook himself, and his vision cleared, he saw the desk; and behind the desk, a man.

The sight of that lean, dark, saturnine figure shocked electrically along his nerves, instantly galvanized a measure of strength back into his body. He leaned forward, his attention gathered on the man; and that was like a signal.

Dr. Lell said derisively: "I know. You've decided to cooperate. It was in your mind even before we left the present of . . . er . . . pardon the familiarity . . . of Norma, to whose rescue you came with such impetuous gallantry. Unfortunately, it isn't only a matter of making up *your* mind."

There was a quality of sneer in the man's voice that sent
an uneasy current through Garson. He shook himself
mentally, trying to clear the remnants of weakness out of
his system.

He thought, not coherently, not even chronologically:
Lucky he was here in this room. Damned lucky they
hadn't sprung a complication of futuristic newness on him,
and so disorganized his concentration. Now there was
time to gather his thoughts, harden his mind to every
conceivable development, discount surprises, *and stay
alive.*

He said: "It's quite simple. You've got Norma. You've
got me in your power, here in your own age. I'd be a fool
to resist."

Dr. Lell regarded; him almost pityingly for a moment.
And then—there was no doubt of the sneer as he spoke:

"My dear Professor Garson, discussion at this point
would be utterly futile. My purpose is merely to discover
if you are the type we can use in our laboratories. If you
are not, the only alternative is the depersonalizing
chamber. I can say this much: men of your character type
have not, on the average, been successful in passing our
tests."

That was real; every word like a penetrating edged
thing. Actually, in spite of his sneers and his amused
contempt—actually this man was indifferent to him.
There was only the test, whatever that was; and his own
conscious life at stake. The important thing was to stay
calm, and to stick leechlike to this one tremendous
subject. Before he could speak, Dr. Lell said in a curiously
flat voice:

"We have a machine that tests human beings for degree of recalcitrancy. The Observer Machine will speak to you now!"

"What is your name?" said a voice out of the thin air beside Garson.

Garson jumped; his brain staggered, literally; and there was a terrible moment of unbalance. The dim, dismayed thought came that, in spite of determination, he had been caught off guard; and there was the still vaguer thought that, without his being aware of it, he had actually been in a state of dangerous tension.

With a terrific effort, he caught himself. He saw that Dr. Lell was smiling again, and that helped! Trembling, he leaned back in his chair; and, after a moment, he was sufficiently recovered to feel a surge of anger at the way the chill clung to his body, and at the tiny quaver in his voice, as he began to answer:

"My name is John Bellmore Garson—age thirty-three—professor of physics at the University of—research scientist—blood type number—"

There were too many questions, an exhaustive drain of detail out of his mind, the history of his life, his aspirations. In the end, the deadly truth was a cold weight inside him. His life, his conscious life, was at stake *now*— this minute! Here was not even the shadow of comedy, but a precise, thorough, machinelike grilling. He must pass this test or—

"Dr. Lell!" The insistent voice of the machine broke in. "What is the state of this man's mind at this moment?"

Dr. Lell said promptly, coolly: "A state of tremendous doubt. His subconscious is in a turmoil of uncertainty. I need hardly add that his subconscious knows his character."

Garson drew a deep breath. He felt utterly sick at the simple way he had been disintegrated. And by one *newness!* A machine that needed neither telephone nor radio—if it was a machine! His voice was a rasping thing in his own ears, as he snapped:

"My subconscious can go straight to hell! I'm a reasonable person. I've made up my mind. I play ball with your organization to the limit."

The silence that followed was unnaturally long; and when at last the machine spoke, his relief lasted only till its final words penetrated. The disembodied voice said coldly:

"I am pessimistic—but bring him over for the test after the usual preliminaries!"

Preliminaries! Was it possible that this mindshaking test had been but the preliminary to the preliminary of the real test?

Rigid with dismay, he stood up to follow the bleakly smiling Dr. Lell out of the room.

He began to feel better, as he walked behind Dr. Lell along the gray-blue hallway. In a small way, he had won. Whatever these other tests were, how *could* they possibly ignore his determined conviction that he must cooperate? As for himself—

For himself, there was this colossal world of the future. Surely, he could resign himself to his lot for the duration of this silly war and lose himself in the amazing immensity of a science that included time machines, fireballs, and Observer Machines that judged men with a cold, remorseless logic and spoke out of thin air.

He frowned. There must be some trick to that, some "telephone" in the nearby wall. Damned if he'd believe that any force could focus sound without intermediary instruments, just as Norma couldn't have been made older in the police station without—

The thought collapsed.

For a paralyzed moment, he stared down where the floor had been.

It wasn't there!

With a gasp, Garson grabbed at the opaque wall; and then, as a low laugh from the doctor, and the continued hardness beneath his feet, told the extent of the illusion, he controlled himself—and stared in utter fascination.

Below him was a section of a room, whose limits he could not see because the opaque walls barred his vision on either side. A milling pack of men filled every available foot of space that he could see. Men, oh— The ironic voice of Dr. Lell pierced his stunned senses, echoing his thoughts with brittle words:

"Men, yes, men! Recruits out of all times. Soldiers-to-be from the ages, and not yet do they know their destiny."

The voice ended, but the indescribable scene went on. Men squirmed, shoved, fought. Upturned faces showed stark puzzlement, anger, fear, amusement, and all the combinations of all the possible emotions. There were men in clothes that sparkled with every color of the rainbow; there were the drab-clothed, the in-betweens; there were—

Garson caught his flitting mind into an observant tightness. In spite of the radical difference in the dress styles of the men who floundered down there like sheep in a slaughterhouse pen, there was a sameness about them that could only mean one thing. They were all—

"You're right!" It was that cool, taunting voice again. "They're all Americans, all from this one city now called Delpa. From our several thousand machines located in the various ages of Delpa, we obtain about four thousand men an hour during the daylight hours. What you see below is the main receiving room.

"The recruits come sliding down the time chutes, and are promptly revived and shoved in there. Naturally at this stage there is a certain amount of confusion. But let us proceed further."

Garson scarcely noticed as the solid floor leaped into place beneath his feet. The vague thought did come that at no time had he seen Dr. Lell press a button or manipulate a control of any kind, neither when the Observer Machine spoke with ventriloquistic wizardry, nor when the floor was made invisible, nor now when it again became opaque. Possibly here was some form of mental control. His mind leaped to a personal danger:

What was the purpose of this—preliminary? Were they showing him horror, then watching his reactions? He felt abrupt rage. What did they expect from a man brought up in twentieth-century environment? Nothing here had anything to do with his intellectual conviction that he was caught and that therefore he must cooperate. But—four thousand men in one hour from one city! Why, it meant—

"And here," Dr. Lell said, and his voice was as calm as the placid waters of a pond, "we have one of several hundred smaller rooms that make a great circle around the primary time machine. You can see the confusion has diminished."

Truth, Garson thought, had never suffered greater understatement than those words. There was absolute absence of confusion. Men sat on chesterfields. Some were looking at books; others chatted like people in a silent movie; their lips moved, but no sound penetrated the illusive transparency of the floor.

"I didn't," came that calm, smooth, confident voice, "show you the intermediate stage that leads up to this clublike atmosphere. A thousand frightened men confronted with danger could make trouble. But we winnow them down psychologically and physically till we have one man going through that door at the end of the room—ah, there's one going now. Let us by all means follow him. You see, at this point we dispense with coddling and bring forth the naked reality."

The reality was a metal, boiler-shaped affair, with a furnacelike door; and four beast humans simply grabbed the startled newcomer and thrust him feet first into the door.

The man must have screamed; for, once, his face twisted upward, and the contorted fear, the almost idiotic gaping and working of the mouth came at Garson like some enormous physical blow. As from a great distance, he heard Dr. Lell say:

"It helps at this stage to disorganize the patient's mind, for the depersonalizing machine can then do a better job."

Abruptly, the impersonalness went out of his voice. In an icily curt tone, he said: "It is useless continuing this little lecture tour. To my mind, your reactions have fully justified the pessimism of the Observer. There will be no further delay."

The deadly words scarcely touched him. He was drained of emotion, of hope; and that first blaze of scientific eagerness was a dull, aching ember.

After that incredible succession of blows, he accepted the failure verdict as—merited!

It was consciousness of the sardonic profile of his captor that brought the first emergence from that dark defeatism. Damn it, there was still the fact that he was logistically committed to this world. He'd have to harden himself, narrow his emotions down to a channel that would include only Norma and himself. If these people and their machine condemned on the basis of feelings, then he'd have to show them how stony-cold his intellect could be.

He braced himself. Where the devil was this all-knowing machine?

The corridor ended abruptly in a plain, black door, exactly like all the other doors, that held not the faintest promise of anything important beyond.

Amazingly, it opened onto a street! A street of the city of the future!

Garson stiffened. His brain soared beyond contemplation of his own danger in a burning anticipation; and then, almost instantly, began to sag.

Puzzled, he stared at a scene that was utterly different from his expectations. In a vague way, mindful of the effects of war, he had pictured devastated magnificence. Instead—

Before his gaze stretched a depressingly narrow, unsightly street. Dark, unwashed buildings towered up to hide the sun. A trickle of the squat, semi-human men and women, beastlike creatures, moved stolidly along narrow areas of pavement marked off by black lines, that constituted the only method of distinguishing the road from the sidewalk.

The street stretched away for miles; and it was all like that, as far as he could see clearly. Intensely disappointed, conscious even of disgust, Garson turned away—and grew aware that Dr. Lell was staring at him with a grim smile. The doctor said laconically:

"What you are looking for, Professor Garson, you will not find, not in this or similar cities of the 'Slaves,' but in the palace cities of the Glorious and the Planetarians—"

He stopped, as if his words had brought an incredibly unpleasant thought; to Garson's amazement, his face twisted with rage; his voice almost choked, as he spat: "Those damnable Planetarians! When I think what their so-called ideals are bringing the world to, I—"

The spasm of fury passed; he said quietly: "Several hundred years ago, a mixed commission of Glorious and Planetarians surveyed the entire physical resources of the Solar System. Men had made themselves practically immortal; theoretically, this body of mine will last a million years, barring major accidents. It was decided available resources would maintain ten million men on Earth, ten million on Venus, five million on Mars and ten million altogether on the moons of Jupiter for one million years at the then existing high standard of consumption, roughly amounting to about four million dollars a year per person at 1941 values.

"If in the meantime Man conquered the stars, all these

figures were subject to revision, though then, as now, the latter possibility was considered as remote as the stars themselves. Under examination, the problem, so apparently simple, has shown itself intricate beyond the scope of our mathematics."

He paused, and Garson ventured: "We had versions of planned states in our time, too, but they always broke down because of human nature. That seems to have happened again."

Not for a second had Garson considered his statement dangerous. The effect of his words was startling. The lean, handsome face became like frozen marble. Harshly, Dr. Lell said:

"Do not dare to compare your Naziism or Communism to—us! We are the rulers of all future time, and who in the past could ever stand against us if we chose to dominate? We shall win this war, in spite of being on the verge of defeat, for we are building the greatest time-energy barrier that has ever existed. With it, we shall destroy—or no one will win! We'll teach those moralistic scum of the planets to prate about man's rights and the freedom of the spirit. Blast them all!"

It was stunning. There was a passion of pride here, a violence of emotion altogether outside any possible anticipation. And yet—the fact remained that his own opinions were what they were, and he could not actually hope to conceal them from either Dr. Lell or the Observer; so—

He said: "I see an aristocratic hierarchy and a swarm of beast-men slaves. How do they fit into the picture, anyway? What about the resources they require? There certainly seem to be hundreds of thousands in this city alone." The man was staring at him in rigid hostility that brought a sudden chill to Garson's spine. Genuinely, he hadn't expected that any reasonable statement he might make would be used against him. Dr. Lell said too quietly: "Basically, they do not use any resources. They live in cities of stone and brick, and eat the produce of the indefatigable soil."

His voice was suddenly as sharp as steel. "And now, Professor Garson, I assure you that you have already condemned yourself. The Observer is located in that metal building across the street because the strain of energy from the great primary time machine would affect its sensitive parts if it was any nearer. I can think of no other explanation that you require, and I certainly have no desire to remain in the company of a man who will be an automaton in half an hour. *Come along!*"

Briefly, there was no impulse in him to argue, nothing but awareness of this monstrous city. Here it was again, the old, old story of the aristocrat justifying his black crime against his fellow man. Originally, there must have been deliberate physical degradation, deliberate misuse of psychology. The very name by which these people called themselves, the Glorious, seemed a heritage from days when dastardly and enormous efforts must have been made to arouse hysterical hero worship in the masses.

Dr. Lell's dry voice said: "Your disapproval of our slaves is shared by the Planetarians. They also oppose our methods of depersonalizing our recruits. It is easy to see that they and you have many things in common, and if only you could escape to their side—"

With an effort, Garson pulled himself out of his private world. He was being led on, not even skillfully; and it was only too apparent now that every word Dr. Lell spoke had the purpose of making him reveal himself. For a moment, he was conscious of genuine impatience; then puzzlement came.

"I don't get it," he said. "What you're doing cannot be bringing forth any new facts. I'm the product of my environment. You know what that environment is, and what type of normal human being it must inevitably produce. As I've said, my whole case rests on cooper—"

It was the difference in the texture of the sky at the remote end of that street that snatched his attention. A faint, unnormal, scarlet tinge it was, like a mist, an unnatural, unearthly sunset, only it was hours yet before the sun would set.

Astoundingly, he felt himself taut, growing tauter. He said in a tense voice:

"What's that?"

"That," Dr. Lell's curt, amused voice came at him, "is the war."

Garson restrained a crazy impulse to burst out laughing. For weeks, speculation about this gigantic war of the future had intertwined with his gathering anxiety about Norma. And now this—this red haze on the horizon of an otherwise undamaged city—the war!

The dark flash of inner laughter faded, as Dr. Lell said:

"It is not so funny as you think. Most of Delpa is intact because it is protected by a local time-energy barrier. Delpa is actually under siege fifty miles inside enemy territory."

He must have caught the thought that came to Garson. He said good-humoredly: "You're right. All you have to do is get out of Delpa, and you'll be safe."

Garson said angrily, "It's a thought that would occur naturally to any intelligent person. Don't forget you have Miss Matheson."

Dr. Lell seemed not to have heard. "The red haze you see is the point where the enemy has neutralized our energy barrier. It is there that they attack us unceasingly day and night with an inexhaustible store of robot machines.

"We are unfortunate in not having the factory capacity in Delpa to build robot weapons, so we use a similar type manned by depersonalized humans. Unfortunately, again, the cost in lives is high: ninety-eight percent of recruits. Every day, too, we lose about forty feet of the city, and, of course, in the end, Delpa will fall."

He smiled, an almost gentle smile. Garson was amazed to notice that he seemed suddenly in high good humor. Dr. Lell said:

"You can see how effective even a small time-energy barrier is. When we complete the great barrier two years hence, our entire front line will be literally impregnable. And now, as for your cooperation argument, it's worthless. Men are braver than they think, braver than reason. But let's forget argument. In a minute, the machine will give us the truth of this matter—" At first sight, the Observer Machine was a solid bank of flickering lights that steadied oddly, seemed almost to glare as they surveyed him. Garson stood quite still, scarcely breathing; a dim thought came that this—this wall of black metal machine and lights was utterly unimpressive.

He found himself analyzing the lack: It was too big and too stationary. If it had been small and possessed of shape, however ugly, and movement, there might have been a suggestion of abnormal personality.

But here was nothing, but a myriad of lights. As he watched, the lights began to wink again. Abruptly, they blinked out, all except a little colored design of them at the bottom right-hand corner.

Behind him, the door opened, and Dr. Lell came into the silent room. "I'm glad," he said quietly, "that the result was what it was. We are desperately in need of good assistants.

"To illustrate," he went on, as they emerged into the brightness of the unpleasant street, "I am, for instance, in charge of the recruiting station in 1941, but I'm there only when an intertime alarm system has warned me. In the interim, I am employed on scientific duties of the second order—first order being work that, by its very nature, must continue without interruption."

They were back in the same great building from which he had come; and ahead stretched the same gray-blue, familiar corridor, only this time Dr. Lell opened the first of several doors. He bowed politely.

"After you, professor!"

A fraction too late, Garson's fist flailed the air where that dark, strong face had been. They stared at each other, Garson tight-lipped, his brain like a steel bar. The superman said softly:

"You will always be that instant too slow, professor. It is a lack you cannot remedy. You know, of course, that my little speech was designed to keep you quiet during the trip back here, and that, actually, you failed the test. What you do not know is that you failed startlingly with a recalcitrancy grading of 6, which is the very worst, and intelligence AA plus, almost the best. It is too bad because we genuinely need capable assistants. I regret—"

"Let me do the regretting!" Garson cut him off roughly. "If I remember rightly, it was just below here that your beast men were forcing a man into the depersonalizing machine. Perhaps, on the staircase going down, I can find some way of tripping you up, and knocking that little gun you're palming right out of your hand."

There was something in the smile of the other that should have warned him—a hint of sly amusement. Not that it would have made any difference. Only—

He stepped through the open doorway toward the gray-blue, plainly visible stairway. Behind him, the door clicked with an odd finality. Ahead there was—

Amazingly, the staircase was gone. Where it had been was a large boilerlike case with a furnace-shaped door. Half a dozen beast men came forward—a moment later, they were shoving him toward that black hole of a door—

The second day Norma took the risk. The windows of the recruiting station still showed the same blank interior; walls stripped by the police of Calonian slogans, and signs and newspaper clippings trampled all over the floor. The door to the back room was half closed—too dark to see the interior.

It was noon. With drummed-up courage, Norma walked swiftly to the front entrance. The lock clicked open smoothly, and she was inside—pushing at that back door.

The machine was not there. Great dents showed in the floor, where it had malignantly crouched for so many months. But it was gone, as completely as Dr. Lell, as completely as the creaturemen and Jack Garson.

Back in her rooms, she collapsed onto the bed, and lay quivering from the dreadful nervous reaction of that swift, illegal search.

On the afternoon of the fourth day, as she sat staring at the meaningless words of a book, there was an abrupt tingling in her body. Somewhere a machine—*the machine*—was vibrating softly.

She climbed to her feet, the book forgotten on the windowsill, where, freakishly, it had fallen. But the sound was gone. Not a tremor touched her taut nerves. The thought came: imagination! The pressure was really beginning to get her.

As she stood there stiff, unable to relax, there came the thin squeal of a door opening downstairs. She recognized the sound instantly. It was the back door that led onto the vacant back lot, which her window overlooked. The back door opening and shutting!

She stared, fascinated, as Dr. Lell stalked into view. Her thought of awareness of him was so sharp that he must have caught it—but he did not turn. In half a minute he was gone, out of her line of vision.

On the fifth day, there was hammering downstairs, carpenters working. Several trucks came, and there was the mumbling sound of men talking. But it was evening before she dared venture downstairs. Through the window, then, she saw the beginning of the changes that were being wrought.

The old bench had been removed. The walls were being redone; there was no new furniture yet, but a rough, unfinished sign leaned against one wall. It read:

EMPLOYMENT BUREAU
MEN WANTED

Men wanted! So that was it. Another trap for men! Those ravenous armies of the Glorious must be kept glutted with fodder. The incredible war up there in that incredible future raged on. And she—

Quite dumbly, she watched as Dr. Lell came out of the back room. He walked toward the front door, and there was not even the impulse in her to run. She stood there, as he opened the door, came out, meticulously closed the door behind him, and then, after a moment, stood beside her, as silent as she, staring into the window. Finally:

"I see you've been admiring our new set-up!"

His voice was matter-of-fact, completely lacking in menace. She made no reply; he seemed to expect none, for he said almost immediately, in that same conversational tone:

"It's just as well that it all happened as it did. Nothing I ever told you has been disproved. I said that investigation had shown the machine to be here several years hence. Naturally, we could not examine every day or week of that time. This little episode accordingly escaped our notice, but did not change the situation.

"As for the fact that it will be an employment bureau henceforth, that seemed natural at the period of our investigation because this war of your time was over then."

He paused, and still there was no word that she could think of saying. In the gathering darkness, he seemed to stare at her.

"I'm telling you all this because it would be annoying to have to train someone else for your position, and because you must realize the impossibility of further opposition.

"Accept your situation. We have thousands of machines similar to this, and the millions of men flowing through them are gradually turning the tide of battle in our favor. We must win; our cause is overwhelmingly just; we are Earth against all the planets; Earth protecting herself against the aggression of a combination of enemies armed as no powers in all time have ever been armed. We have the highest moral right to draw on the men of Earth of every century to defend their planet.

"However"—his voice lost its objectivity, grew colder— "if this logic does not move you, the following rewards for your good behavior should prove efficacious. We have Professor Garson; unfortunately, I was unable to save his personality. Definite tests proved that he would be a recalcitrant, so—

"Then there is your youth. It will be returned to you on a salary basis. Every three weeks you will become a year younger. In short, it will require two years for you to return to your version of twenty."

He finished on a note of command: "A week from today, this bureau will open for business. You will report at nine o'clock. This is your last chance. Good-by."

In the darkness, she watched his shape turn; he vanished into the gloom of the building.

She had a purpose. At first it was a tiny mindgrowth that she wouldn't admit into her consciousness. But gradually embarrassment passed, and the whole world of her thought began to organize around it.

It began with the developing realization that resistance was useless. Not that she believed in the rightness of the cause of Dr. Lell and of this race that called itself the Glorious, although his story of Earth against the planets had put the first doubt into her brain. As—she knew—he had intended it should.

The whole affair was simpler than that. One woman had set herself against the men of the future—what a silly thing for one woman to do!

There remained Jack Garson!

If she could get him back, poor, broken, strange creature that he must be now with his personality destroyed—somehow she would make amends for having been responsible, but—

She thought: What madness to hope that they'd give him back to her, ever! She was the tiniest cog in a vast war machine. Nevertheless, the fact remained:

She must get him back!

The part of her brain that was educated, civilized, thought: What an elemental purpose, everything drained out of her but the basic of basics, one woman concentrating on the one man.

But the purpose was there, unquenchable!

The slow months dragged; and, once gone, seemed to

have flashed by. Suddenly, the Great War was over—and swarms of returned soldiers made the streets both dangerous and alive.

One night she turned a corner and found herself on a street she hadn't visited for some time. She stopped short, her body stiffening. The street ahead was thick with men—but their presence scarcely touched her mind.

Above all that confusion of sound, above the catcalls, above the roar of streetcars and automobiles, above the totality of the cacophonous combination, there was another sound, an incredibly softer sound—the whisper of a time machine.

She was miles from the employment bureau with its machine, but the tiny tremor along her nerves was unmistakable.

She pressed forward, blind to everything but the brilliantly lighted building that was the center of the attention of the men. A man tried to put his arm through hers. She jerked free automatically. Another man simply caught her in an embrace, and for brief seconds she was subjected to a steel-hard hug and a steel-hard kiss.

Purpose gave her strength. With scarcely an effort, she freed one arm and struck at his face. The man laughed good-humoredly, released her, but walked beside her.

"Clear the way for the lady!" he shouted.

Almost magically, there was a lane; and she was at the window. There was a sign that read:

WANTED
RETURNED SOLDIERS FOR DANGEROUS ADVENTURE
GOOD PAY!

No emotion came to the realization that here was another trap for men. In her brain, she had space only for impression.

The impression was of a large square room, with a dozen men in it. Only three of the men were recruits; of the other nine, one was an American soldier dressed in the uniform of World War I. He sat at a desk pounding a typewriter. Over him leaned a Roman legionnaire of the time of Julius Caesar, complete with toga and short sword. Beside the door, holding back the pressing throng of men, were two Greek soldiers of the time of Pericles. The men and the times they represented were unmistakable to her, who had taken four years of university Latin and Greek, and acted in plays of both periods in the original languages.

There was another man in an ancient costume, but she was unable to place him. At the moment, he was at a short counter interviewing one of the three recruits.

Of the four remaining men, two wore uniforms that could have been developments of the late twentieth century: the cloth was a light-yellow texture, and both men had two pips on their shoulders. The rank of lieutenant was obviously still in style when they were commissioned.

The remaining two men were simply strange, not in face, but in the cloth of their uniforms. Their faces were of sensitive, normal construction; their uniforms consisted of breeches and neatly fitting coats all in blue, a blue that sparkled as from a million needlelike diamond points. In a quiet, blue, intense way, they shone.

One of the recruits was led to the back door, as she watched, her first awareness that there was a back door.

The door opened; she had the briefest glimpse of a towering machine and a flashing picture of a man who was tall and dark of face, and who might have been Dr. Lell. Only he wasn't. But the similarity of race was unmistakable.

The door closed, and one of the Greeks guarding the outer entrance said: "All right, two more of you fellows can come in!"

There was a struggle for position, brief but incredibly violent. And then the two victors, grinning and breathing heavily from their exertion, were inside. In the silence that followed, one of the Greeks turned to the other, and said in a tangy, almost incomprehensible version of ancient Greek:

"Sparta herself never had more willing fighters. This promises to be a good night's catch!"

It was the rhythm of the words, and the colloquial gusto with which they were spoken that almost destroyed the meaning for her. After a moment, however, she made the mental translation. And now the truth was unmistakable. The men of Time had gone back even to old Greece, probably much farther back, for their recruits. And always they had used every version of bait, based on all the weaknesses and urgencies in the natures of men.

"Fight for Calonia"—an appeal to idealism! "Men wanted"—the most basic of all appeals, work for food, happiness, security. And now, the appeal variation was for returned soldiers. Adventure—with pay!

Diabolical! And yet so effective that they could even use men who had formerly been caught on the same brand of fly paper as recruiting officers. These men must be of the recalcitrant type, who fitted themselves willingly into the war machine of the Glorious One.

Traitors!

Abruptly ablaze with hatred for all nonrecalcitrants, who still possessed their personalities, she whirled away from the window.

She was thinking: Thousands of such machines. The figures had been meaningless before, but now, with just one other machine as a tremendous example, the reality reared up into a monstrous thing.

To think that there was a time when she had actually set her slim body and single, inadequate mind against *them*!

There remained the problem of getting Jack Garson out of the hell of that titanic war of the future!

At night, she walked the streets, because there was always the fear that in the apartment her thoughts, her driving deadly thoughts, would be—tapped. And because to be enclosed in those narrow walls above the machine that had devoured so many thousands of men was— intolerable!

She thought as she walked—over and over she thought of the letter Jack Garson had written her before he came in person. Long destroyed, that letter, but every word was emblazoned on her brain; and of all the words of it, the one sentence that she always returned to was: "In your position, I would ask myself one question: Was there anything, any metal, *anything*, upon my person, that might have been placed there?"

One day, as she was wearily unlocking the door of her apartment, the answer came. Perhaps it was the extra weariness that brought her briefly closer to basic things.

Perhaps her brain was simply tired of slipping over the same blind spot. Or perhaps the months of concentration had finally earned the long-delayed result.

Whatever the reason, she was putting the key back into her purse when the hard, metallic feel of it against her fingers brought wild, piercing realization.

The key, metal, the key, metal, the key—

Desperately, she stopped the mad repetition. The apartment door slammed behind her, and like some terrorized creature she fled down the dark stairs into the glare of the night streets.

Impossible to return till she had calmed the burning, raging chaos that was in her mind. Until she had made sure!

After half an hour, the first flash of coherence came. In a drugstore, she bought a night bag and a few fill-ins to give it weight. A pair of small pliers, a pair of tweezers—in case the pliers were too large—and a small screwdriver completed her equipment. Then she went to a hotel.

The pliers and the tweezers were all she needed. The little bulbous cap of the skeleton-type key yielded to the first hard pressure. Her trembling fingers completed the unscrewing—and she found herself staring at a tiny, glowing point, like a red-hot needle protruding from the very center of the tube that was the inside of the key.

The needle vanished into an intricate design of spiderlike wires, all visible in the glow that shed from them—

The vague thought came that there was probably terrific, communicable energies here. But somehow there came no sense of restraint from the idea. Only enough reality of danger struck her to make her wrap her flimsy lace handkerchief around the tweezers—and then she touched the shining, protruding needle point.

It yielded the slightest bit to her shaky touch. Nothing happened. It just glowed there.

Dissatisfied, she put the key down and stared at it. So tiny, so delicate a machine actually disturbed to the extent of one sixteenth of an inch displacement—and nothing happened. She—

A sudden thought sent her to the dresser mirror. A forty-year-old face stared back at her.

Months now since she had returned to twenty. And now, in a flash, she was forty. The little touch of the pin against the needle's end, pushing, had aged her twenty years.

That explained what had happened at the police station. It meant—if she could only pull it back— She fought to steady her fingers, then applied the tweezers.

She was twenty again!

Abruptly weak, she lay down on the bed. She thought:

Somewhere in the world of time and space was the still-living body of the man that had been Jack Garson. But for him she could throw this key thing into the river three blocks away, take the first train East or West or South—anywhere—and the power of the machine would be futile against her. Dr. Lell would not even think of searching for her once she had lost herself in the swarm of humankind.

How simple it all really was. For three long years, their power over her had been the key and its one devastating ability to age her.

Or was that all?

Startled, she sat up. Did they count, perhaps, on their victims believing themselves safe enough to keep the key and its magic powers of rejuvenation? She, of course, because of Jack Garson, was bound to the key as if it was still the controller and not she. But the other incentive, now that she had thought of it, was enormous. And—

Her fingers shook as she picked up the dully gleaming key with its glowing, intricate interior. Incredible that they could have allowed so precious an instrument to pass so easily into the hands of an alien, when they must have known that the probability of discovery was not— improbable!

An idea came; and, with it, abrupt calm. With suddenly steady fingers, she picked up the tweezers, caught the protruding glow point of the key between the metal jaws, and, making no attempt to pull or push, twisted screw-wise. There was a tiny, almost inaudible click. Her body twanged like a taut violin string, and she was falling— falling into dark, immeasurable distance. Out of the night, a vaguely shining body drifted toward her, a body human yet not human; there was something about the head and the shoulders, something physically different that somehow eluded her slow thought; and in that strange, superhuman head were eyes that blazed like jewels, seemed literally to pierce her. The voice that came couldn't have been sound, for it was inside her brain, and it said:

"With this great moment, you enter upon your power and your purpose. I say to you, the time-energy barrier must not be completed. It will destroy all the ages of the

Solar System. The time-energy barrier must not, not, NOT be completed—"

The body faded and was gone into remoteness. The very memory of it became a dim mind-shape. There remained the darkness, the jet, incredible darkness.

Abruptly, she was in a material world. She seemed to be half-slumped, half-kneeling, one leg folded under her in the exact position she had occupied on the bed. Only she must have drooped there unconscious for long moments; her knees ached and ached with the hard, pressing pain of position. And—beneath the silk of her stockings was, not the hotel bed, but—metal!

It was the combination of surprise, the aloneness, and the stark fact of the mind-destroying thing that was going to happen that unnerved Garson. Involuntarily, he started to squirm, then he was writhing, his face twisting in strange mental agony; and then the strength of those rough, stolid hands holding him seemed to flow somehow into his nerves.

Almost literally, he clenched his mind, and was safe from madness!

There were no hands touching him now. He lay, face downward on a flat, hard surface; and at first there was only the darkness and a slow return of the sense of aloneness.

Vague thoughts came, thoughts of Norma and of the coincidence that had molded his life, seemingly so free for so many years, yet destined to find its ending here in this black execution chamber—for he *was* being destroyed here, though his body might live on for a few brief mindless hours. Or days. Or weeks. It mattered not.

The thing was fantastic. This whole damned business was a nightmare, and in a minute he'd wake up and—

At first the sound was less than a whisper, a stealthy noise out of remoteness, that prodded with an odd insistence at Garson's hearing. It quivered toward him in the blackness, edging out of inaudibility, a rasping presence that grew louder, louder—voices!

It exploded into a monstrous existence, a billion voices clamoring at his brain, a massive blare that pressed at him, *pressed him!*

Abruptly, the ferocity of the voices dimmed. They faded into distance, still insistent, somehow reluctant to leave, as if there was something still left unsaid.

The end of sound came, and briefly there was utter silence. Then—there was a click. Light flooded at him from an opening a scant foot from his head. Garson twisted and stared, fascinated. Daylight! From his vantage point, he could see the edge of a brick-and-stone building, a wretchedly old, worn building, a street of Delpa.

It was over. Incredibly it was over.

And nothing had happened. No, that wasn't it exactly. There were things in his mind, confusing things about the importance of loyalty to the Glorious, a sense of intimacy with his surroundings, pictures of machines and—nothing clear, except—

A harsh voice broke his amazed blur of thought. "Come on out of there, you damned slow poke!"

A square, heavy, brutal face was peering into the open door, a big, square-built young man with a thick neck, a boxer's flat nose, and unpleasant blue eyes.

Garson lay quite still. It was not that he intended to

disobey. All his reason urged instant, automatic obedience until he could estimate the astounding things that had happened.

What held him there, every muscle stiff, was a new, tremendous fact that grew, not out of the meaning of the man's words, but out of the words themselves.

The language was not English. Yet he had understood— every word!

The sudden squint of impatient rage that flushed the coarse face peering in at him brought life to Garson's muscles. He scrambled forward, but it was the man's truck-driver hands that actually pulled him clear and deposited him with a jarring casualness face downward on the paved road.

He lay there for an electric instant, tense with an anger that congealed reluctantly before the thought: He dare not get mad. Or act the fool!

The terrific reality was that something had gone wrong. Somehow the machine hadn't worked all the way, and if he was crazy enough to wreck the great chance that offered—

He stood up slowly, wondering how an automaton, a depersonalized human being, should look and act.

"This way, damn you," said that bullying voice from behind him. "You're in the army now."

Satisfaction came into the voice: "Well, you're the last for me today. I'll get you fellows to the front, and then—"

"This way" led to a dispirited-looking group of men, about a hundred of them, who stood in two rows alongside a great, gloomy, dirty building. He walked stolidly to the end of the rear line, and for the first time realized how surprisingly straight the formation of men were holding their lines, in spite of their dulled appearance.

"All right, all right," bellowed the square-jawed young man. "Let's get going. You've got some hard fighting ahead of you before this day and night are over—"

The contemptuous thought came to Garson, as he stared at the leader: this, then, was the type *they* picked for nonrecalcitrant training: the ignorant, blatant, amoral, sensual pigmen. No wonder he himself had been rejected by the Observer.

His eyes narrowed to slits as he watched the line of dead-alive men walk by him in perfect rhythm; he fell in step, his mind deliberately slow and ice-cold, cautiously exploring the strange knowledge in his brain that didn't fit with his—freedom!

That didn't fit with anything! A little group of sentences that kept repeating inside him:

"The great time-energy barrier is being built in Delpa. It must not be completed, for it will destroy the Universe. Prepare to do your part in its destruction; try to tell the Planetarians, but take no unnecessary risks. To stay alive, to tell the Planetarians: those are your immediate purposes. The time-energy barriers must not—NOT—"

Funny, he thought, funny! He squeezed the crazy thing out of his consciousness.

No trucks came gliding up to transport them; no streetcar whispered along in some superdevelopment of street-railway service; there was simply no machinery, nothing but those narrow avenues with their gray, side-walkless length, like back alleys.

They walked to war; and it was like being in a dead, old, deserted city—deserted except for the straggle of short, thick, slow, stolid men and women who plodded heavily by, unsmiling, without so much as a side glance. As if they were but the pitiful, primitive remnant of a once-great race, and this city the proud monument to— No!

Garson smiled wryly. Of all the fools, getting romantic about this monstrosity of a city. All too evident it was, even without Dr. Lell's words as a reminder, that every narrow, dirty street, every squalid building had been erected—to be what it was.

And the sooner he got out of the place, and delivered to the Planetarians the queer, inexplicable message about the great time-energy barrier—

With a half shudder, with deliberate abruptness, he cut the thought. Damn it, he'd have to be careful. If one of the Glorious should happen to be around, and accidentally catch the free thought of what was supposed to be an automaton—next time there'd be no mistake.

Tramp, tramp, tramp! The pavement echoed with the strange lifeless hollowness of a ghost city; and the tremendous thought came that he was here centuries, perhaps millenniums, into the future. What an awful realization to think that Norma, poor, persecuted, enslaved Norma, whose despairing face he had seen little more than an hour ago, was actually dead and buried in the dim ages of the long ago.

And yet she was alive. Those six hundred billion bodies per minute of hers were somewhere in space and time, alive because the great time energy followed its casual, cosmic course of endless repetition, because life was but an accident as purposeless as the immeasurable energy that plunged grandly on into the unknown night that must be—somewhere!

Tramp, tramp— On and on, and his thought was a rhythm to the march— With an ugly start he came out of his reverie, and instantly grew abnormally aware of the nearness of the red haze in the sky ahead. Why, it wouldn't take ten minutes now, and they'd be *there!*

Machines glinted in the slanting rays of the warm, golden, sinking sun; machines that moved and—fought! A sick thrill struck Garson, the first shock of realization that this—this tiny segment of the battle of the ages was real, and near, and deadly.

Up there, every minute men were dying miserably for a cause their depersonalized minds did not even comprehend. Up there, too, was infinitesimal victory for the Planetarians, and a small, stinging measure of defeat for the Glorious. Forty feet a day, Dr. Lell had said.

Forty feet of city conquered every day. What a murderous war of attrition, what a bankruptcy of strategy. Or was it the ultimate nullification of the role of military genius, in that each side knew and practiced every rule of military science without error?—and the forty feet was simply the inevitable mathematical outcome of the difference in the potential in striking power of the two forces.

Forty feet a day. In a blaze of wonder, Garson stood finally with his troop a hundred yards from that unnatural battle front. Like a robot he stood stiffly among those robot men, but his eyes and mind fed in undiminished fascination at the deadly mechanical routine that was the offense and defense.

The Planetarians had seven major machines, and there were at least half a hundred tiny, swift, glittering craft as escort for each of the great—battleships! That was it: battleships and destroyers.

Against them, the Glorious had only destroyers, a host of darting, shining, torpedo-shaped craft that hugged the ground, and fought in an endlessly repeated, complicated maneuver.

Maneuver against maneuver! An intricate chess game—it was a game, an incredibly involved game whose purpose and method seemed to quiver just beyond reach of his reason.

Everything revolved around the battleships. In some way they must be protected from energy guns, because no attempt was made to use anything like that. Somehow, too, cannon must be useless against them. There was none in sight, no attempt to hurtle great gobs of metal either at the machines or—by the Planetarians at the more than a hundred troops like his own, who stood at stiff attention so close to the front, so bunched that a few superexplosive shells of the future would have smashed them all.

Nothing but the battleships and the destroyers!

The battleships moved forward and backward and forward and backward and in and out, intertwining among themselves; and the destroyers of the Glorious darted in when the battleships came forward, and hung back when the battleships retreated; and always the destroyers of the Planetarians were gliding in to intercept the destroyers of the Glorious; and as the sun sank in a blaze of red beyond the green hills to the west, the battleships in their farthest forward thrust were feet closer than they had been at the beginning; and the sharply delineated red line of haze, that must be the point where the time-energy barrier was neutralized, was no longer lying athwart a shattered slab of rock—but on the ground feet nearer.

That was it. The battleships somehow forced the time-energy barrier to be withdrawn. Obviously, it would only be withdrawn to save it from a worse fate, perhaps from a complete neutralization over a wide front. And so a city was being won, inch by inch, foot by foot, street by street—only the intricate evolution of the battle, the why of that almost immeasurably slow victory, was as great a mystery as ever.

The grim thought came: If the odd, tremendous message that had come into his brain in that out-of-order depersonalizing machine was true, then the final victory would never come in time. Long before the forty-foot-a-day conquerors had gained the prize that was Delpa, the secret, super, time-energy barrier would be completed; and the devilish spirit of war would at last have won its senseless goal—complete elimination of the human race and all its works.

Night fell, but a glare of searchlights replaced the sun, and that fantastic battle raged on. No one aimed a gun or a weapon at the lights; each side concentrated with that strange, deadly intentness on its part of that intricate, murderous game; and troop after troop dissolved into the ravenous, incredible conflagration.

Death came simply to the automatons. Each in turn crowded into one of the torpedo-shaped destroyers; and knowing—as he did—from the depersonalizing machine, that the tiny, man-sized tank was operated by thought control, flashed out into battle line.

Sometimes the end came swiftly, sometimes it was delayed, but sooner or later there was metallic contact with the enemy; and that was all that was needed. Instantly, the machine would twist and race toward the line of waiting men; the next victim would drag out the corpse, crawl in himself and—

There were variations. Machines clashed with the enemy and died with their drivers; or darted with frantic aimlessness, out of control. Always, swift, metallic scavengers raced from both sides to capture the prize; and sometimes the Planetarians succeeded, sometimes the Glorious.

Garson counted: one, two, three—less than four hundred men ahead of him—and the realization of how close his turn was brought the perspiration coldly to his face. Minutes! Damn it, *damn it*, he had to solve the rules of this battle, or go in there, without plan, without hope.

Seven battleships, scores of destroyers to each battleship and all acting as one unit in one involved maneuver and—

And, by heaven, he had a part of the answer. One unit. Not seven battleships out there, but one in the form of seven. One superneutralizing machine in its seven-dimensional maneuver. No wonder he had been unable to follow the intertwinings of those monsters with each other, the retreats, the advances. Mathematicians of the twentieth century could only solve easily problems with four equations. Here was a problem with seven; and the

general staff of the Glorious could never be anything but
a step behind in their solution—and that step cost them
forty feet a day—

His turn! He crept into the casing of the torpedo cycle;
and it was smaller even than he had thought. The machine
fitted him almost like a glove. Effortlessly, it glided
forward, too smoothly, too willingly, into that dazzle of
searchlights, into that maelstrom of machines.

One contact, he thought, one contact with an enemy
meant death; and his plan of breaking through was as
vague as his understanding of how a seven-dimensional
maneuver actually worked.

Amazed wonder came that he was even letting himself
hope.

Norma began to notice the difference, a strange,
vibrant, flamelike quality within herself, a rich, warm
aliveness, like an electric wire quiescent with latent force
tremendous— It was utterly different, alien, as new as life
returning to a dead body. Only it was added life to the life
that had always existed within her.

Physically, she was still crouching there tautly, her legs
twisted under her, vision still blinded; and the hard pain
of the metal beneath her was an unchanged pressure
against the bone and muscle of her knees. But—

Along every nerve that wonderful sense of well-being,
of strange, abnormal power quivered and grew—and
yielded abruptly to the violence of the thought that
flashed into her mind:

Where was she? What had happened? What—
The thought snapped in the middle because,

amazingly, an alienness—intruded into it, another thought, not out of her own mind, not even directed at her, not—human!

"—Tentacle 2731 reporting to the Observer. A warning light has flashed on the ... (meaningless) ... xxxxx time machine. Action!"

The answer came instantly, coldly:

"An intruder—on top of the primary time machine. Warning from, and to, Dr. Lell's section. Tentacle 2731, go at once—destroy intruder. Action!" There were stunning immensities in those hard wisps of message and answering message, that echoed back along the dim corridors of her mind. The stupefying fact that she had effortlessly intercepted thought waves momentarily blotted out the immediacy of the greater fact that every chilling word of that death threat was meant for her. But then—

Before that colossal menace, even the knowledge of where she was came with a quiet unobtrusiveness, like a minor harmony in a clash of major discord. Her present location was only too obvious. Twisting the key the way she had, had sent her hurtling through time to the age of the Glorious, to the primary-time machine, where fantastic things called tentacles and observers guarded—

If only she could see! She *must* see, or she was lost before she could begin to hope.

Frantically, she strained against the blackness that lay so tight against her eyes and—

She could see!

It was as simple as that. One instant, blindness! The next, the urge to see. And then, sight, complete, without preliminary blur, like opening her eyes after a quiet sleep.

The simplicity part of it was crowded out of her brain by a whirling confusion of impression. There were two swift thoughts that clung—the brief wonder at the way sight had come back to her, merely from the wish that it would—and a flashing memory of the face that had floated at her out of the blackness of time. *With this great moment you enter upon your power and your purpose*—

The picture, all connecting thoughts, fled. She saw that she was in a room, a vast, domed room, and that she was on top of a gigantic machine. There were transparent walls! and beyond—

Her mind and vision leaped beyond the room, through the transparent walls. There was something out there, something tremendous! A shimmering, roseate fire, like a greater dome that covered the near sky and hid the night universe beyond.

The effort of staring tired her. Her gaze came down out of the sky; and, back in the room, she saw that all the transparent wall that faced her was broken into a senseless pattern of small balconies, each mounting glittering, strangely menacing machinery—weapons!

So many weapons—for what?

With a jar that shocked her brain, the thought disintegrated. She stared in blank horror at a long, thick, tube-shaped metal thing that floated up from below the rim of the time machine. A score of gleaming, insectlike facets seemed to glare at her.

"Tentacle 2731, destroy the intruder—"

"No!" It was her own desperate negation, product of pure devastating panic, product of newness, of a hideous, alien threat that wrecked on the instant all the bravery that had made her experiment with the key in the first place.

Her mind spun like a dizzily spinning wheel, her body shrank from the sodden, abnormal fear that this—metal— would spray her with some incredible flame weapon before she could think, before she could turn or run, or even move!

Of all her pride and accumulated courage, there remained only enough to bring a spasm of shame at the words that burst senselessly from her lips: "No! No! You can't! Go away—go back—where you came from! Go—"

She stopped, blinked, and stared wildly. The thing was gone!

The reality of that had scarcely touched her when a crash sounded. It came from beyond and below the rim of the machine. Quite instinctively, Norma ran forward to peer down.

The hundred-foot, precipicelike slope of metal time machine that greeted her startled gaze made her draw back with a gasp, but instantly she was creeping forward again, more cautiously, but with utter fascination to see again what that first brief glimpse had revealed.

And there it was, on the distant floor, the tube-shaped thing. Even as she watched, hope building up in her, there came a weak impulse of alien thought:

"Tentacle 2731 reporting—difficulty. Female human using Insel mind rays—power 100—no further action possible by this unit—incapacitation 74 mechanical—"

Hope grew gigantic, and there was a wild burst of surmise and a desperate, wondering half belief in the miracle that was taking place. She was doing this; her wish had brought instant return of sight, her despairing thought had sent the tentacle thing crashing to mechanical ruin, Insel mind rays, power 100! Why, it meant—it could mean—

The leaping thought sagged. One of a series of doors in the wall facing her opened, and a tall man emerged hurriedly. Quite automatically, she pressed back, tried to lie flat on the metal, out of sight; but it seemed to her those familiar, sardonic eyes were staring straight up at her. Dr. Lell's hard, tight, superbly confident thought came then like a succession of battering blows against the crumbling structure of her hope:

"This is a repetition of the x time and space manipulation. Fortunately, the transformation center this seventeenth time is a Miss Norma Matheson, who is utterly incapable, mathematically, of using the power at her disposal. She must be kept confused, kept on the run. The solution to her swift destruction is a concentration of forces of the third order, nonmechanical, according to Plan A4. Action!"

"Action immediate!" came the cold, distinctive thought of the Observer.

That was like death itself. Hope abandoned her; she lay flat on that flat metal, her mind blank, and not a quiver of strength in her body.

A minute passed; and that seemed an immense time. So much that the swift form of her thought had time to change, to harden. Fear faded like a dream; and then came returning awareness of that curious, wonderful sense of power.

She stood up, and the way her legs trembled with the

effort brought the automatic memory of the way she had regained her vision. She thought tensely, consciously:

"No more physical weakness. Every muscle, every nerve, every organ of my body must function perfectly from now on and—"

A queer thrill cut the thought. It seemed to start at her toes and sweep up, a delicious sense of warmth, like an all-over blush.

And the weakness was gone.

She stood for a moment, fascinated, utterly absorbed by this—toy! And hesitated to try it too far. Yet—

She thought: "No more mental weakness, no confusion; my brain must function with all the logic of which I am capable!"

It was strange, and not altogether satisfactory, what happened then. Her mind seemed to come to a dead stop. For an instant the blankness was complete; and then, a single, simple idea came into it:

Danger! For her there was nothing but danger and the getting out of that danger. Find the key. Go back to 1944. Get out of this world of Dr. Lell and gain time to solve the secrets of the mighty power centralized in her. She jerked, as a lean, yard-long flame struck the metal beside her, and caromed away toward the ceiling. She watched it bounce from the ceiling, out of sight beyond the precipicelike edge of the machine. It must have struck the floor, but instantly it was in sight again, leaping toward the ceiling with undiminished ardor.

Up, down, up, down, up, it went as she watched; then abruptly it lost momentum and collapsed like an empty flaming sack toward the floor, out of her line of vision.

A second streamer of flame soared up from where Dr. Lell had been heading when last she saw him. It struck the ceiling, and like an elongated billiard ball, darted down—and this time she was ready for it. Her brain reached out: *Stop! Whatever the energy that drives you, it is powerless against me. Stop!*

The flame missed her right hand by inches, and soared on up to the ceiling; and from below, strong and clear and satirical, came the voice, or was it the thought of Dr. Lell:

"My dear Miss Matheson, that's the first of the third-order energies, quite beyond your control. And have you noticed that your mind isn't quite so cool as you ordered it to be. The truth is that, though you have power unlimited, you can only use it when you understand the forces involved, either consciously or unconsciously. Most people have a reasonably clear picture of their bodily processes, which is why your body reacted so favorably, but your brain—its secrets are largely beyond your understanding.

"As for the key"—there was laughter in the words— "you seem to have forgotten it is geared to the time machine. The Observer's first act was to switch it back to 1944. Accordingly, I can promise you death—"

Her brain remained calm; her body steady, unaffected. No blood surged to her head; there was the barest quickening of her heartbeat; her hands clenched with the tense knowledge that she must act faster, think faster—

If only Jack Garson were here, with his science, his swift, logical brain—

Strangely, then, she could feel her mind slipping out of

her control, like sand between her fingers. Her body remained untroubled, untouched, but her mind was suddenly gliding down, down, into dark depths.

Terror came abruptly, as a score of flame streamers leaped into sight toward the ceiling, bounced and—

"Jack, Jack, help me! I need you! Oh, Jack, come—" The slow seconds brought no answer; and the urgency of her need could brook no waiting. "Back home," she thought. "I've got to get back home, back to 1944, back—"

Her body twanged. There was blackness, and a horrible sensation of falling.

The blow of the fall was not hard; and that unaffected, almost indestructible body of hers took the shock in a flash of pain-absorbing power. Awareness came of a floor with a rug on it. A vague light directly in front of her lost its distortion and became—a window!

Her own apartment! Like a young tigress she scrambled to her feet; and then poised motionless with dismay as the old, familiar, subtle vibration thrilled its intimate way along her nerves. The machine! The machine was in the room below and working!

Her will to safety had sent her back to her own time, but her call to Jack Garson had passed unheeded, unheard; and here she was, alone with only a strange unwieldy power to help her against the gathering might of the enemy. And that was her hope, that it was only gathering! Even Dr. Lell must have time to transport his forces. If she could get out of this building, use her power to carry her, as it had already borne her from the time and space of the future—

Carry her where? There was only one other place she

could think of: To the hotel! To the hotel room from where she had launched herself with the key.

It wasn't death that came then, but a blow so hard that she was sobbing bitterly with the pain even as her mind yielded reluctantly to unconsciousness; even as she was realizing in stark dismay that she had struck the wall of her apartment and this power she possessed had been betrayed once again by her inability to handle it. And now Dr. Lell would have time to do everything necessary—

Blackness came—

There was a memory in Garson of the night, and of the rushing machine that had carried him, the wonderful little metal thing that darted and twisted far to the left, as close to the red haze of the time-energy barrier as he dared to go—and not a machine had followed him. In seconds he was through the blazing gap, out of Delpa, safe from Dr. Lell—only something had struck at him then, a crushing blow—

He came out of sleep without pain, and with no sense of urgency. Drowsily, he lay, parading before his mind the things that had happened; and the comfortable realization came that he must be safe or he wouldn't be—like this!

There were things to do, of course. He must transmit the information to the Planetarians that they must conquer Delpa more swiftly, that final victory waited nowhere but in Delpa. And then, somehow, he must persuade them to let him return to 1941, to Norma and—

For a while he lay peacefully, his eyes open, gazing

thoughtfully at a gray ceiling. From nearby, a man's voice said:

"There's no use expecting it."

Garson turned his head, his first alert movement. A row of hospital-like cots stretched there, other rows beyond. From the nearest bed, a pair of fine, bright, cheerful eyes stared at him. The man lay with his head crotched in a bunched, badly rumpled pillow. He said:

"Expecting to feel surprised, I mean. You won't. You've been conditioned into recovering on a gradual scale, no excitement, no hysteria, nothing that will upset you. The doctors, though Planetarian trained, are all men of the past; and up to a day ago, they pronounced you—"

Quite amazingly, the man paused; his brown eyes darkened in frown, then he smiled with an equally amazing grimness:

"I nearly said too much there. Actually you may be strong enough to stand any shock now, conditioning or no. But the fact is you'll learn the hard truths of your predicament soon enough, without getting yourself into a nervous state now. Here's a preliminary warning: Toughen your mind for bad news." Strangely, he felt only the dimmest curiosity, and no sense of alarm at all. After what Dr. Lell had said directly and by implication of the Planetarians, no danger here could surpass what he had already been through. The only emotion he could sense within himself had to do with his double purpose of rescuing Norma from the recruiting station and—

He said aloud: "If I should be asleep the next time a doctor or Planetarian comes in, will you waken me? I've got something to tell them."

The odd, mirthless smile of the other made Garson frown. His voice was almost sharp, as he asked:

"What's the matter?"

The stranger shook his head half pityingly: "I've been twenty-seven days in this stage, and I've never seen a Planetarian. As for telling anyone on the Planetarian side anything, I've already told you to expect bad news. I know you have a message to deliver. I even know from Dra Derrel what it is, but don't ask me how he found out. All I can say is, you'll have to forget about delivering any message to anyone. Incidentally, my name is Mairphy—Edard Mairphy."

Garson lay quite still. For the moment he wasn't interested in names or the mystery of how they knew his message. There was a vague thrill of worry in the back of his mind. Every word this gentle-faced, gentle-voiced young man had spoken was packed with dark, tremendous implications.

He stared at Mairphy, but there was only the frank, open face, the friendly, half-grim smile, the careless wisp of bright, brown hair coming down over one temple—nothing at all of danger.

Besides, where could any danger be coming from? From the Planetarians?

That was ridiculous. Regardless of their shortcomings, the Planetarians were the one race of this "time" that must be supported. They might have curious, even difficult habits, but the other side was evil almost beyond imagination. Between them, there was no question of choice.

His course was simple. As soon as he was allowed to

get up—and he felt perfectly well now—he would set out
to make contact with a Planetarian in a reasonable
persistent manner. The whole affair was beginning to
show unpleasant, puzzling aspects, but—

He grew aware of Mairphy's voice: "The warning is all
I'll say on that subject for the time being. There's
something else, though. Do you think you'll be able to get
up in about an hour? I mean, do you feel all right?"

Garson nodded, puzzled: "I think so. Why?"

"We'll be passing the Moon about then, and I
understand it's a sight worth—"

"*What?*"

Mairphy was staring at him. He said slowly: "I forgot. I
was so busy not telling you about our main danger, it didn't
occur to me that you were unconscious when we started."

He shrugged. "Well, we're on our way to Venus; and
even if there was nothing else, the cards would be stacked
against you by that fact alone. There are no Planetarians
aboard this ship, only human beings out of the past and
tentacles of the Observer. There's not a chance in the
world of you speaking to any of them because—"

He stopped; then: "There I nearly went again, damn
it! I'll let out the devilish truth yet, before you ought to
hear it."

Garson scarcely heard. The shock wouldn't go away.
He lay in a daze of wonder, overwhelmed by the
incredible fact that he was in space. In space! He felt
suddenly outmaneuvered. Even the events he knew about
were abruptly a million miles ahead of his plans.

At first, the very idea was incredibly shocking. Pain
pulsed in his temples from the wave of blood that charged

there. He sat, rigidly, awkwardly, in the bed; and, finally, in a choked voice he said:

"How long will it take to get to Venus?"

"Ten days, I believe!"

Very cautiously, Garson allowed the figures to penetrate. Hope surged through him. It wasn't so bad as his first despairing thought had pictured it. Ten days to get there, ten days to persuade someone to let a Planetarian have a glimpse of his mind, ten days to get back to Earth.

A month! He frowned. Actually, that wasn't so good. Wars had been lost, great empires collapsed in less time than that. Yet, how could he deliver his message—on a spaceship. Venus-bound? Courses of initial action suggested themselves, but—

He said in a troubled tone, "If I was back in 1941, at this point I would try to see the captain of the ship. But you've made me doubt that normal procedures apply on a Planetarian space liner. Frankly, what are my chances?" He saw that the young man was grim. "Exactly none!" Mairphy replied. "This is no joke, Garson. As I said before, Derrel knows and is interested in your message, don't ask me how or what or when. He was a political leader in his own age, and he's a marvel at mechanics, but, according to him, he knows only the normal, everyday things of his life. You'll have to get used to the idea of being in with a bunch of men from past ages, some queer ducks among them, Derrel the queerest of them all.

"But forget that! Just remember that you're on a spaceship in an age so far ahead of your own that there's not even a record of your time in the history books and—"

Abruptly, that was what got him. Garson lay back,

breathlessly still, dazzled once again by his strange, tremendous environment, straining for impression. But there was no sense of movement, no abnormality at all. The world was quiet; the room seemed like an unusually large dormitory in a hospital.

After a moment of tenseness, he allowed his body to relax, and the full, rich flood of thought to flow in. In that eager tide, the danger to which Mairphy had referred was like a figment of imagination, a dim, darkling shadow in remoteness.

There was only the wonder, only Venus and—this silent, swift-plunging spaceship.

Venus! He let the word roll around in his mind, and it was like rich, intellectual food, luscious beyond reason to a mind shaped and trained as was his.

Venus—For ages the dreams of men had reached longingly into the skies, immeasurably fascinated by the mind-staggering fact of other worlds as vast as their own; continents, seas, rivers, treasure beyond estimate.

And now for him there was to be glittering reality. Before that fact, other urgencies faded. Norma must be rescued, of course; the strange message delivered; but if it was to be his destiny to remain in this world 'till the end of war, then he could ask nothing more of those years than this glowing sense of adventure, this shining opportunity to learn and see and know in a scientist's heaven.

He grew aware that Mairphy was speaking: "You know"—the young man's voice was thoughtful—"it's just possible that it might be a good idea if you did try to see the captain. I'll have to speak to Derrel before any further action is taken and—"

Garson sighed wearily. He felt suddenly genuinely exhausted, mentally and physically, by the twisting courses of events.

"Look," he said, "a minute ago you stated it was absolutely impossible for me to see the captain; now it seems it might be a good idea and so the impossible becomes poss—"

A sound interrupted his words, a curious hissing sound that seemed to press at him. With a start he saw that men were climbing out of bed, groups that had been standing in quiet conversation were breaking up. In a minute, except for some three dozen who had not stirred from their beds, the manpower of that great room had emptied through a far door. As the door closed, Mairphy's tense voice stabbed at him:

"Quick! Help me out of bed and into my wheelchair. Damn this game leg of mine, but I've got to see Derrel. The attack must not take place until you've tried to see the captain. Quick, man!"

"*Attack!*" Garson began, then with an effort, caught himself. Forcing coolness through the shock that was gathering in his system, he lay back; he said in a voice that teetered on the edge of tremble:

"I'll help you when you tell me what all this is about. Start talking! Fast!"

Mairphy sighed: "The whole thing's really very simple. They herded together a bunch of skeptics—that's us; it means simply men who know they are in another age, and aren't superstitious about it, always potential explosive, as the Planetarians well understood. But what they didn't realize was that Derrel was what he was.

"The mutiny was only partially successful. We got the

control room, the engine room, but only one of the arsenals. The worst thing was that one of the tentacles escaped our trap, which means that the Observer Machine has been informed, and that battleships have already been dispatched after us. Unless we can gain full control fast, we'll be crushed; and the whole bunch of us will be executed out of hand."

Mairphy finished with a bleak smile: "That includes you and every person in this room, lame, sick or innocent. The Planetarians leave the details of running their world in the hands of a monster machine called the Observer; and the Observer is mercilessly logical.

"That's what I meant by bad news. All of us are committed to victory or to death—and now, quick, let me get to Derrel, and stop this attack!"

His mind felt a swollen, painful thing with the questions that quivered there: skeptics—tentacles—mutiny— Good heavens!

It was not until after Mairphy's power-driven wheelchair had vanished through the door that had swallowed the men that he realized how weary he was. He lay down on the bed, and there didn't seem to be a drop of emotion in him. He was thinking, a slow, flat, gray thought, of the part of the message that had come to him in the depersonalizing machine, the solemn admonishment: "—Take no unnecessary risks—*stay alive!*"

What a chance!

The Moon floated majestically against the backdrop of black space, a great globe of light that grew and grew. For a solid hour it clung to size, but at last it began to retreat into distance.

It was the gathering immensity of that distance that brought to Garson a sudden empty sense, a dark consciousness that he was again a tiny pawn in this gigantic struggle of gigantic forces.

He watched until the glowing sphere of Moon was a shadowy, pea-sized light half hidden by the dominating ball of fire that was the Earth. His immediate purpose was already a waxing shape in his mind, as he turned to stare down at Mairphy in his wheelchair; it struck him there were lines of fatigue around the other's eyes; he said:

"And now that the attack has been called off, I'd like to meet this mysterious Derrel. After which you'd better go straight to sleep."

The younger man drooped. "Help me to my bed, will you?"

From the bed, Mairphy smiled wanly. "Apparently, I'm the invalid, not you. The paralyzer certainly did you no real harm, but the energy chopper made a pretty job of my right leg. By the way, I'll introduce you to Derrel when I wake up."

His slow, deep breathing came as a distinct shock to Garson. He felt deserted, at a loss for action, and finally annoyed at the way he had come to depend on the company of another man.

For a while, he wandered around the room, half aimlessly, half in search of the extraordinary Derrel. But gradually his mind was drawn from that undetermined purpose, as the men, the incredible men, grew into his consciousness.

They swaggered, these chaps. When they stood, they leaned with casual grace, thumbs nonchalantly tucked into belts or into the armpits of strangely designed vests. Not more than half a dozen of that bold, vigorous-looking crew seemed to be the introvert, studious type.

Here were men of the past, adventurers, soldiers of fortune, who had mutinied as easily as, under slightly different circumstances, they might have decided to fight for, instead of against, their captors.

Bad psychology on the part of the Planetarians?

Impossible because they were perfectionists in the art.

The explanation, of course, was that an intelligence and ability as great as their own, or nearly as great, had entered the scene unknown to them, and easily duped the men of the past who operated the spaceship.

Derrel!

The whole thing was strangely, breathlessly exciting, a glittering facet of the full, violent aliveness of the life that had raged over the Earth through the ages; here were men come full grown out of their own times, loving life, yet by their casual, desperate attempt at mutiny proving that they were not remotely afraid of death.

One man was the responsible, the activating force and—

Three times Garson was sure that he had picked out Derrel, but each time he changed his mind before actually approaching the stranger.

It was only gradually that he grew aware of a lank man. The first coherent picture he had was of a tall, gawky man with a long face that was hollow-cheeked. The fellow was dressed casually in a gray shirt and gray trousers. Except for the cleanness of the clothes, he could have stepped out of a 1936 dust-bowl farmhouse.

The man half stood, half leaned, awkwardly against the side of one of the hospital-type beds, and he said nothing. Yet, somehow, he was the center of the group that surrounded him. The leader!

After a moment Garson saw that the other was surreptitiously studying him; and that was all he needed. Quite frankly, quite boldly, he surveyed the man. Before that searching gaze, the deceptive, farmerish appearance of the other dissolved like dark fog in a bright sun.

The hollow cheeks showed suddenly as a natural strength that distorted the almost abnormal strength of that face. The line of jaw ceased to be merely framework supporting the chin, showed instead in all its grim hardness, like the blunt edge of an anvil, not too prominently thrust forward. The nose—

At that point somebody addressed the man as Mr. Derrel; and it was as if Derrel had been waiting for the words as for a signal.

He stepped forward; he said in the calmest voice Garson had ever heard:

"Professor Garson, do you mind if I speak to you"—he motioned forcefully yet vaguely—"over there?"

Garson was amazed to find himself hesitating. For nearly an hour he had had the purpose of finding this man, but now—it was simply not in his nature to yield readily to the leadership of others. It struck him sharply that even to agree to Derrel's simple request was to place himself, somehow, subtly under the man's domination.

Their eyes met, his own hard with thought, Derrel's at first expressionless, then smiling. The smile touched his face and lighted it in astounding fashion. His entire countenance seemed to change; briefly, his personality was like a flame that burned away opposition.

Garson was startled to hear himself say: "Why, yes, what is it you wish?"

The answer was cool and tremendous: "You have received a warning message, but you need look no further for its source. I am Dra Derrel of the Wizard race of Lin. My people are fighting under great difficulties to save a universe threatened by a war whose weapons are based on the time energy itself."

"Just a minute!" Garson's voice was harsh in his own ears. "Are you trying to tell me you . . . your people sent that message?"

"I am!" The man's face was almost gray-steel in color. "And to explain that our position is now so dangerous that your own suggestion that you see Captain Gurradin has become the most important necessity and the best plan—"

Strangely, it was that on which his mind fastened, not the revelation, but the mind picture of himself leaving the placid security of this room, delivering himself into the ruthless clutches of men of some other, more merciless past than his own—and to tentacles—

Like a monstrous shadow overhanging every other emotion, the dark realization came that the law of averages would not permit him to face death again without—death!

Slowly, the other thought—Derrel's revelation—began to intrude. He examined it, at first half puzzled that it continued to exist in his mind; somehow, it wasn't really adequate, and certainly far from satisfactory as an explanation of all that had happened.

A message delivered into the black narrowness of a Glorious depersonalizing machine, hurtled across distance, through a web of Glorious defenses from—

Derrel!

Garson frowned, his dissatisfaction growing by the second. He stared at the man from slitted eyes; and saw that the other was standing in that peculiar easy-awkward posture of his, gazing at him coolly as if—the impression was a distinct one—as if waiting patiently for his considered reaction. That was oddly reassuring, but it was far, far from being enough. Garson said:

"I can see I've got to be frank, or this thing's going to be all wrong. My angle goes like this: I've been building a picture in my mind, an impossible picture I can see now, of beings with tremendous powers. I thought of them as possibly acting from the future of this future, but, whatever their origin, I had the uttermost confidence that they were superhuman, super-Glorious and—"

He stopped because the long-faced man was smiling in twisted fashion. "And now," Derrel said wryly, "the reality does not come up, to your expectations. An ordinary man stands before you, and your dreams of god-power interfering in the affairs of men becomes what it always was basically: wishful hallucination!"

"And in its place—what?" Garson questioned coolly.

Derrel took up the words steadily: "In its place is a man who failed to take over a spaceship, and now faces a sordid death himself."

Garson parted his lips to speak, then closed them again,

puzzled. There was nothing so far but honesty almost excessive. Still—confession was far from being satisfactory explanation.

Derrel's voice, rich with the first hint of passion the man had shown, beat at him: "Are you sure it was such a great failure? One man manipulating strangers who had no reason to fight—many of them invalids—and winning a partial success against the highly trained crew of a completely mechanized space cruiser, a crew supported by no less than four tentacles of the omniscient Observer."

Stripped as the account was, it brought a vivid fascinating flash of what the reality of that fight must have been. Flesh-and-blood men charging forward in the face of—energy—weapons, dealing and receiving desperate wounds, overwhelming the alert and abundant staff of an armored ship, and four tentacles, whatever they were. Tentacle—a potent, ugly word, inhuman— Nevertheless—

"If you're going to use logic on this," Garson said slowly, "you'll have to put up with my brand for another minute. Why did you go in for mutiny in the first place under such difficult conditions?"

Amazingly, the man's eyes flashed with contemptuous fire. When he spoke, his voice was thick with passion: "Can you reasonably ask for more than the reality, which is that our position is desperate because we took risks? We took risks because"—he paused, as if gathering himself; then his words flamed on—"because I am of the race of Wizards; and we were masters of the Earth of our time because we were bold. As was ever the way with the Wizards, I chose the difficult, the dangerous path; and I tell you that victory with all that it means is not yet beyond our grasp. I—"

In the queerest fashion, the glowing voice died. An intent expression crept into the man's eyes; he tilted his head, as if listening for a remote sound. Garson shook the odd impression out of his mind, and returned to the thoughts that had been gathering while the other was speaking; he said coolly:

"Unfortunately, for all that emotion, I was—trained to be a scientist; and I was never taught to accept justification as a substitute for explanation. I—"

It was his turn to fall silent. With startled gaze, he watched the tall, gawky figure stride at top speed along the wall. The Wizard man halted as swiftly as he had started, but now his fingers were working with a strangely frantic speed at a section of the wall.

As Garson came up, the wall slid free; and Derrel, half lowered, half dropped it to the floor. In the hollow space revealed, wires gleamed; and a silver, shining glow point showed. Unhesitatingly, Derrel grasped at the white-hot-looking thing, and jerked. There was a faint flash of fire; and when his hand came away the glow was gone.

Derrel stared at Garson grimly: "Those seeming wires are not wires at all, but a pure energy web, an electron mold that, over a period of about an hour, can mold a weapon where nothing existed before. Tentacles can focus that type of mold anywhere; and the mold itself is indestructible, but up to a certain stage the molded thing can be destroyed."

Garson braced himself instinctively, as the other faced him squarely. Derrel said:

"You can see that, without my special ability to sense energy formations, there would have been surprise tragedy."

"Without you," Garson interjected, "there would have been no mutiny. I'm sorry, but I've got the kind of mind that worries about explanations. So—"

The man gazed at him without hostility; he said finally earnestly: "I know your doubts, but you can see yourself that I must go around examining our rather large territory for further electron-mold manifestations. Briefly, we Wizards are a race of the past who developed a science that enabled us to tap the time ways of the Glorious, though we cannot yet build a time machine. In many ways, we are the superiors of either Planetarians or Glorious. Our mathematics showed us that the time energy could not stand strains beyond a certain point; accordingly we have taken and are taking every possible action to save the Universe, the first and most important necessity being that of establishing a base of operations, preferably a spaceship."

He finished quietly: "For the rest, for the time being you must have faith. Regardless of your doubts, you must go to see the captain; we must win this ship before we are overwhelmed. I leave you now to think it over."

He whirled and strode off; and behind him he left half conviction, half confidence, but—Garson thought wryly— no facts!

What a vague, unsatisfactory basis on which to risk the only life he had!

He found himself straining for sounds, but there was no movement, nothing but a straggle of words that came at him from the other men. The ship itself, the wondrous ship, was quiet. It seemed to be suspended in this remote coign of the Universe; and it at least was not restless. It flashed on in tireless, stupendous flight, but basically it was unhurried, isolated from mechanical necessities, knowing neither doubt nor hope, nor fear nor courage.

Doubt! His brain was a dark opaque mass flecked with the moving lights of thoughts, heavy with the gathering pall of his doubt, knowing finally only one certainty:

With so much at stake, he must find out more about the so-called Wizard of Lin. It would be utterly ridiculous to make some move against the Planetarians, the hope of this war, on the glib say-so of—anyone! But what to do? Where to find out?

The urgent minutes fled. There was the black, incredible vista of space—but no answers offered there. There was lying in bed and staring at the gray ceiling; that was worse. Finally, there was the discovery of the library in a room adjoining the long dormitory; and that held such an immense promise that, for a brief hour, even the sense of urgency faded out of him.

Only gradually did awareness come that the books were a carefully selected collection. At any other time, every word of every page would have held him in thrall, but not now. For a while, with grim good humor, he examined volume after volume to verify his discovery. At last, weary with frustration, he returned to his bed—and saw that Mairphy was awake.

His mind leaped; then he hesitated. It was possible he would have to approach the subject of Derrel warily. He said finally:

"I suppose you've been through the library."

Mairphy shook his head, brown eyes slightly sardonic. "Not that one. But on the basis of the two I have seen, I'll venture to guess they're elementary scientific books, travel books about the planets, but no histories, and nowhere is there a reference to what year this is. They're not even letting us skeptics know that."

Garson cut in almost harshly: "These Planetarians are not such good angels as I thought. In an entirely different, perhaps cleverer way, this ship is organized to press us into their mold just as the Glorious used the deperson—"

He stopped, startled by the hard tenor of his thoughts. Good heavens! At this rate he'd soon work himself into an anti-Planetary fury. Deliberately, he tightened his mind. His job was not to hate, but to ask careful questions about Derrel—and stay alive!

He parted his lips, but before he could speak, Mairphy said: "Oh, the Planetarians are all right. If we hadn't gone in for this damned mutiny, we'd have been treated all right in the long run, provided we kept our mouths shut and conformed."

Garson's mind literally wrenched itself from thought of Derrel. "Mouths shut!" he said. "What do you mean?"

Mairphy laughed mirthlessly: "We're the skeptics who, in a general way, know where we are. The great majority of recruits *don't* know anything except that it's a strange place. For psychological reasons, they've got to feel that they're in perfectly rational surroundings. Their own superstitions provide the solutions.

"A slew of ancient Greeks think they're fighting on the side of Jupiter in the battle of the gods. Religious folks from about four hundred different ignorant ages think for reasons of their own that everything is as it should be. The Lerdite Moralists from the thirtieth century believe this is the war of the Great Machine to control its dissident elements. And the Nelorian Dissenter of the year 7643 to 7699 who— What's the matter?"

Garson couldn't help it. The shock was physical rather than mental. He hadn't, somehow, thought of it when Derrel talked of the Wizards of Lin, but now— His nerves shivered from that casual, stunning array of words. He said finally, shakily:

"Don't mind me. It's those damned dates you've been handing out. I suppose it's really silly to think of time as being a past and a future. It's all there, spread out, six hundred billion earths and universes created every minute." He drew a deep breath. Damn it, he'd stalled long enough. Any minute, Derrel would be coming back and—

He said stiffly: "What about the Wizards of Lin? I heard somebody use the phrase, and it intrigued me."

"Interesting race," Mairphy commented; and Garson sighed with relief. The man suspected no ulterior motive. He waited tensely, as Mairphy went on: "The Wizards discovered some connection between sex and the mind, which gave them superintellect including mental telepathy. Ruled the Earth for about three hundred years, just before the age of Endless Peace set in. Power politics and all that, violence, great on mechanics, built the first spaceship which, according to description, was as good as any that has ever existed since. Most of their secrets were lost. Those that weren't became the property of a special priest clique whose final destruction is a long story and—"

He paused, frowning thoughtfully, while Garson wondered bleakly how he ought to be taking all this. So far, Derrel's story was substantiated practically word for word. Mairphy's voice cut into his indecision:

"There's a pretty story about how the spaceship was invented. In their final struggle for power, a defeated leader, mad with anxiety about his beautiful wife who had been taken as a mistress by the conqueror, disappeared, returned with the ship, got his wife and his power back; and the Derrel dynasty ruled for a hundred years after that—"

"Derrel!" Garson said. "The Derrel dynasty!"

And that, simply yet devastatingly, was that.

The echo of the shock yielded to time and familiarity and died— They talked about it in low tones; and their hushed baritones formed a queer, deep-throated background to the measured beat of Garson's thoughts.

He stepped back, finally, as Mairphy eagerly called other men. With bleak detachment, he listened while Mairphy's voice recast itself over and over into the same shape, the same story, though the words and even the tone varied with each telling. Always, however, the reaction of the men was the same—joy! Joy at the certainty of victory! And what did it matter what age they went to afterward?

Garson grew abruptly aware that Mairphy was staring at him sharply. Mairphy said: "What's the matter?"

He felt the weight of other gazes on him, as he shrugged and said:

"All this offers little hope for me. History records that we won this ship. But I have still to confront the captain; and history is silent as to whether I lived or died—

Frankly, I consider the message that I received in the Glorious depersonalizing machine more important than ever, and accordingly my life is of more importance than that of anyone else on this ship.

"I repeat, our only certainty is that Derrel escaped with the spaceship. Who else lived, we don't know. Derrel—"

"Yes!" said the calm voice of Derrel behind him. "Yes, Professor Garson."

Garson turned slowly. He had no fixed plan; there was the vaguest intention to undermine Derrel's position; and that had made him stress the uncertainty of any of the men escaping. But it wasn't a plan because—there was the unalterable fact that the ship had gotten away; Derrel had won.

No plan— The only factors in his situation were his own tremendous necessities and the inimical environment in which they existed.

For a long moment, he stared at the gangling body, studied the faint triumph that gleamed in the abnormally long yet distinctive face of the Wizard man. Garson said:

"You can read minds. So it's unnecessary to tell you what's going on. What are your intentions?"

Derrel smiled, the glowing, magnetic smile that Garson had already seen. His agate eyes shone, as he surveyed the circle of men; then he began to speak in a strong, resonant voice. There was command in that voice, and a rich, powerful personality behind it, the voice of a man who had won:

"My first intention is to tell everyone here that we are going to an age that is a treasure house of spoils for bold men. Women, palaces, wealth, power for every man who follows me to the death. You know yourself what a damned, barren world we're in now. No women, never anything for us but the prospect of facing death fighting the Glorious still entrenched on Venus or Earth! And a damned bunch of moralists fighting a war to the finish over some queer idea that men ought or ought not to have birth control. Are you with me?"

It was a stirring, a ringing appeal to basic impulses; and the answer could not have been more satisfactory. A roar of voices, cheers; and finally: "What are we waiting for? Let's get going!"

The faint triumph deepened on Derrel's face as he turned back to Garson. He said softly:

"I'm sorry I lied to you, professor, but it never occurred to me that Mairphy or anybody aboard would know my history. I told you what I did because I had read in your mind some of the purposes that moved your actions. Naturally, I applied the first law of persuasion, and encouraged your hopes and desires."

Garson smiled grimly. The little speech Derrel had just given to the men was a supreme example of the encouragement of hopes and desires, obviously opportunistic, insincere and—reliable only if it served the other's future purposes.

He saw that Derrel was staring at him, and he said:

"You know what's in my mind. Perhaps you can give me some of that easy encouragement you dispense. But remember, it's got to be based on logic. That includes convincing me that, if I go to the captain, it is to your self-interest to set me down near a Planetarian stronghold, and that furthermore—"

The words, all the air in his lungs, hissed out of his body. There was a hideous sense of pressure. He was jerked off his feet; and he had the flashing, incomprehending vision of two beds passing by beneath him. Then he was falling.

Instinctively, he put out his hand—and took the desperate blow of the crash onto a third bed. He sprawled there, stunned, dismayed, but unhurt and safe.

Safe from what?

He clawed himself erect, and stood swaying, watching other men pick themselves up, becoming aware for the first time of groans, cries of pain and—

A voice exploded into the room from some unseen source: "Control room speaking! Derrel—the damnedest thing has happened. A minute ago, we were thirty million miles from Venus. Now, the planet's just ahead, less than two million miles, plainly visible. What's happened?"

Garson saw Derrel then. The man was lying on his back on the floor, his eyes open, an intent expression on his face. The Wizard man waved aside his extended hands.

"Wait!" Derrel said sharply. "The tentacle aboard this ship has just reported to the Observer on Venus; and is receiving a reply, an explanation of what happened. I'm trying to get it."

His voice changed, became a monotone: "—the seventeenth x space and time manipulations . . . taking place somewhere in the future . . . several years from now. Your spaceship either by accident or design caught in the eddying current in the resulting time storm— Still not the faintest clue to the origin of the mighty powers being exercised. That is all . . . except that battleships are on the way from Venus to help you—"

Derrel stood up; he said quietly: "About what you were saying, Garson, there is no method by which I can prove that I will do anything for you. History records that I lived out my full span of life. Therefore, no self-interest, no danger to the Universe can affect my existence in the past. You'll have to act on the chance that the opportunity offers for us to give you assistance later, and there's no other guarantee I can give."

That at least was straightforward. Only—to the opportunist, even truth was but a means to an end, a means of lulling suspicion. There remained the hard fact that *he* must take the risks.

He said: "Give me five minutes to think it over. You believe, I can see, that I will go."

Derrel nodded: "Both your conscious and subconscious minds are beginning to accept the idea." There was utterly no premonition in him of the fantastic thing that was going to happen. He thought a gray, cold thought:

So he was going! In five minutes.

He stood finally at the wall visiplate, staring out at the burnished silver immensity of Venus. The planet, already vast, was expanding visibly, like a balloon being blown up. Only it didn't stop expanding and, unlike an overgrown balloon, it didn't explode.

The tight silence was broken by the tallest of the three handsome Ganellians. The man's words echoed, not Garson's thoughts, but the tenor, the dark mood of them:

"So much beauty proves once again that war is the most completely futile act of man. And the worst of it is that, somewhere in the future of this 'future' there are people who know who won this war; and they're doing nothing—damn them!"

His impulse was to say something, to add once more his own few facts to that fascinating subject. But instead he held his thought hard on the reality of what he must do—in a minute!

Besides, Mairphy had described the Ganellians as emotional weaklings, who had concentrated on beauty, and with whom it was useless to discuss anything. True, he himself had given quite a few passable displays of emotionalism. Nevertheless—

The thought ended, as Mairphy said almost impatiently: "We've discussed all that before, and we're agreed that either the people of the future do not exist at all—which means the Universe was blown up in due course by the Glorious time-energy barrier—or, on the other hand, if the people of the future exist, they're simply older versions of the million-year-old bodies of the Planetarians or Glorious. If they exist, then the Universe was not destroyed, so why should they interfere in the war?

"Finally, we're agreed that it's impossible that the people of the future, whatever their form, are responsible for the message that came through to Professor Garson. If they can get through a message at all, why pick Garson? Why not contact the Planetarians direct? Or even warn the Glorious of the danger!"

Garson said: "Derrel, what is your plan of attack?"

The reply was cool: "I'm not going to tell you that. Reason: at close range a tentacle can read an unwary mind. I want you to concentrate on the thought that your purpose is aboveboard, don't even think of an attack in connection with it. Wait—don't reply! I'm going to speak to Captain Gurradin!"

"Eh," Garson began, and stopped.

The Wizard man's eyes were closed, his body rigid. He said, half to Garson, half to the others: "A lot of this stuff here works by mind control—" His voice changed: "Captain Gurradin!"

There was a tense silence; then a steel-hard voice literally spat into the room: "Yes!"

Derrel said: "We have an important communication to make. Professor Garson, one of the men who was unconscious when—"

"I know who you mean!" interrupted that curt voice. "For God's sake, get on with your communication!"

"Not later than the twenty-fourth century," Mairphy whispered to Garson. "Note his reference to God. God was expunged from the dictionary in the 2300s. And is he boiling at this mutiny and what it's done to his prestige!" It wasn't funny. For all this was going to be real to him. The thought drained; Mairphy became a vague background figure. There was only Derrel and Captain Gurradin; Derrel saying:

"Professor Garson has just become conscious; and he has the answer to the phenomena that carried this spaceship thirty million miles in thirty seconds. He feels that he must see you immediately and communicate his message to the Planetarians at once."

There was a wave of chill laughter: "What fools we'd be to let any of you come here until after the battleships arrive! And that's my answer: He'll have to wait till the battleships arrive."

"His message," said Derrel, "cannot wait. He's coming down now, alone."

"He will be shot on sight."

"I can well imagine," Derrel said scathingly, "what the Planetarians would do to you if he is shot. This has nothing to do with the rest of us. He's coming because he must deliver that message. That is all."

Before Garson could speak, Mairphy said in a distinct voice: "I'm opposed to it. I admit it was my idea in the first place, but I couldn't favor it under such circumstances."

The Wizard man whirled on him. His vibrant voice was a drumming thing as he raged:

"That was a stab in the back to all of us. Here is a man trying to make up his mind on a dangerous mission, and you project a weakening thought. You have said that you come from the stormy period following the 13,000 years of Endless Peace. That was after my time, and I know nothing about the age, but it is evident that the softness of the peace period still corroded your people. As a cripple, a weakling, who is not going to do any of the fighting, you will kindly refrain from further advice—to men!"

It could have been devastating, but Mairphy simply shrugged, smiled gently, unaffectedly, at Garson, and said: "I withdraw from the conversation." He finished: "Good luck, friend!"

Derrel, steely-eyed and cold-voiced, said to Garson: "I want to point out one thing. History says we conquered this ship. The only plan we have left revolves around you. Therefore you went to see the captain."

To Garson, to whom logic was the great prime mover, that thought had already come. Besides, his mind had been made up for five minutes.

The second corridor was empty, too; and that strained his tightening nerves to the breaking point. Garson paused stiffly and wiped the thin line of perspiration from his brow.

And still there was no premonition in him of the incredible ending that was coming—for him; nothing but the deadly actuality of his penetration into the depths of a ship that seemed of endless length, and grew vaster with each step that he took.

A door yielded to his touch; and he peered into a great storeroom, piled with freight, thousands of tons, silent and lifeless as the corridors ahead— He walked on, his mind blanker now, held steady far from the thought of Derrel's intended attack.

He thought vaguely: If Norma could keep from Dr. Lell her action of writing a letter to him, then he could keep any thought from *anything* and—

He was so intent that he didn't see the side corridor till the men burst from it—and had him before he could think of fighting. Not that he intended to fight—

"Bring him in here!" said a hard, familiar voice; and after a moment of peering into the shadows of the receding corridor, he saw a slender man in uniform standing beside—

A tentacle!

That thick, pipe-shaped thing could be nothing else— It rolled forward, as if wheels held it up, and its faceted eyes glared at him. It spoke abruptly in a clear, passionless voice:

"I can catch no thoughts, which is unusual. It presupposes schooling, preparation for mindreading attempts. The Observer advises execution—"

The hard, young man's voice said impatiently: "To hell with the Observer. We can always execute. Bring him in here!"

A door opened; and light splashed out. The door closed behind him; and he saw that the room was no more than a small anteroom to some vaster, darkened room beyond.

But he scarcely noticed that. He was thinking with a stinging shock of fury: The logical Observer advising executions without a hearing. Why, that wasn't reasonable. Damn the stupid Observer!

His fury faded into vast surprise, as he stared at the captain. His first impression had been that the other was a young man, but at this closer view, he looked years older, immeasurably more mature. And, somehow, in his keyed-up state, that observation brought immense astonishment. Amazement ended, as his mind registered the blazing question in Captain Gurradin's eyes. Quite automatically, he launched into his story.

When he had finished, the commander turned his hard face to the tentacle: "Well?" he said.

The tentacle's voice came instantly, coldly: "The Observer recalls to your memory its earlier analysis of this entire situation: The destruction of Tentacles 1601, 2 and 3 and the neutralization of electron molds could only have been accomplished with the assistance of a mind reader. Accordingly, unknown to us, a mind reader was aboard.

"Four races in history solved the secret of the training

essential to mental telepathy. Of these, only the Wizards of Lin possessed surpassing mechanical ability—"

It was the eeriness that held his whole mind—at first— the fantastic reality of this thing talking and reasoning like a human being. The Observer Machine of the Glorious that he had seen was simply a vast machine, too big to grasp mentally; like some gigantic number, it was there, and that was all. But this—this long, tubular monstrosity with its human voice and—

Eeriness ended in hard, dismaying realization that a creature that could analyze Derrel's identity might actually prove that death was his own logical lot, and that all else was illusion—

The dispassionate voice went on:

"Wizard men are bold, cunning and remorseless, and they take no action in an emergency that is not related to their purpose. Therefore, this man's appearance is part of a plot. Therefore destroy him and withdraw from the ship. The battleships will take all further action necessary, without further loss of life."

That was stunning. With a sudden, desperate fear, Garson saw that Captain Gurradin was hesitating. The commander said unhappily: "Damn it, I hate to admit defeat."

"Don't be tedious!" said the tentacle. "Your forces might win, but the battleships *will* win."

Decision came abruptly. "Very well," said the captain curtly, "Willant, deenergize this prisoner and—"

Garson said in a voice that he scarcely recognized, an abnormally steady voice: "What about my story?"

Strangely, there was a moment of silence.

"Your story," the tentacle said finally—and Garson's mind jumped at the realization that it was the tentacle, and not the captain who answered—"your story is rejected by the Observer as illogical. It is impossible that anything went wrong with a Glorious depersonalizing machine. The fact that you were repersonalized after the usual manner on reaching our lines is evidence of your condition, because the repersonalizing machine reported nothing unusual in your case.

"Furthermore, even if it was true, the message you received was stupid, because no known power or military knowledge could force the surrender of Delpa one minute sooner. It is impossible to neutralize a time-energy barrier at more than one point at one time without destroying the neutralizing machine. Consequently, the attack can only be made at one point; the military maneuver being used is the ultimate development of dimensional warfare in a given area of space. And so—"

The words scarcely penetrated, though all the sense strained through, somehow. His mind was like an enormous weight, dragging at one thought, one hope. He said, fighting for calmness now:

"Commander, by your manner to this tentacle and its master, I can see that you have long ago ceased to follow its conclusions literally. Why: because it's inhuman; the Observer is a great reservoir of facts that can be coordinated on any subject, but it is limited by the facts it knows. It's a machine, and, while it may be logical to destroy me before you leave the ship, you know and I know that it is neither necessary nor just, and what is overwhelmingly more important, it can do no harm to hold me prisoner, and make arrangements for a Planetarian to examine the origin of the message that came to me."

He finished in a quiet, confident tone: "Captain, from what one of the men told me, you're from the 2000s A.D. I'll wager they still had horse races in your day. I'll wager furthermore that no machine could ever understand a man getting a hunch and betting his bottom dollar on a dark horse. You've already been illogical in not shooting me at sight, as you threatened on the communicator; in not leaving the ship as the Observer advised; in letting me talk on here even as the attack on your enemies is beginning—for there is an attack of some kind, and it's got the best brain on this ship behind it. But that's unimportant because you're going to abandon ship.

"What is important is this: You must carry your illogic to its logical conclusion. Retrieve your prestige, depend for once in this barren life here on luck and luck alone—"

The hard eyes did not weaken by a single gleam, but the hard voice spoke words that sounded like purest music:

"Willant, take this prisoner into the lifeboat and—"

It was at that moment it happened. With victory in his hands, the knowledge that more than two years remained before the time-energy barrier would be threatening the Universe, the whole, rich, tremendous joy that he had won—everything. All of that, and unutterable relief, and more, was in his brain when—

A voice came into his mind, strong and clear and as irresistible as living fire, a woman's voice—Norma's!

"Jack! Jack! Help me! I need you! Oh, Jack, come—"

The Universe spun. Abruptly, there was no ship; and he was pitching into a gulf of blackness. Inconceivable distance fell behind him and—just like that—the fall ended.

There was no ship, no earth, no light—

Time must have passed; for slow thought was in him; and the night remained.

No, not night. He could realize that now, for there was time to realize. It was not night; it was—emptiness. Nothingness!

Briefly, the scientist part of his brain grasped at the idea; the possibility of exploring, of examining this nonspace. But there was nothing to examine, nothing in him to examine with, no senses that could record or comprehend—nothingness!

Dismay came, a black tidal wave that surged in wild confusion through his being; his brain shrank from the sheer, terrible strain of impression. But, somehow, time passed; the flood of despair streamed out of him. There remained *nothingness!*

Change came abruptly. One instant there was that complete isolation; the next—

A man's voice said matter-of-factly: "This one is a problem. How the devil did he get into the configuration of the upper arc? You'd think he fell in."

"No report of any planes passing over Delpa!" said a second voice. "Better ask the Observer if there's any way of getting him out."

Figuratively, gravely, his mind nodded in agreement to that. He'd have to get out, of course, and—

His brain paused. *Out* of where? Nothingness?

For a long, tense moment, his thought poised over that tremendous question, striving to penetrate the obscure depths of it, that seemed to waver just beyond the reach of his reason. There had been familiar words spoken—

Delpa! An ugly thrill chased through his mind. He wasn't in Delpa, or—he felt abruptly, horribly, sick—*or was he?*

The sickness faded into a hopeless weariness, almost a chaotic dissolution: what did it matter where he was? Once more, he was a complete prisoner of a powerful, dominating environment, prey to forces beyond his slightest control, unable to help Norma, unable to help himself and—Norma! He frowned mentally, empty of any emotion, unresponsive even to the thought that what had happened implied some enormous and deadly danger—for Norma! There was only the curious, almost incredible way that she had called him; and nightmarishly he had fallen—toward Delpa! Fallen into an insane region called the configuration of the upper arc—

With a start, he realized that the Observer's voice had been speaking for some seconds:

"—it can be finally stated that no plane, no machine of any kind, has flown over Delpa since the seventeenth time and space manipulation four weeks ago. Therefore the man you have discovered in the upper arc is an enigma, whose identity must be solved without delay. Call your commander."

He waited, for there was nothing to think about—at least not at first. Memory came finally that the spaceship had been pulled a million miles a second by the mysterious seventeenth manipulation of time and space;

only Derrel had distinctly described it as a repercussion from several years in the future. Now, the Observer talked as if it had happened four weeks ago. Funny!

"Nothing funny about it!" said a fourth voice, a voice so finely pitched, so directed into the stream of his thought that he wondered briefly, blankly, whether he had thought the words, or spoken them himself; then:

"Professor Garson, you are identified. The voice you are hearing is that of a Planetarian who can read your mind."

A Planetarian! Wave on wave of relief made a chaos of his brain. With a dreadful effort, he tried to speak, but there was not even a sense of tongue, or lips, or body, nothing but his mind there in that—emptiness; his mind revolving swiftly, ever more swiftly around the host of things he simply had to know. It was the voice, the cool, sane voice, and the stupendous things it was saying, that gradually quieted the turmoil that racked him:

"The answer to what worries you most is that Miss Matheson was the center of the seventeenth space and time manipulation, the first time a human being has been used.

"The manipulation consisted of withdrawing one unit of the entire Solar System from the main stream without affecting the continuity of the main system; one out of the ten billion a second was swung clear in such a fashion that the time energy with its senseless, limitless power began to recreate it, carrying on two with the same superlative ease as formerly with only one.

"Actually, there are now eighteen solar systems existing roughly parallel to each other—seventeen manipulated creations and the original. My body, however, exists in only two of these because none of the previous sixteen manipulations occurred in my lifetime. Naturally, these two bodies of mine exist in separate worlds and will never again have contact with each other.

"Because she was the center of activity, Norma Matheson has her being in the main solar system only. The reason your physical elements responded to her call is that she now possesses the Insel mind power. Her call merely drew you toward her and not to her, because she lacks both the intelligence and the knowledge necessary to a competent employment of her power. As she did not protect you from intermediate dangers, you fell straight into the local time-energy barrier surrounding the city of Delpa, which promptly precipitated you into the time emptiness where you now exist.

"Because of the angle of your fall, it will require an indefinite period for the machines to solve the equation that will release you. Until then, have patience!"

"Wait!" Garson thought urgently. "The great time-energy barrier! It should be completed about now!"

"In two weeks at most," came the cool reply. "We received your story, all right, and transmitted the startling extent of the danger to the Glorious. In their pride and awful determination, they see it merely as a threat to make us surrender—or else! To us, however, the rigidly controlled world they envision means another form of death—a worse form. No blackmail will make us yield, and we have the knowledge that people of the future sent the warning. Therefore—we won!"

There was no time to think that over carefully. Garson

projected his next question hurriedly: "Suppose they're not of the future, not of this seventeenth, or is it eighteenth, solar system? What will happen to me if this solar system explodes out of existence?"

The answer was cooler still: "Your position is as unique as that of Miss Matheson. You fell out of the past into the future; you missed the manipulation. Therefore you exist, not in two solar systems, but only where you are, attached in a general way to us. Miss Matheson exists only in the main system. There is no way in my knowledge that you two can ever come together again. Accustom yourself to that idea."

That was all. His next thought remained unanswered. Time passed; and his restless spirit drooped. Life grew dim within him. He lay without thought on the great, black deep.

Immense, immeasurable time passed; and he waited, but no voices came to disturb his cosmic grave. Twice, forces tugged at him. The first time he thought painfully:

The time-energy barrier of the Glorious had been completed, and the pressure, the tugging was all he felt of the resulting destruction.

If that had happened, nothing, no one would ever come to save him!

That first tugging, and the thought that went with it, faded into remoteness, succumbed to the weight of the centuries, was lost in the trackless waste of the eons that slid by. And finally, when it was completely forgotten, when every thought had been repeated uncountable times, when every plan of action, every theory, every hope and despair—everything—had been explored to the nth degree—the second tug of pressure came.

A probing sensation it was, as if he was being examined; and finally a flaming, devastatingly powerful thought came at him from—outside!

"I judge it an extrusion from a previous universe, a very low form of life, intelligence .007, unworthy of our attention. It must be registered for its infinitesimal influence and interference with energy flowage—and cast adrift."

Returning consciousness stirred in her body. She felt the sigh that breathed from her lips, as dim awareness came that she must leave this place. But there was not yet enough life in her nerves, no quickening of the co-ordination, the concentration, so necessary to the strange, masochistic power she had been given.

She thought drearily: If only she had gone to a window instead of projecting her weak flesh against an impenetrable wall.

She must get to the breakfast-nook window that overlooked the roof.

She stood at the window, weary with pain, vaguely startled by the swift reaction to her thought. Hope came violently, and the thought that she had been briefly crushed by the hard reality of the wall revived—"Pain—No pain can touch me—"

Behind her, footsteps and other—stranger—sounds crashed on the stairway; behind her, the outer door blinked into ravenous flame; ahead—was the dark, lonely night.

She scrambled to the sill— In her ears was the sound of the things that were swarming into her apartment, forcing her to swift *will*. From the edge of the roof she could see the milling beast men on the sidewalk below, and she could see the street corner a hundred yards away.

Instantly, she was at the corner, standing lightly, painlessly, on the pavement. But there were too many cars for further "power" travel, cars that would make devastatingly hard walls.

As she stood in a passion of uncertainty, one of the cars slowed to a stop; and it was the simplest thing to run forward, open the door and climb in, just as it started forward again. There was a small man crouching in the dimness behind the steering wheel. To him, she said, almost matter-of-factly:

"Those men! They're chasing me!"

A swarm of the beast men wallowed awkwardly into the revealing glow of the corner light, squat, apelike, frightening things. Her driver yelped shrilly: "Good God!" The car accelerated.

Almost instantly, the man was babbling: "Get out! Get out! I can't afford to get mixed up in a thing like this! I've got a family—wife—children—waiting for me this instant at home. Get out!"

He shoved at her with one hand, as if he would somehow push her through the closed door. And, because her brain was utterly pliant, utterly geared to flight, she felt scarcely a quiver of resistance. A neon light a block away caught her gaze, her attention, and fitted completely into her automatic yielding to this man's desire. She said:

"There's a taxi stand. Let me off there—"

By the time she climbed out, tentacles were glittering shapes in the air above the dim street behind her. She struck at them with her mind, but they only sagged back, like recoiling snakes, still under control, obviously prepared now for her power.

In the taxi, her mind reverted briefly in astounded thought: That mouse of a man! Had she actually let him control her, instead of forcing the little pipsqueak of a human to her mighty will—

Will! She must use her will. No tentacle can come within—within— She'd have to be practical. How far had they retreated from her power—half a mile? No tentacle can come within half a mile of this car—

Eagerly, she stared out of the rear window, and her eyes widened as she saw they were a hundred yards away and coming closer. *What was wrong?* In brief, shrinking expectation she waited for the devastating fire of third-order energies; and when it did not come, she thought: This car, it must be made to go faster!

There were other cars ahead, and some passing, but altogether not many. There was room for terrible speeds if she had courage, didn't lose control and if the power would work.

"Through there," she directed, *"and through there and around that corner—"*

She heard shrill yells from the driver, but for a time the very extent of his dismay brought encouragement—that faded bleakly as the tentacles continued their glittering course behind her, sometimes close, sometimes far away, but always relentlessly on her trail, unshakably astute in frustrating every twist of her thought, every turn of the car, every hope, only—

Why didn't they attack?

There was no answer to that, as the long night of flight dragged on, minute by slow minute. Finally, pity touched her for the almost mad driver, who half sat, half swooned behind the steering wheel, held to consciousness and to sanity—she could see in his mind—only by the desperate knowledge that this car was his sole means of livelihood, and nothing else mattered besides that, not even death.

Let him go, she thought. It was sheer cruelty to include him in the fate that was gathering out of the night for her. Let him go, but not yet.

At first, she couldn't have told what the purpose was that quivered in her mind. But it was there, deep and chill and like death itself, and she kept directing the car without knowing exactly where she was going.

Conscious understanding of her unconscious will to death came finally, as she climbed to the ground and saw the glint of river through the trees of a park. She thought then, quite simply:

Here in this park, beside this river, where nearly four years before she had come starving and hopeless to commit suicide—here she would make her last stand!

She watched the tentacles floating toward her through the trees, catching little flashing glimpses of them, as the dim, electric lights of the park shimmered against their metallic bodies; and the vast wonder came, untainted by fear:

Was this real? Was it possible that these living, miasmaticlike emanations from the most dreadful nightmare conceivable were actually surrounding her, and that in all this great world of 1944 there was no one, no weapon, no combination of air, land and sea forces, nothing that could offer her even a husk of protection?

In a sudden, wild exasperation, she thrust her power at the nearest glint and laughed a curt, futile laugh when the thing did not even quiver. So far as the tentacles were concerned, her power had been nullified. The implications were ultimate: when Dr. Lell arrived, he would bring swift death with him, unless—

She scrambled down the steep bank to the dark edge of the sullen river; and the intellectual mood that had brought her here to this park where once she had wanted death filled her being. She stood taut, striving for a return of the emotion, for the thought of it was not enough.

If only she could recapture the black, *emotional* mood of that other dark night!

A cool, damp breeze whisked her cheeks—but there was not a fraction of real desire to taste those ugly waters. She wanted, not death, nor power, nor the devastation of third-order energies, but marriage, a home with green grass and a flower garden; she wanted life, contentment, Garson!

Garson!

It was more of a prayer than a command that rose from her lips in that second call for help, an appeal from the depths of her need to the only man whom all these long, deadly years had been in her thoughts:

"Jack, wherever you are, come to me here on Earth, come through the emptiness of time, come safely without pain, without body hurt or damage and with mind clear. Come now!"

With a dreadful start, she jerked back. For a man stood beside her there by the dark waters!

The breeze came stronger. It brought a richer, more tangy smell of river stingingly into her nostrils. But it wasn't physical revival she needed. It was her mind again that was slow to move, her mind that had never yet reacted favorably to her power, her mind lying now like a cold weight inside her. For the figure stood with stonelike solidity, like a lump of dark, roughly shaped clay given a gruesome half-life; she thought in a ghastly dismay: Had she recalled from the dead into dreadful existence a body that may have been lying in its grave for generations?

The thing stirred and became a man. Garson said in a voice that sounded hesitant and huskily unnatural in his own ears:

"I've come—but my mind is only clearing now. And speech comes hard after a quadrillion years." He shuddered with the thought of the countless ages he had spent in eternity; then: "I don't know what happened, I don't know what danger made you call me a second time or whether any exists; but, whatever the situation, I've thought it all out.

"You and I are being used by the mysterious universe manipulators because, according to their history, we were used. They would not have allowed us to get into such desperate straits if they could come to us physically, and yet it is obvious that everything will fail for them, for us, unless they can make some direct physical contact and show us how to use the vast power you have been endowed with.

"They must be able to come only through some outside

force; and only yours exists in our lives. Therefore, call them, call them in any words, for they must need only the slightest assistance. Call them, and afterward we can talk and plan and hope."

Thought began to come to her, and questions, all the questions that had ever puzzled her: Why had Dr. Lell kept repeating that she had made no trouble, according to the Glorious historical record of her, when trouble was all she had ever given? Why had she been able to defeat the first tentacle, and yet now her power that had called *the* man from some remote time was futile against them? And where was Dr. Lell?

With an effort she finally roused her brain from its slough of pondering over paradox. What words she used then, she could not have repeated, or no memory of them remained a moment after they were spoken. In her mind was only a fascinated horror of expectation that grew and grew, as a sound came from the water near her feet.

The water stirred; it sighed as if yielding to some body that pressed its dark elements; it gurgled with a queer, obscene horror; and a body blacker than itself, and bigger than any man made a glinting, ugly rill of foam. It was Jack Garson's fingers, strong and unflinching, grasping her, and his hard determined voice that prevented her from uttering the panicky words of demon exorcise that quivered at the verge of her mind.

"Wait!" he said. "It's victory, not defeat. Wait!"

"Thank you, Professor Garson!" The voice that came out of the darkness held a strange, inhuman quality that kept her taut and uneasy. It went on: "For your sakes, I could approach in no other way. We of the four hundred and ninetieth century A.D. are human in name only. There is a dreadful irony in the thought that war, the destroyer of men, finally changed man into a beastlike creature. One solace remains: We saved our minds and our souls at the expense of our bodies.

"Your analysis was right, Professor Garson, as far as it went. The reason we cannot use so much as a single time machine from our age is that our whole period will be in a state of abnormal unbalance for hundreds of thousands of years; even the tiniest misuse of energy could cause unforeseeable changes in the fabric of time energy, which is so utterly indifferent to the fate of men. Our method could only be the indirect and partially successful one of isolating the explosion on one of eighteen solar systems, and drawing all the others together to withstand the shock. This was not so difficult as it sounds, for time yields easily to simple pressures.

"Miss Matheson, the reason the tentacles could trail you is that you were being subjected to psychological terrors. The tentacles that have been following you through the night were not real but third-order light projections of tentacles, designed to keep you occupied till Dr. Lell could bring his destroyer machines to bear. Actually, you have escaped all their designs. How? I have said time yields easily to proper pressures. Such a pressure existed as you stood by the river's edge trying to recall the black mood of suicide. It was easier for you who have power to slip through time to that period nearly four years ago than for you to recapture an unwanted lust for self-inflicted death."

"Good heavens!" Garson gasped. "Are you trying to tell

us that this is the night of 1941, and that a few minutes from now Dr. Lell will come along and hire a desperate girl sitting on a park bench to be a front for a fake Calonian recruiting station?"

"And this time," said that inhuman voice, "the history of the Glorious will be fulfilled. She will make no trouble."

Garson had the sudden desperate sensation of being beyond his depth. He literally fought for words. "What ... what about our bodies that existed then? I thought two bodies of the same person couldn't exist in the same time and space."

"They can't!"

"But—"

The firm, alien voice cut him off, cut off, too, Norma's sudden, startled intention to speak. "There are no paradoxes in time. I have said that, in order to resist the destruction of the isolated eighteenth solar system, the other seventeen were brought together into one—this one! The only one that now exists! But the others were, and in some form you were in them, but now you are here; and this is the real and only world.

"I leave you to think that over, for now you must act. History says that you two took out a marriage license— tomorrow. History says Norma Garson had no difficulty leading the double life of wife of Professor Garson and slave of Dr. Lell; and that, under my direction, she learned to use her power until the day came to destroy the great energy barrier of Delpa and help the Planetarians to their rightful victory."

Garson was himself again. "Rightful?" he said. "I'm not so convinced of that. They were the ones who precipitated the war by breaking the agreement for population curtailment."

"Rightful," said the voice firmly, "because they first denounced the agreement on the grounds that it would atrophy the human spirit and mind; they fought the war on a noble plane, and offered compromise until the last moment. No automatons on their side; and all the men they directly recruited from the past were plainly told they were wanted for dangerous work. Most of them were unemployed veterans of past wars."

Norma found her voice: "That second recruiting station I saw, with the Greeks and the Romans—"

"Exactly. But now you must receive your first lesson in the intricate process of mind and thought control, enough to fool Dr. Lell—"

The odd part of it was that, in spite of all the words that had been spoken, the warm glow of genuine belief in—everything—didn't come to her until she sat in the dim light on the bench and watched the gaunt body of Dr. Lell stalking out of the shadowed path. Poor, unsuspecting superman!

THE OLDEST SOLDIER
by Fritz Leiber

One of Fritz Leiber's stories is titled "The Haunted
Future," and while it is not part of his Changewar series,
the title aptly describes the eerie mood of that series,
which includes the Hugo-winning novel, The Big Time.
Leiber's opposing sides, called the "Snakes" and "Spiders"
after the identifying patterns on their foreheads, stalk like
ghosts through our past and present, struggling to change
it to bring about a desired, if not quite desirable future.
I'm not sure that "The Oldest Soldier" is part of that series,
though it has been grouped with them in the collection
Changewar (Ace, 1983), but it does involve a man who
says he is a time-traveling soldier. His yarns are taken for
just tall tales intended to amuse the patrons of a local
watering hole—until evidence of his veracity arrives for
the narrator. And, Leiber having been a master of horror
as well as science fiction, it is very unsettling evidence . . .

The one we called the Leutnant took a long swallow of his
dark Löwensbräu. He'd just been describing a battle of

307

infantry rockets on the Eastern Front, the German and Russian positions erupting bundles of flame.

Max swished his paler beer in its green bottle and his eyes got a faraway look and he said, "When the rockets killed their thousands in Copenhagen, they laced the sky with fire and lit up the steeples in the city and the masts and bare spars of the British ships like a field of crosses."

"I didn't know there were any landings in Denmark," someone remarked with an expectant casualness.

"This was in the Napoleonic wars," Max explained. "The British bombarded the city and captured the Danish fleet. Back in 1807."

"Vas you dere, Maxie?" Woody asked, and the gang around the counter chuckled and beamed. Drinking at a liquor store is a pretty dull occupation and one is grateful for small vaudeville acts.

"Why bare spars?" someone asked.

"So there'd be less chance of the rockets setting the launching ships afire," Max came back at him. "Sails burn fast and wooden ships are tinder anyway—that's why ships firing red-hot shot never worked out. Rockets and bare spars were bad enough. Yes, and it was Congreve rockets made the 'red glare' at Fort McHenry," he continued unruffled, "while the 'bombs bursting in air' were about the earliest precision artillery shells, fired from mortars on bomb ketches. There's a condensed history of arms in the American anthem." He looked around smiling.

"Yes, I was there, Woody—just as I was with the South Martians when they stormed Copernicus in the Second Colonial War. And just as I'll be in a foxhole outside

Copeybawa a billion years from now while the blast waves from the battling Venusian spaceships shake the soil and roil the mud and give me some more digging to do."

This time the gang really snorted its happy laughter and Woody was slowly shaking his head and repeating, "Copenhagen and Copernicus and—what was the third? Oh, what a mind he's got," and the Leutnant was saying, "Yah, you vas there—in books," and I was thinking, *Thank God for all the screwballs, especially the brave ones who never flinch, who never lose their tempers or drop the act, so that you never do quite find out whether it's just a gag or their solemnest belief. There's only one person here takes Max even one percent seriously, but they all love him because he won't ever drop his guard....*

"The only point I was trying to make," Max continued when he could easily make himself heard "was the way styles in weapons keep moving in cycles."

"Did the Romans use rockets?" asked the same light voice as had remarked about the landings in Denmark and the bare spars. I saw now it was Sol from behind the counter.

Max shook his head. "Not so you'd notice. Catapults were their specialty." He squinted his eyes. "Though now you mention it, I recall a dogfoot telling me Archimedes faked up some rockets powered with Greek fire to touch off the sails of the Roman ships at Syracuse—and none of this romance about a giant burning glass."

"You mean," said Woody, "that there are other gazebos besides yourself in this fighting-all-over-the-universe-and-to-the-end-of-time racket?" His deep whiskey voice was at its solemnest and most wondering.

"Naturally," Max told him earnestly. "How else do you suppose wars ever get really fought and refought?"

"Why should wars ever be refought?" Sol asked lightly. "Once ought to be enough."

"Do you suppose anybody could time-travel and keep his hands off wars?" Max countered.

I put in my two cents' worth. "Then that would make Archimedes' rockets the earliest liquid-fuel rockets by a long shot."

Max looked straight at me, a special quirk in his smile. "Yes, I guess so," he said after a couple of seconds. "On this planet, that is."

The laughter had been falling off, but that brought it back and while Woody was saying loudly to himself, "I like that refighting part—that's what we're all so good at," the Leutnant asked Max with only a moderate accent that fit North Chicago, "And zo you aggshually have fought on Mars?"

"Yes, I have," Max agreed after a bit. "Though that ruckus I mentioned happened on our moon— expeditionary forces from the Red Planet."

"Ach, yes. And now let me ask you something—"

I really mean that about screwballs, you know. I don't care whether they're saucer addicts or extrasensory perception bugs or religious or musical maniacs or crackpot philosophers or psychologists or merely guys with a strange dream or gag like Max—for my money they are the ones who are keeping individuality alive in this age of conformity. They are the ones who are resisting the encroachments of the mass media and motivation research and the mass man. The only really bad thing about crack pottery and screw-ballistics (as with dope and prostitution) is the coldblooded people who prey on it for money. So I say to all screwballs: Go it on your own. Don't take any wooden nickels or give out any silver dimes. Be wise and brave—like Max.

He and the Leutnant were working up a discussion of the problems of artillery in airless space and low gravity that was a little too technical to keep the laughter alive. So Woody up and remarked, "Say, Maximillian, if you got to be in all these wars all over hell and gone, you must have a pretty tight schedule. How come you got time to be drinking with us bums?"

"I often ask myself that," Max cracked back at him. "Fact is, I'm on a sort of unscheduled furlough, result of a transportation slip-up. I'm due to be picked up and returned to my outfit any day now—that is, if the enemy underground doesn't get to me first."

It was just then, as Max said that bit about enemy underground, and as the laughter came, a little diminished, and as Woody was chortling "Enemy underground now. How do you like that?" and as I was thinking how much Max had given me in these couple of weeks—a guy with an almost poetic flare for vivid historical reconstruction, but with more than that . . . it was just then that I saw the two red eyes low down in the dusty plate-glass window looking in from the dark street.

Everything in modern America has to have a big plate-glass display window, everything from suburban mansions, general managers' offices and skyscraper apartments to barber shops and beauty parlors and ginmills—there are even gymnasium swimming pools with plate-glass

windows twenty feet high opening on busy boulevards—
and Sol's dingy liquor store was no exception; in fact I
believe there's a law that it's got to be that way. But I was
the only one of the gang who happened to be looking out
of this particular window at the moment. It was a dark
windy night outside and it's a dark untidy street at best
and across from Sol's are more plate-glass windows that
sometimes give off very odd reflections, so when I got a
glimpse of this black formless head with the two eyes like
red coals peering in past the brown pyramid of empty
whiskey bottles, I don't suppose it was a half second
before I realized it must be something like a couple of
cigarette butts kept alive by the wind, or more likely a
freak reflection of taillights from some car turning a
corner down street, and in another half second it was
gone, the car having finished turning the corner or the
wind blowing the cigarette butts away altogether. Still, for
a moment it gave me a very goosey feeling, coming right
on top of that remark about an enemy underground.

And I must have shown my reaction in some way, for
Woody, who is very observant, called out, "Hey, Fred, has
that soda pop you drink started to rot your nerves—or are
even Max's friends getting sick at the outrageous lies he's
been telling us?"

Max looked at me sharply and perhaps he saw
something too. At any rate he finished his beer and said,
"I guess I'll be taking off." He didn't say it to me
particularly, but he kept looking at me. I nodded and put
down on the counter my small green bottle, still one-third
full of the lemon pop I find overly sweet, though it was
the sourest Sol stocked. Max and I zipped up our

Windbreakers. He opened the door and a little of the wind came in and troubled the tanbark around the sill. The Leutnant said to Max, "Tomorrow night we design a better space gun;" Sol routinely advised the two of us, "Keep your noses clean;" and Woody called, "So long space soldiers." (And I could imagine him saying as the door closed, "That Max is nuttier than a fruitcake and Freddy isn't much better. Drinking soda pop—ugh!")

And then Max and I were outside leaning into the wind, our eyes slitted against the blown dust, for the three-block trudge to Max's pad—a name his tiny apartment merits without any attempt to force the language.

There weren't any large black shaggy dogs with red eyes slinking about and I hadn't quite expected there would be.

Why Max and his soldier-of-history gag and our outwardly small comradeship meant so much to me is something that goes way back into my childhood. I was a lonely timid child, with no brothers and sisters to spar around with in preparation for the battles of life, and I never went through the usual stages of boyhood gangs either. In line with those things I grew up into a very devout liberal and "hated war" with a mystical fervor during the intermission between 1918 and 1939—so much so that I made a point of avoiding military services in the second conflict, though merely by working in the nearest war plant, not by the arduously heroic route of out-and-out pacifism.

But then the inevitable reaction set in, sparked by the liberal curse of being able, however, belatedly, to see both sides of any question. I began to be curious about and cautiously admiring of soldiering and soldiers. Unwillingly at first, I came to see the necessity and romance of the spearmen—those guardians, often lonely as myself, of the perilous camps of civilization and brotherhood in a black hostile universe... necessary guardians, for all the truth in the indictments that war caters to irrationality and sadism and serves the munition makers and reaction.

I commenced to see my own hatred of war as in part only a mask for cowardice, and I started to look for some way to do honor in my life to the other half of the truth. Though it's anything but easy to give yourself a feeling of being brave just because you suddenly want that feeling. Obvious opportunities to be obviously brave come very seldom in our largely civilized culture, in fact they're clean contrary to safety drives and so-called normal adjustment and good peacetime citizenship and all the rest, and they come mostly in the earliest part of a man's life. So that for the person who belatedly wants to be brave it's generally a matter of waiting for an opportunity for six months and then getting a tiny one and muffing it in six seconds.

But however uncomfortable it was, I had this reaction to my devout early pacifism, as I say. At first I took it out only in reading. I devoured war books, current and historical, fact and fiction. I tried to soak up the military aspects and jargon of all ages, the organization and weapons, the strategy and tactics. Characters like Tros of Samothrace and Horatio Hornblower became my new secret heroes, along with Heinlein's space cadets and Bullard and other brave rangers of the spaceways.

But after a while reading wasn't enough. I had to have

some real soldiers and I finally found them in the little gang that gathered nightly at Sol's liquor store. It's funny but liquor stores that serve drinks have a clientele with more character and comradeship than the clienteles of most bars—perhaps it is the absence of juke-boxes, chromium plate, bowling machines, trouble-hunting, drink-cadging women, and—along with those—men in search of fights and forgetfulness. At any rate, it was at Sol's liquor store that I found Woody and the Leutnant and Bert and Mike and Pierre and Sol himself. The casual customer would hardly have guessed that they were anything but quiet souses, certainly not soldiers, but I got a clue or two and I started to hang around, making myself inconspicuous and drinking my rather symbolic soda pop, and pretty soon they started to open up and yarn about North Africa and Stalingrad and Anzio and Korea and such and I was pretty happy in a partial sort of way.

And then about a month ago Max had turned up and he was the man I'd really been looking for. A genuine soldier with my historical slant on things—only he knew a lot more than I did, I was a rank amateur by comparison—and he had this crazy appealing gag too, and besides that he actually cottoned to me and invited me on to his place a few times, so that with him I was more than a tavern hanger-on. Max was good for me, though I still hadn't the faintest idea of who he really was or what he did.

Naturally Max hadn't opened up the first couple of nights with the gang, he'd just bought his beer and kept quiet and felt his way much as I had. Yet he looked and felt so much the soldier that I think the gang was inclined to accept him from the start—a quick stocky man with big hands and a leathery face and smiling tired eyes that seemed to have seen everything at one time or another. And then on the third or fourth night Bert told something about the Battle of the Bulge and Max chimed in with some things he'd seen there, and I could tell from the looks Bert and the Leutnant exchanged that Max had "passed"—he was now the accepted seventh member of the gang, with me still as the tolerated clerical-type hanger-on, for I'd never made any secret of my complete lack of military experience.

Not long afterwards—it couldn't have been more than one or two nights—Woody told some tall tales and Max started matching him and that was the beginning of the time-and-space-soldier gag. It was funny about the gag. I suppose we just should have assumed that Max was a history nut and liked to parade his bookish hobby in a picturesque way—and maybe some of the gang did assume just that—but he was so vivid yet so casual in his descriptions of other times and places that you felt there had to be something more and sometimes he'd get such a lost, nostalgic look on his face talking of things fifty million miles or five hundred years away that Woody would almost die laughing, which was really the sincerest sort of tribute to Max's convincingness.

Max even kept up the gag when he and I were alone together, walking or at his place—he'd never come to mine—though he kept it up in a minor-key sort of way, so that it sometimes seemed that what he was trying to get across was not that he was the Soldier of a Power that was fighting across all of time to change history, but simply that we men were creatures with imaginations and it was our highest duty to try to feel what it was really like to live in other times and places and bodies. Once he said to me, "The growth of consciousness is everything, Fred—the seed of awareness sending its roots across space and time. But it can grow in so many ways, spinning its web from mind to mind like the spider or burrowing into the unconscious darkness like the snake. The biggest wars are the wars of thought."

But whatever he was trying to get across, I went along with his gag—which seems to me the proper way to behave with any other man, screwball or not, so long as you can do it without violating your own personality. Another man brings a little life and excitement into the world, why try to kill it? It is simply a matter of politeness and style.

I'd come to think a lot about style since knowing Max. It doesn't matter so much what you do in life, he once said to me—soldiering or clerking, preaching or picking pockets—so long as you do it with style. Better fail in a grand style than succeed in a mean one—you won't enjoy the successes you get the second way.

Max seemed to understand my own special problems without my having to confess them. He pointed out to me that the soldier is trained for bravery. The whole object of military discipline is to make sure that when the six seconds of testing come every six months or so, you do the brave thing without thinking, by drilled second nature. It's not a matter of the soldier having some special virtue or virility the civilian lacks. And then about fear. All men are afraid, Max said, except a few psychopathic or suicidal types and they merely haven't fear at the conscious level. But the better you know yourself and the men around you and the situation you're up against (though you can never know all of the last and sometimes you have only a glimmering), then the better you are prepared to prevent fear from mastering you. Generally speaking, if you prepare yourself by the daily self-discipline of looking squarely at life, if you imagine realistically the troubles and opportunities that may come, then the chances are you won't fail in the testing. Well, of course I'd heard and read all those things before, but coming from Max they seemed to mean a lot more to me. As I say, Max was good for me.

So on this night when Max had talked about Copenhagen and Copernicus and Copeybawa and I'd imagined I'd seen a big black dog with red eyes and we were walking the lonely streets hunched in our jackets and I was listening to the big clock over at the University tolling eleven...well, on this night I wasn't thinking anything special except that I was with my screwball buddy and pretty soon we'd be at his place and having a nightcap. I'd make mine coffee.

I certainly wasn't expecting anything.

Until, at the windy corner just before his place, Max suddenly stopped.

Max's junky front room-and-a-half was in a smoky brick building two flights up over some run-down stores. There is a rust-flaked fire escape on the front of it, running past the old-fashioned jutting bay windows, its lowest flight a counter-balanced one that only swings down when somebody walks out onto it—that is, if a person ever had occasion to.

When Max stopped suddenly, I stopped too of course. He was looking up at his window. His window was dark and I couldn't see anything in particular, except that he or somebody else had apparently left a big black bundle of something out on the fire escape and and—it wouldn't be the first time I'd seen that space used for storage and drying wash and whatnot, against all fire regulations, I'm sure.

But Max stayed stopped and kept on looking.

"Say, Fred," he said softly then, "how about going over to your place for a change? Is the standing invitation still out?"

"Sure Max, why not," I replied instantly, matching my voice to his. "I've been asking you all along."

My place was just two blocks away. We'd only have to turn the corner we were standing on and we'd be headed straight for it.

"Okay then," Max said. "Let's get going." There was a touch of sharp impatience in his voice that I'd never heard there before. He suddenly seemed very eager that we should get around that corner. He took hold of my arm.

He was no longer looking up at the fire escape, but I was. The wind had abruptly died and it was very still. As we went around the corner—to be exact as Max pulled me around it—the big bundle of something lifted up and looked down at me with eyes like two red coals.

I didn't let out a gasp or say anything. I don't think Max realized then that I'd seen anything, but I was shaken. This time I couldn't lay it to cigarette butts or reflected taillights, they were too difficult to place on a third-story fire escape. This time my mind would have to rationalize a lot more inventively to find an explanation, and until it did I would have to believe that something...well, alien...was at large in this part of Chicago.

Big cities have their natural menaces—hold-up artists, hopped-up kids, sick-headed sadists, that sort of thing— and you're more or less prepared for them. You're not prepared for something...alien. If you hear a scuttling in the basement you assume it's rats and although you know rats can be dangerous you're not particularly frightened and you may even go down to investigate. You don't expect to find bird-catching Amazonian spiders.

The wind hadn't resumed yet. We'd gone about a third of the way down the first block when I heard behind us, faintly but distinctly, a rusty creaking ending in a metallic jar that didn't fit anything but the first flight of the fire escape swinging down to the sidewalk.

I just kept walking then, but my mind split in two— half of it listening and straining back over my shoulder, the other half darting off to investigate the weirdest notions, such as that Max was a refugee from some unimaginable concentration camp on the other side of the stars. If there were such concentration camps, I told myself in my cold hysteria, run by some sort of supernatural SS men, they'd have dogs just like the one I'd thought I'd seen...and, to be honest, thought I'd *see* padding along if I looked over my shoulder now.

It was hard to hang on and just walk, not run, with this insanity or whatever it was hovering over my mind, and the fact that Max didn't say a word didn't help either.

Finally, as we were starting the second block, I got hold of myself and I quietly reported to Max exactly what I thought I'd seen. His response surprised me.

"What's the layout of your apartment, Fred? Third floor, isn't it?"

"Yes. Well . . ."

"Begin at the door we'll be going in," he directed me.

"That's the living room, then there's a tiny short open hall, then the kitchen. It's like an hour-glass, with the living room and kitchen the ends, and the hall the wasp waist. Two doors open from the hall: the one to your right (figuring from the living room) opens into the bathroom; the one to your left, into a small bedroom."

"Windows?"

"Two in the living room, side by side," I told him. "None in the bathroom. One in the bedroom, onto an air shaft. Two in the kitchen, apart."

"Back door in the kitchen?" he asked.

"Yes. To the back porch. Has glass in the top half of it. I hadn't thought about that. That makes three windows in the kitchen."

"Are the shades in the windows pulled down now?"

"No."

Questions and answers had been rapid-fire, without time for me to think, done while we walked a quarter of a block. Now after the briefest pause Max said, "Look, Fred, I'm not asking you or anyone to believe in all the things I've been telling as if for kicks at Sol's—that's too much for all of a sudden—but you do believe in that black dog, don't you?" He touched my arm warningly. "No, don't look behind you!"

I swallowed. "I believe in him right now," I said.

"Okay. Keep on walking. I'm sorry I got you into this, Fred, but now I've got to try to get both of us out. *Your* best chance is to disregard the thing, pretend you're not aware of anything strange happened—then the beast won't know whether I've told you anything, it'll be hesitant to disturb you, it'll try to get at me without troubling you, and it'll even hold off a while if it thinks it will get me that way. But it won't hold off forever—it's only imperfectly disciplined. *My* best chance is to get in touch with headquarters—something I've been putting off—and have them pull me out. I should be able to do it in an hour, maybe less. You can give me that time, Fred."

"How?" I asked him. I was mounting the steps to the vestibule. I thought I could hear, very faintly, a light pad-padding behind us. I didn't look back.

Max stepped through the door I held open and we started up the stairs.

"As soon as we get in your apartment," he said, "you turn on all the lights in the living room and kitchen. Leave the shades up. Then start doing whatever you might be doing if you were staying up at this time of night. Reading or typing, say. Or having a bite of food, if you can manage it. Play it as naturally as you can. If you hear things, if you feel things, try to take no notice. Above all, don't open the windows or doors, or look out of them to see anything, or go to them if you can help it—you'll probably feel drawn to do just that. Just play it naturally. If you can hold them . . . it . . . off that way for half an hour or so—until midnight, say—if you can give me that much time, I should be able to handle my end of it. And remember, it's the best chance for you as well as for me. Once I'm out of here, you're safe."

"But you—" I said, digging for my key, "—what will you—?"

"As soon as we get inside," Max said, "I'll duck in your bedroom and shut the door. Pay no attention. Don't come after me, whatever you hear. Is there a plug-in in your bedroom? I'll need juice."

"Yes," I told him, turning the key. "But the lights have been going off a lot lately. Someone has been blowing the fuses."

"That's great," he growled, following me inside.

I turned on the lights and went in the kitchen, did the same there and came back. Max was still in the living room, bent over the table beside my typewriter. He had a sheet of light-green paper. He must have brought it with him. He was scrawling something at the top and bottom of it. He straightened up and gave it to me.

"Fold it up and put it in your pocket and keep it on you the next few days," he said.

It was just a blank sheet of cracklingly thin light-green paper with "Dear Fred" scribbled at the top and "Your friend, Max Bournemann" at the bottom and nothing in between.

"But what—?" I began, looking up at him.

"Do as I say!" He snapped at me. Then, as I almost flinched away from him, he grinned—a great big comradely grin.

"Okay, let's get working," he said, and he went into the bedroom and shut the door behind him.

I folded the sheet of paper three times and unzipped my Windbreaker and tucked it inside the breast pocket. Then I went to the bookcase and pulled at random a volume out of the top shelf—my psychology shelf, I remembered the next moment—and sat down and opened the book and looked at a page without seeing the print.

And now there was time for me to think. Since I'd spoken of the red eyes to Max there had been no time for anything but to listen and to remember and to act. Now there was time for me to think.

My first thoughts were: *This is ridiculous! I saw something strange and frightening, sure, but it was in the dark, I couldn't see anything clearly, there must be some simple natural explanation for whatever it was on the fire escape. I saw something strange and Max sensed I was frightened and when I told him about it he decided to play a practical joke on me in line with that eternal gag he lives by. I'll bet right now he's lying on my bed and chuckling, wondering how long it will be before I—*

The window beside me rattled as if the wind had suddenly risen again. The rattling grew more violent— and then it abruptly stopped without dying away, stopped with a feeling of tension, as if the wind or something more material were still pressing against the pane.

And I did not turn my head to look at it, although (or perhaps because) I knew there was no fire escape or other support outside. I simply endured that sense of a presence at my elbow and stared unseeingly at the book in my hands, while my heart pounded and my skin froze and flushed.

I realized fully then that my first skeptical thoughts had been the sheerest automatic escapism and that, just as I'd told Max, I believed with my whole mind in the black dog. I believed in the whole business insofar as I could imagine it. I believed that there are undreamed of powers warring in this universe. I believed that Max was a stranded time-traveller and that in my bedroom he was now frantically operating some unearthly device to signal for help from some unknown headquarters. I believed that the impossible and the deadly was loose in Chicago.

But my thoughts couldn't carry further than that. They kept repeating themselves, faster and faster. My mind felt like an engine that is shaking itself to pieces. And the impulse to turn my head and look out the window came to me and grew.

I forced myself to focus on the middle of the page where I had the book open and start reading.

Jung's archetypes transgress the barriers of time and space. More than that: they are capable of breaking the shackles of the laws of causality. They are endowed with frankly mystical "prospective" faculties. The soul itself, according to Jung, is the reaction of the personality to the unconscious and includes in every person both male and female elements, the animus and anima, as well as the persona or the person's reaction to the outside world. . . .

I think I read that last sentence a dozen times, swiftly at first, then word by word, until it was a meaningless jumble and I could no longer force my gaze across it.

Then the glass in the window beside me creaked.

I laid down the book and stood up, eyes front, and went into the kitchen and grabbed a handful of crackers and opened the refrigerator.

The rattling that muted itself in hungry pressure followed. I heard it first in one kitchen window, then the other, then in the glass in the top of the door. I didn't look.

I went back in the living room, hesitated a moment

beside my typewriter, which had a blank sheet of yellow paper in it, then sat down again in the armchair beside the window, putting the crackers and the half carton of milk on the little table beside me. I picked up the book I'd tried to read and put it on my knees.

The rattling returned with me—at once and peremptorily, as if something were growing impatient.

I couldn't focus on the print any more. I picked up a cracker and put it down. I touched the cold milk carton and my throat constricted and I drew my fingers away.

I looked at my typewriter and then I thought of the blank sheet of *green* paper and the explanation for Max's strange act suddenly seemed clear to me. Whatever happened to him tonight, he wanted me to be able to type a message over his signature that would exonerate me. A suicide note, say. Whatever happened to him . . .

The window beside me shook violently, as if at a terrific gust.

It occurred to me that while I must not look out of the window as if expecting to see something (that would be the sort of give-away against which Max warned me) I could safely let my gaze slide across it—say, if I turned to look at the clock behind me. Only, I told myself, I musn't pause or react if I saw anything.

I nerved myself. After all, I told myself, there was the blessed possibility that I would see nothing outside the taut pane but darkness.

I turned my head to look at the clock.

I saw *it* twice, going and coming back, and although my gaze did not pause or falter, my blood and my thoughts started to pound as if my heart and mind would burst.

It was about two feet outside the window—a face or mask or muzzle of a more gleaming black than the darkness around it. The face was at the same time the face of a hound, a panther, a giant bat, and a man—in between those four. A pitiless, hopeless man-animal face alive with knowledge but dead with a monstrous melancholy and a monstrous malice. There was the sheen of needlelike white teeth against black lips or dewlaps. There was the dull pulsing glow of eyes like red coals.

My gaze didn't pause or falter or go back—yes—and my heart and mind didn't burst, but I stood up then and stepped jerkily to the typewriter and sat down at it and started to pound the keys. After a while my gaze stopped blurring and I started to see what I was typing. The first thing I'd typed was:

the quick red fox jumped over the crazy black dog . . .

I kept on typing. It was better than reading. Typing I was doing something, I could discharge. I typed a flood of fragments: "Now is the time for all good men—", the first words of the Declaration of Independence and the Constitution, the Winston Commercial, six lines of Hamlet's "To be or not to be," without punctuation, Newton's Third Law of Motion, "Mary had a big black—"

In the middle of it all the face of the electric clock that I'd looked at sprang into my mind. My mental image of it had been blanked out until then. The hands were at quarter to twelve.

Whipping in a fresh yellow sheet, I typed the first stanza of Poe's "Raven," the Oath of Allegiance to the American Flag, the lost-ghost lines from Thomas Wolfe, the Creed and the Lord's prayer, "Beauty is truth; truth, blackness—"

The rattling made a swift circuit of the windows— though I heard nothing from the bedroom, nothing at all—and finally the rattling settled on the kitchen door. There was a creaking of wood and metal under pressure.

I thought: *You are standing guard. You are standing guard for yourself and for Max.* And then the second thought came: *If you open the door, if you welcome it in, if you open the kitchen door and then the bedroom door, it will spare you, it will not hurt you.*

Over and over again I fought down that second thought and the urge that went with it. It didn't seem to be coming from my mind, but from the outside. I typed Ford, Buick, the names of all the automobiles I could remember, Overland, Moon, I typed all the four-letter words, I typed the alphabet, lower case and capitals. I typed the numerals and punctuation marks, I typed the keys of the keyboard in order from left to right, top to bottom, then in from each side alternately. I filled the last yellow sheet I was on and it fell out and I kept pounding mechanically, making shiny black marks on the dull black platen.

But then the urge became something I could not resist. I stood up and in the sudden silence I walked through the hall to the back door, looking down at the floor and resisting, dragging each step as much as I could.

My hands touched the knob and the long-handled key in the lock. My body pressed the door, which seemed to surge against me, so that I felt it was only my counter-pressure that kept it from bursting open in a shower of splintered glass and wood.

Far off, as if it were something happening in another universe, I heard the University clock tolling one . . . two . . .

And then, because I could resist no longer, I turned the key and the knob.

The lights all went out.

In the darkness the door pushed open against me and something came in past me like a gust of cold black wind with streaks of heat in it.

I heard the bedroom door swing open.

The clock completed its strokes. Eleven . . . twelve . . .

And then . . .

Nothing . . . nothing at all. All pressures lifted from me. I was aware only of being alone, utterly alone. I knew it, deep down.

After some . . . minutes, I think, I shut and locked the door and I went over and opened a drawer and rummaged out a candle, lit it, and went through the apartment and into the bedroom.

Max wasn't there. I'd known he wouldn't be. I didn't know how badly I'd failed him. I lay down on the bed and after a while I began to sob and, after another while, I slept.

Next day I told the janitor about the lights. He gave me a funny look.

"I know," he said. "I just put in a new fuse this morning. I never saw one blown like that before. The window in the fuse was gone and there was a metal sprayed all over the inside of the box."

That afternoon I got Max's message. I'd gone for a walk in the park and was sitting on a bench beside the lagoon, watching the water ripple in the breeze when I felt something burning against my chest. For a moment I thought I'd dropped my cigarette butt inside my Windbreaker. I reached in and touched something hot in my pocket and jerked it out. It was the sheet of green paper Max had given me. Tiny threads of smoke were rising from it.

I flipped it open and read, in a scrawl that smoked and grew blacker instant by instant:

Thought you'd like to know I got through okay. Just in time. I'm back with my outfit. It's not too bad. Thanks for the rearguard action.

The handwriting (thought-writing?) of the blackening scrawl was identical with the salutation above and the signature below.

And then the sheet burst into flame. I flipped it away from me. Two boys launching a model sailboat looked at the paper flaming, blackening, whitening, disintegrating...

I know enough chemistry to know that paper smeared with wet white phosphorus will burst into flame when it dries completely. And I know there are kinds of invisible writing that are brought out by heat. There are those general sorts of possibility. Chemical writing.

And then there's thoughtwriting, which is nothing but a word I've coined. Writing from a distance—a literal telegram.

And there may be a combination of the two—chemical writing activated by thought from a distance... from a great distance.

I don't know. I simply don't know. When I remember

that last night with Max, there are parts of it I doubt. But there's one part I never doubt.

When the gang asks me, "Where's Max?" I just shrug.

But when they get to talking about withdrawals they've covered; rearguard actions they've been in, I remember mine. I've never told them about it, but I never doubt that it took place.

HOUSE OF BONES
by Robert Silverberg

*"Never volunteer" is an old rule among soldiers, and
ignoring it had left this soldier irrevocably far from home
and his own time. And then his new companions insisted
he go on another mission, not technological this time, but
apparently dangerous... "House of Bones" won the 1989
Locus Award for the year's best short story.*

✳ ✳ ✳

After the evening meal Paul starts tapping on his drum
and chanting quietly to himself, and Marty picks up the
rhythm, chanting too. And then the two of them launch
into that night's installment of the tribal epic, which is
what happens, sooner or later, every evening.

It all sounds very intense but I don't have a clue to the
meaning. They sing the epic in the religious language,
which I've never been allowed to learn. It has the same
relation to the everyday language, I guess, as Latin does
to French or Spanish. But it's private, sacred, for insiders
only. Not for the likes of me.

"Tell it, man!" B.J. yells.

"Let it roll!" Danny shouts.

Paul and Marty are really getting into it. Then a gust of fierce stinging cold whistles through the house as the reindeer-hide flap over the doorway is lifted, and Zeus comes stomping in.

Zeus is the chieftain. Big burly man, starting to run to fat a little. Mean-looking, just as you'd expect. Heavy black beard streaked with gray and hard, glittering eyes that glow like rubies in a face wrinkled and carved by windburn and time. Despite the Paleolithic cold, all he's wearing is a cloak of black fur, loosely draped. The thick hair on his heavy chest is turning gray too. Festoons of jewelry announce his power and status: necklaces of seashells, bone beads, and amber, a pendant of yellow wolf teeth, an ivory headband, bracelets carved from bone, five or six rings.

Sudden silence. Ordinarily when Zeus drops in at B.J.'s house it's for a little roistering and tale-telling and butt-pinching, but tonight he has come without either of his wives, and he looks troubled, grim. Jabs a finger toward Jeanne.

"You saw the stranger today? What's he like?"

There's been a stranger lurking near the village all week, leaving traces everywhere—footprints in the permafrost, hastily covered-over campsites, broken flints, scraps of charred meat. The whole tribe's keyed. Strangers aren't common. I was the last one, a year and a half ago. God only knows why they took me in: because I seemed so pitiful to them, maybe. But the way they've been talking, they'll kill this one on sight if they can. Paul and

Marty composed a Song of the Stranger last week and Marty sang it by the campfire two different nights. It was in the religious language so I couldn't understand a word of it. But it sounded terrifying.

Jeanne is Marty's wife. She got a good look at the stranger this afternoon, down by the river while netting fish for dinner. "He's short," she tells Zeus. "Shorter than any of you, but with big muscles, like Gebravar." Gebravar is Jeanne's name for me. The people of the tribe are strong, but they didn't pump iron when they were kids. My muscles fascinate them. "His hair is yellow and his eyes are gray. And he's ugly. Nasty. Big head, big flat nose. Walks with his shoulders hunched and his head down." Jeanne shudders. "He's like a pig. A real beast. A goblin. Trying to steal fish from the net, he was. But he ran away when he saw me."

Zeus listens, glowering, asking a question now and then—did he say anything, how was he dressed, was his skin painted in any way. Then he turns to Paul.

"What do you think he is?"

"A ghost," Paul says. These people see ghosts everywhere. And Paul, who is the bard of the tribe, thinks about them all the time. His poems are full of ghosts. He feels the world of ghosts pressing in, pressing in. "Ghosts have gray eyes," he says. "This man has gray eyes."

"A ghost, maybe, yes. But what kind of ghost?"

"What *kind*?"

Zeus glares. "You should listen to your own poems," he snaps. "Can't you see it? This is a Scavenger Folk man prowling around. Or the ghost of one."

General uproar and hubbub at that.

Time Troopers

I turn to Sally. Sally's my woman. I still have trouble saying that she's my wife, but that's what she really is. I call her Sally because there once was a girl back home who I thought I might marry, and that was her name, far from here in another geological epoch.

I ask Sally who the Scavenger Folk are.

"From the old times," she says. "Lived here when we first came. But they're all dead now. They—"

That's all she gets a chance to tell me. Zeus is suddenly looming over me. He's always regarded me with a mixture of amusement and tolerant contempt, but now there's something new in his eye. "Here is something you will do for us," he says to me. "It takes a stranger to find a stranger. This will be your task. Whether he is a ghost or a man, we must know the truth. So you, tomorrow: you will go out and you will find him and you will take him. Do you understand? At first light you will go to search for him, and you will not come back until you have him."

I try to say something, but my lips don't want to move. My silence seems good enough for Zeus, though. He smiles and nods fiercely and swings around, and goes stalking off into the night.

They all gather around me, excited in that kind of animated edgy way that comes over you when someone you know is picked for some big distinction. I can't tell whether they envy me or feel sorry for me. B.J. hugs me, Danny punches me in the arm, Paul runs up a jubilant-sounding number on his drum. Marty pulls a wickedly sharp stone blade about nine inches long out of his kit-bag and presses it into my hand.

"Here. You take this. You may need it."

I stare at it as if he had handed me a live grenade.

"Look," I say. "I don't know anything about stalking and capturing people."

"Come *on*," B.J. says. "What's the problem?"

B.J. is an architect. Paul's a poet. Marty sings, better than Pavarotti. Danny paints and sculpts. I think of them as my special buddies. They're all what you could loosely call Cro-Magnon men. I'm not. They treat me just like one of the gang, though. We five, we're some bunch. Without them I'd have gone crazy here. Lost as I am, cut off from I am from everything I used to be and know.

"You're strong and quick," Marty says. "You can do it."

"And you're pretty smart, in your crazy way," says Paul. "Smarter than *he* is. We aren't worried at all."

If they're a little condescending sometimes, I suppose I deserve it. They're highly skilled individuals, after all, proud of the things they can do. To them I'm a kind of retard. That's a novelty for me. I used to be considered highly skilled too, back where I came from.

"You go with me," I say to Marty. "You and Paul both. I'll do whatever has to be done but I want you to back me up."

"No," Marty says. "You do this alone."

"B.J.? Danny?"

"No," they say. And their smiles harden, their eyes grow chilly. Suddenly it doesn't look so chummy around here. We may be buddies but I have to go out there by myself. Or I may have misread the whole situation and we aren't such big buddies at all. Either way this is some kind of test, some rite of passage maybe, an initiation. I don't know. Just when I think these people are exactly like us except for a few piddling differences of customs and languages, I realize how alien they really are. Not savages, far from it. But they aren't even remotely like modern people. They're something entirely else. Their bodies and their minds are pure *Homo sapiens* but their souls are different from ours by 20,000 years.

To Sally I say, "Tell me more about the Scavenger Folk."

"Like animals, they were," she says. "They could speak but only in grunts and belches. They were bad hunters and they ate dead things that they found on the ground, or stole the kills of others."

"They smelled like garbage," says Danny. "Like an old dump where everything was rotten. And they didn't know how to paint or sculpt."

"This was how they screwed," says Marty, grabbing the nearest woman, pushing her down, pretending to hump her from behind. Everyone laughs, cheers, stamps his feet.

"And they walked like this," says B.J., doing an ape-shuffle, banging his chest with his fists.

There's a lot more, a lot of locker-room stuff about the ugly shaggy stupid smelly disgusting Scavenger Folk. How dirty they were, how barbaric. How the pregnant women kept the babies in their bellies twelve or thirteen months and they came out already hairy, with a full mouth of teeth. All ancient history, handed down through the generations by bards like Paul in the epics. None of them has ever actually seen a Scavenger. But they sure seem to detest them.

"They're all dead," Paul says. "They were killed in the migration wars long ago. That has to be a ghost out there."

Of course I've guessed what's up. I'm no archaeologist at all—West Point, fourth generation. My skills are in electronics, computers, time-shift physics. There was such horrible political infighting among the archaeology boys about who was going to get to go to the past that in the end none of them went and the gig wound up going to the military. Still, they sent me here with enough crash-course archaeology to be able to see that the Scavengers must have been what we call the Neanderthals, that shambling race of also-rans that got left behind in the evolutionary sweepstakes.

So there really had been a war of extermination between the slow-witted Scavengers and clever *Homo sapiens* here in Ice Age Europe. But there must have been a few survivors left on the losing side, and one of them, God knows why, is wandering around near this village.

Now I'm supposed to find the ugly stranger and capture him. Or kill him, I guess. Is that what Zeus wants from me? To take the stranger's blood on my head? A very civilized tribe, they are, even if they do hunt huge woolly elephants and build houses out of their whitened bones. Too civilized to do their own murdering, and they figure they can send me out to do it for them.

"I don't think he's a Scavenger," Danny says. "I think he's from Naz Glesim. The Naz Glesim people have gray eyes. Besides, what would a ghost want with fish?"

Naz Glesim is a land far to the northeast, perhaps near what will someday be Moscow. Even here in the

Paleolithic the world is divided into a thousand little nations. Danny once went on a great solo journey through all the neighboring lands: he's a kind of tribal Marco Polo.

"You better not let the chief hear that," B.J. tells him. "He'll break your balls. Anyway, the Naz Glesim people aren't ugly. They look just like us except for their eyes."

"Well, there's that," Danny concedes. "But I still think—"

Paul shakes his head. That gesture goes way back, too. "A Scavenger ghost," he insists.

B.J. looks at me. "What do you think, Pumangiup?" That's his name for me.

"Me?" I say. "What do I know about these things?"

"You come from far away. You ever see a man like that?"

"I've seen plenty of ugly men, yes." The people of the tribe are tall and lean, brown hair and dark shining eyes, wide faces, bold cheekbones. If they had better teeth they'd be gorgeous. "But I don't know about this one. I'd have to see him."

Sally brings a new platter of grilled fish over. I run my hand fondly over her bare haunch. Inside this house made of mammoth bones nobody wears very much clothing, because the structure is well insulated and the heat builds up even in the dead of winter. To me Sally is far and away the best looking woman in the tribe, high firm breasts, long supple legs, alert, inquisitive face. She was the mate of a man who had to be killed last summer because he became infested with ghosts. Danny and B.J. and a couple of the others bashed his head in, by way of a mercy killing, and then there was a wild six-day wake, dancing and wailing around the clock. Because she needed a change of luck they gave Sally to me, or me to her, figuring a holy fool like me must carry the charm of the gods. We have a fine time, Sally and I. We were two lost souls when we came together, and together we've kept each other from tumbling even deeper into the darkness.

"You'll be all right," B.J. says. "You can handle it. The gods love you."

"I hope that's true," I tell him.

Much later in the night Sally and I hold each other as though we both know that this could be our last time. She's all over me, hot, eager. There's no privacy in the bone-house and the others can hear us, four couples and I don't know how many kids, but that doesn't matter. It's dark. Our little bed of fox-pelts is our own little world.

There's nothing esoteric, by the way, about these people's style of love-making. There are only so many ways that a male human body and a female human body can be joined together, and all of them, it seems, had already been invented by the time the glaciers came.

At dawn, by first light, I am on my way, alone, to hunt the Scavenger man. I rub the rough strange wall of the house of bones for luck, and off I go.

The village stretches for a couple of hundred yards along the bank of a cold, swiftly-flowing river. The three round bone-houses where most of us live are arranged in a row, and the fourth one, the long house that is the residence of Zeus and his family and also serves as the temple and house of parliament, is just beyond them. On the far side of it is the new fifth house that we've been building this past week. Further down, there's a workshop where tools are made and hides are scraped, and then a butchering area, and just past that there's an immense garbage dump and a towering heap of mammoth bones for future construction projects.

A sparse pine forest lies east of the village, and beyond it are the rolling hills and open plains where the mammoths and rhinos graze. No one ever goes into the river, because it's too cold and the current is too strong, and so it hems us in like a wall on our western border. I want to teach the tribesfolk how to build kayaks one of these days. I should also try to teach them how to swim, I guess. And maybe a few years farther along I'd like to see if we can chop down some trees and build a bridge. Will it shock the pants off them when I come out with all this useful stuff? They think I'm an idiot, because I don't know about the different grades of mud and frozen ground, the colors of charcoal, the uses and qualities of antler, bone, fat, hide, and stone. They feel sorry for me because I'm so limited. But they like me all the same. And the gods *love* me. At least B.J. thinks so.

I start my search down by the riverfront, since that's where Jeanne saw the Scavenger yesterday. The sun, at dawn on this Ice Age autumn morning, is small and pale, a sad little lemon far away. But the wind is quiet now. The ground is still soft from the summer thaw, and I look for tracks. There's permafrost five feet down, but the topsoil, at least, turns spongy in May and gets downright muddy by July. Then it hardens again and by October it's like steel, but by October we live mostly indoors.

There are footprints all over the place. We wear leather

sandals, but a lot of us go barefoot much of the time, even now, in 40-degree weather. The people of the tribe have long, narrow feet with high arches. But down by the water near the fish-nets I pick up a different spoor, the mark of a short, thick, low-arched foot with curled-under toes. It must be my Neanderthal. I smile. I feel like Sherlock Holmes. "Hey, look, Marty," I say to the sleeping village. "I've got the ugly bugger's track. B.J.? Paul? Danny? You just watch me. I'm going to find him faster than you could believe."

Those aren't their actual names. I just call them that, Marty, Paul, B.J., Danny. Around here everyone gives everyone else his own private set of names. Marty's name for B.J. is Ungklava. He calls Danny Tisbalalak and Paul is Shibgamon. Paul calls Marty Dolibog. His name for B.J. is Kalamok. And so on all around the tribe, a ton of names, hundreds and hundreds of names for just forty or fifty people. It's a confusing system. They have reasons for it that satisfy them. You learn to live with it.

A man never reveals his true name, the one his mother whispered when he was born. Not even his father knows that, or his wife. You could put hot stones between his legs and he still wouldn't tell you that true name of his, because that'd bring every ghost from Cornwall to Vladivostok down on his ass to haunt him. The world is full of angry ghosts, resentful of the living, ready to jump on anyone who'll give them an opening and plague him like leeches, like bedbugs, like every malign and perverse bloodsucking pest rolled into one.

We are somewhere in western Russia, or maybe Poland. The landscape suggests that: flat, bleak, a cold grassy steppe with a few oaks and birches and pines here and there. Of course a lot of Europe must look like that in this glacial epoch. But the clincher is the fact that these people build mammoth-bone houses. The only place that was ever done was Eastern Europe, so far as anybody down the line knows. Possibly they're the oldest true houses in the world.

What gets me is the immensity of this prehistoric age, the spans of time. It goes back and back and back and all of it is alive for these people. We think it's a big deal to go to England and see a cathedral a thousand years old. They've been hunting on this steppe thirty times as long. Can you visualize 30,000 years? To you, George Washington lived an incredibly long time ago.

George is going to have his 300th birthday very soon. Make a stack of books a foot high and tell yourself that that stands for all the time that has gone by since George was born in 1732. Now go on stacking up the books. When you've got a pile as high as a ten-story building, that's 30,000 years.

A stack of years almost as high as that separates me from you, right this minute. In my bad moments, when the loneliness and the fear and the pain and the remembrance of all that I have lost start to operate on me, I feel that stack of years pressing on me with the weight of a mountain. I try not to let it get me down. But that's a hell of a weight to carry. Now and then it grinds me right into the frozen ground.

The flatfooted track leads me up to the north, around the garbage dump, and toward the forest. Then I lose it.

The prints go round and round, double back to the garbage dump, then to the butchering area, then toward the forest again, then all the way over to the river. I can't make sense of the pattern. The poor dumb bastard just seems to have been milling around, foraging in the garbage for anything edible, then taking off again but not going far, checking back to see if anything's been caught in the fish net, and so on. Where's he sleeping? Out in the open, I guess. Well, if what I heard last night is true, he's as hairy as a gorilla; maybe the cold doesn't bother him much.

Now that I've lost the trail, I have some time to think about the nature of the mission, and I start getting uncomfortable.

I'm carrying a long stone knife. I'm out here to kill. I picked the military for my profession a long time ago, but it wasn't with the idea of killing anyone, and certainly not in hand-to-hand combat. I guess I see myself as a representative of civilization, somebody trying to hold back the night, not as anyone who would go creeping around planning to stick a sharp flint blade into some miserable solitary tramp.

But I might well be the one that gets killed. He's wild, he's hungry, he's scared, he's primitive. He may not be very smart, but at least he's shrewd enough to have made it to adulthood, and he's out here earning his living by his wits and his strength. This is his world, not mine. He may be stalking me even while I'm stalking him, and when we catch up with each other he won't be fighting by any rules I ever learned. A good argument for turning back right now.

On the other hand if I come home in one piece with the Scavenger still at large, Zeus will hang my hide on the bone-house wall for disobeying him. We may all be great buddies here but when the chief gives the word, you hop to it or else. That's the way it's been since history began and I have no reason to think it's any different back here.

I simply have to kill the Scavenger. That's all there is to it.

I don't want to get killed by a wild man in this forest, and I don't want to be nailed up by a tribal court-martial either. I want to live to get back to my own time. I still hang on to the faint chance that the rainbow will come back for me and take me down the line to tell my tale in what I have already started to think of as the future. I want to make my report.

The news I'd like to bring you people up there in the world of the future is that these Ice Age folk don't see themselves as primitive. They know, they absolutely *know*, that they're the crown of creation. They have a language—two of them, in fact—they have history, they have music, they have poetry, they have technology, they have art, they have architecture. They have religion. They have laws. They have a way of life that has worked for thousands of years, that will go on working for thousands more. You may think it's all grunts and war-clubs back here, but you're wrong. I can make this world real to you, if I could only get back there to you.

But even if I can't ever get back, there's a lot I want to do here. I want to learn that epic of theirs and write it down for you to read. I want to teach them about kayaks and bridges, and maybe more. I want to finish building

the bone-house we started last week. I want to go on
horsing around with my buddies B.J. and Danny and
Marty and Paul. I want Sally. Christ, I might even have
kids by her, and inject my own futuristic genes into the
Ice Age gene pool.

I don't want to die today trying to fulfill a dumb
murderous mission in this cold bleak prehistoric forest.

The morning grows warmer, though not warm. I pick
up the trail again, or think I do, and start off toward the
east and north, into the forest. Behind me I hear the
sounds of laughter and shouting and song as work gets
going on the new house, but soon I'm out of earshot. Now
I hold the knife in my hand, ready for anything. There are
wolves in here, as well as a frightened half-man who may
try to kill me before I can kill him.

I wonder how likely it is that I'll find him. I wonder
how long I'm supposed to stay out here, too—a couple of
hours, a day, a week?—and what I'm supposed to use for
food, and how I keep my ass from freezing after dark, and
what Zeus will say or do if I come back empty-handed.

I'm wandering around randomly now. I don't feel like
Sherlock Holmes any longer.

Working on the bone-house, that's what I'd rather be
doing now. Winter is coming on and the tribe has grown
too big for the existing four houses. B.J., directs the job
and Marty and Paul sing and chant and play the drum and
flute, and about seven of us do the heavy labor.

"Pile those jawbones chin down," B.J. will yell, as I try
to slip one into the foundation the wrong way around.

"*Chin down*, bozo! That's better." Paul bangs out a terrific riff on the drum to applaud me for getting it right the second time. Marty starts making up a ballad about how dumb I am, and everyone laughs. But it's loving laughter. "Now that backbone over there," B.J. yells to me. I pull a long string of mammoth vertebrae from the huge pile. The bones are white, old bones that have been lying around a long time. They're dense and heavy. "Wedge it down in there good! Tighter! Tighter!" I huff and puff under the immense weight of the thing, and stagger a little, and somehow get it where it belongs, and jump out of the way just in time as Danny and two other men come tottering toward me carrying a gigantic skull.

The winter-houses are intricate and elaborate structures that require real ingenuity of design and construction. At this point in time B.J. may well be the best architect the world has ever known. He carries around a piece of ivory on which he has carved a blueprint for the house, and makes sure everybody weaves the bones and skulls and tusks into the structure just the right way. There's no shortage of construction materials. After 30,000 years of hunting mammoths in this territory, these people have enough bones lying around to build a city the size of Los Angeles.

The houses are warm and snug. They're round and domed, like big igloos made out of bones. The foundation is a circle of mammoth skulls with maybe a hundred mammoth jawbones stacked up over them in fancy herringbone patterns to form the wall. The roof is made of hides stretched over enormous tusks mounted overhead as arches. The whole thing is supported by a

wooden frame and smaller bones are chinked in to seal
the openings in the walls, plus a plastering of red clay.
There's an entranceway made up of gigantic thighbones
set up on end. It may all sound bizarre but there's a weird
kind of beauty to it and you have no idea, once you're
inside, that the bitter winds of the Pleistocene are howling
all around you.

The tribe is semi-nomadic and lives by hunting and
gathering. In the summer, which is about two months
long, they roam the steppe, killing mammoths and rhinos
and musk oxen, and bagging up berries and nuts to get
them through the winter. Toward what I would guess is
August the weather turns cold and they start to head for
their village of bone houses, hunting reindeer along the
way. By the time the really bad weather arrives—think
Minnesota-and-a-half—they're settled in for the winter
with six months' worth of meat stored in deep-freeze pits
in the permafrost. It's an orderly, rhythmic life. There's a
real community here. I'd be willing to call it a civilization.
But—as I stalk my human prey out here in the cold—I
remind myself that life here is harsh and strange. Alien.
Maybe I'm doing all this buddy-buddy nickname stuff
simply to save my own sanity, you think? I don't know.

If I get killed out here today the thing I'll regret most
is never learning their secret religious language and not
being able to understand the big historical epic that they
sing every night. They just don't want to teach it to me.
Evidently it's something outsiders aren't meant to
understand.

The epic, Sally tells me, is an immense account of

everything that's ever happened: the *Iliad* and the *Odyssey* and the *Encyclopedia Britannica* all rolled into one, a vast tale of gods and kings and men and warfare and migrations and vanished empires and great calamities. The text is so big and Sally's recounting of it is so sketchy that I have only the foggiest idea of what it's about, but when I hear it I want desperately to understand it. It's the actual history of a forgotten world, the tribal annals of thirty millennia, told in a forgotten language, all of it as lost to us as last year's dreams.

If I could learn it and translate it I would set it all down in writing so that maybe it would be found by archaeologists thousands of years from now. I've been taking notes on these people already, an account of what they're like and how I happen to be living among them. I've made twenty tablets so far, using the same clay that the tribe uses to make its pots and sculptures, and firing it in the same beehive-shaped kiln. It's a godawful slow job writing on slabs of clay with my little bone knife. I bake my tablets and bury them in the cobblestone floor of the house. Somewhere in the 21st or 22nd century a Russian archaeologist will dig them up and they'll give him one hell of a jolt. But of their history, their myths, their poetry, I don't have a thing, because of the language problem. Not a damned thing.

Noon has come and gone. I find some white berries on a glossy-leaved bush and, after only a moment's hesitation, gobble them down. There's a faint sweetness there. I'm still hungry even after I pick the bush clean.

If I were back in the village now, we'd have knocked

off work at noon for a lunch of dried fruit and strips of preserved reindeer meat, washed down with mugs of mildly fermented fruit juice. The fermentation is accidental, I think, an artifact of their storage methods. But obviously there are yeasts here and I'd like to try to invent wine and beer. Maybe they'll make me a god for that. This year I invented writing, but I did it for my sake and not for theirs and they aren't much interested in it. I think they'll be more impressed with beer.

A hard, nasty wind has started up out of the east. It's September now and the long winter is clamping down. In half an hour the temperature has dropped fifteen degrees, and I'm freezing. I'm wearing a fur parka and trousers, but that thin icy wind cuts right through. And it scours up the fine dry loose topsoil and flings it in our faces. Some day that light yellow dust will lie thirty feet deep over this village, and over B.J. and Marty and Danny and Paul, and probably over me as well.

Soon they'll be quitting for the day. The house will take eight or ten more days to finish, if early-season snowstorms don't interrupt. I can imagine Paul hitting the drum six good raps to wind things up and everybody making a run for indoors, whooping and hollering. These are high-spirited guys. They jump and shout and sing, punch each other playfully on the arms, brag about the goddesses they've screwed and the holy rhinos they've killed. Not that they're kids. My guess is that they're 25, 30 years old, senior men of the tribe. The life expectancy here seems to be about 45. I'm 34. I have a grandmother alive back in Illinois. Nobody here could possibly believe that. The one I call Zeus, the oldest and richest man in town, looks to be about 53, probably is younger than that, and is generally regarded as favored by the gods because he's lived so long. He's a wild old bastard, still full of bounce and vigor. He lets you know that he keeps those two wives of his busy all night long, even at his age. These are robust people. They lead a tough life, but they don't know that, and so their souls are buoyant. I definitely will try to turn them on to beer next summer, if I last that long and if I can figure out the technology. This could be one hell of a party town.

Sometimes I can't help feeling abandoned by my own time. I know it's irrational. It has to be just an accident that I'm marooned here. But there are times when I think the people up there in 2013 simply shrugged and forgot about me when things went wrong, and it pisses me off tremendously until I get it under control. I'm a professionally trained hard-ass. But I'm 20,000 years from home and there are times when it hurts more than I can stand.

Maybe beer isn't the answer. Maybe what I need is a still. Brew up some stronger stuff than beer, a little moonshine to get me through those very black moments when the anger and the really heavy resentment start breaking through.

In the beginning the tribe looked on me, I guess, as a moron. Of course I was in shock. The time trip was a lot more traumatic than the experiments with rabbits and turtles had led us to think.

There I was, naked, dizzy, stunned, blinking and gaping, retching and puking. The air had a bitter acid smell to it—who expected that, that the air would smell different in the past?—and it was so cold it burned my nostrils. I knew at once that I hadn't landed in the pleasant France of the Cro-Magnons but in some harsher, bleaker land far to the east. I could still see the rainbow glow of the Zeller Ring, but it was vanishing fast, and then it was gone.

The tribe found me ten minutes later. That was an absolute fluke. I could have wandered for months, encountering nothing but reindeer and bison. I could have frozen; I could have starved. But no, the men I would come to call B.J. and Danny and Marty and Paul were hunting near the place where I dropped out of the sky and they stumbled on me right away. Thank God they didn't see me arrive. They'd have decided that I was a supernatural being and would have expected miracles from me, and I can't do miracles. Instead they simply took me for some poor dope who had wandered so far from home that he didn't know where he was, which after all was essentially the truth.

I must have seemed like one sad case. I couldn't speak their language or any other language they knew. I carried no weapons. I didn't know how to make tools out of flints or sew a fur parka or set up a snare for a wolf or stampede a herd of mammoths into a trap. I didn't know anything, in fact, not a single useful thing. But instead of spearing me on the spot they took me to their village, fed me, clothed me, taught me their language. Threw their arms around me and told me what a great guy I was. They made me one of them. That was a year and a half ago. I'm a kind of holy fool for them, a sacred idiot.

I was supposed to be here just four days and then the Zeller Effect rainbow would come for me and carry me home. Of course within a few weeks I realized that something had gone wonky at the uptime end, that the experiment had malfunctioned and that I probably wasn't ever going to get home. There was that risk all along. Well, here I am, here I stay. First came stinging pain and anger and I suppose grief when the truth finally caught up with me. Now there's just a dull ache that won't go away.

In early afternoon I stumble across the Scavenger Man. It's pure dumb luck. The trail has long since given out—the forest floor is covered with soft pine duff here, and I'm not enough of a hunter to distinguish one spoor from another in that—and I'm simply moving aimlessly when I see some broken branches, and then I get a whiff of burning wood, and I follow that scent twenty or thirty yards over a low rise and there he is, hunkered down by a hastily thrown-together little hearth roasting a couple of ptarmigans on a green spit. A scavenger he may be, but he's a better man than I am when it comes to skulling ptarmigans.

He's really ugly. Jeanne wasn't exaggerating at all.

His head is huge and juts back a long way. His mouth is like a muzzle and his chin is hardly there at all and his forehead slopes down to huge brow-ridges like an ape's. His hair is like straw, and it's all over him, though he isn't really shaggy, no hairier than a lot of men I've known. His eyes are gray, yes, and small, deep-set. He's built low and thick, like an Olympic weight-lifter. He's wearing a strip of fur around his middle and nothing else. He's an honest-to-God Neanderthal, straight out of the textbooks, and when I see him a chill runs down my spine as though up till this minute I had never really believed that I had traveled 20,000 years in time and now, holy shit, the whole concept has finally become real to me.

He sniffs and gets my wind, and his big brows knit and his whole body goes tense. He stares at me, checking me out, sizing me up. It's very quiet here and we are primordial enemies, face to face with no one else around. I've never felt anything like that before.

We are maybe twenty feet from each other. I can smell him and he can smell me, and it's the smell of fear on both sides. I can't begin to anticipate his move. He rocks back and forth a little, as if getting ready to spring up and come charging, or maybe bolt off into the forest.

But he doesn't do that. The first moment of tension passes and he eases back. He doesn't try to attack, and he doesn't get up to run. He just sits there in a kind of patient, tired way, staring at me, waiting to see what I'm going to do. I wonder if I'm being suckered, set up for a sudden onslaught.

I'm so cold and hungry and tired that I wonder if I'll be able to kill him when he comes at me. For a moment I almost don't care.

Then I laugh at myself for expecting shrewdness and trickery from a Neanderthal man. Between one moment and the next all the menace goes out of him for me. He isn't pretty but he doesn't seem like a goblin, or a demon, just an ugly thick-bodied man sitting alone in a chilly forest.

And I know that sure as anything I'm not going to try to kill him, not because he's so terrifying but because he isn't.

"They sent me out here to kill you," I say, showing him the flint knife.

He goes on staring. I might just as well be speaking English, or Sanskrit.

"I'm not going to do it," I tell him. "That's the first thing you ought to know. I've never killed anyone before and I'm not going to begin with a complete stranger. Okay? Is that understood?"

He says something now. His voice is soft and indistinct, but I can tell that he's speaking some entirely other language.

"I can't understand what you're telling me," I say, "and you don't understand me. So we're even."

I take a couple of steps toward him. The blade is still in my hand. He doesn't move. I see now that he's got no weapons and even though he's powerfully built and could probably rip my arms off in two seconds, I'd be able to put the blade into him first. I point to the north, away from the village, and make a broad sweeping gesture. "You'd be wise to head off that way," I say, speaking very slowly and loudly, as if that would matter. "Get yourself out of the neighborhood. They'll kill you otherwise. You understand? *Capisce? Verstehen Sie?* Go. Scat. Scram. I won't kill you, but they will."

I gesture some more, vociferously pantomiming his route to the north. He looks at me. He looks at the knife. His enormous cavernous nostrils widen and flicker. For a moment I think I've misread him in the most idiotically

naive way, that he's been simply biding his time getting
ready to jump me as soon as I stop making speeches.

Then he pulls a chunk of meat from the bird he's been
roasting, and offers it to me.

"I come here to kill you, and you give me lunch?"

He holds it out. A bribe? Begging for his life?

"I can't," I say. "I came here to kill you. Look, I'm just
going to turn around and go back, all right? If anybody
asks, I never saw you." He waves the meat at me and I
begin to salivate as though it's pheasant under glass. But
no, no, I can't take his lunch. I point to him, and again to
the north, and once more indicate that he ought not to let
the sun set on him in this town. Then I turn and start to
walk away, wondering if this is the moment when he'll
leap up and spring on me from behind and choke the life
out of me.

I take five steps, ten, and then I hear him moving
behind me.

So this is it. We really are going to fight.

I turn, my knife at the ready. He looks down at it sadly.
He's standing there with the piece of meat still in his hand,
coming after me to give it to me anyway.

"Jesus," I say. "You're just lonely."

He says something in that soft blurred language of his
and holds out the meat. I take it and bolt it down fast, even
though it's only half cooked—dumb Neanderthal!—and I
almost gag. He smiles. I don't care what he looks like, if
he smiles and shares his food then he's human by me. I
smile too. Zeus is going to murder me. We sit down
together and watch the other ptarmigan cook, and when
it's ready we share it, neither of us saying a word. He has

trouble getting a wing off, and I hand him my knife, which he uses in a clumsy way and hands back to me.

After lunch I get up and say, "I'm going back now. I wish to hell you'd head off to the hills before they catch you."

And I turn, and go.

And he follows me like a lost dog who has just adopted a new owner.

So I bring him back to the village with me. There's simply no way to get rid of him short of physically attacking him, and I'm not going to do that. As we emerge from the forest a sickening wave of fear sweeps over me. I think at first it's the roast ptarmigan trying to come back up, but no, it's downright terror, because the Scavenger is obviously planning to stick with me right to the end, and the end is not going to be good. I can see Zeus' blazing eyes, his furious scowl. The thwarted Ice Age chieftain in a storm of wrath. Since I didn't do the job, they will. They'll kill him and maybe they'll kill me too, since I've revealed myself to be a dangerous moron who will bring home the very enemy he was sent out to eliminate.

"This is dumb," I tell the Neanderthal. "You shouldn't be doing this."

He smiles again. You don't understand shit, do you, fellow?

We are past the garbage dump now, past the butchering area. B.J. and his crew are at work on the new house. B.J. looks up when he sees me and his eyes are bright with surprise.

He nudges Marty and Marty nudges Paul, and Paul

taps Danny on the shoulder. They point to me and to the
Neanderthal. They look at each other. They open their
mouths but they don't say anything. They whisper, they
shake their heads. They back off a little, and circle around
us, gaping, staring.

Christ. Here it comes.

I can imagine what they're thinking. They're thinking that
I have really screwed up. That I've brought a ghost home
for dinner. Or else an enemy that I was supposed to kill.
They're thinking that I'm an absolute lunatic, that I'm an
idiot, and now they've got to do the dirty work that I was too
dumb to do. And I wonder if I'll try to defend the
Neanderthal against them, and what it'll be like if I do. What
am I going to do, take them all on at once? And go down
swinging as my four sweet buddies close in on me and
flatten me into the permafrost? I will. If they force me to it,
by God I will. I'll go for their guts with Marty's long stone
blade if they try anything on the Neanderthal, or on me.

I don't want to think about it. I don't want to think
about any of this.

Then Marty points and claps his hands and jumps
about three feet in the air.

"Hey!" he yells. "Look at that! He brought the ghost
back with him!"

And then they move in on me, just like that, the four
of them, swarming all around me, pressing close,
pummelling hard. There's no room to use the knife. They
come on too fast. I do what I can with elbows, knees, even
teeth. But they pound me from every side, open fists
against my ribs, sides of hands crashing against the meat
of my back. The breath goes from me and I come close to

toppling as pain breaks out all over me at once. I need all of my strength, and then some, to keep from going down under their onslaught, and I think, this is a dumb way to die, beaten to death by a bunch of berserk cave men in 20,000 B.C.

But after the first few wild moments things become a bit quieter and I get myself together and manage to push them back from me a little way, and I land a good one that sends Paul reeling backward with blood spouting from his lip, and I whirl toward B.J. and start to take him out, figuring I'll deal with Marty on the rebound. And then I realize that they aren't really fighting with me any more, and in fact that they never were.

It dawns on me that they were smiling and laughing as they worked me over, that their eyes were full of laughter and love, that if they had truly wanted to work me over it would have taken the four of them about seven and a half seconds to do it.

They're just having fun. They're playing with me in a jolly roughhouse way.

They step back from me. We all stand there quietly for a moment, breathing hard, rubbing our cuts and bruises. The thought of throwing up crosses my mind and I push it away.

"You brought the ghost back," Marty says again.

"Not a ghost," I say. "He's real."

"Not a ghost?"

"Not a ghost, no. He's live. He followed me back here."

"Can you believe it?" B.J. cries. "Live! Followed him back here! Just came marching right in here with him!" He turns to Paul. His eyes are gleaming and for a second

I think they're going to jump me all over again. If they do I don't think I'm going to be able to deal with it. But he says simply, "This has to be a song by tonight. This is something special."

"I'm going to get the chief," says Danny, and runs off.

"Look, I'm sorry," I say. "I know what the chief wanted. I just couldn't do it."

"Do what?" B.J. asks. "What are you talking about?" says Paul.

"Kill him," I say. "He was just sitting there by his fire, roasting a couple of birds, and he offered me a chunk, and—"

"*Kill* him?" B.J. says. "You were going to kill him?"

"Wasn't that what I was supposed—"

He goggles at me and starts to answer, but just then Zeus comes running up, and pretty much everyone else in the tribe, the women and the kids too, and they sweep up around us like the tide. Cheering, yelling, dancing, pummelling me in that cheerful bone-smashing way of theirs, laughing, shouting. Forming a ring around the Scavenger Man and throwing their hands in the air. It's a jubilee. Even Zeus is grinning. Marty begins to sing and Paul gets going on the drum. And Zeus comes over to me and embraces me like the big old bear that he is.

"I had it all wrong, didn't I?" I say later to B.J. "You were all just testing me, sure. But not to see how good a hunter I am."

He looks at me without any comprehension at all and doesn't answer. B.J., with that crafty architect's mind of his that takes in everything.

"You wanted to see if I was really human, right? If I had compassion, if I could treat a lost stranger the way I was treated myself."

Blank stares. Deadpan faces.

"Marty? Paul?"

They shrug. Tap their foreheads: the timeless gesture, ages old.

Are they putting me on? I don't know. But I'm certain that I'm right. If I had killed the Neanderthal they almost certainly would have killed me. That must have been it. I need to believe that that was it. All the time that I was congratulating them for not being the savages I had expected them to be, they were wondering how much of a savage *I* was. They had tested the depth of my humanity; and I had passed. And they finally see that I'm civilized too.

At any rate the Scavenger Man lives with us now. Not as a member of the tribe, of course, but as a sacred pet of some sort, a tame chimpanzee, perhaps. He may very well be the last of his kind, or close to it; and though the tribe looks upon him as something dopey and filthy and pathetic, they're not going to do him any harm. To them he's a pitiful bedraggled savage who'll bring good luck if he's treated well. He'll keep the ghosts away. Hell, maybe that's why they took me in, too.

As for me, I've given up what little hope I had of going home. The Zeller rainbow will never return for me, of that I'm altogether sure. But that's all right. I've been through some changes. I've come to terms with it.

We finished the new house yesterday and B.J. let me put the last tusk in place, the one they call the ghost-bone, that keeps dark spirits outside. It's apparently a big honor to be the one who sets up the ghost-bone. Afterward the four of them sang the Song of the House, which is a sort of dedication. Like all their other songs, it's in the old language, the secret one, the sacred one. I couldn't sing it with them, not having the words, but I came in with oom-pahs on the choruses and that seemed to go down pretty well.

I told them that by the next time we need to build a house, I will have invented beer, so that we can all go out when it's finished and get drunk to celebrate properly.

Of course they didn't know what the hell I was talking about, but they looked pleased anyway.

And tomorrow, Paul says, he's going to begin teaching me the other language. The secret one. The one that only the members of the tribe may know.

FREE TIME
by Sarah A. Hoyt & Robert A. Hoyt

Technology has been decisive in battles, going back to when someone realized that a pointed stick might beat out fists, or even thrown rocks. That lasted until the guy with the pointed stick went up against the state-of-the-art bow and arrow. If high tech loses to higher tech, R&D is essential, and if a bunch of promising tech types could be living at a faster time rate than the outside world experienced, they might make the government that put them there invincible in war. Except that living in isolation at a different time rate might make them feel unconnected to that government. And even more so for their descendants . . .

The dull thump descended into the subsonic as the metronome in the breacher fell into line with the big metronome inside the rologium. The grinding wheels shrieked around in a perfect arc, ripping the side open with geometric precision. Then they stopped. In a breathless moment, time inside the breacher snapped into synchrony—and with little fanfare, time was passing at seven hundred times the rate that prevailed in the world outside. A plug of steel and concrete wheeled aside weightlessly on automated servos.

The men charged inside. Or rather, twelve men charged—one walked in. Clad in mechanical armor, rifles raised, their feet shattered the tile and their servos made the air buzz. Forward Alliance was not taking chances this time.

They entered the living quarters of the rologium.

The plan was simple. Make a mess, take some hostages, get the attention of whomever was in charge of the rologium, and start making some demands. The Forward Alliance had already sent in a group of men via the front door. They hadn't come back out. The Central Committee was getting extremely impatient with their errant research staff.

There was the expected disarray when their party entered the compound. They'd evidently caught the researchers during the rologium's night cycle. Nevertheless, there were people about in the common area, dressed in unfamiliar and garish styles of sleepware.

The Central Committee of the Forward Alliance had some time ago deemed brightly colored clothing to be an unnecessary and garish extravagance. It meant extra dye factories of varying kinds, not to mention that it disturbed the unity of the people to have so many ways of differentiating themselves from one another. It was a shock to Adam Swessinger to see supposed citizens dressed up as garishly as a sunset in spring.

Merril Greyland, the team leader, a great bear of a man who it seemed impossible to imagine smiling even when he was not dressed in a meshwork of mechanical parts, was up at the fore of the group shouting orders. He fired his gun in the air just to keep the locals baffled. The group started methodically cornering people, forcing them up against the wall, restraining them in a prone position with their arms behind them. They gained control of a corner and worked their way outward. The common areas led by a series of large hallways out through a honeycomb of rooms, but the place they had targeted faced directly onto "Main Street" and had only one angle of approach.

Then, to their great surprise, there was an all too recognizable *ping*.

Adam, not himself a military man by training, turned white, and ducked behind a wall. The rebels were armed! That was unthinkable. He had no idea what they armed themselves with. Although, then again, hadn't they been locked in here with fine fabrication facilities and ample supplies? Hah! What had they been thinking? Making weapons had probably been entirely trivial to these dissenters.

Adam looked around the corner in time to see a device clatter to the ground in front of them.

"Grenade!" someone shouted. The device popped open.

And then there was a terrible sensation of slowness. Suddenly the rebels down the hallway seemed to be moving much faster toward them.

"What the hell?"

"It's some kind of—time bomb. I don't know. Lay down

suppressive fire. The bullets move fast enough it won't make any difference," said Merril.

It would be wrong to say that the actual soldiers in the group didn't bat an eye, because nobody is entirely sanguine when being shot at by people who can take three shots to their one. But the few bullets that connected bounced harmlessly off the mechanical carapaces. Still, they took cover.

Merril shouted back at Adam.

"Dammit Swessinger, earn your keep."

This startled Adam enough to shock him into action. Keeping himself well away from the corner, where a hail of bullets was even now raining for the hallway, he started casting for the Q-Net channels looking for a network that he could connect with, using the Forward Alliance protocol as his basis. He reasoned that even if the rebels had reprogrammed the machines, there was no particular reason for them to develop entirely new protocols.

He turned out to be correct. As he scanned through channel 2687, suddenly his sensors let up. His occipital screen began displaying a set of readouts which would've been meaningless to the layperson, but which to him lay open all of the inner workings of the rologium.

With the skill of a trained technician, he identified power relays on the fire doors in this area. Being fire doors, their failure mode was to close. If, then, someone were to systematically overload them with electricity, causing all the fuses inside them to burst, they would slam shut.

They did so. One of them slammed on the little device and crushed it. Normal time came back.

The hail of fire from the hallway ceased.

The men emerged from cover, keeping their guns trained on the door. Merril circled back and dragged one of the hostages up by his shirt collar.

"I will only say this once," he said. "Who's leading this place?"

The man looked confused.

"Comrade, answer the question," Merril growled, practically shoving a rifle up the man's nose.

"Nobody is leading this place," the man said.

Merril stared.

"Are you deaf, or stupid? Who is in charge? Who gives the orders?"

It is very hard to draw oneself up, while being held by the shirt collar, and with all one's limbs restrained. Nevertheless, the man somehow managed it.

"Nobody, sir. Nobody gives us orders."

Merril growled, and tossed the man backwards. Then, as an apparent afterthought, he shot him.

"Listen up!" he shouted at the arrayed bodies prone on the floor. "We are here to dictate terms to the ringleaders of this place. Do we understand each other? Give me a name."

He kicked one of the hostages. The mechanical suit amplified the movement. The helpless man rolled across the room and into a wall. Nobody said anything.

Then, a small voice came from the side of the group.

"If you're going to shoot us for not declaring our leaders, you might as well get started."

It was an alto voice, although it nevertheless was colored with a dusky timbre that Adam found immediately intriguing. He looked for its source. It turned out to be a redheaded woman in a green nightgown made of slightly silken material. She had rolled upright and was addressing the ceiling.

"You volunteering, miss?" said Merril threateningly.

"Just between the eyes, dirtbag. Make it quick."

Merril started to raise his gun. Without quite knowing why, Adam stepped into his path. Merril swore.

"Sir, just a second, please," he said. He turned to the woman.

"You seem very sure that nobody will betray your leaders even on pain of death, comrade," he looked over at the body and shuddered. "Demonstrated pain of death. Why is that?" he asked.

The woman looked at him. A chill ran down Adam's spine. It seemed for a moment that the woman was reading his life story off the back of his skull. She didn't seem that impressed.

"You can't betray what does not exist. The man spoke truthfully. We have no leaders."

"The hell you don't. You swore an oath to the Forward Alliance, comrade!" shouted one of the soldiers.

The woman eyed him levelly.

"Then call up your Central Committee and dictate your terms to them. Anyway, *comrade*, I am twenty-three years old," she said, the word dripping with sarcasm. "My grandfather swore loyalty to the Forward Alliance, and only because of what you'd do if he didn't."

Merril swept Adam aside and hit her with his rifle butt.

"Enough," he said. He took aim with his rifle.

Once again, not feeling entirely under his own control, Adam moved to push the rifle aside.

Merril raised the weapon to point at him. Adam's blood ran cold. He was armored, but these were armor-piercing rounds. The Forward Alliance had no idea what the threat would be inside the rologium, so they'd prepared for the worst.

"I *will* kill you if you interfere again," he said coldly.

"Sir, the hostages are our leverage. We don't have anything to bargain with if you kill them all," he said, his voice shaking.

Merril stared at Adam for a moment through his helmet. Then he stepped smartly forward, grabbed him by the head and threw him face-first into the ground.

"Take that as a warning," he said, quietly. "For the last time, who is *leading* this rabble?" he roared at the group.

There was laughter, from someone who clearly didn't want to laugh but couldn't believe what they were hearing. Merril turned around in rage, but before he had identified who it was, all the hostages were laughing.

Another voice in the group of prone people shouted defiantly.

"I reckon the gunfire made 'em deaf. One more time with feeling, guys? Three, two, one—"

"We have no leader!" the group of hostages shouted in almost-chorus.

. . . In synchrony with which, the fire door nearest them burst.

Adam awoke in a cell with a pounding headache.

His last waking moments had been a blur. The rebels,

breaking through the door. Merril and his men, countercharging, breaking through the line of advancing men before they knew what was happening. Charging down into the hallway, advancing toward less well-enforced positions.

Leaving Adam alone, and very much surrounded by angry rebels.

The thump on the back of the head, before he could finish standing from where Merril had laid him low.

"Good morning, Corporal. That insignia does mean you're a corporal, doesn't it?"

Adam fought to get his eyes to focus.

He looked up into the eyes of a man who looked about forty, except for neatly combed steel gray hair, and watery blue eyes. He was sitting outside—yes, this was a cell. And that meant—

"You are, from our perspective, a prisoner of war, son. Of course we'll need Forward Alliance to actually recognize our claims of independence first. I guess in the meantime you're our—guest."

Adam sat back in his cell and took stock. He'd been stripped of his suit—obviously—and left only with the long underwear he kept on beneath it, for decency's sake. If the rebels knew their business they'd done a cavity search before letting him wake up, although it wouldn't avail him if they hadn't since he didn't have any life-saving devices secreted away.

Although he felt understandably vulnerable, a small part of him was happy to be out of the metal shell. Unlike the rest of the team he didn't live and work in it every day. He'd mostly been employed for design work on things like

the time rologiums—and the breaching device for the
time rologiums, which the Forward Alliance had
contracted for *in a hurry* after the thousand odd
individuals in the time-accelerated rologium who were
supposed to be designing a superweapon to give them a
definitive edge over World Unity unexpectedly declared
independence just one year into the project. Of course,
that was a hundred and fifty years from the perspective of
the people inside. And would quickly become a lot more,
since they'd sped up the metronome.

He was only in the military because practically
everyone in the Forward Alliance with technical training
was in the military. Whereas Greyland and his men were
notorious for being sent in, not so much when you wanted
to get a job done, as when you wanted to make a point.
He had never seen a dead man until—well, he didn't
know how long he'd been out, but recently. And he wasn't
keen to do it again.

"So what happens now?"

The man shrugged "I suppose we interrogate you."

Adam considered this.

"I'd been hoping to avoid that."

"You could tell us everything you know in advance, if
you like."

Adam also gave this due consideration. He thought of
Ashley, and little Annabelle. Bombs falling in the darkness
five hundred miles away from where he labored for the
Forward Alliance, designing rologiums so they could gain
a research edge on their opponents.

The Forward Alliance said that it had been done by
World Unity. Sometimes, at 2:00 AM, sitting under the

fluorescent lamps and staring at the plans projected through his occipital computer into 3D space in front of them, he needed to believe that. He needed to think that in some small way, his work was helping to avenge their deaths.

He looked up at the man. "I'd like to, but I don't think that I can."

The man nodded, understandingly.

"Torture it is, I'm afraid."

There was a knock at the door.

The man looked over.

"Come in," he said.

To Adam's amazement, the person who entered was the woman who had been mouthing off at Merril.

"What are you doing here, Theresa?"

"I asked to see this gentleman, Phillip."

"It's a bit of a wrench. We were just about to torture him."

The woman gave him a look.

"Phillip, have you ever tortured anyone?"

The man shrugged.

"You never know until you try," he said glibly. "You got a better idea?"

"Give me ten minutes to talk to him."

"Do *you* have any experience torturing people?"

She smiled.

"It's practically in the job description for the female of the species."

"Theresa—"

"Just trust me, please?" she said.

"Make it quick. We don't have a lot of time," he said, standing up. He left.

Theresa sat down across from Adam, demurely sitting with her legs crossed on the stool in front of him.

He smiled grimly.

"Ah, let me see. So that was stick, and you are carrot, I suppose?"

She smiled. It was a surprisingly nice smile. "Should I thank you for the compliment or make a joke about my hair being more a dark red."

It was a very nice dark red. Glossy too, in a way no one in the outside world had. He wondered why. "I meant the first. You're supposed to pretend to like me, so I'll open up?"

"That would be a good idea for next time. We're not as advanced at dealing with prisoners as the Forward Alliance, I'm afraid. I'm just . . . me," the way she said the last part sounded less brazen, and a bit more uncertain. After a moment she said:

"Thank you."

"For what?"

"For keeping me from getting a bullet in the brain. I was raised as a free woman, and expected to die one. There is no freedom without consequences, as my grandfather always said. That doesn't mean I'm not grateful."

Adam looked around at his surroundings.

"That hasn't done me a lot of good."

She snorted.

"The hell it hasn't. You almost got your throat slit, do you know?"

"I didn't."

"*That*, people have had plenty of practice on. Ever

since Forward Alliance sent the first set of bully boys through the front door."

"Ah, so that would be where Team One went."

"Yes," she said, flatly. There was another pause. "I expect you'd do the same if I invaded your home, and rightly so."

Adam grunted.

"I'm not here to ask you for information"—she looked at his shirt—"Swessinger," she said.

"Adam is fine."

"Adam, then. I'm Theresa. Theresa Lamb. I'm here to give you some information."

Adam cleared his throat. "I can't imagine what sort of information you'd offer a man in my position."

"Your team is the devil to kill, did you know that?"

"Only by reputation. I don't usually work with the likes of them."

"I suspected that. What was it that made you stick your neck out for me, anyway? I can't work that out."

He shrugged. He didn't know. He felt a pang in the memory of Ashley as he watched Theresa shift positions on the chair, her limbs sliding easily out of and back into her silken clothing. He didn't know, and he didn't dare ask.

"Very well, then. Well, let me get you up to speed."

Merril shouted orders at the group and called them into order.

They'd killed everyone who stood in their way. As far as Merril was concerned, an enemy was an enemy. The rebels had at least learned not to charge in the open. They were taking potshots every so often, which were as inconsequential as mosquitoes, so far. Little flanking groups were turning out, but they were easily dealt with.

"Sir, without Swessinger it's going to be hard to stop the metronome," a corporal named Hans pointed out.

"Forget him. There's another way."

They brought up the plans of the rologium on their 3D screens and figured out a way down to the power generators.

"They'll be equally vulnerable if the power goes out. Something has to run the metronome."

They tried the elevators at first, but found that the rebels had cut the cables. It was inconvenient but not unexpected.

They found the nearest stairwell and began advancing downward.

But, rabble though they were, the soldiers were only able to advance a short way in that direction before someone clearly sussed out their new plan. This place was so honeycombed with hallways—designed to ease logistical flow around an area designed first and foremost with the research and manufacturing of novel technologies in mind—that it was impossible to stop people getting around them.

A door slammed shut in front of them when they were no more than a few stairways down. Not a fire door, either, but a blast door, designed specifically to form a seal in the event that a reactor went critical.

A moment later, the door slammed shut upstream, behind them.

"Shit. And we don't have anyone who can hack it."

"Screw hacking it."

"You want to blow it?"

"I say we see what these suits can do."

A man named Svenson stepped forward and experimentally flexed his fingers against the metal. There were a few agonizing seconds as the metal protested. Then, it gave way all at once, and he forced his fingers into the gap. Pushing the suit to its limits, he started to draw his hands apart. Giant cogs designed with the idea of keeping the power of the sun at bay fought to the death. Sparks poured out as he wrenched them apart. Beyond them, a kid no more than sixteen years old looked out with frightened eyes from a piece of circuit paneling on the wall which he had just sabotaged. He turned and started to run. Svenson lifted his gun and shot him in the back. His body convulsed, hit the ground, and slid to a halt.

There was a thump in the distance. Further down the hall, another door slid closed. A moment later, there was another pair of thumps to their left and right. And then a series of thumps, duller and duller as they continued on into the distance.

Merril shook his head.

"Idiots. Proceed forward, men. They're going to run out of doors eventually.

"That's bought us time, but it hasn't stopped them," Theresa said. "They're ripping the doors open one at a time with those damned suits of yours. It's not fast, but it's effective. And anyone who tries to flank them is getting cut down."

"I suppose they're thinking that once they get in the

generator room, they'll be able to shut down the power which is keeping the metronome ticking," Adam said, blandly. "You could have worked that out yourself."

"Was that not the plan all along, then?"

It hadn't been the plan, Adam thought to himself. The plan had been to make their way directly to the metronome. It was infinitely more accessible from the living quarters than the generator area, precisely because of the doors Theresa had mentioned. But also, without his expertise, Greyland and his team very likely could not disable it. It probably wouldn't be any deadlier than the clockstopper to disable the metronome haphazardly, but Merril was clearly still thinking he could win this. And he might be right.

He didn't say any of this aloud, but something in his expression must have given Theresa a clue.

"No, huh? Well, could have fooled us."

She shook her head, and then looked at the ground.

"People are gathering for a final defense. There are other ways down besides the main stairwell. We've been monitoring from the cameras. But, you'll be pleased to know, your entire team is still alive."

Theresa was watching him very carefully as she said this. He wasn't sure what to feel in response to it. Apparently this was noted. She smiled and leaned forward.

"That sentence doesn't mean anything to you. You already said you don't usually work with this team, but that's only half the story, isn't it? You're not a soldier, Adam. You're dressed in a soldier's uniform, that's all. We caught you jacked into our Q-Net. You're a technical specialist of some kind, aren't you?"

Adam said nothing.

"Do you know why my grandfather renounced his citizenship, Adam?"

"Do you usually do all the talking during your interrogations?" he interjected blandly.

"What can I say, I'm practicing," she said, "and anyway, getting all the information that I want. Do you know why?"

"No. Why?"

"Because about three years after he started working inside this rologium—which in outside time would have been probably just a week—he got a letter. Communicated over the Q-Net. It told him that his wife and little son had been killed in a bombing by World Unity. He was all alone in the world."

Adam froze.

"But, you see, in a little rologium like this, they can't keep the researchers from talking to one another in their spare time.

Joshua Lamb was, by nature, a neurotic man, with a tendency toward external processing. This usually fatal tendency had not gotten him killed in the Forward Alliance only because he had an exceptional gift for mathematics. Forward Alliance felt that the time rologium was a perfect fit for a man of his excitable temperament. He was the sort to get loose lips when nervous, but if he was bottled up with a bunch of other researchers who were also on a top secret project with him, he remained annoying, but far less actively dangerous.

He was in the lunch room with his closest friend in

the rologium, Leonard Stevens, a physicist from Ohio, and made no attempt to hide the fact that he was upset. Eventually Stevens decided to put Lamb out of his misery.

"What's eating you?" Stevens said, carefully. Though the science fiction stories the Forward Alliance had provided in the hopes of sparking their imaginations had been extensively dampened by a heavy rain of censorship on their journey into the rologium, certain essential ideas had managed to filter through. Joshua Lamb impressed many of his colleagues as a man likely to be a Dr. Ledbetter—the creator of a perfect matter transmuter in one of the old tales—in the flesh, but his roaring engine of a brain heavily overtaxed the two-speed gearbox of his emotions. He was not infrequently at wit's end, and it was often hard to guess why.

Joshua pulled out the letter that had been delivered over the Q-Net. Translation protocols over the time breach were easier on the way in than the way out. To a quantum network it didn't matter at all that time went faster in one place than another—the states flipped from one point to another in synchrony with one another no matter where the two sides were. The only issue was that the time was passing one hundred fifty times slower outside, which meant that a message that took a minute to process and decode outside would take over two and a half hours if being transferred inside. This inconvenience notwithstanding, the Forward Alliance found it helpful to have a means of continuing to send directives into the rologium. Sending directives was in fact a primary function of the Forward Alliance, in the same way that swimming is a primary function of fish. They would hardly know what to do with themselves if they could not.

Leonard read over the letter. His mouth quirked into a grim line. He read over it again. Like most people in the Forward Alliance he'd learned not to wear his emotions on his sleeve. Where Lamb had been forced in, he had volunteered out of patriotic duty. But now, years of training were breaking down. Slowly, carefully, he reached into his pocket and picked out a nearly identical letter. He laid it silently on the table besides Joshua's.

Joshua was from California. He wasn't much of a military strategist or a geographer but Leonard knew something odd when he saw it. And though he didn't show it as much as Joshua, he too was grieving.

Over the course of the next few days the men began to make quiet inquiries around the base. And slowly, the terrible truth began to emerge.

"And that, Adam, is how they all found out that all their loved ones, spread 'cross thousands of miles, in every part of the country, had somehow been mysteriously killed in one night by what one has to suppose was World Unity's most ingeniously coordinated attack yet."

Adam shut his eyes. It was like being punched in the gut.

There was a heavy silence between the two of them. After a while, Theresa said:

"My grandfather never learned what really happened to his wife and son. Some people think that the Forward Alliance just shot them in order to cut the loose ends. They'd promised people who entered the rologium, knowing they would grow old and die without seeing their loved ones again, that those loved ones would be taken care of forever. And they meant it, Mr. Swessinger."

"Shut up," said Adam. Theresa turned her head slightly to the side.

"Now what's gotten into you?"

He took a deep breath and sat upright. He opened his eyes and looked at her.

"Shut. Up."

Theresa gave him a long look. But Adam couldn't find a trace of gloating in it. There was only pity. After another moment she said:

"I'm sorry for your loss."

"They weren't killed by our side."

"Of course. What was I thinking?...anyway. Afterwards, you know, my grandfather wasn't quite the same. He did end up finding a fellow researcher in the rologium who—helped comfort him, I suppose."

Adam stared at her. Theresa looked back.

"What is the point of telling me all this?" Adam said, at last. He blinked, and tears ran down his cheeks. But he stiffened his jaw and set his face like stone. He was a man like all men, and his heart felt cracked in two. But he was not a weak man.

"I suppose I wanted somebody to know, Adam. You see, once your team makes its way to the generator, I give our people maybe fifty-fifty odds against them."

"That's tragically optimistic," he said bluntly. "I'm not keen to test your bullets myself but the ones that did catch us bounced off. It will be a massacre or a miracle, and I'm betting on the massacre."

"*And if* they shut it down," said Theresa, "we're going to fall back into normal time. There are hundreds of people in here who couldn't name the Central Committee members on a bet. *We* certainly don't think of ourselves as part of the Forward Alliance anymore! But they think of us as part of them, you see. And once they flood in here, they're going to expand on what your team is doing. I expect they'll kill us all, and that's if we get lucky. Stories have gotten passed down, you know?"

"And?"

"They might not kill you. You're my chance to pass the story on. To get a little piece of what we learned here out. Who knows? It's all I can do."

She stood up, and turned toward the door. She took a few steps toward it, and then paused.

"I suppose I shouldn't say, but—I don't really think Phillip has it in him to torture you."

She opened the door. Phillip was nearby. He got up, and looked over her shoulder at Adam, sitting tensely with tears in his eyes.

"What did you do?"

"Interrogated him," she said, glumly.

She went to close the door.

Adam stood up.

"Wait," he said. He looked up at Theresa. "I'll talk."

Merril and his team had not come in without contingencies. That was the difference between them and Team One.

"They've got something with them. It's called a clockstopper."

"Ah. That would be that weird device full of Tempux that the first group of you had. We have no idea what it was for but we appreciated the donation toward our metronome. We hoped we'd be able to speed it up enough to buy us some time but, evidently, not enough."

Adam started.

"That was really your whole plan? Extend your time and hope something shows up?"

"Why not? It was the Forward Alliance's whole concept for building this place. Really it still *is* our plan."

Phillip grabbed her arm.

"Theresa," he said, warningly.

She looked back at him.

"Do you see any way we're going to get through this anyway?"

His mouth worked silently. She turned defiantly toward Adam and continued.

"We've been working to manufacture more Tempux to *really* accelerate the metronome. If we can speed up time arbitrarily fast, Forward Alliance's opinion won't matter. We will, de facto, be free, for as long as we wish to be free. I'm happy to hear your team brought another donation to our supply, though I have to ask, why?"

"The clockstopper is designed in such a way that it will cause a catastrophic explosion that propagates in direct proportion to the speed of the time it's moving through. It will scythe the rologium clean if it goes off."

"The Forward Alliance is asking their men to commit suicide?"

"Only in extremis. But they've learned from Team One. Their clockstopper was designed to need manual activation if things went south. This one's on a timer, and without my expertise, it will stay on a timer," said Adam.

"Ah."

"You aren't going to outfight them by conventional means," he said blandly, "and all they have to do is survive long enough for the clockstopper to go. I don't imagine they relish it but the little I've learned of these men suggests they won't flinch from it either." He paused. "You don't happen to have some kind of superweapon that you've developed in here, do you? That *was* supposed to be the whole point. And the Central Committee is convinced that you do."

"Afraid not."

"What about that time grenade someone used on us earlier?"

"That? That's practically a toy. Popular with excitable young boys."

"Can I see one?"

Phillip balked. "I'm pretty sure you're not supposed to give weapons to prisoners of war," he said."

Adam rolled his eyes.

"You caught me. It's part of my devious plan to kill both of you. I'm really hoping that the Forward Alliance will give me a medal"—his voice became bitter—"I'll lay it on my wife's grave. Assuming I ever learn where it is." He looked over at Theresa.

Theresa looked at Phillip.

"Find a damned time grenade."

Grudgingly, Phillip went into the next room. He came back with a little handmade device.

Adam asked for a screwdriver, and disassembled it

rapidly. He poked around at its internals for a few moments.

"This wasn't designed by an engineer," he said at last.

Theresa nodded.

"More a tinkerer. The design is something that was developed by trial and error, really. It's basically like our food storage devices, except it radiates out from a point.

"That was a nontrivial achievement, mind you," Adam admitted. The rologium was designed as it was because shaping an area that was having its tick rate changed by a metronome was difficult. It became infinitely harder without some sort of a rigid frame. Really, as far as the engineers outside the rologium knew, it was impossible. But now that he saw how it was done—simple, but beautiful. He wasn't sure if it was a piece of genius insight or blind luck, but there was a breakthrough here, in infant form.

"They aren't very dangerous the way they are. A trained fighting man still reacts fast enough to be able to deal with untrained people taking potshots at him across that time differential. But I think I see the principle at work. If you can find me a couple more of these and a larger power supply, I think I can fix that."

They could.

"What's your plan?"

Adam and Theresa made their way down the hall. Giant turbines hummed on either side of them. The rologium was self-contained with nuclear reactors designed for a thousand years of continuous operation. The Forward Alliance felt that if a thousand years of continuous work relative to the outside was not enough for the people in the rologium to come up with a superweapon, probably no superweapon was forthcoming.

Adam made no effort to conceal himself. He stood right by the reactor nearest to the front, directly in the path from the doors. Hundreds of people were milling around.

Theresa passed the message down the line that everyone was to fall back. The rebels did indeed not have any leaders. That did not mean they had no organization. But they didn't need much additional encouragement to follow common sense.

When Merril and his team arrived at the bottom of the stairs they found Adam, apparently alone in his suit, standing and waiting for them. The overhead lights cast his shadow far in front of him, overlapping the doorway as the men wrenched open the door with their mechanical arms and advanced.

They slowed down as they recognized him.

"Swessinger? How in the hell did you get down here?"

"I walked. These rebels aren't much good at fighting."

"You're a bad liar, you know that?"

Theresa, prone in the shadows behind them, took aim with an anti-tank gun that had sat in the armory of the rologium for some time. One advantage of defending a place designed explicitly to engineer weaponry was that many experiments had been left lying around. She picked out the man with the pack that Adam had pointed out as the clockstopper. There was a deafening *thump* as she fired the weapon, catapulting the man out of the group. As the soldiers turned, Adam rolled his modified clockstopper into the midst of the crowd.

It popped open. This time, a purple light flared at the

center of the device as it dissolved its entire Tempux load in one go. The group dissolved into dust.

Adam and Theresa took a few deep breaths and walked over to what was left of the man hit by the tank killer. Adam regarded the remains for a second, then turned away. He still hadn't developed much stomach for dead bodies, especially not such incredibly dead bodies. Nonetheless, he eventually managed to collect himself.

"Well done. If we hadn't gotten him separated from the group the clockstopper would have run out its clock in nanoseconds."

"What do we do now?"

The last modifications to the metronome clicked into place. Adam and Theresa looked over the final checks.

The rebels had done a good job by themselves, and had pushed the metronome to limits that nobody had dared before. It had been designed to get one hundred fifty years to the year. They had pushed it to rather more than seven hundred with the Tempux that they had harvested from the first clockstopper. Now—

"This is going to be the fastest metronome in human history."

"They'll be making plans to follow up their last mission, you know."

Theresa shrugged.

"Let them. By the time this thing comes online—and with the design optimizations you contributed—we're going to be doing ten thousand years in here to one *day* out there."

"Even so—do you think there's a chance—?"

Theresa pulled him close.

"Not in a million years," she said, and kissed him. Above them, the Republic of Free Time, an hourglass in the blue field of an old-fashioned American flag, was being prepared to be raised up.

General Vonner was having an extremely bad day. He had lost two military incursion teams in the past week, and he had just heard from the people monitoring the rologium that not only had they lost contact with Team Two, but the metronome inside the rologium had actually just sped up considerably. The teams said—well, anyway, the numbers were unbelievable. The instruments had to be broken. There was no way the metronome could be going that fast.

He was on the phone directly to the Central Committee.

"I don't know what they have in there, but they've made two strike teams vanish. Like they weren't even there."

"Those strike teams were your direct responsibility, General."

"I'm fighting one hundred fifty years of technological development. This is as bad as fighting the gun with a bow and arrow. I don't know what it is, but—"

"It *cannot* be allowed to fall into the hands of World Unity, you understand that, comrade?"

"Yes, sir."

"Send in a second breacher with just a clockstopper. Take no chances. Perhaps we will be able to work out what this miracle technology was from its slag."

"I—yes, sir."

He turned off the Q-Net, and walked out of the forward base to regard the front door of the rologium, when, to his surprise, alarms started going off, and the front door of the rologium started to open.

His mouth dropped open. Could they really be surrendering? Just like that?

Out of the blinding light beyond walked a humanoid figure. It was eight feet tall if it was an inch. It was clad in shining white armor that didn't show a seam anywhere, yet bent easily, so that at each moment its owner seemed to be a shining alabaster statue in motion. It was carrying some kind of strange device in its right hand and a flag of the old corrupt republic, with an hourglass in the blue field, in its left.

Men fired at it, but the bullets created a brief blue glow and were swallowed up.

The figure gestured casually at the troops, and to the amazement of the general, they turned into gold, and then crumbled into dust. The figure strode toward him and stopped a few feet in front of him. For a moment he got a sense this suit—this thing—was being worn by a petite redheaded woman. He couldn't tell how because he didn't precisely see her.

He drew his service pistol and fired, but it had no effect other than pretty blue sparkles. It stopped. It seemed to regard him for a long while. It was hard to tell because he couldn't tell where the eyes were.

"My name is Jennifer Lamb Swessinger," it said in a beautiful tone with metallic overtones.

"Millenia ago, my ancestor charged us with delivering a message—"

The figure gestured back to hundreds of similar creatures emerging from the front door of the rologium.

"—message goes—the Republic of Free Time greets you. The invasion begins now."

She pointed at the luckless general.

And by the power of technologies thousands of years beyond his understanding, he was reduced to a pile of gold.

CHOOSERS OF THE SLAIN
by John C. Wright

The Valkyries, of Norse mythology, were choosers of the slain, carrying worthy but no longer breathing warriors off to Valhalla. This warrior was still breathing, but the heroic act he was planning might put a stop to that... unless a time-traveling Valkyrie equivalent could tempt him to put valor aside...

The time was Autumn, and what few beech trees had been spared, released gold leaves into the chilly air, to swirl and dance and fall. Defoliants, and poisons, had reduced the greater number of the trees to leafless, sickly hulks, unwholesome to behold; and where the weapons of the enemy had fallen, running walls of fire had consumed them, leaving stands of wood and smoking ash. But here and there within the ruin, defying destruction, a kingly tree raised up a bounty of leaves, shining green-gold in the setting sun. Through the ruins of the forest came a man. He was past his youth, and past the middle

393

of his age, but not yet old. His posture was erect, untiring, unbowed, and strong. His hair was iron-grey with age, his face was lined and careworn. The sternness of his glance showed he had been a leader of men, used to command. The sorrow and cold rage kindled in his eye showed he was no more. The furtive silence of his footstep, the quick grace of his flight, showed that he was hunted.

He wore the uniform of a warrior of his day and age. The fabric was soft dove-grey, broken into unpatterned lines and shadows. The fabric faded to dull green when he stood near a flowering bush, or darkened to grey-black when he ran across an open space thick with piles of ash.

Across his back he bore a weapon which could fire a dozen missiles no larger than his littlest finger. The missiles could be programmed to seek and dive, circle and evade; or to search out specific individuals, whose signatures of heat, or auranetic patterns, matched those locked within the little bullets. The little bullets could fly for hundreds of yards, hunting, or, if fired with a booster, reach enemies miles away. On his shoulder, he wore his medical appliance, with needles stabbed into the great veins of his arm, and colored tabs to show what plagues and viruses of the enemy had been found and contradicted in his blood.

Hanging open at his throat, there hung a mask to filter poisoned air. He left it dangling loose now as he walked, for the wind was fresh, and smelled of the salt sea, and blew into the east, toward the patrols he fled. When he came clear of the trees, he saw a rushing mountain stream, but poisoned now, and clogged with stinking fish and blood. He had climbed higher than he knew. Not a dozen

paces to his left, the stream fell out into the air, and let a
bloody waterfall tumbled down high cliffs once green with
trees.

He knew these cliffs; he had climbed and played upon
them as a boy. Once he had climbed their craggy sides to
a high place not far from here, and felt such crowning
triumph and such joy as he had not felt again, not even
when the many fighting factions of his land had united all
beneath his hand to join in common bond to repel the
invaders from over the sea.

For many years he had ruled a turbulent people, united
them in one cause, and laid down strict laws to govern
them, laws he prayed were fair and just. Now,
remembering the way, he climbed the rocks again to find,
unchanged, that wide and grassy ledge where once he
viewed in triumph the green field of his youth.

When he turned and looked out upon the world, he
saw the hills and deep-delved valleys fall away into the
roads and fields and cottages, now blackened and
deserted. By the river in the distance, he could see the
city burning which once had been his capital. The bridges
leading to the city had been shattered; the tall towers
beyond had been thrown down, or tilted on their
foundations like senile drunks. The airfield, bare of ships,
was cracked and torn. Where once his mansion stood, a
crater smoked.

Sirens wailed to no avail. There was no one to answer.

On the far horizon, red with sunset, was the sea.
Against the clouds stained red with dying light loomed
angular, grim silhouettes; the warships of the enemy were
gathered in great force. Midmost, and taller than the

others, was the flagship, a giant vessel, whose every armored deck and deckhouse held up dark muzzle-bores of many cannons.

He took his weapon into his lap and lit its tiny screen. The symbols showed the codes and patterns for the five highest officers of the enemy forces, as well as that for their commander. Only on the last day of the war, now, too late, had his spies discovered what those patterns were; only now, too late, would vengeance be fulfilled. He gently touched the button with his thumb which programmed his ammunition.

The man took out his knife and turned it on, and scratched into the rock these words: OWEN PENTHANE SEPTEMBER THIRD STOOD HERE AND FIRED A FINAL VOLLEY INTO THE FLAGSHIP 'ATLAS'

He paused in thought a while, and watched the setting sun. Already the lowlands were in shadows. The rocks and trees around him gleamed cherry-pink. Now he wrote more words into the stone: THAT ALL WOULD KNOW BY THIS, THAT WE HAVE BEEN DESTROYED, BUT NOT DEFEATED, AND EVEN TO THE LAST MAN, LAST BULLET, FOUGHT EVER ON.

He stood and raised the weapon to his cheek. The magnified image on the screen before his eye displayed the deckhouse of the mighty warship, and the moving figures bent over their controls. Webs of wire covered all the windows; these would detect incoming shots, and control the massive counter fire.

He wondered if he should step away from the rock which bore his epitaph; were it to crack or melt within the counter-fire, no future generations would read his final words.

And yet again, the circuits woven in the fabric of his suit were designed to bewilder and confuse the electric brains of approaching fire. It was possible he would not be harmed at all.

Nonetheless, he stepped aside for many paces. Now he raised the weapon once again.

A touch of his finger spun tiny gyroscopes within the stock. His weapon was now as firm on target as if it rested on a tripod. The computer built inside adjusted for the minute pitch and roll of the warship's deck, and for the vibration of the intervening air. The image on the aiming screen grew steady, clear, and fixed. A woman's voice spoke gently from behind him: "Lord Owen Penthane. Hold your fire." His thumb twitched on the programming dial. "I can fire behind as easily as ahead." He had programmed the first bullet to circle.

"Fear not." her voice answered softly. "I am unarmed."

He looked behind him. He squinted in astonishment, switched the weapon to stand-by, and studied her closely.

Her hair was yellow as corn silk, held on top within a web of silver wires set with pearls, but escaping on the sides to fall loose about her shoulders to her waist. Two long red ribbons dangled from the back of her pearly corona, and lifted in the breeze which stirred her hair into a fragrant cloud.

Her face was fair; her eyes were grey-blue as a stormy sea; her lips were red as sweet roses. Down to her feet white vesture flowed, shimmering like sea-mist, of some fabric he had never seen nor dreamed. Tight around her narrow waist she wore a wide embroidered belt of red; red slippers held slim feet. On her finger was a silver ring, whose stone gleamed with a point of light, burning like a star. It was not electric nor atomic nor any energy he could describe. He knew enough to know she came from places far beyond his knowing.

She watched him watching her, and softly smiled, as if pleased.

"There is rock wall behind you." he said, "And no place to climb except up in front of me. You were not here before I came."

"Not before, but after." she said, "Many ages hence, I shall stand within this place, and use the art we know to travel eons backward in a single step. I am a child of the future many centuries unborn. My name is Sigrune." She smiled, for a moment, at the rock he had inscribed, as if pleased to see the inscription freshly cut.

"Your accent is peculiar."

"I learned your speech from books, in my time, ancient, in yours, not yet composed."

He glanced at the medical apparatus on his shoulder. She laughed; a gay and lovely sound; and said, "No hallucinogen is in your blood. What you see before you is most real."

He laughed. "Flattering to think myself so famous that posterity will fly out of the deeps of time to talk to me! Flattering, but impossible."

"Impossible to the science of this age, perhaps. Be assured: your works shall not be forgotten, but preserved, and what you have said and done and thought shall shine through all the ages with clear light, and, in days to come, young students shall wonder what it would be like to see and to talk with you."

And now Sigrune blushed and faltered. Owen Penthane was perceptive. He could imagine some young student of time drowsing over her history books, waiting for the opportunity to meet the man whom time has lent the luster of myth and hero worship. A famous man in his own day, he had seen such blushes, and received such hero-worship, before.

Somehow, her shy look convinced him she was what she claimed.

"All this is most pleasing to me." he said, nodding to her, gravely. "Since all my work, till now, has been futile, and led to nothing more than ruin, I take your presence here as a sign that great things are left for me to accomplish in what few years a man of my age has remaining. Perhaps my scattered folk will rally, or my treacherous allies repent, and combine to drive the invaders from our soil. Now stand away; for with this shot, I hope to signal the return of hope to my oppressed nation. Having seen so fair a child from the future, I now have cause to think that hope shall not be vain."

She looked down, smiling uncertainly. It was a demure gesture, but also betrayed a strange hesitation, a hint of fear and sorrow. He stood, weapon in hand, staring at her for a long moment. Her fingers were twined together before her, and her head was bowed.

Owen Penthane said, "If you are a time traveler, how is it that your ventures do not imperil you? Any smallest change could unravel all the history you know, or thwart the marriage of your ancestors, undo the founding of your nations, and make you fade away like ghosts. What make you proof from change?" There was a steely edge within his voice.

"There are two precautions that we undertake." she said, still not daring to look up. "The first is this: our grandchildren and their grandchildren have the government of our span of time, warning us of bad results to come, and wiping out mistakes, to make them as if they had never been. If any ill were fated to befall us on any of our journeyings, the Museum of Man at the End of Time would warn us of the outcome, long before it ever could arise. Their knowledge is perfect, for they cannot ever err."

"And the second?" he said, grimly.

Now she raised her head and met his eye. "We show ourselves only to those who are about to die."

He was silent, frowning, while she looked on. Her gaze was steady, calm, and sad.

"I meant to cause you no pain, Lord Owen." she said. Soft breeze sent ripples through her hair. "Bid your world farewell: a finer world awaits you; a world which lacks no joy."

"You have told me nothing I did not foresee. The soldier is a fool who thinks to live forever. I suppose if I do not fire upon the flagship . . . ?"

"There are enemies lurking in the woods below. The result is much the same."

"Indeed." He turned and put the weapon to his shoulder. "Again I thank you, madam. Now that no hope torments me, my mind is put to rest. I am resolved."

"Wait! I beg you, wait!" She stepped forward suddenly,

and put her hands on his weapon. He caught her one wrist with a hard grasp, and stared angrily at her.

"Why now do you interfere?" he asked. Her skin was soft, untouched by any scar or plague. Since the bombardments, he had not seen many women with unblemished skin.

She put her other hand gently on his rough fingers, and gazed at him with wide eyes. "Set your weapon on its timer." she said. "And hold my hand and come with me into my land, beyond all history. At the Museum of Man, the arts and sciences of every age are gathered, the bravest of men, the most beautiful of women, the greatest of philosophers, and the most lucid of all poets. Our medicine can restore your vanished youth to you; it is a country of the young, where aging is unknown, and death by accident is undone before it can occur. In the twilight of all time, sorrow is unknown to us, and all those wise and great and glorious enough to join our company have been called up from out of the abyss of history. You will sit in our feast-hall, to eat whatever meats or breads delight you, or drink our sweet and endless wine. A place has been reserved for you, next to the seats of Brian Boru, Alfred the Great, and Charlemagne. We feast and know no lack, we who can change time to restore drained goblets back to fullness, or resurrect the slaughtered beast to roast again. Only for us, the flame of a blown-out candle can be unblown, and brightly burn again."

He released her wrist. She saw the cold and unmoved expression of his face.

Grief made her voice grow shrill, but no less lovely. She knelt, and clasped her shaking hands around his waist.

"Come away with me, I pray you, Owen! I offer what all men have dreamed in vain! Our joys do not pall, cannot grow stale and wearisome like other joys, for we can change unhappy days not ever to have been! All great men, except for those who died in public places, in the witness of many eyes, are gathered there. All these great men, your peers, will cheer your coming to our halls. You shall hear the thousand poems, each grander than the last, which Dante and which Homer have composed in all the many centuries since they have dwelt among us, or sample the deep wisdom Aristotle has deduced in his thousand years of subtlest debate with Gotuma, Lao Tsu, Descartes, and John Locke."

He said sternly, "What chance have I to open fire, and survive? To gather up my scattered people, and lead them once again against a foe, which, if my bullets find their aim, will be, for now, leaderless and demoralized? What chance?"

She rose slowly. "I was told to tell you, you have none."

"But you cannot know for certain. You know only that, in the version of the history you know, I did not fire, but went away with you."

She bowed her head and whispered a half-silent, "Yes." But then she raised her head again. Her eyes now shone with unwept tears, and now she raised her hand to brush her straying hair aside. "But come with me, not because you must, but because I ask. Give up your world: you have lost it. You have failed. I have been promised that, should I return with you, great love would grow between us. We are destined. Is this ruined land so fair that you will not renounce it for eternal youth, and love?"

"Renounce your world instead, and stay with me. Teach me all the secrets of your age, and we will sweep my enemies away with the irresistible weapons of the future. No? If you change the past, you cannot return to find the future that you knew, can you?"

"It is so." she said.

"You will not renounce your world for love? Just so. Nor will I, mine. Now stand away, my dear. Before the sun is set, I mean to fire."

She whirled away from him in a shimmer of pale fabric, and strode to stand where she had been when first he saw her. Now she spoke in anger, "You cannot resist my will in this! I need but step a moment back ago, and play this scene again, till I find right words, or what wiles or arguments I must to bend your stiff neck, and persuade you from your folly. Foolish man! Foolish and vain man! You have done nothing to defy me! I shall make it never to have been, till finally you must change your mind!"

Now he smiled. "Let my other versions worry what they shall do. I am myself; I shall concern myself with me. But I suspect I am not the first of me who has declined your sweet temptation; I deem that you have played this scene before. I cannot think that any words or promises could stay me from my resolve."

She hid her face behind her hands and wept.

He said, "Be comforted. If I were not the man you so admire, then, perhaps, I would depart with you. But if you love me for my bravery, then do not seek to rob me of this last, brave, final, act."

She said from behind her hands, "It may be that you

will survive; but the future which will come of that shall not have me in it."

And with these words, she vanished like a dream.

The sun was sinking downward into night. Against the bloody glimmer of its final rays, the warship which held his enemies rose up in gloomy silhouette. Now he raised his weapon to his shoulder, took careful aim, and depressed the trigger. There came a clasp of thunder.

And because he knew not what might come next, his mind was utterly at peace.

AGAINST THE
LAFAYETTE ESCADRILLE
by Gene Wolfe

*Some say everyone should have a hobby, but this one led
to an accidental foray into the past in which no shots were
fired, but a wound was taken, the sort of wound that heals
slowly, if ever. Grand master Gene Wolfe shows a
distinctly Bradburyesque touch in this gentle tale.*

I have built a perfect replica of a Fokker triplane, except
for the flammable dope. It is five meters, seventy-seven
centimeters long and has a wingspan of seven meters,
nineteen centimeters, just like the original. The engine is
an authentic copy of an Oberursel UR II. I have a lathe
and a milling machine and I made most of the parts for
the engine myself, but some had to be farmed out to a
company in Cleveland, and most of the electrical parts
were done in Louisville, Kentucky.

In the beginning I had hoped to get an original engine,

and I wrote my first letters to Germany with that in mind, but it just wasn't possible; there are only a very few left, and as nearly as I could find out none in private hands. The Oberursel Worke is no longer in existence. I was able to secure plans though, through the cooperation of some German hobbyests. I redrew them myself translating the German when they had to be sent to Cleveland. A man from the newspaper came to take pictures when the Fokker was nearly ready to fly, and I estimated then that I had put more than three thousand hours into building it. I did all the airframe and the fabric work myself, and carved the propeller.

Throughout the project I have tried to keep everything as realistic as possible, and I even have two 7.92 mm Maxim "Spandau" machineguns mounted just ahead of the cockpit. They are not loaded of course, but they are coupled to the engine with the Fokker Zentralsteuerung interrupter gear.

The question of dope came up because of a man in Oregon I used to correspond with who flies a Nieuport Scout. The authentic dope, as you're probably aware, was extremely flammable. He wanted to know if I'd used it, and when I told him I had not he became critical. As I said then, I love the Fokker too much to want to see it burn authentically, and if Antony Fokker and Reinhold Platz had had fireproof dope they would have used it. This didn't satisfy the Oregon man and he finally became so abusive I stopped replying to his letters. I still believe what I did was correct, and if I had it to do over my decision would be the same.

I have had a trailer specially built to move the Fokker,

and I traded my car in on a truck to tow it and carry parts and extra gear, but mostly I leave it at a small field near here where I have rented hangar space, and move it as little as possible on the roads. When I do because of the wide load I have to drive very slowly and only use certain roads. People always stop to look when we pass, and sometimes I can hear them on their front porches calling to others inside to come and see. I think the three wings of the Fokker interest them particularly, and once in a rare while a veteran of the war will see it—almost always a man who smokes a pipe and has a cane. If I can hear what they say it is often pretty foolish, but a light comes into their eyes that I enjoy.

Mostly the Fokker is just in its hangar out at the field and you wouldn't know me from anyone else as I drive out to fly. There is a black cross painted on the door of my truck, but it wouldn't mean anything to you. I suppose it wouldn't have meant anything even if you had seen me on my way out the day I saw the balloon.

It was one of the earliest days of spring, with a very fresh, really indescribable feeling in the air. Three days before I had gone up for the first time that year, coming after work and flying in weather that was a little too bad with not quite enough light left; winter flying, really. Now it was Saturday and everything was changed. I remember how my scarf streamed out while I was just standing on the field talking to the mechanic.

The wind was good, coming right down the length of the field to me, getting under the Fokker's wings and lifting it like a kite before we had gone a hundred feet. I did a slow turn then, getting a good look at the field with all the new, green grass starting to show, and adjusting my goggles.

Have you ever looked from an open cockpit to see the wing struts trembling and the ground swinging far below? There is nothing like it. I pulled back on the stick and gave it more throttle and rose and rose until I was looking down on the backs of all the birds and I could not be certain which of the tiny roofs I saw was the house where I live or the factory where I work. Then I forgot looking down, and looked up and out, always remembering to look over my shoulder especially, and to watch the sun where the S.E. 5a's of the Royal Flying Corps love to hang like dragonflies, invisible against the glare.

Then I looked away and I saw it, almost on the horizon, an orange dot. I did not, of course, know then what it was; but I waved to the other members of the Jagstaffel I command and turned toward it, the Fokker thrilling to the challenge. It was moving with the wind, which meant almost directly away from me, but that only gave the Fokker a tailwind, and we came at it—rising all the time.

It was not really orange-red as I had first thought. Rather it was a thousand colors and shades, with reds and yellows and white predominating. I climbed toward it steeply with the stick drawn far back, almost at a stall. Because of that I failed, at first, to see the basket hanging from it. Then I leveled out and circled it at a distance. That was when I realized it was a balloon. After a moment I saw, too, that it was of very old-fashioned design with a wicker basket for the passengers and that someone was in it. At the moment the profusion of colors interested me more, and I went slowly spiraling in until I could see them better, the Easter egg blues and the blacks as well as the reds and whites and yellows.

It wasn't until I looked at the girl that I understood. She was the passenger, a very beautiful girl, and she wore crinolines and had her hair in long chestnut curls that hung down over her bare shoulders. She waved to me, and then I understood.

The ladies of Richmond had sewn it for the Confederate army, making it from their silk dresses. I remembered reading about it. The girl in the basket blew me a kiss and I waved to her, trying to convey with my wave that none of the men of my command would ever be allowed to harm her; that we had at first thought that her craft might be a French or Italian observation balloon, but that for the future she need fear no gun in the service of the Kaiser's Flugzeugmeisterei.

I circled her for some time then, she turning slowly in the basket to follow the motion of my plane, and we talked as well as we could with gestures and smiles. At last when my fuel was running low I signaled her that I must leave. She took, from a container hidden by the rim of the basket, a badly shaped, corked brown bottle. I circled even closer, in a tight bank, until I could see the yellow, crumbling label. It was one of the very early soft drinks, an original bottle. While I watched she drew the cork, drank some, and held it out symbolically to me.

Then I had to go. I made it back to the field, but I landed dead stick with my last drop of fuel exhausted when I was half a kilometer away. Naturally I had the Fokker refueled at once and went up again, but I could not find her balloon.

I have never been able to find it again, although I go up almost every day when the weather makes it possible. There is nothing but an empty sky and a few jets. Sometimes, to tell the truth, I have wondered if things would not have been different if, in finishing the Fokker, I had used the original, flammable dope. She was so authentic. Sometimes toward evening I think I see her in the distance, above the clouds, and I follow as fast as I can across the silent vault with the Fokker trembling around me and the throttle all the way out; but it is only the sun.

DOCTOR QUIET
by Jacob Holo

Terrorists and time machines make for a deadly combination, and the mastermind calling himself "Doctor Quiet" needs to be taken alive if these criminals are to be brought to justice. The newbie time soldier Susan Cantrell has muffed one chance already, but nothing expands opportunities—and danger—like traveling through time. This story is set in the continuing Gordian Division series created by David Weber and Jacob Holo, featuring the best-selling novels The Gordian Protocol *and* The Valkyrie Protocol, *both from Baen Books.*

★ ★ ★

"Agent Cantrell?" Captain Jason Elifritz asked, appraising the empty space above Susan Cantrell's shoulders. A space that should have been occupied by her head.

"Yes, sir," Susan replied through simulated speech across their shared virtual senses. Her current body—a Type-92 combat frame—took the form of a black skeletal humanoid festooned with maneuvering boosters and weaponry. She squared her shoulders and stood at attention within the captain's office aboard Chronoport *Defender-Two*. "You wished to speak with me?"

"I did." The chronoport captain removed the blue peaked cap of his Admin Peacekeeper uniform as he continued to regard Susan's headless status with barely a tick on his face. "I know I asked to see you immediately after we returned to the True Present, but perhaps our discussion can wait."

"Why's that, sir? Is something wrong?"

"Well . . ." The faintest hint of a grimace leaked through his cool professionalism. "I had assumed you'd switch back into your general purpose synthoid before coming here."

"Oh, right." Susan nodded in understanding. Or rather, tried to. Instead, the severed power and data cables of her neck trunk wiggled back and forth. "I'm sorry to report I'm unable to switch bodies at the moment."

"And why is that?"

"It's my armor." She gestured with a thumb over her shoulder. "One of the explosions melted the malmetal plates on my back. Fused them together. The operators need to saw me open before they can retrieve my connectome case. I thought you wouldn't want to wait that long, so I came to see you straight away."

"I see." Elifritz glanced down and dusted off the top of his cap. "I suppose I can't fault your thought process there, though that still leaves the matter of your head."

"What about it, sir?"

"It appears to have been shot off."

"You should see the other guy."

"Yes..." Elifritz ran his fingers through long hair tied back in a ponytail, then refitted his cap with the utmost precision and care. He clasped his hands behind his back before continuing. "Funny you should mention that."

"Sir?"

"Before I continue, a question for you, Agent. How, precisely, are you still getting around without your head?"

"Oh, that's easy. I'm using the aux camera in my grenade launcher." She tapped the shoulder-mounted weapon.

Elifritz glanced to the grenade launcher, which gave him a little up-and-down nod as if to say that, yes, she was using it as a backup head.

"I hate to have to inquire, but did you unload that thing before coming to see me?"

"No need."

"And why would that be?"

"Because I discharged all my ordnance during the mission."

"Ah." Elifritz let out a resigned sigh. "I should have guessed."

"Sir, is something wrong?" Susan asked, genuinely curious and a bit worried at this point. "Am I in trouble?"

"In a manner of speaking." Elifritz made eye contact with the grenade launcher's camera. "Do you recall the state of the guy who shot off your head—the 'other guy,' as you put it—last you saw him?"

"You mean besides the crater?"

"Yes." One of his eyes twitched. "Besides the crater."

"Well, I'm not too sure." Susan raised a hand to her chin in an attempt to strike a thoughtful pose, but then

fumbled around for her missing head and decided to drop
the arm back down. "I think some of him may have ended
up smeared across the ceiling before I . . ." She trailed off,
now acutely aware of where her description was headed.

"Yes? Please continue."

"Before I blew up the ceiling." She paused
uncomfortably. "Is that what this is about?"

"No. We had the building tagged as non-vital, so
damage to it in service of the mission was acceptable. The
occupants, though, were a separate matter."

"Sir." Susan tried to stand a little straighter. "Even
though I'd suffered damage and was still under fire, I
made sure to check my target before retaliating. That
terrorist was not listed as a capture priority, and therefore,
I was free to respond with lethal force."

"That may be so, but I think your situational awareness
needs some work."

"Sir?"

"Agent, do you recall our mission parameters?"

"Of course, I do, sir."

"Then indulge me. What were they?"

"We were executing a standard intelligence grab. Go
into the past, crash a terrorist party, and retrieve vital intel,
be it people or material. This particular mission took us
back to August the twenty-third, 2971—negative sixty
days back from the True Present—to a Free Luna cell.
The targets were operating out of an automated
warehouse just south of the capital's Block F20." She
paused before continuing. "Sir, I'm sorry, but I'm not sure
what this is about. As I said, I checked my target before
returning fire."

Elifritz raised his chin ever so slightly. "What about the individual standing *next* to him?"

"The individual . . . next to him?"

Elifritz held out his palm, and a window opened in their shared virtual vision. Susan recognized the logistical warehouse interior: the nearest wall taken up by multistoried storage racks and robot cranes suspended from the ceiling on rails. A group of terrorists hastily retrieved heavy weapons from a pallet of "food printer cartridges," and one already had an anti-materiel rail-rifle aimed at her.

The image shuddered as her combat frame took incoming fire. Damage indicators flashed in the window periphery, and the view swung toward her assailant and focused in.

Elifritz paused the video, then slowly panned the image to the side until a second terrorist came into view, partially obscured by the logistical scaffold. He was a tall and somewhat lanky man with sunken cheeks and long, dark hair, gray creeping in at the temples and trim salt-and-pepper goatee. Despite the attack, his dark eyes were focused and cold, fixated on the source of the commotion without a hint of fear in them.

Those chilling eyes belonged to Cameron Nist: Capture Target Priority One.

"Oh." Her shoulders slumped. "Oh, shit."

Elifritz raised a chastising eyebrow.

"Shoot," she corrected hastily. "Sorry, sir."

"As you can see," the captain began, "not only did you blow up the unlucky idiot shooting at you, you *also* reduced our mission objective to a form of abstract art on the warehouse ceiling. Do you see the problem, Agent?"

"Yes, sir. I believe I do. But why didn't we try again? We could have performed a temporal microjump and reset the local timeline."

"Because the team on *Defender-Prime* had markedly more success than we did." He sighed and shook his head. "*They* managed to retrieve a copy of Nist from negative fifty-six days, and since their version is older than the one we found, our capture attempt became redundant. So, with us looking at both *Defender-Prime*'s success and the local version of Nist atomized by your grenade barrage—"

Susan tried to lower her head further, but only succeeded in moving her neck trunk.

"—I made the call to abort and return to base."

"I see, sir. I think I have a clear understanding of the problem."

"Anything to say for yourself, Agent?"

"I will . . . endeavor to show more restraint in the future."

"See that you do," Elifritz said stiffly. "Dismissed."

Susan opened her eyes, and they really were *her* eyes this time. Or at least the eyes she *thought of* as hers, even though her old organic body had long since been recycled. Her mind could inhabit the combat frame as easily as any other compatible vessel, but she didn't view the stark, robotic weapon with the same sense of self she bestowed upon her synthoid body.

Sharp hazel eyes stared out of a young oval face framed by red hair in a pixie cut.

Her eyes, and *her* face, and *her* hair.

They might all have been as artificial as the combat frame, but the synthoid's cosmetic layer matched her original body in just about every detail, even while the mechanisms underneath granted her enhanced speed and strength. Not on the same level as the combat frame, but far superior to any natural human.

"You back with us?" Specialist Erika Nishi asked from her seat behind Susan. They both sat in a maintenance bay within the main tower for the Department of Temporal Investigation.

"Yes, thank you."

"Good. Let's get you buttoned up." Nishi pressed hard against Susan's naked spine, her palms tracking downward, forcing the flap in the cosmetic layer to stick firmly against the port for her connectome case, which contained the neural map of her mind.

Susan glanced to the side and took in the inert combat frame next to her, its back armor warped and cut open by Nishi. She still found it odd to see the combat frame from the outside after spending hours—sometimes days— operating it. As a member of the Admin's Special Training and Nonorganic Deployment command, she could swap bodies the way most people swapped coats, but her transition from organic to synthetic had occurred barely a month ago, and many aspects of this new life jarred with her old flesh-and-blood sensibilities.

"I suppose I'll get used to it eventually," she muttered under her breath.

"Used to what?" Nishi asked.

"Seeing one of my bodies from the outside," Susan said over her shoulder.

"Hell, I still can't believe you volunteered for this." Nishi picked up a tool with a pistol grip and used it to apply a bead of fleshlike glue. She traced the tip slowly around a U-shaped seam in Susan's back.

"*I* still can't believe STAND accepted my application," Susan admitted. "I mean, I only transferred to the DTI a year ago, and I've only been a Peacekeeper for three."

"Then why bother applying in the first place?"

"Because there was no harm in trying."

"Sure, except for the whole fry-your-original-brain part of the process."

"It wasn't bad at all. I closed my eyes in my old body and woke up in this." Susan tapped her collarbone. "Didn't feel a thing."

"That you *remember*," Nishi pointed out. "Here." She handed Susan her uniform jacket.

"Thanks." Susan smiled and slipped her arms into the sleeves. "Honestly, all the interviews and psych evals leading up to it were more of a pain than the actual process. But even then, the approval moved a lot faster than I expected."

"That's just the DTI for you." Nishi put her tools away and stood up. "It's amazing how fast this place is growing, and I don't think it's slowing down. In fact, it might even be *accelerating*. From what I hear, they've already started construction on a *third* chronoport squadron."

"You mean instead of the suppression tower network?"

"No. In addition to!" Nishi said brightly.

"Wow. Yeah, that's fast." Susan pulled her jacket snug, then joined Nishi at the exit. "Still, back to the whole

STAND thing, it can't be that hard to find people more experienced than me."

"Maybe they didn't apply," Nishi commented.

"Maybe." Susan let out a slow sigh.

"You still bummed about the mission?"

"A little."

"Don't let it bother you. Elifritz is just upset Okunnu and the rest of *Defender-Prime* showed us up."

"Somehow," Susan began with a frown, "I don't think that's why he chewed me out. By the way, where are you headed?"

"The mess." She rubbed her stomach, which let out a faint rumble as if on cue. "I should really stop skipping meals on missions. You?"

"Nowhere I need to be. Mind if I join you?"

"You sure it won't bother you?"

"Why would it?" Susan asked.

"Oh, you know." Nishi cracked a half-smile. "Us organics and all our organic drama?"

"I'm sorry." Susan crinkled her brow. "You lost me."

"Do I have to spell it out for you?" Nishi leaned in and lowered her voice, even though they were alone. "Eating and pooping."

"I'd hardly classify those as 'organic drama.'"

"Listen, Susan." Nishi placed a hand on her shoulder. "I'll admit joining STAND *does* have a few perks. You'll never go hungry and, if you so choose, you never have to take a dump ever again. Granted, those are about the *only* perks that could convince me to join STAND, and even then I'd have to be blackout drunk when they asked."

"I think I can manage," Susan replied dryly.

"You sure?" Nishi asked with that same half-smile.

"Look." Susan sighed and rolled her eyes. "I've been eating and pooping my entire life. Besides, I still have all my senses, and some comfort food sounds good right about now."

"Well, as long as you're fine with our drama." Nishi started down the corridor toward the elevators.

"It's *not* drama," Susan insisted.

Susan gazed down at her plate of chicken flautas topped with salsa fresca, sour cream, and guacamole. She breathed in the aroma, and her mouth watered, bringing a smile to her face. Her synthoid's cosmetic layer, which included everything inside her mouth, truly was an impressive piece of engineering, given how it interacted seamlessly with the biochemical simulation running parallel to her neural runtime. That simulation allowed the smell of delicious food to brighten her mood, for example, by simulating an organic body's response to stimulus.

She leaned a little closer and breathed in once more.

It had been ... two days since she last ate? Three, maybe? She wondered if eating on a regular schedule might help restore some of the normalcy to her life, at least until she acclimated to this new, synthetic existence.

"Are you going to do anything besides sniff it?" Nishi asked, already halfway through one of her three flautas.

"I'm savoring the aroma," Susan defended. "Would you mind passing the hot sauce?"

"Sure." Nishi leaned over to snag a bottle further down the table. The mess was only about a fifth full with some occupants finishing their meals while others headed to the printers to order up late lunches. "Here you go."

"Thanks."

"Mind if I join you?"

Susan looked up to find the imposing frame of a gray-skinned, yellow-eyed synthoid made somewhat less intimidating by the tray of beef enchiladas in his big hands. Like Susan, Special Agent Miguel Pérez was a part of the STAND force assigned to the DTI, but unlike her, he'd joined STAND back when synthoid technology had been relatively new and it had been illegal for them to resemble organic humans too closely, hence his unnatural skin and eye coloration.

Susan wasn't sure how old Pérez was; she could have looked it up in his service record, but that just seemed rude and unnecessary to her. However old he was, he was *old* old. Not exactly as old as dirt, but maybe old enough to be one of dirt's grandkids.

"Sure, Miguel," Susan responded.

"Thank you." The big STAND set his tray down and sat next to Nishi, whose fork had frozen halfway to her mouth.

"Umm." Susan's brow creased as she took in the awkward scene.

Pérez had what might best be described as a reputation for violence. Very *discriminating* violence, always directed at enemies of the Admin, but violence nonetheless. Couple that with his imposing appearance and how he could snap Nishi's neck with ease, and Susan could understand her friend's . . . discomfort at sitting next to him.

Granted, Susan was physically capable of the same acts—if she disengaged her safety limiters—but *she* didn't look the part. And besides, Nishi knew her from before her transition. Susan doubted *anyone* knew Pérez from his meat-and-bone days, except perhaps other old STANDs.

"Specialist Nishi, you're welcome to stay with us," Pérez remarked in what was almost a soothing tone. "There's just a little bit of business I need to discuss with Agent Cantrell."

"I . . ." She set her fork down and picked up her tray. "You know, maybe I should make this a working lunch. Gotta replace your frame's armor. Later!"

Nishi rose abruptly and left without another word. Susan and Pérez watched her exit the mess hall with the haste of someone eager to enjoy her meal somewhere else.

Susan turned back to her fellow STAND. "You scared her off on purpose."

"Did not."

"Did too."

"Susan, I didn't say anything . . . unnecessarily hostile, as you like to put it. Look." He gestured to his meal. "I even grabbed a tray of food I'm not going to eat, all in an effort to look normal and nonthreatening."

"Uh huh." Susan rested her cheek on a fist.

Pérez was Susan's mentor in STAND, and she'd come to believe he was a big softy on the inside, once one pushed past the badass synthoid act. It was penetrating the act that gave most people problems.

"Did I say something wrong?" he asked, perhaps more amused by the situation than distressed.

"I think it's more how you hovered menacingly behind her."

"Hovered? With menace?" He placed a splayed hand on his chest. "Me? Why, I'm as unthreatening as they come."

"Whatever." Susan rolled her eyes. "You said you had some business to discuss?"

"I do, though it's not quite business. More like"—he paused ever so slightly—"news."

"Why do I sense you left out a word there?"

"It's not *bad* news." He paused again, his face contemplative for a moment. "Well, maybe it is."

Susan sighed and shook her head. "Just hit me with it."

"As you wish." He leaned forward. "I've been transferred to *Defender-Two*'s ground team."

"Shit!" Susan put a hand to her forehead and rubbed.

"Temporarily," Pérez added, holding up a hand.

"Yeah. I'll bet." She looked up. "This come from the captain?"

Pérez nodded. "Elifritz thought it might be beneficial to have a more experienced STAND on the team. Temporarily," he stressed again.

"Thank you for the vote of confidence, everyone." She shook her head and grabbed the hot sauce.

"It's not that, Susan. He's doing what he thinks is best. Both for the DTI and for your development. That's all this is. You still have his confidence, and mine. He just wants to see . . . fewer hasty mistakes from you."

"I had my head shot off!" Susan unscrewed the bottle and began drenching her meal in hot sauce. "So, okay, yeah, I responded with a bit too much firepower. I freely admit that, but those weren't peashooters I was up against!" She set the bottle down. "I sure as hell needed to neutralize the threat *somehow*."

"Of course. Just not with all of your grenades."

"I know that *now*!" She stabbed a fork into a flauta and lifted the whole thing to her mouth.

"Uhhh, Susan?" Pérez asked, sounding worried all of a sudden.

"What?"

"Do you plan to eat that?"

"Sure do. Why?"

"Well, it's just..." He tilted his head to the side. "Maybe they fixed that problem with the newer synthoid versions."

"What problem?"

"The spicy problem. Didn't anyone mention food restrictions to you?"

"I have no idea what you're talking about." She stuffed the whole flauta into her mouth, chewed and swallowed.

"Well, I guess we'll know soon enough."

"Know wha—"

A sudden, searing heat assaulted Susan's senses. It started on her tongue, then spread insidiously from there, sending tendrils of unpleasantness across the inside of her mouth and down her throat. Her artificial eyes watered, and her face twisted up as if she'd sucked on a lemon.

"Yeah, there's the look," Pérez remarked hopelessly.

Susan grabbed her glass of water and chugged it, but the cool fluid provided scant relief. She stole the glass from Pérez's tray and chugged that, too, but the additional water only seemed to smear the pain across a wider area.

"More!" she said desperately, and bolted up from her seat.

"I think there're drink machines that—"

Pérez had only begun to point when Susan started sprinting.

Pérez found Susan alone in a side room lined with drink machines, her head stuck underneath one of the dispensers with a finger jammed against the drink select. The machine poured a continuous stream of water, while she alternated between swallowing, swishing, and spitting it out.

"Feel any better?" he asked with genuine empathy.

"What the hell *was* that?!" Susan spat before starting another gurgling cycle.

"Pain, which I think you haven't felt in a month or so." Pérez shrugged. "Spicy food is one of the few ways we can still feel pain. I suppose someone thinks it's a good idea. I'm not a fan, but some STANDs apparently love it."

She pulled her head out. "But I like spicy food!"

"Not anymore, I think."

"Oh, fuck this!" she exclaimed before sticking her head back under the dispenser.

"You going to be okay?"

"*Glugfergurgglgup.*"

"What?"

Susan contorted under the drink machine and gave him a thumbs up with her free hand.

"That's the spirit."

An alert pinged across both their virtual senses.

"Hmm." Pérez eyed the message header hovering in his virtual vision. "Wonder what that could be?"

Susan extracted herself from the dispenser and stood up straight. She grabbed a paper towel and wiped her face off. In the absence of moisture, her uniform's smart fabric morphed out of its waterproof mode.

"How do you feel?" Pérez asked.

"Like I suddenly hate spicy food." She pointed to the alert. "What's that?"

"Haven't checked it yet."

Susan raised an open palm, and the alert expanded. "Emergency mission brief for *Defender-Two*'s command staff and ground team," she read.

"Then let's not keep the rest of them waiting."

"One second." Susan entered an order into the drink machine. "I'm taking one to go, just in case."

Susan and Pérez filed into the briefing room and took a pair of empty desks near the back. The automatic door locked shut behind them.

"Good. I believe that's everyone," Elifritz said, surveying the room. "Let's get started."

He placed a hand on the podium, linking his Personal Implant Network with the surrounding closed-circuit infostructure. Susan planted her own hand on the desk, and the classified briefing appeared in her virtual vision. An image of Cameron Nist popped up first, his dark eyes glaring straight ahead in the cramped interrogation room while two agents from the DTI's espionage ops sat across from him.

"The good news," Elifritz began, "is the interrogation of the past version of Cameron Nist, a.k.a. Doctor Quiet, is substantively complete."

Susan let out a little snort.

Doctor Quiet, she thought. *What a stupid, pretentious name. Like some video game supervillain.*

"The bad news is it proved less productive than we'd hoped. We've been able to confirm the relatively small size of this terrorist cell, less than ten members, and that Nist serves as their leader, but he didn't reveal much else of value. It seems that under Nist's command, this Free Luna cell has adapted their operating parameters to reduce the intelligence we can gather by raiding their old hangouts."

"How'd they pull that off, Captain?" asked a member of the chronoport's bridge crew.

"By leaving a portion of their plan up to random chance. Quite literally in this case. They're taking a list of about a thousand potential targets—most of them officials at various levels of our government—and using random number generation to pick their next target. While this method has clear disadvantages, it also means that past-Nist doesn't know who they'll hit next. At least, not that far back in the timeline."

"Sir, do we have the breakdown on their new weapon?"

"We do." Elifritz pulled up a picture of a complex microscopic machine that resembled a fat, metallic beetle. "Here's the culprit. It's a modified version of a common surgical microbot, adapted for assault on the victim's nervous system, which is where Doctor Nist's previous career as a neurosurgeon comes into play. Upon introduction to the body, the microbots travel to the brain's speech center and cause significant damage, resulting in global aphasia for most victims." He turned to his team. "During his interview, Doctor Nist insisted this approach was more 'humane' since it doesn't kill anyone."

Murmurs of disgust circulated the briefing room.

"Can the weapon self-replicate?" Susan asked.

"A good question, and fortunately not," Elifritz answered. "The modifications are entirely software-based, so the technical capabilities of the original remain unchanged. *Unfortunately*, this also means the terrorists will have no issues creating more, as these microbots are commonly used in medical facilities all across the globe."

"What's the threat level to the ground team?" Pérez asked.

"Low, since the weapon has to be injected into the victim." He pointed to the microbot schematic.

Susan felt her concentration waver due to the agony in her mouth, and she raised the drink straw as stealthily as she could.

"Our organic operators should be safe—"
Schlooorp.

Elifritz paused and frowned. "Should be safe—"
Shlurp.

"Should be—"
Shlrp.

The captain turned and swept his gaze over the room, but Susan moved her drink under the desk with superhuman speed.

"Did anyone else hear that?" the captain asked.

"Hear what, sir?" Pérez asked innocently.

"I . . . never mind." Elifritz cleared his throat and

pointed once more to the microbot picture. "As I was saying, the risk to our ground team should be minimal. The weapon is intended for civilian targets, not armored operators or STANDs in combat frames. We expect conventional weapons to be the main threat to the ground team."

"What are we hitting, sir?"

"A public infostructure tower seven days ago, which if you recall, will place us one day after the initial attack on our government. Our goal is to infiltrate the tower in the past and record the Free Luna software making its next target selection before distributing its orders to the cell."

"Sounds like we don't expect to meet resistance," Pérez noted.

"Yes and no." Elifritz brought up a new image. It took Susan a few moments to realize the abstract graph represented chronometric activity as detected by a chronoport's dish. "On its way back to the True Present, *Defender-Prime* detected what might be the wake of an illegal time machine. Furthermore, Doctor Nist revealed his Free Luna cell somehow got its hands on a makeshift chronoton impeller. That was fifty-six days ago, which is conceivably enough time for them to attach a basic power plant and crew cabin to the impeller."

"Free Luna has a *time machine*?" Nishi exclaimed.

"That's one possibility," Elifritz said. "And given how savvy this cell is to our methods, I think it's possible they're using it to guard key events in the past, in case we come snooping around."

"What if their junker time machine shows itself?" Pérez asked.

"Your orders are to destroy it, if possible," Elifritz stated firmly. "If not, *Defender-Two* will engage the craft directly."

"Understood, sir," Pérez said with a nod.

Chronoport *Defender-Two* hovered out of the DTI tower hangar, held aloft by directional exhaust from its twin fusion thrusters. The craft's ninety-meter length resembled the silhouette of a manta ray with a thick delta wing expanding outward from the main body and the long, narrow spike of its chronoton impeller protruding from the rear. External racks under its wing were heavy with cannon and missile pods.

Power diverted from the fusion plants to the impeller, which spun up. Chronotons—elementary particles that looped constantly back and forth through time in closed temporal loops—permeated the impeller with ease up until the moment it fully energized.

The exotic matter of the impeller began to block chronotons moving backward in time, and this created intense chronometric pressure along the impeller. The pressure built until the force overcame the chronoport's natural momentum through time, shifting the entire vessel out of phase with the True Present, the newest point in time in the universe, a point past which the future had yet to be created.

The chronoport vanished from the present and sped into the past at ninety-five thousand seconds per second.

"I'm in." Nishi crouched near the server tower's roof access, her armor's variskin reducing her and the other three operators to watery blurs, though the squad's short-ranged infostructure highlighted each friendly with a blue border.

Susan and Pérez stood behind them, flush against the wall, their synthoids swapped out for Type-92 and Type-86 combat frames respectively. Pérez's combat frame might have been older than her model, but that didn't make it any less deadly in a fight. Quite the contrary, since the Type-86 sported heavier armor and weaponry than her Type-92, at the cost of a modest loss in speed and maneuverability.

"The door?" Pérez asked.

"I'll have it disabled in a moment," Nishi replied. "Just double-checking my work so I don't set off any alarms."

Susan scanned their surroundings. The chronoport had dropped them off atop the infostructure tower situated in the outskirts of the sprawling metropolis built over the old Yanluo Blight. The orange glow of dusk melted into the dark of night overhead, and the cityscape glowed with running lights of commuter shuttles. A blue triangle pulsed in the distance, representing *Defender-Two* holding position with all stealth systems engaged.

The ground team could have blown the door open or entered the building with any number of loud, forceful methods. They might have been in the past, but any "changes" they made would vanish as soon as they left, melting back into the immutable march of time. Still, it benefited their work to be discrete, since they were an outside factor on the local timeline. Not only could their presence influence past events, potentially corrupting whatever intelligence they sought, but misunderstandings with other Peacekeeper forces could—and in one case *had*—ended badly.

Notifying the past version of local Peacekeepers was always an option, but even a small change like that could have large and unpredictable consequences. And so, the DTI operated quietly whenever possible.

"Door's power is cut," Nishi reported. "And no building alarms so far."

"Good work."

Pérez nodded to Susan, who nodded back and grabbed the handle. She shoved the heavy door aside, then stepped in, heavy rail-rifle tracking across the interior. The inside was unlit except for the blinking lights of rack-mounted infostructure nodes, but the gloom provided little challenge to her enhanced senses. Pérez followed her in and together they performed a sweep of the level.

"Clear," Susan reported.

"Clear," Pérez echoed.

"Moving in." Nishi and the other operators entered the floor and closed the door behind them. She hurried over to Susan's position.

"This one should work." Susan tapped the master node on the central rack. If it was configured like most, the master node would have administrative functions Nishi could use to her advantage.

"Yeah, that'll do." She crouched down and plugged into the master node. Virtual interfaces materialized around her. "This could take a while."

"I've got your back."

Susan kept watch as Nishi worked. Nothing stirred

except for the constant sound of coolant flowing through the racked nodes. Pérez and the other operators spread out, keeping watch over each of the floor's entrances.

"How's it going?" Susan asked ten minutes later.

"Slow," Nishi admitted. "Whoever coded this put in some false leads. I'm having to eliminate them one by one."

"Well, keep at it. The good thing is we should have all the time in the—"

The ceiling exploded directly above the two women, and hot shrapnel rained down on them. Susan raised her arm in an instant and energized its malmetal armor plates. The hexagonal segments shifted into a wide shield, and shrapnel bounced off before it could cut through Nishi.

"Damn!" the specialist exclaimed as the force of the explosion knocked her to the ground. She yanked out her cable, grabbed her rail-rifle, and scrambled to her feet.

Susan retracted her armor and peered through the clearing smoke. She overlaid the view with infrared, and the profile of a hovering craft came into focus. It looked like someone had grafted the long spike of a chronoton impeller onto a passenger airliner, though the heavy cannon hanging from its chin-mounted turret was most definitely an "aftermarket" addition. She could make out the thermal silhouettes of two people sitting side by side in the cockpit.

"Hostile craft above us!" Susan shouted moments before the enemy fired again.

Its second shot tore through the racks in a swift line of exploding, sparking hardware. Susan grabbed Nishi and pulled her away, and bits of ruined equipment pattered off her back.

"Engage!" Pérez called out as he opened fire. His three-shot burst punched through the cockpit canopy and splattered the thermal signature of one of the pilots. The craft swerved to the side, and its cannon barrel raked through the ceiling.

A twisted metal girder fell, but Susan caught it and tossed it aside. She lit her shoulder boosters and flew up through the smoke, climbing rapidly above the terrorist time machine. She leveled off and fired several shots down into the craft's passenger cabin, but only one of her shots penetrated the hull. Someone had added some "aftermarket" armor, and all the side windows were plated over.

She engaged her boosters again and swung around toward the front of the craft, which finished tearing a ragged groove through the tower's roof and began a lazy spin as it slowly lost altitude, descending into the nearby urban canyon. Her thermal readings brightened where the airliner's main fuselage met the impeller spike.

"Power-up detected!" Susan reported. "I think they're trying to phase out!"

"Stop them!" Pérez ordered, boosting toward the edge of the building. "Take it down!"

Susan followed the time machine's spin and lined up a shot on the cockpit. Her optics focused in on the pilot, but then she hesitated. Her variskin must have been damaged by the shrapnel, because the lanky man glared at her with fierce eyes and a hateful scowl.

She immediately recognized those intense eyes, even if the man had changed his hair color and style.

The second pilot was Cameron Nist! Their top

capture target was meters away from her! And this version wasn't fifty or sixty days out of date, but from the True Present! He'd know every one of Free Luna's dirty little secrets!

"Hold your fire!" Susan called out.

"Wait, what?" Pérez shouted from the edge of the tower roof. "Susan, what's wrong?"

She lit her shoulder boosters and crashed feetfirst onto the time machine's roof moments before its impeller activated. Everything but her combat frame and the Free Luna time machine blurred, and the city's day and night cycle played out once every ten seconds, even as the time machine continued its barely controlled descent down the urban canyon.

Susan clambered along the roof toward the back of the craft. She stopped by one of the dents she'd shot into it, found a seam, and punched it with all the might her combat frame could muster. Then again and again.

The armor bowed inward, and she poked her rail-rifle into the gash and pumped shot after shot into where her thermal vision said the power plant should be. A gout of plasma scorched her armor through the gash, and she backed away as the impeller faltered.

Their surroundings snapped back into sharp clarity, and a bright noon sun shone down into the urban canyon. The time machine's nose tipped upward, and the impeller spike dragged across the building roofs at the bottom of the canyon. Side thrusters strained to keep the craft aloft, but then they puttered out, and the whole craft levered down onto its belly.

Susan held on until the craft came to rest, then she

hurried back to the cockpit. Nist had retreated into the vessel's interior, but that wouldn't stop her.

"Cameron Nist, you are under arrest!" She shot up the window and shattered it with a swift kick, then jumped into the cockpit next to the gooey remains of the doctor's copilot. "Come out with your hands up!"

"Go to hell!" Nist swung into the open at the rear of the cockpit, pistol leveled at her. She engaged her boosters. Nist fired, but her armor deflected the shot moments before she tackled him. The gun flew out of his hand, and she pinned him to the floor.

He scrambled under her grip and kicked her in the leg, but then winced in pain, as he discovered how little protection the soft toe of his shoe provided for his foot.

"Ouch! Damn it!"

"Really?" she asked. "You tried to kick a STAND? Were you really a neurosurgeon?"

"Fuck you!"

"Yeah, yeah."

She turned him over and forced his arms behind his back, then retrieved a malmetal strip from her waist. Once in place, the strip constricted around his wrists.

"Agent Cantrell, do you read me?" Captain Elifritz radioed in from *Defender-Two*.

"Loud and clear, sir."

"We tracked the rogue time machine's movements and are now in phase with your temporal position. What's your status?"

"I managed to disable the enemy time machine and capture one of the pilots."

"Good work. We're heading your way now. We

should be in position to pick you up in about three minutes."

"Understood, sir. Also, I have something else to report, and I think you're going to like it."

"And what would that be?"

"The pilot I captured? It's Nist, sir."

"*Really.*" She could almost see the wide grin on Elifritz's face. "Well, well, well. Isn't this a fortunate turn of events? Fine work out there, Agent. Prep the prisoner for extraction."

"Yes, sir!" She stood up and lifted Nist to his feet. "We'll be waiting outside the time machine."

"This is all so pointless," the doctor snarled at her. "You might have caught me, but others will rise to take my place! The Admin will fall, and Luna will be independent once more! It's only a matter of time!"

"Save it, Nist." She hauled him toward the busted window.

"Try to ignore me all you want, but it'll do you no good! You're nothing but a soulless machine! A windup caricature of a corrupt thug, built to serve a corrupt government! I'd spit in your eyes if you still had them! You and the rest of your ill-conceived kind are a sickening perversion of humanity! The universe would be a better place if you were all deleted!"

She paused at the threshold, then chuckled.

"What the hell is so funny?" he snapped at her.

"Nothing." She chuckled again. "It's just, for someone calling himself 'Doctor Quiet,' you sure do run your mouth a lot."

REMEMBER THE ALAMO
by T.R. Fehrenbach

When this story appeared in the December 1961 issue of
Analog, *legendary editor John W. Campbell preceded it
with this observation, "This is, I think, one of the most
powerful comments on the modern social philosophy I
have seen. A really blood-chilling little tale." Very true
then, and even more on target six decades later. For some
reason, the author, renowned historian T.R. Fehrenbach,
was listed as "R.R. Fehrenbach" in the magazine, perhaps
a typo.*

Toward sundown, in the murky drizzle, the man who called
himself Ord brought Lieutenant Colonel William Barrett
Travis word that the Mexican light cavalry had completely
invested Bexar, and that some light guns were being set up
across the San Antonio River. Even as he spoke, there was
a flash and bang from the west, and a shell screamed over
the old mission walls. Travis looked worried.

"What kind of guns?" he asked.

"Nothing to worry about, sir," Ord said. "Only a few one-pounders, nothing of respectable siege caliber. General Santa Anna has had to move too fast for any big stuff to keep up." Ord spoke in his odd accent. After all, he was a Britainer, or some other kind of foreigner. But he spoke good Spanish, and he seemed to know everything. In the four or five days since he had appeared he had become very useful to Travis.

Frowning, Travis asked, "How many Mexicans, do you think, Ord?"

"Not more than a thousand, now," the dark-haired, blue-eyed young man said confidently. "But when the main body arrives, there'll be four, five thousand."

Travis shook his head. "How do you get all this information, Ord? You recite it like you had read it all some place—like it were history."

Ord merely smiled. "Oh, I don't know *everything*, colonel. That is why I had to come here. There is so much we don't know about what happened. . . . I mean, sir, what will happen—in the Alamo." His sharp eyes grew puzzled for an instant. "And some things don't seem to match up, somehow—"

Travis looked at him sympathetically. Ord talked queerly at times, and Travis suspected he was a bit deranged. This was understandable, for the man was undoubtedly a Britainer aristocrat, a refugee from Napoleon's thousand-year Empire. Travis had heard about the detention camps and the charcoal ovens . . . but once, when he had mentioned the *Empereur's* sack of London in '06, Ord had gotten a very queer look in his eyes, as if he had forgotten completely.

But John Ord, or whatever his name was, seemed to be the only man in the Texas forces who understood what William Barrett Travis was trying to do. Now Travis looked around at the thick adobe wall surrounding the old mission in which they stood. In the cold, yellowish twilight even the flaring cook fires of his hundred and eighty-two men could not dispel the ghostly air that clung to the old place. Travis shivered involuntarily. But the walls were thick, and they could turn one-pounders. He asked, "What was it you called this place, Ord . . . the Mexican name?"

"The Alamo, sir." A slow, steady excitement seemed to burn in the Britainer's bright eyes. "Santa Anna won't forget that name, you can be sure. You'll want to talk to the other officers now, sir? About the message we drew up for Sam Houston?"

"Yes, of course," Travis said absently. He watched Ord head for the walls. No doubt about it, Ord understood what William Barrett Travis was trying to do here. So few of the others seemed to care.

Travis was suddenly very glad that John Ord had shown up when he did.

On the walls, Ord found the man he sought, broad-shouldered and tall in a fancy Mexican jacket. "The commandant's compliments, sir, and he desires your presence in the chapel."

The big man put away the knife with which he had been whittling. The switchblade snicked back and disappeared into a side pocket of the jacket, while Ord watched it with fascinated eyes. "What's old Bill got his britches hot about this time?" the big man asked.

"I wouldn't know, sir," Ord said stiffly and moved on.

Bang-bang-bang roared the small Mexican cannon from across the river. *Pow-pow-pow!* The little balls only chipped dust from the thick adobe walls. Ord smiled.

He found the second man he sought, a lean man with a weathered face, leaning against a wall and chewing tobacco. This man wore a long, fringed, leather lounge jacket, and he carried a guitar slung beside his Rock Island rifle. He squinted up at Ord. "I know...I know," he muttered. "Willy Travis is in an uproar again. You reckon that colonel's commission that Congress up in Washington-on-the-Brazos give him swelled his head?"

Rather stiffly, Ord said, "Colonel, the commandant desires an officers' conference in the chapel, now." Ord was somewhat annoyed. He had not realized he would find these Americans so—distasteful. Hardly preferable to Mexicans, really. Not at all as he had imagined.

For an instant he wished he had chosen Drake and the Armada instead of this pack of ruffians—but no, he had never been able to stand sea sickness. He couldn't have taken the Channel, not even for five minutes.

And there was no changing now. He had chosen this place and time carefully, at great expense—actually, at great risk, for the X-4-A had aborted twice, and he had had a hard time bringing her in. But it had got him here at last. And, because for a historian he had always been an impetuous and daring man, he grinned now, thinking of the glory that was to come. And he was a participant— much better than a ringside seat! Only he would have to be careful, at the last, to slip away.

John Ord knew very well how this coming battle had ended, back here in 1836.

He marched back to William Barrett Travis, clicked heels smartly. Travis' eyes glowed; he was the only senior officer here who loved military punctilio. "Sir, they are on the way."

"Thank you, Ord," Travis hesitated a moment. "Look, Ord. There will be a battle, as we know. I know so little about you. If something should happen to you, is there anyone to write? Across the water?"

Ord grinned. "No, sir. I'm afraid my ancestor wouldn't understand."

Travis shrugged. Who was he to say that Ord was crazy? In this day and age, any man with vision was looked on as mad. Sometimes he felt closer to Ord than to the others.

The two officers Ord had summoned entered the chapel. The big man in the Mexican jacket tried to dominate the wood table at which they sat. He towered over the slender, nervous Travis, but the commandant, straight-backed and arrogant, did not give an inch. "Boys, you know Santa Anna has invested us. We've been fired on all day—" He seemed to be listening for something. *Wham!* Outside, a cannon split the dusk with flame and sound as it fired from the walls. "There is my answer!"

The man in the lounge coat shrugged. "What I want to know is what our orders are. What does old Sam say? Sam and me were in Congress once. Sam's got good sense; he can smell the way the wind's blowin'." He stopped speaking and hit his guitar a few licks. He winked across the table at the officer in the Mexican jacket who took out his knife. "Eh, Jim?"

"Right," Jim said. "Sam's a good man, although I don't think he ever met a payroll."

"General Houston's leaving it up to me," Travis told them.

"Well, that's that," Jim said unhappily. "So what you figurin' to do, Bill?"

Travis stood up in the weak, flickering candlelight, one hand on the polished hilt of his saber. The other two men winced, watching him. "Gentlemen, Houston's trying to pull his militia together while he falls back. You know, Texas was woefully unprepared for a contest at arms. The general's idea is to draw Santa Anna as far into Texas as he can, then hit him when he's extended, at the right place, and right time. But Houston needs more time— Santa Anna's moved faster than any of us anticipated. Unless we can stop the Mexican Army and take a little steam out of them, General Houston's in trouble."

Jim flicked the knife blade in and out. "Go on."

"This is where we come in, gentlemen. Santa Anna can't leave a force of one hundred eighty men in his rear. If we hold fast, he must attack us. But he has no siege equipment, not even large field cannon." Travis' eye gleamed. "Think of it, boys! He'll have to mount a frontal attack, against protected American riflemen. Ord, couldn't your Englishers tell him a few things about that!"

"Whoa, now," Jim barked. "Billy, anybody tell you there's maybe four or five thousand Mexicaners comin'?"

"Let them come. Less will leave!"

But Jim, sour-faced turned to the other man. "Davey? You got something to say?"

"Hell, yes. How do we get out, after we done pinned Santa Anna down? You thought of that, Billy boy?"

Travis shrugged. "There is an element of grave risk, of course. Ord, where's the document, the message you wrote up for me? Ah, thank you." Travis cleared his throat. "Here's what I'm sending on to general Houston." He read, "Commandancy of the Alamo, February 24, 1836 . . . are you sure of that date, Ord?"

"Oh, I'm sure of that," Ord said.

"Never mind—if you're wrong we can change it later. 'To the People of Texas and all Americans in the World. Fellow Freemen and Compatriots! I am besieged with a thousand or more Mexicans under Santa Anna. I have sustained a continual bombardment for many hours but have not lost a man. The enemy has demanded surrender at discretion, otherwise, the garrison is to be put to the sword, if taken. I have answered the demand with a cannon shot, and our flag still waves proudly over the walls. I shall never surrender or retreat. Then, I call on you in the name of liberty, of patriotism and everything dear to the American character—'" He paused, frowning, "This language seems pretty old-fashioned, Ord—"

"Oh, no, sir. That's exactly right," Ord murmured.

"'. . . To come to our aid with all dispatch. The enemy is receiving reinforcements daily and will no doubt increase to three or four thousand in four or five days. If this call is neglected, I am determined to sustain myself as long as possible and die like a soldier who never forgets what is due his honor or that of his homeland. VICTORY OR DEATH!'"

Travis stopped reading, looked up. "Wonderful! Wonderful!" Ord breathed. "The greatest words of defiance ever written in the English tongue—and so much more literate than that chap at Bastogne."

"You mean to send that?" Jim gasped.

The man called Davey was holding his head in his hands.

"You object, Colonel Bowie?" Travis asked icily.

"Oh, cut that 'colonel' stuff, Bill," Bowie said. "It's only a National Guard title, and I like 'Jim' better, even though I am a pretty important man. Damn right I have an objection! Why, that message is almost aggressive. You'd think we wanted to fight Santa Anna! You want us to be marked down as warmongers? It'll give us trouble when we get to the negotiation table—"

Travis' head turned. "Colonel Crockett?"

"What Jim says goes for me, too. And this: I'd change that part about all Americans, et cetera. You don't want anybody to think we think we're better than the Mexicans. After all, Americans are a minority in the world. Why not make it 'all men who love security?' That'd have world-wide appeal—"

"Oh, Crockett," Travis hissed.

Crockett stood up. "Don't use that tone of voice to me, Billy Travis! That piece of paper you got don't make you no better'n us. I ran for Congress twice, and won. I know what the people want—"

"What the people want doesn't mean a damn right now," Travis said harshly. "Don't you realize the tyrant is at the gates?"

Crockett rolled his eyes heavenward. "Never thought

I'd hear a good American say that! Billy, you'll never run for office—"

Bowie held up a hand, cutting into Crockett's talk. "All right, Davey. Hold up. You ain't runnin' for Congress now. Bill, the main thing I don't like in your whole message is that part about victory or death. That's got to go. Don't ask us to sell that to the troops!"

Travis closed his eyes briefly. "Boys, listen. We don't have to tell the men about this. They don't need to know the real story until it's too late for them to get out. And then we shall cover ourselves with such glory that none of us shall ever be forgotten. Americans are the best fighters in the world when they are trapped. They teach this in the Foot School back on the Chatahoochee. And if we die, to die for one's country is sweet—"

"Hell with that," Crockett drawled. "I don't mind dyin', but not for these big landowners like Jim Bowie here. I just been thinkin'—I don't own nothing in Texas."

"I resent that," Bowie shouted. "You know very well I volunteered, after I sent my wife off to Acapulco to be with her family." With an effort, he calmed himself. "Look, Travis. I have some reputation as a fighting man— you know I lived through the gang wars back home. It's obvious this Alamo place is indefensible, even if we had a thousand men."

"But we must delay Santa Anna at all costs—"

Bowie took out a fine, dark Mexican cigar and whittled at it with his blade. Then he lit it, saying around it, "All right, let's all calm down. Nothing a group of good men can't settle around a table. Now listen. I got in with this revolution at first because I thought old Emperor Iturbide would listen to reason and lower taxes. But nothin's worked out, because hot-heads like you, Travis, queered the deal. All this yammerin' about liberty! Mexico is a Republic, under an Emperor, not some kind of democracy, and we can't change that. Let's talk some sense before it's too late. We're all too old and too smart to be wavin' the flag like it's the Fourth of July. Sooner or later, we're goin' to have to sit down and talk with the Mexicans. And like Davey said, I own a million hectares, and I've always paid minimum wage, and my wife's folks are way up there in the Imperial Government of the Republic of Mexico. That means I got influence in all the votin' groups, includin' the American Immigrant, since I'm a minority group member myself. I think I can talk to Santa Anna, and even to old Iturbide. If we sign a treaty now with Santa Anna, acknowledge the law of the land, I think our lives and property rights will be respected—" He cocked an eye toward Crockett.

"Makes sense, Jim. That's the way we do it in Congress. Compromise, everybody happy. We never allowed ourselves to be led nowhere we didn't want to go, I can tell you! And Bill, you got to admit that we're in better bargaining position if we're out in the open, than if old Santa Anna's got us penned up in this old Alamo."

"Ord," Travis said despairingly. "Ord, you understand. Help me! Make them listen!"

Ord moved into the candlelight, his lean face sweating. "Gentlemen, this is all wrong! It doesn't happen this way—"

Crockett sneered, "Who asked you, Ord? I'll bet you ain't even got a poll tax!"

Decisively, Bowie said, "We're free men, Travis, and we won't be led around like cattle. How about it, Davey? Think you could handle the rear guard, if we try to move out of here?"

"Hell, yes! Just so we're movin'!"

"O.K. Put it to a vote of the men outside. Do we stay, and maybe get croaked, or do we fall back and conserve our strength until we need it? Take care of it, eh, Davey?"

Crockett picked up his guitar and went outside.

Travis roared, "This is insubordination! Treason!" He drew his saber, but Bowie took it from him and broke it in two. Then the big man pulled his knife.

"Stay back, Ord. The Alamo isn't worth the bones of a Britainer, either."

"Colonel Bowie, please," Ord cried. "You don't understand! You *must* defend the Alamo! This is the turning point in the winning of the west! If Houston is beaten, Texas will never join the Union! There will be no Mexican War. No California, no nation stretching from sea to shining sea! This is the Americans' manifest destiny. You are the hope of the future . . . you will save the world from Hitler, from Bolshevism—"

"Crazy as a hoot owl," Bowie said sadly. "Ord, you and Travis got to look at it both ways. We ain't all in the right in this war—we Americans got our faults, too."

"But you are free men," Ord whispered. "Vulgar, opinionated, brutal—but free! You are still better than any breed who kneels to tyranny—"

Crockett came in. "O.K., Jim."

"How'd it go?"

"Fifty-one per cent for hightailin' it right now."

Bowie smiled. "That's a flat majority. Let's make tracks."

"Comin', Bill?" Crockett asked. "You're O.K., but you just don't know how to be one of the boys. You got to learn that no dog is better'n any other."

"No," Travis croaked hoarsely. "I stay. Stay or go, we shall all die like dogs, anyway. Boys, for the last time! Don't reveal our weakness to the enemy—"

"What weakness? We're stronger than them. Americans could whip the Mexicans any day, if we wanted to. But the thing to do is make 'em talk, not fight. So long, Bill."

The two big men stepped outside. In the night there was a sudden clatter of hoofs as the Texans mounted and rode. From across the river came a brief spatter of musket fire, then silence. In the dark, there had been no difficulty in breaking through the Mexican lines.

Inside the chapel, John Ord's mouth hung slackly. He muttered, "Am I insane? It didn't happen this way—it couldn't! The books can't be *that* wrong—"

In the candlelight, Travis hung his head. "We tried, John. Perhaps it was a forlorn hope at best. Even if we had defeated Santa Anna, or delayed him, I do not think the Indian Nations would have let Houston get help from the United States."

Ord continued his dazed muttering, hardly hearing.

"We need a contiguous frontier with Texas," Travis continued slowly, just above a whisper. "But we Americans have never broken a treaty with the Indians, and pray God we never shall. *We* aren't like the Mexicans, always pushing, always grabbing off New Mexico, Arizona,

California. *We* aren't colonial oppressors, thank God! No, it wouldn't have worked out, even if we American immigrants had secured our rights in Texas—" He lifted a short, heavy, percussion pistol in his hand and cocked it. "I hate to say it, but perhaps if we hadn't taken Payne and Jefferson so seriously—if we could only have paid lip service, and done what we really wanted to do, in our hearts . . . no matter. I won't live to see our final disgrace."

He put the pistol to his head and blew out his brains.

Ord was still gibbering when the Mexican cavalry stormed into the old mission, pulling down the flag and seizing him, dragging him before the resplendent little general in green and gold.

Since he was the only prisoner, Santa Anna questioned Ord carefully. When the sharp point of a bayonet had been thrust half an inch into his stomach, the Britainer seemed to come around. When he started speaking, and the Mexicans realized he was English, it went better with him. Ord was obviously mad, it seemed to Santa Anna, but since he spoke English and seemed educated, he could be useful. Santa Anna didn't mind the raving; he understood all about Napoleon's detention camps and what they had done to Britainers over there. In fact, Santa Anna was thinking of setting up a couple of those camps himself. When they had milked Ord dry, they threw him on a horse and took him along.

Thus John Ord had an excellent view of the battlefield when Santa Anna's cannon broke the American lines south of the Trinity. Unable to get his men across to safety, Sam Houston died leading the last, desperate charge against

the Mexican regulars. After that, the American survivors
were too tired to run from the cavalry that pinned them
against the flooding river. Most of them died there. Santa
Anna expressed complete indifference to what happened
to the Texans' women and children.

Mexican soldiers found Jim Bowie hiding in a hut,
wearing a plain linen tunic and pretending to be a civilian.
They would not have discovered his identity had not some
of the Texan women cried out, "Colonel Bowie—Colonel
Bowie!" as he was led into the Mexican camp.

He was hauled before Santa Anna, and Ord was
summoned to watch. "Well, don Jaime," Santa Anna
remarked, "You have been a foolish man. I promised your
wife's uncle to send you to Acapulco safely, though of
course your lands are forfeit. You understand we must
have lands for the veterans' program when this campaign
is over—" Santa Anna smiled then. "Besides, since Ord
here has told me how instrumental you were in the
abandonment of the Alamo, I think the Emperor will
agree to mercy in your case. You know, don Jaime, your
compatriots had me worried back there. The Alamo might
have been a tough nut to crack . . . *pues*, no matter."

And since Santa Anna had always been broadminded,
not objecting to light skin or immigrant background, he
invited Bowie to dinner that night.

Santa Anna turned to Ord. "But if we could catch this
rascally war criminal, Crockett . . . however, I fear he has
escaped us. He slipped over the river with a fake passport,
and the Indians have interned him."

"Sí, *Señor Presidente*," Ord said dully.

"Please, don't call me that," Santa Anna cried, looking

around. "True, many of us officers have political ambitions, but Emperor Iturbide is old and vain. It could mean my head—"

Suddenly, Ord's head was erect, and the old, clear light was in his blue eyes. "Now I understand!" he shouted. "I thought Travis was raving back there, before he shot himself—and your talk of the Emperor! American respect for Indian rights! Jeffersonian form of government! Oh, those ponces who peddled me that X-4-A—the *track jumper*! I'm not back in my own past. I've jumped the time track—*I'm back in a screaming alternate!*"

"Please, not so loud, *Señor* Ord," Santa Anna sighed. "Now, we must shoot a few more American officers, of course. I regret this, you understand, and I shall no doubt be much criticized in French Canada and Russia, where there are still civilized values. But we must establish the Republic of the Empire once and for all upon this continent, that aristocratic tyranny shall not perish from the earth. Of course, as an Englishman, you understand perfectly, Señor Ord."

"Of course, excellency," Ord said.

"There are soft hearts—soft heads, I say—in Mexico who cry for civil rights for the Americans. But I must make sure that Mexican dominance is never again threatened north of the Rio Grande."

"*Seguro*, excellency," Ord said, suddenly. If the bloody X-4-A *had* jumped the track, there was no getting back, none at all. He was stuck here. Ord's blue eyes narrowed. "After all, it . . . it is manifest destiny that the Latin peoples of North America meet at the center of the continent. Canada and Mexico shall share the Mississippi."

Santa Anna's dark eyes glowed. "You say what I have often thought. You are a man of vision, and much sense. You realize the *Indios* must go, whether they were here first or not. I think I will make you my secretary, with the rank of captain."

"*Gracias*, Excellency."

"Now, let us write my communique to the capital, *Capitán* Ord. We must describe how the American abandonment of the Alamo allowed me to press the traitor Houston so closely he had no chance to maneuver his men into the trap he sought. *Ay, Capitán*, it is a cardinal principle of the Anglo-Saxons, to get themselves into a trap from which they must fight their way out. This I never let them do, which is why I succeed where others fail . . . you said something, *Capitán*?"

"*Sí*, Excellency. I said, I shall title our communique: 'Remember the Alamo,'" Ord said, standing at attention.

"*Bueno!* You have a gift for words. Indeed, if ever we feel the *gringos* are too much for us, your words shall once again remind us of the truth!" Santa Anna smiled. "I think I shall make you a major. You have indeed coined a phrase which shall live in history forever!"

COMRADES OF TIME
by Edmond Hamilton

Edmond Hamilton's writing spanned a sizable chunk of the twentieth century, so it's not surprising that his writing changed, or "matured" (as the lit crit types like to say), beginning with fast-paced action yarns, later changing to more reflective works with subtler mood and characterization. This is one of the early pieces, with noble heroes and even a not-quite mad scientist and his beautiful daughter, but Hamilton's gift for action keeps the set pieces in headlong motion. And nowadays, the story might even get points for being "multicultural." At the time, it was popular enough to merit a sequel, "Armies from the Past," which I wish I could have included, though a little poking around online by the reader will turn it up.

I
Men from the Past

Ethan Drew's rifle was hot in his hand, and not from the scorching desert sun but from desperate firing. There were just two of them left, just two of this patrol of the Foreign Legion that had been ambushed here deep in the Sahara.

As he crouched in the scant shelter of the sandy gully, firing at the white-burnoosed riders out there in front of him, he laughed harshly. His browned, aquiline young face was taut, his nostrils flaring, gray eyes icy, as he called to his single companion.

"They're going to charge, Emil! Looks as if we won't be seeing the cafes at Sidi again."

"We're going to die!" wailed the other legionnaire, a swarthy, stocky Swiss, terror on his features. "We're going to—"

Thuck! The Swiss tumbled sidewise with a hole in his face and lay sprawled half across the bodies of the other dead men. And the Tuaregs were now riding forward in their charge, white-garbed, veiled demons, flourishing their rifles and sabers and yelling like fiends as they came on.

Ethan Drew savagely aimed and pulled trigger. At the first shot, a horse and rider crashed. The second time he squeezed the trigger, there was only a click. The Lebel was empty. He grabbed a sword from a dead officer and stood up, his blond head bare in the blazing sunlight as he yelled recklessly.

"Come on, damn you!"

"Muhammad rasul Allah!" screamed the Tuaregs, racing each other for the honor of cutting down this last survivor.

Ethan Drew had a momentary vision of them thundering down on him, horses' eyes rolling wildly, upraised sabers glinting, veiled riders leaning forward. Then the whole world seemed suddenly to explode in blinding light, and he knew nothing more.

He awoke to dim consciousness that he was lying on a cold, hard surface. The air was chill, with a pungent, unfamiliar quality. Now this was a strange thing, Ethan thought dully, to awake from death. For he knew the Tuaregs must have killed him in that charge—indeed, he had wanted to be killed rather than to be captured and tortured.

Yet he did not feel dead, at all. He could feel the cold floor under him distinctly and was also aware that his head was aching badly. Also, he could hear the voices of men close beside him.

He lay, feeling too dazed to open his eyes, and listened.

"No use buttin' your horns against a tree, Pedro," a dry, nasal voice was drawling. "This Injun don't like bein' cooped up here no more than you do, but that ain't anything we can do about it."

"But, *Dios*, I shall go mad in this cursed cell!" swore another, angry voice with a strong Spanish accent. "It's no place for a *conquistador*. I'd welcome the devil himself if he got me out of here."

"Cease blaspheming, man," commanded a harsh, deep voice. "If it is the Lord's will that we escape from here, we shall do so."

Ethan Drew listened with gathering amazement. Then he stirred, struggling to sit up.

"The new one is awakening!" someone called. There was a rush of feet toward the young American as he sat up and looked around. He found that he still held the officer's sword clutched in his hand.

He was sitting on the floor of a large room of black stone. There was but one window, a tiny, heavily barred one through which came an oblique shaft of dusky *red* sunlight. The only door was a small metal trap-door in the ceiling, sixteen feet overhead.

The men in the room were crowding eagerly around Ethan Drew. The dazed young American looked bewilderingly at the foremost of them, who was bending keenly forward.

He was a tall, lank man of forty, dressed in greasy buckskin shirt, trousers and moccasins, and a shabby coonskin cap. A big hunting knife was stuck in his belt, and he held a long, old-fashioned muzzle-loading rifle in the hollow of his arm. He had a weathered, saturnine face with jutting jaw and cool, wise blue eyes.

"Feelin' all right?" he asked Ethan. "It shore takes the tucker out of you when you first get here. This child knows."

"Who—who are you?" Ethan asked haltingly.

"Me, I'm Hank Martin, the best trapper an' scout in the Rockies, barrin' my friend, Kit Carson," drawled the tall figure.

"A mountain-man of Kit Carson's time?" gasped. Ethan Drew. "Why, you're crazy! That was a hundred years ago!"

"That's what *you* think," drawled Hank Martin dryly. "You've got a lot to learn, young feller. Why, just a week ago, it seems, I was trappin' up in the Utes with Kit and ol' Bill Williams and the rest."

Ethan stared at the man unbelievingly. His stare

became more incredulous as he saw the man standing beside the trapper. This was a stalwart, broad-shouldered figure with a stern, somber, massive face, dressed in drab homespun uniform, high leather boots and a plain black hat. A huge broadsword swung at his wide belt.

"I am John Crewe, formerly corporal in the Ironsides of that man of God, Oliver Cromwell," he said in his deep, harsh voice. "Say, do you know anything of how we were brought here, or for what reason?"

"Aye, if you know who has done this, just tell me his name!" roared another voice before Ethan could answer. "*Por Dios*, I'll gut him like a rat, whoever he is! I'll teach him what it means to play his enchanter's tricks upon Pedro Lopez!"

Lopez was a fierce-mustached, eagle-eyed, swearing Spaniard who wore the iron helmet and breastplate and baggy boots and long sword of a Sixteenth Century *conquistador*.

"I'll make the wizard who played this trick on me wish he'd never been born!" he roared. "Am I, one of the valiant followers of the peerless Don Hernando Cortez, to be snatched out of my own time by black magic, without slitting a few throats in return?"

"Aw, cool down, Pedro," drawled Hank Martin. "Can't you see I want to interduce the rest of the boys to this tenderfoot?"

"This *must* be a crazy joke of some kind!" Ethan exclaimed hoarsely. "You men—from times centuries apart—it's impossible!"

"Shore, mebbe it's impossible, but it's true," Hank Martin drawled coolly. "We've been in here for days together, most of us, and we've got pretty well acquainted, and Crewe and I hev larned the others some English. Speak up, boys, and tell our new pardner who you are."

A small, wiry man with a dark face and cunning eyes, wearing the bronze armor and shortsword of a soldier of ancient Egypt, stepped forward and spoke calmly to the dazed Ethan in halting English.

"I am Ptah, soldier of the great Thothmes the Third," he said proudly. "I followed him to the conquest of Syria."

"And I," added a heavy, rumbling voice, "am Swain Njallson, seafarer and raider, whose beaked ships have been feared form my own Northland south even to Mikligard."

Swain was a huge giant of a man, a Tenth Century viking whose blond hair flowed from under his horned helmet, whose blue eyes were icy cold as his native seas. An enormous axe was gripped in his hand.

Ethan Drew's eyes roamed dazedly over the weirdly assorted five men. He still felt that all of this was utterly unreal, yet the men before him were no hallucination. Ancient Egyptian and viking and Spanish *conquistador*, Rocky Mountain trapper and Puritan trooper, they stood before him as real as himself.

"I'm Ethan Drew, and I'm from a later time than any of you," he said unsteadily. "From the year 1938. I was fighting off enemies, about to be killed, when there was a blaze of light; then I awoke here."

"Same thing happened to all of us," Hank Martin told him. "Me, I was heelin' it out of Ute Pass with a bunch of redskins after me when somethin' hit me, and I woke up here. I was alone at first—later on, the trap-door in the ceilin' opened, and they let down this little fellow Ptah, from Egypt. The others here came the same way, one after another, through the trap-door. And now you, too."

"Then you've never seen the person or persons who brought us here?" Ethan cried bewilderedly.

Hank Martin shook his head. "Nary once. The trap-door is opened, and grub and water are let down to us once a day, but that's all."

"Isn't there any way to escape from here?" Ethan exclaimed. "What about that window?"

"Look for yourself," Hank drawled.

Ethan went to the little window. He was at once that escape by it was impossible. It was only a foot square and barred with heavy rods of metal. But the was stricken with awe and wonder by the weird vista outside.

Before him, black rock cliffs sloped down steeply toward a vast expanse of flat country thickly blanketed by dense green jungle. As far as the eye could reach stretched that silent, mighty wilderness, unearthly and forbidding.

Across the limitless jungle struck the level crimson rays of the descending sun. Huge and blood-red and weirdly glowing, it was sinking toward the horizon. It might have been a different sun entirely, setting upon a wild and unknown planet.

"This isn't my own time—this isn't 1938," Ethan Drew muttered in awe. "We've all been drawn somehow into the far future."

"The future?" repeated John Crewe, frowning. "What makes you think that?"

"Look at the sun," Ethan said quickly. "It is far redder, which means it is older—millions of years older."

"How in the devil's name *could* we be dragged across millions of years?" Pedro Lopez demanded loudly. "It is impossible."

"It is the work of Loki, the demon god," rumbled Swain Njallson with conviction. "Only he could do this to us."

John Crewe, the big Puritan, cast a gloomy glance at the huge viking.

"Talk not of your heathen gods doing this," he said harshly. "No vain idols brought us here but Satan, the Evil One, himself."

"Wal, how we got here don't bother me much," drawled Hank Martin. "What bothers me is how we're going to get back to our own times. Me, I don't cotton to the looks of this world much—I'd ruther be back in the Rockies, trappin' beaver and dodgin' Injuns."

Ethan Drew looked up keenly at the little metal trap-door in the high stone ceiling.

"Have you tried to reach that door, by standing on each other's shoulders?" he asked.

"Yes, but we could never reach it," Pedro Lopez told him. "*Sangre de Dios*, I'm still sore all over from the falls I had on this cursed stone floor."

"But now there is another of us to help!" Ptah, the Egyptian, exclaimed, pointing at Ethan. "We might be able to make it now!"

"Let us make the attempt, then," rumbled Swain. "Anything is better than rotting away to a cow's death in this cell."

The six men began to form a human pyramid beneath

the trap-door. Swain, John Crewe and Hank Martin, as the three biggest of them, formed the base. Pedro Lopez and Ethan climbed onto their shoulders. And then Ptah, the smallest and wiriest of them, mounted precariously upon the shoulders of Ethan and the *conquistador*.

The whole pyramid swayed hazardously as the little Egyptian attacked the trap-door with his bronze shortsword. But the huge shoulders of the viking, down at the heart of the human tower's base, steadied them. And presently they heard a clang from above, and an exultant cry from Ptah.

"I have it open!" he cried to them.

They felt the little Egyptian scramble up through the opening. Then he unfastened and let down his leather belt and hauled Ethan and the Spaniard up.

By fastening together all their belts, they were able to pull up Hank Martin and John Crewe and Swain, though the huge weight of the viking almost snapped the improvised leather rope. Then, panting from their efforts, they stared excitedly around them.

They stood in a narrow, dusky stone corridor.

It turned in a sharp angle a few yards away, preventing them from seeing any distance along it.

But as they stood panting, there came dimly to them down this corridor a sound familiar to all these men—one that made them stiffen—the clash of steel against steel, of sword against sword!

"Fightin' goin' on!" exclaimed Hank Martin, the trapper's leathery face tightening.

They heard a bull voice in the distance shouting orders, then a woman's sharp scream.

"Odin, at least there is battle in this world!" exclaimed Swain, blue eyes gleaming. "Let us go to it, comrades!"

"Aye, for I still crave the blood of the wizard who brought us here," cried Pedro Lopez fiercely.

The viking's great axe raised, Hank Martin's long rifle under his arm, the swords of the others gleaming in the dusk, they started along the corridor.

II
Rumble of Doom

The clash of swords bad ceased, but the feminine scream was repeated as the six fighting-men advanced. Then as they rounded the turn in the corridor, they beheld the source of those screams.

Two black-bearded, black-armored men with wolfish faces held a white-faced girl. Laughing at her wild struggles, one of them tore away the neck of her short white robe, exposing an ivory shoulder and breast. The girl, her dark eyes blazing and her black hair wildly disheveled, struck in vain with tiny fists.

Ethan Drew's blood heated in swift anger at the sight. He started ahead, sword raised.

"We can't let *that* go on!" he rasped.

"They are godless men—sons of Belial," said John Crewe harshly. "Forward!"

The two black-bearded soldiers looked up and saw that grim, weirdly assorted little company of six men coming down the corridor toward them. They released the girl and yelled in alarm, at the same time drawing their swords.

Other black-armored soldiers came hurrying into the farther cell of the corridor in answer to the call.

Then Ethan Drew's sword clashed the blade of one of the two warriors. The swift anger that boiled in the young American brought all his remembered fencing skill into his muscles as he parried a vicious blow and then stabbed fiercely.

His opponent went down, his throat transfixed by Ethan's blade. At the same moment the other of the two who had held the girl sank in a lifeless heap, his neck half severed by John Crewe's broad blade.

"Thus die all followers of Satan!" shouted the big Puritan with fanatic fervor.

"Here come the others!" yelled Ptah.

The girl had sunk fainting to the floor. Ethan hastily swept her behind them, then faced with his comrades the dozen warriors racing down the corridor. They were bellowing with rage, those fierce-faced men in black armor. Their swords gleamed in the dusky light, lust to kill written on their faces.

Crack! One of them fell with a neat little hole drilled between his eyes.

"Easy shootin'," drawled Hank Martin. "I wish Kit and ol' Bill was here."

Then the charging warriors met the line of six men. Sparks flew through the dusk as sword clashed fiercely against sword.

Ethan Drew fought with forced coolness, his brown, lean face set in a mirthless grin as he stabbed and feinted. The first man to oppose him reeled back with his shoulder impaled, howling.

Another raised his blade to slash sidewise at the American. Before the man could complete the stroke, Ptah's bronze shortsword bit into his vitals. The swarthy little Egyptian calmly attacked another man.

A hell of battle raged in that dusky hallway for minutes. Hank Martin had clubbed his long rifle and was smashing faces into red pulp with its butt. John Crewe's somber, massive face held a stern light of battle as he struck with his big broadsword.

"Spawn of Beelzebub!" muttered the big Puritan as he fought. "Men without righteousness!"

"Come on, dogs!" Lopez was roaring. The *conquistador* cursed as he hacked. "I'll make you sorry your mothers ever bore you!"

But it was Swain Njallson who was doing most execution in that cramped, terrific fight. The huge viking's axe whirled in circles of blinding death, smashing helmet after helmet, his blue eyes blazing.

It was too much for the black armored attackers. They recoiled, leaving more than half their number dead, then turned and ran down the corridor.

"Flee, vermin!" Lopez shouted after them. "Now you know what it means to meet a cavalier of Spain."

"Haw! haw!" chuckled Hank Martin, reloading his rifle. "They sure bit off more'n they could chew."

Ethan Drew, while the others stood panting, was bending over the unconscious girl, seeking to revive her. The ripe curves of her body were hardly concealed by the short, torn white robe. There were still red marks of rude fingers on her creamy shoulders.

She opened great, dark eyes, gazed bewilderedly up

into Ethan's lean face. Her eyes widened in wonder, her soft red lips parted. Then as memory came back, she sprang erect.

"My father!" she cried. "Thorold and his soldiers have captured him!"

Ethan was amazed to find that he could understand her words. For she spoke in a language that seemed descended from English, though it was changed in inflection and accent and in many word-meanings.

"Who are you?" Ethan demanded, "And who are the men who were attacking you?"

"They were some of Thorold's soldiers!" she cried. "I am Chiri, and my father Kim Idim, is the man who brought you all into this time out of your own past ages."

"Ha, so your father did that!" exclaimed Pedro Lopez, scowling fiercely. "The I will see this father of yours. He'll eat six inches of steel if he doesn't—"

"Shut up, Pedro," drawled Hank Martin. "Let the little lady tell us what she's drivin' at."

"You must save Kim Idim, my father!" Chiri was crying desperately to Ethan.

"Come on, boys," the American rasped to his comrades. "I don't know yet what this is all about, but we're going to find out."

They started on a run along the corridor, Chiri frantically leading the way. The corridor soon debouched into a high, domed hall. Gleaming, grotesque machines about it made it look like a laboratory.

Three men who appeared to have been servants lay dead here, swords still clutched in their hands. Chiri ran

around them and through a door into the open air. Ethan
and his comrades followed her closely.

They emerged into the dusky red sunset, on a paved
terrace. Behind them loomed the building in which they
had been confined, a domed structure of black stone,
immeasurably ancient-looking.

In front of them, the steep black cliff slanted down to
the green sea of jungle. A precarious pathway angled
down the cliff.

Chiri cried out and pointed down to the bottom of the
cliff, hundreds of feet below.

"See, there are Thorold and his soldiers! And my
father!"

Ethan peered down and saw a score of men in black
armor at the foot of the cliff, hastily mounting horses
which had been tethered there.

One of these men, apparently the leader Thorold, was
a huge-framed, dark-faced giant who was shouting orders
in a bull voice as he mounted.

A thin, white-haired old man with blood flowing from
his temple had been thrust in front of one of the mounted
warriors. His hands were bound. And a squat, heavy-
looking machine had been hastily loaded into a litter
swung between two of the horses.

"Thorold is taking my father and the time-ray projector
to Tzar!" Chiri cried. "Stop them!"

"Hank, try to drop the big fellow," Ethan said hastily.

Hank Martin quickly raised his long rifle. But as the
trapper did so, the giant Thorold shouted an order and
the whole troop below spurred forward into the jungle
and were instantly hidden under the trees.

"Dang it, I was a mite too slow!" the buckskin-clad trapper exclaimed in vexation.

"We can follow them, and my sword will not be too slow!" exclaimed Pedro Lopez, starting toward the path down the cliff.

"Aye, let us follow," rumbled Swain, the viking's blue eyes still burning with the battle light.

"Wait!" Ethan commanded. "We can't overtake them now, mounted as they are. And we need to know where we stand before we go very far in this world."

"That's right," Hank Martin approved. "Unless we scout the land before we move, we'll run into an ambush and lose our scalps sure."

Ptah and John Crewe nodded agreement, and the viking and the *conquistador* came back.

Chiri grasped Ethan's arm anxiously, her dark eyes looking pleadingly up at him.

"You will follow and save my father from Thorold?" she cried urgently.

"Why should we?" Ethan demanded sternly. "You admit it was some hellish experiment of your father's that drew us out of our own times into this future age. We owe nothing to him, who played that trick upon us.

"It is true," said John Crewe somberly. "And yon old man whom they captured cannot be a godly man, or he would not juggle with time against the will of heaven, as he did."

Chiri's eyes flashed sudden defiance, and she stamped her little foot.

"If you refuse to rescue my father, you will stay in this

time forever!" she told them; "for only he can send you back to your own ages. And now Thorold has him and his time-ray projector."

"That kinder changes things," muttered Hank Martin thoughtfully. "Me, I don't want to stay in this queer layout forever."

"Nor I either!" Pedro Lopez declared. "I was assisting the valiant Don Hernando Cortez in the conquest of those dogs, the Aztecs, when l was drawn into this age. I must get back to my own time—the peerless Don Hernando will miss my help sorely."

"Where has this fellow Thorold taken your father and the machine?" Ethan asked Chiri.

"To the city of Tzar," she said.

"And where is that?" he demanded.

"It lies thirty miles from here, upon the coast of this land," she told him. "Thorold is the king of Tzar, under the Wise One."

She saw that they did not understand her references.

"I forgot that you know nothing of this time!" she exclaimed. "I will explain. You are now, by your reckoning, in the year 1,243,665."

"Over a million years in the future?" gasped Ethan. "I suspected it, yet—"

"Witchcraft, an unholy business," muttered John Crewe, looking sternly at the girl.

"Aye, black magic of Set," whispered Ptah.

Chiri continued tensely her dark eyes clinging to Ethan's lean face. "The name of this continent is Tzar. It is the last continent left upon earth, for all other continents have sunk beneath the oceans because of great shifts inside the earth. There are islands, but they are uninhabitable because of fierce beasts and fiercer savages.

"And this land of Tzar is doomed like the other continents. Its rock foundations have been crumbling for ages, with many earth-shocks, and many fear the day close at hand when this last continent will sink also into the sea.

"Once the people of Tzar were a mighty race, strong in wisdom. But with doom staring them in the face, they have neglected their science until most of their wisdom is forgotten, and they now use the weapons and ways that are simplest, thinking it folly to seek knowledge when death is approaching. Only a few scientists still keep the ancient learning alive.

"My father, Kim Idim, is one of those scientists. We dwelt in the capital city, Tzar. There reigns Thorold, the king, and there broods the mysterious Wise One, the immortal creature or being who has lived for ages and is almost the deity of our race. None but the king ever sees the Wise One, who remains always in his secret chamber, and only the king even knows what the Wise One looks like, but all Tzar reveres its enigmatic deity.

"My father, Kim Idim, in the course of his secret scientific studies, discovered recently a miraculous power. He had been investigating time. He believed that time is only a dimension and that with the proper force, he could reach into past or future and draw people or objects into this time. And he finally found a force that could do that, an energy he called the time-ray.

"Father tried to keep his tremendous achievement secret. But Thorold, our King, heard of it. He demanded the secret of the time-ray from Father. He wanted to use it so that he could escape with the Wise One from our doomed land into future ages, before Tzar sinks into the sea.

"Father refused Thorold's demand. He knew him to be an evil and ruthless despot, and would not loose such a tyrant upon future ages. Thorold threatened Father with death if he continued to refuse the secret. So my father and I escaped secretly from the city Tzar into this wilderness, with a few servants, taking refuge in this ancient and long-abandoned watchtower.

"Here my father proposed to complete his great experiment of drawing men out of the past, for nothing could dim his passion of scientific curiosity. He built a projector for the time-ray and turned the ray back into the past. Seeing along the ray, he drew you six men out of past ages, one by one. He meant only to learn from you the secrets of the past, and then to send you back to your own times.

"But Thorold must have tracked us to our refuge! For he came today and seized my father and the time-ray projector, as you saw. He has taken them to Tzar. And there he will torture my father until he consents to demonstrate the use of the projector, so that by means of it, Thorold and the Wise One can escape into future ages. And that means a menacing wolf, armed by the immense wisdom of the Wise One, let loose upon the unguessable future!"

Chiri's dark eyes were wide with dread as she finished, her voice sinking almost to a whisper.

Ethan had listened with increasing amazement, as had his five comrades.

"And you want us to follow to the city of Tzar and rescue your father and the machine?" Ethan muttered thoughtfully. "That's a tall order."

Hank Martin shrugged his buckskin shoulders. "It shore is," he drawled, "but we got to do it, if we hanker to get back to our own times."

"Of course!" bellowed Pedro Lopez. "We simply break into this cursed city and take the old man and his devilish contrivance, and that'll be all."

Swain Njallson nodded in cold agreement. But Ptah shook his head, his subtle face frowning.

"It will take stealth and cunning," the little Egyptian said, "but we must try it."

"Aye, it is our duty," said John Crewe harshly. "This Thorold seems an evil tyrant, an Ahab like that Charles Stuart whom I helped pluck from his throne. It is God's work to pull down such a despot."

Ethan nodded, his lean brown face tight and hard as he turned back to the anxious girl.

"We'll do our best to rescue your father, Chiri," he told her. "But you've got to promise that if we succeed, he'll return us to our own times."

"I promise!" she said eagerly. "And I will guide you to Tzar and into it—I know a secret way."

"Good!" cried Pedro Lopez impatiently. "Then let us be off at once. Strike quickly!—that was always the watchword of the incomparable Don Hernando."

Ethan led the way toward the path that angled down the cliff, the girl clinging to his arm, the other fighting-men following. The sun, huge and red, was poised now above the distant horizon, sinking slowly behind the rim of the jungle.

They moved carefully down the risky path. It was dusk when they reached the base of the cliff. Before them yawned the jungle, already dark and mysterious, giant monarchs of the forest rearing two hundred feet into the twilight, shadowy things moving amid the vines that trailed from the trees.

The ground suddenly quivered violently under them. The whole towering cliff and dark jungle rocked like a boat in a storm. They were flung from their feet. And Ethan Drew, as he was sickeningly aware of the rolling and shaking of the rock under him, heard a dim, distant, terrible grinding from far beneath.

The convulsion passed off quickly. They staggered up unsteadily, feeling the ground still trembling under them, and saw that the towering monarchs of the jungle still waved branches wildly in the dusk.

"What in the name of Osiris was *that*?" Ptah gasped.

"'Twas an earth temblor," Pedro Lopez announced. "We felt more than that as we followed Don Hernando up to Tenochtitlan."

"Yes," whispered Chiri. A strange dread, fateful and brooding, was in her dark eyes. "It was another omen that the end of the land of Tzar is near. They come ever more often, these rockings of the Continent under us—"

Then she recovered herself and moved toward a dim trail opening into the shadowy jungle.

"We must hurry!" she declared. "This new shaking of the earth will reinforce Thorold's determination to escape from this time. Unless we rescue my father tonight, we will be too late."

III
In the City of Tzar

The moon had risen soon after midnight, and its brilliant, silvery light penetrated through crevices in the roof of foliage, into the dark jungle in which the six men and the girl pressed forward. The wilderness through which they had been moving for hours was made a weird, unreal fairyland by the broken bars of silver light that slanted between the huge, towering black trees.

Ethan glanced up through the thick foliage as he and his comrades followed Chiri through the forest. He saw that the moon's orb was half again as large as he had ever seen it, and he realized that the long ages that had passed had brought the dead satellite far closer to its parent planet. He could clearly discern the great craters and mountains on its barren face.

Chiri, moving beside him along the vague trail, pressed his hand with her soft fingers.

"We are nearing the city of Tzar, Ethan," she whispered.

He felt her fingers trembling, and quick sympathy for her dread and bravery filled him.

"Keep your chin up, Chiri," he told her encouragingly. "We'll get your father out all right. Good Lord! This outfit is tough enough to lick an army."

"I know," the Tzaran girl whispered fearfully, "yet I am

afraid, not alone of Thorold but of the Wise One, the undying one whom no one knows."

Ethan put his arm protectively around her shoulders as they moved on. Briars whipped their faces, creeping vines and roots tripped them. The breath of the jungle was a damp, steamy exhalation about them, laden with strange scents, alien and sinister.

More than once he heard the crash of great bodies moving in the wilderness, and once the flapping of enormous wings reached his ears and he glimpsed a huge shadow flying over the jungle roof.

He could only guess as to what weird forms of life earth might have produced during the vast period of time across which he and his companions had been drawn.

Ethan could hardly realize that it was all real, that he actually marched through the moonlit jungle of a million years in the future, with a girl of this future day and five hardy fighting-men from past ages. Yet the feel of Chiri's trusting hand in his, the sound of Pedro Lopez cursing in voluble Spanish as he tripped, the heavy tread of the viking and the occasional monosyllables of Ptah and John Crewe and the trapper, reminded the young American that it was all actually happening.

And he and his comrades were in this doomed land of Tzar to stay, unless they could rescue old Kim Idim and his miraculous mechanism. Determination to achieve that hardened in him. He didn't want to stay in this future time, exiled from his own age.

Chiri suddenly came to a halt in the shadows, her fingers tightening again on his hand.

"Yonder lies Tzar," she whispered tensely.

Ethan and his comrades peered eagerly through the foliage. A quarter mile ahead there loomed out of the moonlit jungle an enormous black wall. Inside that titan barrier of ebon stone reared colossal masses of pyramidal structures, some of them rising many hundreds of feet. Monstrous, barbaric-looking city of the far future, looming up into the silver moonlight out of the jungle that hemmed it in! Ruddy lights in the buildings bit holes through the moonlight, and there was a dim, pulsing murmur of life.

"It looks like Babylon," Ptah whispered in awe. "But great as Babylon was when I beheld it, this city is even greater."

"It is true, this place is larger even than Tenochtitlan of the Aztecs," muttered Pedro Lopez.

Swain Njallson had raised his great head, and Ethan saw the viking stiffen suddenly.

"I smell the sea," Swain said, sniffing like a bloodhound suddenly aroused.

"Yes, the ocean laps against the farther side of the city Tzar," Chiri informed him.

"How are we going to get into the place?" Ethan asked her tautly. "I see no gate."

"There is a gate, but it is locked against the beasts of the jungle," Chiri answered. Her face was pale in the white moonlight as she added, "But I know a way inside— the same secret way by which my father and I escaped with our servants. It will take us even to the Citadel of the Wise One, where the king Thorold dwells and where he will have taken my father."

As she spoke, she pointed to one enormous pyramid, far inside the wall of the city, whose truncated summit loomed far above the other buildings into the brilliant moonlight.

"Follow me," she whispered.

Ethan and his comrades slipped after her through the tangled vegetation, toward the looming wall of Tzar. The jungle grew right up to the wall and clawed with vines and creepers at the giant barrier.

They soon stood in the shadows at the base of the wall. Chiri led the way along it until they came to an opening in the wall, a round, dark tunnel-mouth six feet in diameter. It was dark as the pit, and a thin trickle of water ran out of it.

"This is one of the drains of the city," Chiri whispered. "Once there was a grating across it, but it has rusted away and the people of Tzar, who think of naught but pleasure in the face of the coming doom, have not bothered to replace it. This is our way inside the city."

"I ain't exactly pinin' away to go crawlin' up a danged rabbit-hole," muttered Hank Martin.

"Nor I," said Ptah. "One could easily be trapped in such tunnels."

"It is the only way inside," Chiri said anxiously.

"And we're taking it," Ethan declared decisively. "Come on, boys."

They followed without further dissent as he led the way with Chiri into the dark stone tunnel. Their feet splashed in the water as they advanced into the gloomy, lightless passage. After they had gone a few paces, Chiri drew from her robe a tiny tube which shot forth a thin ray of light that partly showed the way.

Ethan saw that the rough stone walls of the great drain were grown with evil-looking white fungi and mosses. White snakes whipped away in front of them, and large white rat-like rodents scuttled ahead. The air here was dank and heavy.

The tunnel forked, dividing into two separate drains. Without hesitation, Chiri led into the left one. They had gone but a short way along this, when Chiri turned and motioned them to observe caution.

They soon saw the reason. Close ahead was a place where the drain protruded up into one of the streets of Tzar, coveted by a stone grating. They reached this spot and cautiously raised their heads so that they could look out into the city street.

Tzar was weirdly beautiful under the huge moon. The vast, somber pyramidal buildings towered out of shadowy gardens and smoothly paved streets, ruddy light blinking from a myriad windows. And in streets and buildings, the people of Tzar were engaged in a mad revelry, a saturnalia of frenzied merry-making, throbbing through the whole city! Music, wild and gay, was pulsing everywhere. There were dancers inside the great buildings, their shadowy forms racing across the windows. And there were music and dancing and drunken laughter in the street into which Ethan and his companions looked.

They saw wantonly laughing girls and women pursued by intoxicated men. Youthful figures stumbled unsteadily past, with wine spilled upon their white robes.

A carnival of utter license seemed unloosed here in the black city beneath the brilliant moon.

"A city of luxury and sin!" muttered John Crewe

harshly, the Puritan's somber face stem and condemnatory in the dim light. "Yes, a city of Belial, its wicked people flown with insolence and wine."

"Hell, I wish I was out there with them," swore Pedro Lopez. "I could enjoy myself out there."

Swain Njallson spat in contempt. "These are a soft, weak race," the viking rumbled scornfully.

"They hold revelry," whispered Chiri, "but it is because they know that this land and city are nearing their doom. It is only in wine and pleasure that my people can forget the dread shadow deepening over them."

And almost as she spoke, there came with startling coincidence an omen of that which she mentioned. A slow, grinding drum-roll sounded from deep within the earth, gathering in volume like a rolling snowball until it broke and crashed in a dull detonation like thunder underground. At the same moment, the whole city shook violently, the great pyramids swaying visibly in the moonlight, rocking Ethan and his comrades from side to side in the tunnel. Then the grinding roll beneath diminished to a dim muttering that died away.

"A sign of God's wrath at this wicked city!" exclaimed John Crewe, his eyes fanatical. "A warning of Jehovah's vengeance!"

"Yes, a warning," whispered Chiri, dread again widening her eyes. "A warning that the doom of Tzar is close—close."

Out in the streets, the carnival of revelry had come to an abrupt halt with the earth-shock. There had been a few screams of terror, followed by an utter silence.

That dead, unnatural silence endured for minutes. The people in the streets seemed stricken to stone. Then suddenly the laughter and music burst forth wilder than before, as though to drown the memory of that ominous shock.

"Fear not, friends—the doom of Tzar has not come yet!" called a drunken voice.

"Aye, it will never come—the Wise One will find a way to save our land," cried another.

"Drink to the Wise One!" yelled an intoxicated soldier in black armor, waving an amphora aloft. "To the Wise One, who will save us!"

The toast was drunk almost frantically, and the wild saturnalia went on at heightened pace.

Ethan and his companions lowered their heads and started forward again in the tunnel.

"They do not really believe that even the Wise One can save them," Chiri murmured as she led the way. "But they clutch at that last straw of hope."

Lighted by her little torch, the six men pressed on through divergent drains, passing cautiously under other gratings open to the streets. Finally the girl halted, her face pale and tense in the little ray of light.

She pointed to a square stone trap-door in the roof of the drain, just over their heads.

"That opens into the cellars in the lowest levels of the Citadel of the Wise One," she whispered. "And now we have come to the most hazardous part. For there are always many people in the Citadel, except in the uppermost level where Thorold and the Wise One dwell."

"We'll have to take our chance of stealing up through

the building unobserved," Ethan said, his lean face tight with desperate resolution. "Keep behind me, Chiri."

Swain reached up, and softly the viking's great arms lifted up the stone trap-door and set it aside. Silently they clambered up through the opening and then looked around.

They stood in dark, gloomy stone cellars, their walls dripping with condensation. From the upper levels of the vast pile, voices and the occasional tread of feet reached them. Through slit-like windows, bright bars of moonlight entered.

"This way to the stair that leads upward," Chiri murmured, starting through the dark crypts. "But I fear now it is madness of us even to attempt to reach the forbidden uppermost level."

Ethan had begun to think so too, but he did not voice this opinion. "Courage, Chiri," he whispered.

They passed through several of the gloomy and apparently unused stone cellars, into one from which a narrow stairway led upward. Ethan was leading toward this when the unexpected happened.

Two soldiers in black armor, warriors of Tzar, emerged suddenly from that stairway. They had evidently been drawn to investigate by some slight sound, for their swords were in their hands and they peered quickly around the dusky crypt as they entered.

One of them saw Ethan and his group, ten feet away. He uttered a cry of alarm.

"Strangers with swords! Warn the guards!"

Before the last words left his lips, the man was tumbling to the floor. Ethan had leaped forward with leopard swiftness, and his sword-point had ripped through the armor joints of the Tzaran warrior and into his heart.

The other man, a little up the steps, turned and started to flee wildly up the stair. Something flashed like a gleaming snake across the moon-shot darkness of the chamber, toward him.

He crashed dead upon the stairs. Swain had hurled his axe with unerring aim, and the viking's heavy weapon had broken the fleeing man's neck.

"A good cast," grunted the Northman.

IV
Citadel of the Wise One

They waited tensely for a moment, swords ready. There was no alarm from above.

"His cry wasn't heard," Ethan rasped. Then as an idea came to him, his eyes lit with excitement, surveying the two dead armored men.

"This gives us a better chance to get to the topmost level!" the young American exclaimed. "Two of us will put on the armor of these men and go up with Chiri. We can pass as Tzaran guards, that way. Pedro, you and I will do it—we look more like Tzarans than the rest of you."

"Good!" approved the *conquistador*. "Our two blades will be enough for the job."

"What do you figger the rest of us are going to do?" Hank Martin demanded aggrievedly.

"You'll wait down here for us," Ethan told the tall trapper. "If we can get Kim Idim and his machine, we'll bring them down and we'll all escape back out of the city by the drains.

"Am I to cower here in darkness while others have the fighting?" Swain rumbled rebelliously.

"Aye," said John Crewe harshly, "we should all go together. God will arm our cause."

Ptah disagreed, the little Egyptian's crafty face earnest. "The plan is a good one," he declared. "Cunning may win where brute force would fail."

But the viking and the trapper were still grumbling as Ethan and Pedro hastily donned the black helmets and armor of the two dead men.

"We should be back soon if we succeed," Ethan told them, pausing on the steps with the Spaniard and Chiri. "If we fail, then you must do as you think best."

"If they count coup over you, we'll take plenty scalps to even the score," Hank Martin promised him grimly.

Then Ethan and Pedro started up the stair, with Chiri's slim white figure between them.

The stairway was a dark, spiral one. Five minutes of climbing brought them suddenly into the main ground level of the Citadel of the Wise One.

Here was a huge labyrinth of dusky halls and corridors, partly illuminated by glowing red torches on the walls. And here, as in the streets outside, were laughter and shouting and drunken calls of intoxicated soldiers and women. It was evident that the discipline of Thorold's soldiery, like everything else, was crumbling as the doom of Tzar neared it.

Chiri led the way toward a great stair. As they passed the revellers at its bottom, Ethan pretended tipsiness himself, stumbled unsteadily with his arm around the girl's slender waist, laughing thickly.

"Stay and drink with us, comrades!" exclaimed a group of armored soldiers and women at the foot of the great stair.

Ethan shook his head drunkenly. One of the men grasped Chiri's arm. The American pushed the fellow away with an unsteady gesture. He fell sprawling and the others laughed loudly.

A supple girl had pressed against Pedro's side and was whispering amorously to him. Ethan gave the Spaniard a warning nudge, and he thrust the girl away. But as they started up the stair, Pedro's voice was rueful.

"Curse it, that wench was a sweet armful! If we only had a little more time—"

"Don't be a fool!" Ethan muttered savagely to the *conquistador*: "We've got to hurry."

As Chiri led the way tensely up the broad, winding stairway, they passed other soldiers lying in drunken sleep on the steps. They climbed through level after level of the vast, shadowy Citadel. Through windows along the way they could look down on the wild carnival of revelry still throbbing in the streets of Tzar—desperate merrymaking of a city doomed to destruction.

And as they mounted higher in the dusky pile, they could look out beyond the city at the moonlit jungle, and on the opposite side, the silvery, heaving ocean, washing against the wall of Tzar as though eager to claw the doomed city down into the deep.

"This temple is like the great teocalli of Huitzilopochtli of the Aztecs," Pedro muttered as they climbed. "*Dios*, it seems but yesterday that I and my fellow cavaliers hacked our way to the top of that temple and cast down its evil idols."

"We are nearing the tenth level, the highest," Chiri whispered tensely. "On that level are Thorold's apartments and also the chamber of the Wise One."

In a few moments they stood amid the dusky network of passages on the topmost story of the great truncated pyramid. A few torches cast ruddy light along the enigmatic passages, but no one was to be seen.

"Where would Thorold have your father?" Ethan demanded in a low voice of the girl.

She shook her head, her face pale. "I do not know. I have never been here before—this level is forbidden to all but the King and his personal guards, because here dwells the Wise One whom none but the king may see."

"We'll have to look for Kim Idim until we find him, then," Ethan rasped. "Come on, Pedro."

He and Pedro had their swords out as they moved blindly through the corridors.

Ethan tried door after door, but behind them were only dark and unoccupied chambers.

Then a distant scream of agony in a high, shrill voice echoed through the corridors, sinking into a long, low wail that died away.

"My, father!" cried Chiri wildly. "Thorold's torturers must be at work on him!"

"That scream came from this direction, I thought," Ethan grated, turning and hurrying down a cross corridor, with Pedro and the girl after him.

***

The scream had not been repeated. Ethan reached the end of the corridor and found himself confronted by a blank silver door in a high, massive frame.

Sword gleaming in the dusk, he pushed the door softly open. Inside was a small antechamber. He and the conquistador and Chiri crossed this silently, and stepped into a dim, high, round room.

It had broad windows that looked across the streets of Tzar, seething with saturnalia far below, and across the moonlit ocean beyond. And in the shafts of moonlight from the windows, there sat alone in this silent room a creature of incredible, unearthly appearance, a creature that riveted their horrified gaze.

"The Wise One!" gasped Chiri in utter horror. "We have blundered into the chamber of the undying one!"

Ethan felt his brain reel at sight of the ghastly creature before them.

He heard Lopez gasp and cross himself.

The Wise One, staring at them, spoke in a low, flat, strange voice. "You are not men of Tzar!" the creature whispered. "You must be some of the strangers whom the scientist Kim Idim drew out of the past.

"Look at me, then, strangers!" the thing commanded, its voice rising weirdly. "I am the Wise One, he who does not die, who holds the wisdom of ages. Look at me, and envy me!"

And appallingly, a burst of high, insane laughter shrilled from the creature, a bitter, maniacal mirth that made the hair bristle on Ethan's neck.

The Wise One was—a human head! A *living* head, great and hairless, whose bald skull bulged in a great dome, whose face was white and plump, whose eyes were enormous, dark orbs staring hypnotically from beneath lashless lids.

This head was without human body. It rested upon a square machine, inside which its neck disappeared from view. And from inside that machine came a faint, ceaseless humming and throbbing.

"A human head!" muttered Ethan in repulsion of horror. "Kept alive for ages, by means of a mechanical heart and body!"

"You have guessed it, stranger," said the Wise One, its insane laughter breaking off, its hypnotic eyes searching the young American's face.

Its haunted voice held the three spellbound in the moonlit chamber.

"Yes, many, many ages ago I was a man like you, stranger," said the Wise One. There was a queer sob of heartbreak in its flat voice. "I walked in the sun and made love beneath the moon, I worked and slept and ate as other people did. Yes, I was human—once.

"But a vaulting, unholy ambition brought this terrible doom upon me. I was a scientist and I had found ways to keep the heads of animals alive, separate from their bodies, by means of mechanical hearts which pumped a synthetic blood-stream through the veins. I wanted to prove that a human head could be kept alive indefinitely in the same way. And so in mad rashness and pride of achievement, I volunteered to submit myself to the experiment.

"The thing was done. My head was severed from my body and attached to this mechanical trunk. I awoke from the operation, no longer a man, but merely a head, a living brain. And I have remained like this ever since, for I cannot die as long as my mechanical heart is kept functioning and my synthetic blood renewed.

"I have seen the generations of man be born and die, for thousands upon thousands of years. I have seen empires and civilizations rise to glory and sink in long decline. And with each year that passed, my wisdom and knowledge grew greater, for while other men had time only to learn the elements of knowledge before they died, I who was immortal could increase my wisdom endlessly.

"But I longed for death, stranger. For thousands on thousands of years I have longed to be free of this wretched mockery of existence and to sink into the blessed peace of death. I have prayed those around me for generations to give me death, but always they have refused.

"They would not kill me, because they wished to profit by my superhuman store of knowledge. They called me the Wise One. And the people who never saw me but worshipped me in awe, also called me the Wise One—me, the half-human thing praying for the release of death!"

A bitterness more than human throbbed in the Wise One's voice, chilled Ethan's brain.

"At last," continued the creature's haunted voice, "I saw a chance of death. This land of Tzar, as I have long known, is destined soon to sink beneath the sea, for its foundations have long been crumbling. Indeed, I think that end is very close at hand, now. I was happy when I learned that, for in that cataclysm I would find death.

"But now the horror of continued life threatens me.

Thorold, the king, seeks the secret of time-projection from the scientist Kim Idim, which will enable him to flee into future ages. And Thorold will take me with him, so that he may continue to profit by my wisdom. The blessed cup of death will be snatched from my thirsty lips!"

The voice of the Wise One was rising wildly, the enormous eyes of the creature terribly distended.

"I knew the secret of the time-ray long before Kim Idim discovered it," the creature raged, "but I disclosed it to no one. But if Thorold gains that secret, my silence will be in vain. Even now Thorold is torturing Kim Idim to make him give up the secret and show him how to operate the projector."

"My father!" cried Chiri, anguish breaking the spell of horror on her face. "Ethan, you must save him from Thorold's tortures!"

Ethan Drew, heart pounding, stepped closer to the monstrous figure of the Wise One.

"I will stop Thorold from obtaining that secret, if I can," he told the creature hoarsely. "Tell us where amid these halls we can find Thorold and Kim Idim, and I swear that I will kill Thorold."

The Wise One's enormous eyes considered the young American.

Then those dark orbs flashed strangely.

"I will tell you where you can find them," said the monstrous thing, "but on one condition only."

"And what is that?" Ethan cried.

"On condition that as soon as I have told you, you kill me!" exclaimed the Wise One. "One stroke of your sword, and I shall be free forever of this travesty of life, safe forever in the arms of death."

Ethan recoiled. "God, I couldn't!"

"You must!" cried the Wise One. "Only if you agree will I tell you what you ask."

And suddenly, grotesquely, there were tears gleaning in the great eyes.

"Do not deny me death!" it whispered. "Do not deny me that for which I have prayed and hoped these thousands on thousands of years."

Ethan shuddered, but he forced himself to speak. "I'll—I'll do it. Where are Thorold and Kim Idim?"

"In Thorold's torture chamber, the fourth door along the third corridor," answered the Wise One swiftly. "At least three of Thorold's torturers will be with him, so you must strike quickly, stranger.

"And now—the death you promised me!" the creature cried.

Ethan advanced sickly, raising his sword. The great head looked up at the blade, eyes gleaming in an ecstasy of anticipation.

"I can't do it," Ethan said thickly.

"You promised!" cried the Wise One. "It will be an act of infinite mercy to me. Strike!"

Chiri and Pedro were watching in a trance of horror. Ethan raised his blade higher, and in the moment before he struck, involuntarily closed his eyes.

"Death!" he heard the Wise One whispering exultantly. "Death, at last—"

Ethan struck. He felt the blade crunch down through bone and flesh and clang against metal.

He opened his eyes, shuddering. He had cloven away the whole rear half of the hideous skull. But upon the dead white face of the Wise One was now a strange expression of peace.

"*Dios*, let us get out of here!" gasped the Spaniard. "This land—it is one of devils!"

Ethan was trembling violently as he stumbled with Chiri and the *conquistador* back out into the dusky corridors.

They hurried toward the third corridor away, then down along it until they came to the fourth door. The trio paused outside that closed door. A voice reached them from within—Thorold's bull voice.

"Will you tell now how the machine is operated?" demanded that voice.

"I—I will never tell you," quavered another shaking voice. "You shall never escape with the Wise One into future times to work evil there."

"Give him another turn," they heard Thorold order. Then there was a sobbing cry from the tortured man.

Softly, soundlessly, Ethan Drew pushed open the door and stepped into the torture chamber.

V
The Hour of Destruction

It was a dusky, red-lit room with a low stone ceiling. Weird, blood-chilling contrivances of torture stood about it, and three wolf-faced men—the torturers employed by the king of Tzar.

Thorold himself stood at the center of the chamber. His giant frame was bent eagerly forward, his dark, ruthless face and black eyes blazing as he watched his torturers at their gruesome work.

They had Kim Idim stretched upon a rack, his toes gripped by the rolls of a contrivance like a great wringer. The old man's white hair was disheveled, his thin face deathly white; his eyes seemed bulging from his sockets as the torturers slowly turned the rolls that gripped and crushed his feet.

"Now will you demonstrate the use of the projector?" Thorold demanded remorselessly.

He pointed as he spoke at a squat mechanism that stood at the side of the room, near a broad window overlooking the moonlit sea.

It was the time-ray projector that had snatched Ethan Drew and his five comrades out of their own ages. The mechanism was a squat complexity of deflection coils and tubes, upon which was mounted a world-globe graven with fine lines. There were vernier controls, and a big copper ring jutted from the bottom of the machine.

"No—not now or ever!" gasped Kim Idim.

The grinning torturers obeyed. Ethan saw the old Tzaran scientist's body arch up to his bonds convulsively from agony, as he and Lopez softly entered.

Chiri screamed. Thorold and the torturers whirled, drawing their swords.

Ethan rushed, red fury lighting his brain, straight at the Tzaran king. One of the torturers stepped between the two—and took the American's blade through his ribs before he could make a thrust.

As Ethan tore out the sword, Pedro was cutting down another of the startled torturers and then rushing upon the third.

"Guards!" yelled Thorold at the top of his voice as his sword clashed with Ethan's.

"They can't hear you," rasped the American. "This is just between us two."

With fierce, resistless attack, he forced Thorold back against the wall.

A savage thrust and twist—and Thorold's blade flew from his hand.

Ethan tensed to lunge in the death stab. But at that moment the room, the whole vast building, rocked wildly about them.

He was flung from his feet. He heard Chiri cry out, and Pedro yell a startled curse. The terrible drum-roll of shifting rock was sounding again deep beneath the city, and the great pile of the Citadel was waving wildly beneath one earth-shock after another.

Ethan staggered to his feet on the quivering floor, and saw Thorold racing out the door.

"Guards!" the Tzaran tyrant was shouting in his bull voice as he ran down the corridors.

"After him!" Pedro cried fiercely, but Ethan held the conquistador back. "No—no time now! We've got to get Kim Idim out before Thorold gets back with soldiers."

They could hear Thorold's great voice shouting for his warriors as he raced down into the lower levels.

Ethan whirled toward the old scientist. Chiri had slashed her father's bonds and was helping him to stand erect on his crushed feet.

"The men from the past!" exclaimed the old man, staring at Ethan and the Spaniard.

Every few moments, now, a new earth-shock was vibrating through the Citadel.

There were distant screams from the people who had been holding carnival in the streets far below. And the fearful grinding from deep in the earth was swelling louder and louder.

"Can you help your father to walk?" Ethan cried to the girl. "Lopez and I can carry the machine and there's still a chance we can get down through the Citadel."

"No—no chance now!" shouted the Spaniard from the door. "Here come the guards!"

Ethan raced to the door. A group of men were running down the dusky corridor toward them. The American and Pedro awaited them desperately with swords raised.

Then one of the men running toward them turned, leveled something. A ringing shot echoed in the shadowy hallway.

"Got that Injun!" yelled a familiar, nasal voice.

"Hank Martin!" Ethan cried. "And the others—"

It was the four they had left in the cellars of the Citadel. Swain's great axe was bloody now, and red-smeared too were the swords of Ptah and John Crewe.

"We heard Thorold a-yelling for his guards, so we figgered you were in trouble and came bustin' up here!" panted the trapper. "But they're after us—a hull tribe of them."

"They've got us trapped up here now—we can't get away," rasped Ptah calmly.

"Odin! What of that when there is good fighting ahead?" shouted Swain, his blue eyes blazing.

A mass of armored men appeared in the farther end of the corridor, and Thorold's bull voice could be heard rallying them forward.

Another tremendous earth-shock rocked the building about them.

The ominous grind of rock underground had now become a loud roar. "The doom of Tzar is at hand!" cried Kim Idim. "Men from the past, I can send you back to your own times with this projector, if you can hold out Thorold and his men until I get it into operation."

"We'll try!" Ethan cried. "But hurry."

"Here they come!" yelled Hank Martin to Ethan, from out in the corridor.

His rifle cracked at the same moment. Then he clubbed the heavy weapon.

"Form a line across the corridor!" Ethan shouted as he joined them. "We must hold them back until Kim Idim gets the machine started."

Thorold was hurrying down the hallway at the head of a solid mass of guards. The soldiers were crazed with fear by the awful earth-shocks that each few moments were shaking the city, and Thorold was playing upon their panic.

"On, men!" the giant king was shouting. "Inside that room is the machine which will enable us to escape from doomed Tzar. Cut down these men who would keep us from it!"

The armored soldiers poured down the hall in a solid living wave—and then stopped.

In a line across that hallway, Ethan Drew and his five comrades were awaiting them. Four swords flashed like bolts of steel lightning. Hank Martin's rifle-butt crashed down, and Swain's great axe clove in red destruction.

Ethan, thrusting and stabbing like a madman, sought to reach Thorold with his sword, but the giant king was out of his reach. Howling, fear-mad warriors who saw their one chance of escape inside the room, kept coming forward, a delirium of wild faces in front of the battling American.

Hank Martin was crushing in skulls and faces like eggshells with the butt of his heavy rifle, uttering a whooping Indian yell each time his iron-shop weapon smashed down.

"Dios!" Pedro swore as he hacked furiously. "Even Don Hernando never led us into a fight like this—"

John Crewe's massive face was flaming crimson as his broadsword flashed in great circles.

"Children of sin!" he was shouting. "Your cup of wickedness has run over—God's wrath is upon you!"

Ptah fought in vicious silence, his swarthy face immobile as a mask as he stabbed and smote with his heavy shortsword. But ever and again a weird, piercing cry arose from the huge viking.

"Aha!" his great voice yelled as his terrible axe smashed down amid the attackers. *"Aha!"*

The Tzaran warriors recoiled from that terrific defense. Bleeding from a dozen cuts, panting and covered with sweat, Ethan glanced around.

Kim Idim was toiling with the projector, fumbling with broken hands, held upright by the bravely encircling arms of Chiri.

"One minute more!" cried the old scientist hoarsely.

Thorold was yelling wildly to his men as new earth-shocks rocked the vast building. "On—they are but six! Cut them down or we sink to doom with Tzar!"

The solid wave of attack smashed back into the thin defending line. And again that line held—six weapons weaving an impassable barrier of death.

Maddened, foaming, Thorold forced forward. His heavy blade clashed that of Ethan, struck past it and pierced the American's left arm.

Heedless of the wound, Ethan stabbed with a low snarl. And his sword drove right through the armor over Thorold's heart. The Tzaran king staggered back, fell sprawling across the pile of bodies.

"You got him, pardner!" yelled Hank Martin exultantly.

"The land is sinking!" screamed a wild voice up through the Citadel.

For now the earth-shocks had become one continuous convulsion, and the great building, racking like a leaf in a wind, was slowly settling downward.

The attackers in the corridor turned and fled in mad panic, seeking a way out of the building. Ethan spun around—and through the window saw the raging, maddened ocean running in mountainous waves that already were washing through the streets of the sinking, moonlit city.

"Doomsday—Jehovah's wrath descends on this accursed land!" yelled Crewe.

"It is Ragnarok!" shouted Swain. "The twilight of the gods!"

Kim Idim cried to them. "The projector is ready. Be quick! Step into the copper ring, one of you!"

"You first, Ptah!" cried Ethan.

The panting little Egyptian made as though to refuse to go first, then stepped into the low copper ring jutting from the bottom of the machine.

"Farewell, comrades!" he shouted.

Kim Idim swiftly moved the stylus touching the world-globe atop the machine, then touched a vernier, threw a switch. A flash of light inside the ring—and Ptah was gone. Then Swain went, waving his red axe in farewell.

Pedro was next. Ethan had to push the *conquistador* into the copper circle.

"*Sangre de Cristo!*" the Spaniard was exclaiming. "I wish—"

He was gone before he could finish. As Kim Idim swiftly changed his controls, Ethan thrust John Crewe toward the machine. But the great Puritan resisted.

"It is not God's will that men should juggle with time," he cried. "I cannot—"

But by main force Ethan shoved him into the copper circle. Kim Idim had already made his adjustments for time and location. The Puritan, still protesting, vanished in the flash of light inside the ring.

"Quickly! Quickly!" cried Kim Idim, his voice almost inaudible amid the thunderous din.

For now, as with long, grinding roll of riven rock, the land of Tzar sank downward, the sea was raging in over the city. There was a crashing of falling walls.

Hank Martin, still gripping his long rifle, had stepped

inside the ring. "Goodbye, pardner!" he called to Ethan, a grin on his lanky, blood-smeared face.

Flash! And he was gone. And Kim Idim motioned Ethan wildly to enter the circle.

"What about you and Chiri?" Ethan demanded hoarsely, grasping the pale girl's arm. "I can't leave you here to die."

"We shall not die—I shall set the machine to hurl Chiri and me into a time a little farther ahead, when I have calculated that new lands will have arisen here!" Kim Idim shouted.

"If ever you need me, you'll know how to call me across time again!" Ethan cried. "Chiri, goodbye!"

A nearer, more ominous crashing sounded.

"The Citadel is beginning to collapse!" Kim Idim yelled.

Ethan loosed the girl, and leaped into the copper circle. The old man flung the switch.

There was a roar as the lower walls of the Citadel began to collapse. But even as that roar struck Ethan's ears, everything exploded in light, and he was hurled into unconsciousness.

Epilogue

He awoke with hot sunlight beating upon his face. He lay upon burning sands, beneath the glare of a midday silence. He could hear a chorus of receding, wild yells.

Ethan staggered up and looked dazedly around. He stood in the desert, the burning Sahara, at the very spot where he had been waiting for the Tuareg charge when he had been snatched into the future. Beside him lay the dead bodies of the other ambushed soldiers of the Foreign Legion patrol.

And a quarter-mile away, a horde of Arabs were riding off with wild yells of terror.

"By heaven, I understand now!" Ethan cried to himself. "Kim Idim sent me back to the identical place and almost the identical time from which he had drawn me. And that's what terrorized those Tuaregs who were charging me—to them, it was as though I vanished from sight for a moment, and then reappeared!"

He looked down wildly at himself. He was still covered with the blood and sweat of that terrific battle in the corridor.

"It was ten minutes ago—and yet it was a million years in the future!" he muttered numbly.

Ethan caught a wandering horse that had belonged to one of the Tuaregs slain in the fight. And soon he was riding across the burning sands, heading toward the French army post a score of miles away.

He would tell them only that his patrol had been ambushed, and all wiped out but himself. There was no use of trying to tell them what had really happened to him. No one would ever believe his story.

And in just the same way, he thought suddenly, Pedro and Swain, and Ptah and John Crewe and Hank Martin, must have got back to their own times, and been forced to keep silent about their incredible experience.

"The best comrades a man ever had," Ethan whispered as he rode. "And now they're all dead and gone, for centuries, even for thousands of years.

"No, it's not true! They're only separated from me by time. And Chiri and Kim Idim, in whatever far future age they fled to, they too are only separated from me by time."

Ethan's head straightened, and a worn smile came for the first time onto his haggard face.

"They're as real and living as I am, all of them. And maybe some day—some day—"

TIME CRIME
by H. Beam Piper

Like Poul Anderson's Time Patrol, the Paratime Police were more cops than soldiers, though with the different mission of keeping the secret of travel between timelines from becoming known to any parallel world other than the one where it had been discovered. So, when it was learned that somebody was capturing people from one timeline to sell as slaves in another, Verkan Vall of the Paratime Police was on the job. But the job was bigger than anticipated, and more than a police operation was urgently needed...

Kiro Soran, the guard captain, stood in the shadow of the veranda roof, his white cloak thrown back to display the scarlet lining. He rubbed his palm reflectively on the checkered butt of his revolver and watched the four men at the table.

"And ten tens are a hundred," one of the clerks in blue jackets said, adding another stack to the pile of gold coins.

503

"Nineteen hundreds," one of the pair in dirty striped robes agreed, taking a stone from the box in front of him and throwing it away. Only one stone remained. "One more hundred to pay."

One of the blue-jacketed plantation clerks made a tally mark; his companion counted out coins, ten and ten and ten.

Dosu Golan, the plantation manager, tapped impatiently on his polished boot leg with a thin riding whip.

"I don't like this," he said, in another and entirely different language. "I know, chattel slavery's an established custom on this sector, and we have to conform to local usages, but it sickens me to have to haggle with these swine over the price of human beings. On the Zarkantha Sector, we used nothing but free wage-labor."

"Migratory workers," the guard captain said. "Humanitarian considerations aside, I can think of a lot better ways of meeting the labor problem on a fruit plantation than by buying slaves you need for three months a year and have to feed and quarter and clothe and doctor the whole twelve."

"Twenty hundreds of *obus*," the clerk who had been counting the money said. "That is the payment, is it not, Coru-hin-Irigod?"

"That is the payment," the slave dealer replied.

The clerk swept up the remaining coins, and his companion took them over and put them in an iron-bound chest, snapping the padlock. The two guards who had been loitering at one side slung their rifles and picked up the chest, carrying it into the plantation house. The slave dealer and his companion arose, putting their money into a leather bag; Coru-hin-Irigod turned and bowed to the two men in white cloaks.

"The slaves are yours, noble lords," he said.

Across the plantation yard, six more men in striped robes, with carbines slung across their backs, approached; with them came another man in a hooded white cloak, and two guards in blue jackets and red caps, with bayoneted rifles. The man in white and his armed attendants came toward the house; the six Calera slavers continued across the yard to where their horses were picketed.

"If I do not offend the noble lords, then," Coru-hin-Irigod said, "I beg their sufferance to depart. I and my men have far to ride if we would reach Careba by nightfall. The Lord, the Great Lord, the Lord God Safar watch between us until we meet again."

Urado Alatena, the labor foreman, came up onto the porch as the two slavers went down.

"Have a good look at them, Radd?" the guard captain asked.

"You think I'm crazy enough to let those bandits out of here with two thousand *obus*—forty thousand Paratemporal Exchange Units—of the Company's money without knowing what we're getting?" the other parried. "They're all right—nice, clean, healthy-looking lot. I did everything but take them apart and inspect the pieces while they were being unshackled at the stockade. I'd like to know where this Coru-hin-Whatshisname got them, though. They're not local stuff. Lot darker, and they're jabbering among themselves in some lingo I never heard before. A few are wearing some rags of clothing, and they have odd-looking sandals. I noticed that most of them showed marks of recent whipping. That may mean they're troublesome, or it may just mean that these Caleras are a lot of sadistic brutes."

"Poor devils!" The man called Dosu Golan was evidently hoping that he'd never catch himself talking about fellow humans like that. The guard captain turned to him.

"Coming to have a look at them, Doth?" he asked.

"You go, Kirv; I'll see them later."

"Still not able to look the Company's property in the face?" the captain asked gently. "You'll not get used to it any sooner than now."

"I suppose you're right." For a moment Dosu Golan watched Coru-hin-Irigod and his followers canter out of the yard and break into a gallop on the road beyond. Then he tucked his whip under his arm. "All right, then. Let's go see them."

The labor foreman went into the house; the manager and the guard captain went down the steps and set out across the yard. A big slat-sided wagon, drawn by four horses, driven by an old slave in a blue smock and a thing like a sunbonnet, rumbled past, loaded with newly-picked oranges. Blue woodsmoke was beginning to rise from the stoves at the open kitchen and a couple of slaves were noisily chopping wood. Then they came to the stockade of close-set pointed poles. A guard sergeant in a red-trimmed blue jacket, armed with a revolver, met them with a salute which Kiro Soran returned: he unfastened the gate and motioned four or five riflemen into positions from which they could fire in between the poles in case the slaves turned on their new owners.

There seemed little danger of that, though Kiro Soran kept his hand close to the butt of his revolver. The slaves, an even hundred of them, squatted under awnings out of the sun, or stood in line to drink at the water-butt. They furtively watched the two men who had entered among them, as though expecting blows or kicks; when none were forthcoming, they relaxed slightly. As the labor foreman had said, they were clean and looked healthy. They were all nearly naked; there were about as many women as men, but no children or old people.

"Radd's right," the captain told the new manager. "They're not local. Much darker skins, and different face-structure; faces wedge-shaped instead of oval, and differently shaped noses, and brown eyes instead of black. I've seen people like that, somewhere, but—"

He fell silent. A suspicion, utterly fantastic, had begun to form in his mind, and he stepped closer to a group of a dozen-odd, the manager following him. One or two had been unmercifully lashed, not long ago, and all bore a few lash-marks. Odd sort of marks, more like burn-blisters than welts. He'd have to have the Company doctor look at them. Then he caught their speech, and the suspicion was converted to certainty.

"These are not like the others: they wear fine garments, and walk proudly. They look stern, but not cruel. They are the real masters here; the others are but servants."

He grasped the manager's arm and drew him aside.

"You know that language?" he asked. When the man called Dosu Golan shook his head, he continued: "That's

Kharanda; it's a dialect spoken by a people in the Ganges Valley, in India, on the Kholghoor Sector of the Fourth Level."

Dosu Golan blinked, and his face went blank for a moment.

"You mean they're from outtime?" he demanded. "Are you sure?"

"I did two years on Fourth Level Kholghoor with the Paratime Police, before I took this job," the man called Kiro Soran replied. "And another thing. Those lash-marks were made with some kind of an electric whip. Not these rawhide quirts the Caleras use."

It took the plantation manager all of five seconds to add that up. The answer frightened him.

"Kirv, this is going to make a simply hideous uproar, all the way up to Home Time Line main office," he said. "I don't know what I'm going to do—"

"Well, I know what I have to do." The captain raised his voice, using the local language: "Sergeant! Run to the guardhouse, and tell Sergeant Adarada to mount up twenty of his men and take off after those Caleras who sold us these slaves. They're headed down the road toward the river. Tell him to bring them all back, and especially their chief, Coru-hin-Irigod, and him I want alive and able to answer questions. And then get the white-cloak lord Urado Alatena, and come back here."

"Yes, captain." The guards were all Yarana people; they disliked Caleras intensely. The sergeant threw a salute, turned, and ran.

"Next, we'll have to isolate these slaves," Kiro Soran said. "You'd better make a full report to the Company as

soon as possible. I'm going to transpose to Police Terminal
Time Line and make my report to the Sector-Regional
Subchief. Then—"

"Now wait a moment, Kirv," Dosu Golan protested.
"After all, I'm the manager, even if I am new here. It's up
to me to make the decisions—"

Kiro Soran shook his head. "Sorry, Doth. Not this one,"
he said. "You know the terms under which I was hired by
the Company. I'm still a field agent of the Paratime Police,
and I'm reporting back on duty as soon as I can transpose
to Police Terminal. Look; here are a hundred men and
women who have been shifted from one time-line, on one
paratemporal sector of probability, to another. Why, the
world from which these people came doesn't even exist in
this space-time continuum. There's only one way they
could have gotten here, and that's the way we did—in a
Ghaldron-Hesthor paratemporal transposition field. You
can carry it on from there as far as you like, but the only
thing it adds up to is a case for the Paratime Police. You
had better include in your report mention that I've
reverted to police status; my Company pay ought to be
stopped as of now. And until somebody who outranks me
is sent here, I'm in complete charge. Paratime
Transposition Code, Section XVII, Article 238."

The plantation manager nodded. Kiro Soran knew how
he must feel; he laid a hand gently on the younger man's
shoulder.

"You understand how it is, Doth; this is the only thing
I can do."

"I understand, Kirv. Count on me for absolutely
anything." He looked at the brown-skinned slaves, and

lines of horror and loathing appeared around his mouth. "To think that some of our own people would do a thing like this! I hope you can catch the devils! Are you transposing out, now?"

"In a few minutes. While I'm gone, have the doctor look at those whip-injuries. Those things could get infected. Fortunately, he's one of our own people."

"Yes, of course. And I'll have these slaves isolated, and if Adarada brings back Coru-hin-Irigod and his gang before you get back, I'll have them locked up and waiting for you. I suppose you want to narco-hypnotize and question the whole lot, slaves and slavers?"

The labor foreman, known locally as Urado Alatena, entered the stockade.

"What's wrong, Kirv?" he asked.

The Paratime Police agent told him, briefly. The labor foreman whistled, threw a quick glance at the nearest slaves, and nodded.

"I knew there was something funny about them," he said. "Doth, what a simply beastly thing to happen, two days after you take charge here!"

"Not his fault," the Paratime Police agent said. "I'm the one the Company'll be sore at, but I'd rather have them down on me rather than old Tortha Karf. Well, sit on the lid till I get back," he told both of them. "We'll need some kind of a story for the locals. Let's see—Explain to the guards, in the hearing of some of the more talkative slaves, that these slaves are from the Asian mainland, that they are of a people friendly to our people, and that they were kidnaped by pirates, our enemies. That ought to explain everything satisfactorily."

On his way back to the plantation house, he saw a clump of local slaves staring curiously at the stockade, and noticed that the guards had unslung their rifles and fixed their bayonets. None of them had any idea, of course, of what had happened, but they all seemed to know, by some sort of ESP, that something was seriously wrong. It was going to get worse, too, when strangers began arriving, apparently from nowhere, at the plantation.

Verkan Vall waited until the small, dark-eyed woman across the circular table had helped herself from one of the bowls on the revolving disk in the middle, then rotated it to bring the platter of cold boar-ham around to himself.

"Want some of this, Dalla?" he asked, transferring a slice of ham and a spoonful of wine sauce to his plate.

"No, I'll have some of the venison," the black-haired girl beside him said. "And some of the pickled beans. We'll be getting our fill of pork, for the next month."

"I thought the Dwarma Sector people were vegetarians," Jandar Jard, the theatrical designer, said. "Most nonviolent peoples are, aren't they?"

"Well, the Dwarma people haven't any specific taboo against taking life," Bronnath Zara, the dark-eyed woman in the brightly colored gown, told him. "They're just utterly noncombative, nonaggressive.

"When I was on the Dwarma Sector, there was a horrible scandal at the village where I was staying. It seems that a farmer and a meat butcher fought over the price of a pig. They actually raised their voices and shouted contradictions at each other. That happened two years before, and people were still talking about it."

"I didn't think they had any money, either," Verkan Vall's wife, Hadron Dalla, said.

"They don't," Zara said. "It's all barter and trade. What are you and Vall going to use for a visible means of support, while you're there?"

"Oh, I have my mandolin, and I've learned all the traditional Dwarma songs by hypno-mech," Dalla said. "And Transtime Tours is fitting Vall out with a bag of tools; he's going to do repair work and carpentry."

"Oh, good; you'll be welcome anywhere," Zara, the sculptress, said. "They're always glad to entertain a singer, and for people who do the fine decorative work they do, they're the most incompetent practical mechanics I've ever seen or heard of. You're going to travel from village to village?"

"Yes. The cover-story is that we're lovers who have left our village in order not to make Vall's former wife unhappy by our presence," Dalla said.

"Oh, good! That's entirely in the Dwarma romantic tradition," Bronnath Zara approved. "Ordinarily, you know, they don't like to travel. They have a saying: 'Happy are the trees, they abide in their own place; sad are the winds, forever they wander.' But that'll be a fine explanation."

Thalvan Dras, the big man with the black beard and the long red coat and cloth-of-gold sash who lounged in the host's seat, laughed.

"I can just see Vall mending pots, and Dalla playing that mandolin and singing," he said. "At least, you'll be getting away from police work. I don't suppose they have anything like police on the Dwarma Sector?"

"Oh, no; they don't even have any such concept,"

Bronnath Zara said. "When somebody does something wrong, his neighbors all come and talk to him about it till he gets ashamed, then they all forgive him and have a feast. They're lovely people, so kind and gentle. But you'll get awfully tired of them in about a month. They have absolutely no respect for anybody's privacy. In fact, it seems slightly indecent to them for anybody to want privacy."

One of Thalvan Dras' human servants came into the room, coughed apologetically, and said:

"A visiphone-call for His Valor, the Mavrad of Nerros."

Vall went on nibbling ham and wine sauce; the servant repeated the announcement a trifle more loudly.

"Vall, you're being paged!" Thalvan Dras told him, with a touch of impatience.

Verkan Vall looked blank for an instant, then grinned. It had been so long since he had even bothered to think about that antiquated title of nobility—

"Vall's probably forgotten that he has a title," a girl across the table, wearing an almost transparent gown and nothing else, laughed.

"That's something the Mavrad of Mnirna and Thalvabar never forgets," Jandar Jard drawled, with what, in a woman, would have been cattishness.

Thalvan Dras gave him a hastily repressed look of venomous anger, then said something, more to Verkan Vall than to Jandar Jard, about titles of nobility being the marks of social position and responsibility which their bearers should never forget. That jab, Vall thought, following the servant out of the room, had been a mistake on Jard's part. A music-drama, for which he had designed the settings, was due to open here in Dhergabar in another ten days. Thalvan Dras would cherish spite, and a word from the Mavrad of Mnirna and Thalvabar would set a dozen critics to disparaging Jandar's work. On the other hand, maybe it had been smart of Jandar Jard to antagonize Thalvan Dras; for every critic who bowed slavishly to the wealthy nobleman, there were at least two more who detested him unutterably, and they would rush to Jandar Jard's defense, and in the ensuing uproar, the settings would get more publicity than the drama itself.

In the visiphone booth, Vall found a girl in a green blouse, with the Paratime Police insigne on her shoulder, looking out of the screen. The wall behind her was pale green striped in gold and black.

"Hello, Eldra," he greeted her.

"Hello, Chief's Assistant: I'm sorry to bother you, but the Chief wants to talk to you. Just a moment, please."

The screen exploded into a kaleidoscopic flash of lights and colors, then cleared again. This time, a man looked out of it. He was well into middle age; close to his three hundredth year. His hair, a uniform iron-gray, was beginning to thin in front, and he was acquiring the beginnings of a double chin. His name was Tortha Karf, and he was Chief of Paratime Police, and Verkan Vall's superior.

"Hello, Vall. Glad I was able to locate you. When are you and Dalla leaving?"

"As soon as we can get away from this luncheon, here. Oh, say an hour. We're taking a rocket to Zarabar, and transposing from there to Passenger Terminal Sixteen, and from there to the Dwarma Sector."

"Well, Vall, I hate to bother you like this," Tortha Karf said, "but I wish you'd stop by Headquarters on your way to the rocketport. Something's come up—it may be a very nasty business—and I'd like to talk to you about it."

"Well, Chief, let me remind you that this vacation, which I've had to postpone four times already, has been overdue for four years," Vall said.

"Yes, Vall, I know. You've been working very hard, and you and Dalla are entitled to a little time together. I just want you to look into something, before you leave."

"It'll have to take some fast looking. Our rocket blasts off in two hours."

"It may take a little longer; if it does, you and Dalla can transpose to Police Terminal and take a rocket for Zarabar Equivalent, and transpose from there to Passenger Sixteen. It would save time if you brought Dalla with you to Headquarters."

"Dalla won't like this," Vall understated.

"No. I'm afraid not." Tortha Karf looked around apprehensively, as though estimating the damage an enraged Hadron Dalla could do to his office furnishings. "Well, try to get here as soon as you can."

Thalvan Dras was holding forth, when Vall returned, on one of his favorite preoccupations.

"... Reason I'm taking such an especially active interest in this year's Arts Exhibitions; I've become disturbed at the extent to which so many of our artists have been content to derive their motifs, even their techniques, from outtime art."

He was using his vocowriter, rather than his conversational, voice. "I yield to no one in my appreciation of outtime art—you all know how devotedly I collect objects of art from all over paratime—but our own artists should endeavor to express their artistic values in our own artistic idioms."

Vall bent over his wife's shoulder.

"We have to leave, right away," he whispered.

"But our rocket doesn't blast off for two hours—"

Thalvan Dras had stopped talking and was looking at them in annoyance.

"I have to go to Headquarters before we leave. It'll save time if you come along."

"Oh, no, Vall!" She looked at him in consternation. "Was that Tortha Karf, calling?" She replaced her plate on the table and got to her feet.

"I'm dreadfully sorry, Dras," he addressed their host. "I just had a call from Tortha Karf. A few minor details that must be cleared up, before I leave Home Time Line. If you'll accept our thanks for a wonderful luncheon—"

"Why, certainly, Vall. Brogoth, will you call—" He gave a slight chuckle. "I'm so used to having Brogoth Zaln at my elbow that I'd forgotten he wasn't here. Wait. I'll call one of the servants to have a car for you."

"Don't bother; we'll take an aircab," Vall told him.

"But you simply can't take a public cab!" The black-bearded nobleman was shocked at such an obscene idea. "I will have a car ready for you in a few minutes."

"Sorry, Dras; we have to hurry. We'll get a cab on the roof. Good-by, everybody; sorry to have to break away like this. See you all when we get back."

★ ★ ★

Hadron Dalla watched dejectedly as the green crags and escarpments of the Paratime Building loomed above the city in front of them, and began slipping under the aircab. She felt like a prisoner recaptured at the moment when attempted escape was about to succeed.

"I knew it," she said. "I knew he'd find something. He's trying to break things up between us, the way he did twenty years ago."

Vall crushed out his cigarette and said nothing. That hadn't been true, and she knew it as well as he did. There had been many other factors involved in the disintegration of their previous marriage, most of them of her own contribution. But that had been twenty years ago, she told herself. This time it would be different, if only—

"Really, Vall, he's never liked me," she went on. "He's jealous of me, I think. You're to be his successor, when he retires, and he thinks I'm not a good influence—"

"Oh, rubbish, Dalla! The Chief has always liked you," Vall replied. "If he didn't, do you think he'd always be inviting us to that farm of his, on Fifth Level Sicily? It's just that this job of ours has no end; something's always turning up, outtime."

The music that the cab had been playing died away. "Paratime Building, just below," it said, in a light feminine voice. "Which landing stage, please?" Vall leaned forward and punched at the buttons in front of him. Something in the cab's electronic brain gave a rapid series of clicks as it shifted from the general Paratime Building beam to the beam of the Paratime Police landing stage, then it said, "Thank you." The building below seemed to rotate upward toward them as it settled down. Then the antigrav-field snapped off, the cab door popped open, and the cab said: "Good-by, now. Ride with me again, sometime."

They crossed the landing stage, entered the antigrav shaft, and floated downward; at the end of a hallway, below, Vall opened the door of Tortha Karf's office and ushered her through ahead of him.

Tortha Karf, inside the semicircle of his desk, was speaking into a recording phone as they approached. He shut off the machine and waved, a cigarette in his hand.

"Come on back and sit down," he invited. "Be with you in a moment." Then he switched on the phone again and went on talking—something about prompter evaluation and transmission of reports and less reliance on robot equipment. "Sign that up, my personal order, and see it's transmitted to everybody down to and including Sector Regional Subchief level," he finished, then hung up the phone and turned to them.

"Sorry about this," he said. "Sit down, if you please. Cigarettes?"

She shook her head and sat down in one of the chairs behind the desk; she started to relax and then caught herself and sat erect, her hands on her lap.

"This won't interfere with your vacation, Vall," Tortha Karf was saying. "I just need a little help before you transpose out."

"We have to catch the rocket for Zarabar in an hour and a half," Dalla reminded him.

"Don't worry about that; if you miss the commercial rocket, our police rockets can give it an hour's start and pass it before it gets to Zarabar," Tortha Karf said. Then he turned to Vall. "Here's what's happened," he said. "One of our field agents on detached duty as guard captain for Consolidated Outtime Foodstuffs on a fruit plantation in western North America, Third Level Esaron Sector, was looking over a lot of slaves who had been sold to the plantation by a local slave dealer. He heard them talking among themselves—in Kharanda."

Dalla caught the significance of that before Vall did. At first, she was puzzled; then, in spite of herself, she was horrified and angry. Tortha Karf was explaining to Vall just where and on what paratemporal sector Kharanda was spoken.

"No possibility that this agent, Skordran Kirv, could have been mistaken. He worked for a while on Kholghoor Sector, himself; knew the language by hypno-mech and by two years' use," Tortha Karf was saying.

"So he ordered himself back on duty, had the slaves isolated and the slave dealers arrested, and then transposed to Police Terminal to report. The SecReg Subchief, old Vulthor Tharn, confirmed him in charge at this Esaron Sector plantation, and assigned him a couple of detectives and a psychist."

"When was this?" Vall asked.

"Yesterday. One-Five-Nine Day. About 1500 local time."

"Twenty-three hundred Dhergabar time," Vall commented.

"Yes. And I just found out about it. Came in in the late morning generalized report-digest; very inconspicuous item, no special urgency symbol or anything. Fortunately, one of the report editors spotted it and messaged Police Terminal for a copy of the original report."

"It's been a long time since we had anything like that," Vall said, studying the glowing tip of his cigarette, his face wearing the curiously withdrawn expression of a conscious memory recall. "Fifty years ago; the time that gang kidnaped some girls from Second Level Triplanetary Empire Sector and sold them into the harem of some Fourth Level Indo-Turanian sultan."

"Yes. That was your first independent case, Vall. That was when I began to think you'd really make a cop. One renegade First Level citizen and four or five ServSec Prole hoodlums, with a stolen fifty-foot conveyer. This looks like a rather more ambitious operation." Dalla got one of her own cigarettes out and lit it. Vall and Tortha Karf were talking cop talk about method of operation and possible size of the gang involved, and why the slaves had been shipped all the way from India to the west coast of North America.

"Always ready sale for slaves on the Esaron Sector," Vall was saying. "And so many small independent states, and different languages, that outtimers wouldn't be particularly conspicuous."

"And with this barbarian invasion going on on the Kholghoor Sector, slaves could be picked up cheaply," Tortha Karf added.

In spite of her determination to boycott the conversation, curiosity began to get the better of her. She had spent a year and a half on the Kholghoor Sector, investigating alleged psychic powers of the local priests. There'd been nothing to it—the prophecies weren't precognition, they were shrewd inferences, and the miracles weren't psychokinesis, they were sleight-of-hand. She found herself asking:

"What barbarian invasion's this?"

"Oh, Central Asian nomadic people, the Croutha," Tortha Karf told her. "They came down through Khyber Pass about three months ago, turned east, and hit the headwaters of the Ganges. Without punching a lot of buttons to find out exactly, I'd say they're halfway to the delta country by now. Leader seems to be a chieftain called Llamh Droogh the Red. A lot of paratime trading companies are yelling for permits to introduce firearms in the Kholghoor Sector to protect their holdings there."

She nodded. The Fourth Level Kholghoor Sector belonged to what was known as Indus-Ganges-Irrawaddy Basic Sector-Grouping—probability of civilization having developed late on the Indian subcontinent, with the rest of the world, including Europe, in Stone Age savagery or early Bronze Age barbarism. The Kharandas, the people among whom she had once done field-research work, had developed a pre-mechanical, animal-power, handcraft, edge-weapon culture. She could imagine the roads jammed with fugitives from the barbarian invaders, the conveyer hidden among the trees, the lurking slavers—

Watch it, Dalla! Don't let the old scoundrel play on your feelings!

"Well, what do you want me to do, Chief?" Vall was asking.

"Well, I have to know just what this situation's likely to develop into, and I want to know why Vulthor Tharn's been sitting on this ever since Skordran Kirv reported it to him—"

"I can answer the second one now," Vall replied.

"Vulthor Tharn is due to retire in a few years. He has a negatively good, undistinguished record. He's trying to play it safe."

Tortha Karf nodded. "That's what I thought. Look, Vall; suppose you and Dalla transpose from here to Police Terminal, and go to Novilan Equivalent, and give this a quick look-over and report to me, and then rocket to Zarabar Equivalent and go on with your trip to the Dwarma Sector. It may delay you eight or ten hours, but—"

"Closer twenty-four," Vall said. "I'd have to transpose to this plantation, on the Esaron Sector. How about it, Dalla? Would you want to do that?"

She hesitated for a moment, angry with him. He didn't want to refuse, and he was trying to make her do it for him.

"I know, it's a confounded imposition, Dalla," Tortha Karf told her. "But it's important that I get a prompt and full estimate of the situation. This may be something very serious. If it's an isolated incident, it can be handled in a routine manner, but I'm afraid it's not. It has all the marks of a large-scale operation, and if this is a matter of mass kidnapings from one sector and transpositions to another, you can see what a threat this is to the Paratime Secret."

"Moral considerations entirely aside," Vall said. "We don't need to discuss them; they're too obvious."

She nodded. For over twelve millennia, the people of her race and Vall's and Tortha Karf's had been existing as parasites on all the innumerable other worlds of alternate probability on the lateral dimension of time. Smart parasites never injure their hosts, and try never to reveal their existence.

"We could do that, couldn't we, Vall?" she asked, angry at herself now for giving in. "And if you want to question these slaves, I speak Kharanda, and I know how they think. And I'm a qualified and licensed narco-hypnotic technician."

"Well, that's splendid, Dalla!" Tortha Karf enthused. "Wait a moment; I'll message Police Terminal to have a rocket ready for you."

"I'll need a hypno-mech for Kharanda, myself," Vall said. "Dalla, do you know Acalan?" When she shook her head, he turned back to Tortha Karf. "Look; it's about a four-hour rocket hop to Novilan Equivalent. Say we have the hypno-mech machines installed in the rocket; Dalla and I can take our language lessons on the way, and be ready to go to work as soon as we land."

"Good idea," Tortha Karf approved. "I'll order that done, right away. Now—"

Oddly enough, she wasn't feeling so angry, now that she had committed herself and Vall. Come to think of it, she had never been on Police Terminal Time Line; very few people, outside the Paratime Police, ever had. And, she had always wanted to learn more about Vall's work, and participate in it with him. And if she'd made him refuse, it would have been something ugly between them all the time they would be on the Dwarma Sector. But this way—

The big circular conveyer room was crowded, as it had been every minute of every day for the past ten thousand years. At the great circular desk in the center, departing or returning police officers were checking in or out with the flat-topped cylindrical robot clerks, or talking to human attendants. Some were in the regulation green uniform; others, like himself, were in civilian clothes; more were in outtime costumes from all over paratime. Fringed robes and cloth-of-gold sashes and conical caps from the Second Level Khiftan Sector; Fourth Level Proto-Aryan mail and helmets; the short tunics and kilts of Fourth Level Alexandrian-Roman Sector; the Zarkantha loincloth and felt cap and daggers; there were priestly vestments stiff with gold, and military uniforms; there were trousers and jackboots and bare legs; blasters, and swords, and pistols, and bows and quivers, and spears. And the place was loud with a babel of voices and the clatter of teleprinters.

Dalla was looking about her in surprised delight; for her, the vacation had already begun. He was glad; for a while, he had been afraid that she would be unhappy about it. He guided her through the crowd to the desk, spoke for a while to one of the human attendants, and found out which was their conveyer. It was a fixed-destination shuttler, operative only between Home Time Line and Police Terminal, from which most of the Paratime Police operations were routed. He put Dall in through the sliding door, followed, and closed it behind him, locking it. Then, before he closed the starting switch, he drew a pistollike weapon and checked it.

In theory, the Ghaldron-Hesthor paratemporal transposition field was uninfluenced by material objects outside it. In practice, however, such objects occasionally intruded, and sometimes they were alive and hostile. The last time he had been in this conveyer room, he had seen a quartet of returning officers emerge from a conveyer dome dragging a dead lion by the tail. The sigma-ray needler, which he carried, was the only weapon which could be used, under the circumstances. It had no effect whatever on any material structure and could be used inside an activated conveyer without deranging the conductor-mesh, as, say, a bullet or the vibration of an ultrasonic paralyzer would do, and it was instantly fatal to anything having a central nervous system. It was a good weapon to use outtime for that reason, also; even on the most civilized time-line, the most elaborate autopsy would reveal no specific cause of death.

"What's the Esaron Sector like?" Dalla asked, as the conveyer dome around them coruscated with shifting light and vanished.

"Third Level; probability of abortive attempt to colonize this planet from Mars about a hundred thousand years ago," he said. "A few survivors—a shipload or so—were left to shift for themselves while the parent civilization on Mars died out. They lost all vestiges of their original Martian culture, even memory of their extraterrestrial origin. About fifteen hundred to two thousand years ago, a reasonably high electrochemical civilization developed and they began working with nuclear energy and developed reaction-drive spaceships. But they'd concentrated so on the inorganic sciences, and so far neglected the bio-sciences, that when they launched their first ship for Venus they hadn't yet developed a germ theory of disease."

"What happened when they ran into the green-vomit fever?" Dalla asked.

"About what you could expect. The first—and only—ship to return brought it back to Terra. Of course, nobody knew what it was, and before the epidemic ended, it had almost depopulated this planet. Since the survivors knew nothing about germs, they blamed it on the anger of the gods—the old story of recourse to supernaturalism in the absence of a known explanation—and a fanatically anti-scientific cult got control. Of course, space travel was taboo; so was nuclear and even electric power. For some reason, steam power and gunpowder weren't offensive to the gods. They went back to a low-order steam-power, black-powder, culture, and haven't gotten beyond that to this day. The relatively civilized regions are on the east coast of Asia and the west coast of North America; civilized race more or less Caucasian. Political organization just barely above the tribal level—thousands of petty kingdoms and republics and principalities and feudal holdings and robbers' roosts. The principal industries are brigandage, piracy, slave-raiding, cattle-rustling and intercommunal warfare. They have a few ramshackle steam railways, and some steamboats on the rivers. We sell them coal and manufactured goods, mostly in exchange for foodstuffs and tobacco. Consolidated Outtime Foodstuffs has the sector franchise. That's one of the companies Thalvan Dras gets his money from."

They had run down through the civilized Second and Third Levels and were leaving the Fourth behind and entering the Fifth, existing in the probability of a world without human population. Once in a while, around them, they caught brief flashes of buildings and rocketports and spaceports and landing stages, as the conveyer took them through narrow paratime belts on which their own civilization had established outposts—Fifth Level Commercial, Fifth Level Passenger, Industrial Sector, Service Sector.

Finally the conveyer dome around them shimmered into visibility and materialized; when they emerged, there were policemen in green uniforms who entered to search the dome with drawn needlers to make sure they had picked up nothing dangerous on the way. The room outside was similar to the one they had left on Home Time Line, even to the shifting, noisy crowd in incongruously-mixed costumes.

The rocketport was a ten minutes' trip by aircar from the conveyer head; when they boarded the stubby-winged strato-rocket, Vall saw that two of the passenger-seats had square metal cabinets bolted in place behind them and blue plastic helmets on swinging arms mounted above them.

"Everything's set up," the pilot told them. "Dr. Hadron, you sit on the left; that cabinet's loaded with language tape for Acalan. Yours is loaded with a tape of Kharanda; that's the Fourth Level Kholghoor language you wanted, Chief's Assistant. Shall I help you get fixed in your seats?"

"Yes, if you please. Here, Dalla, I'll fix that for you."

Dalla was already asleep when the pilot was adjusting his helmet and giving him his injection. He never felt the rocket tilt into firing position, and while he slept, the Kharands language, with all its vocabulary and grammar, became part of his subconscious knowledge, needing only the mental pronunciation of a trigger-symbol to bring it into consciousness. The pilot was already unfastening and raising his helmet when he opened his eyes. Dalla, beside him, was sipping a cup of spiced wine.

On the landing stage of the Sector-Regional Headquarters at Novilan Equivalent, four or five people were waiting for them. Vall recognized the subchief, Vulthor Tharn, who introduced another man, in riding boots and a white cloak, as Skordran Kirv. Vall clasped hands with him warmly.

"Good work, Agent Skordran. You got onto this promptly."

"I tried to, sir. Do you want the dope now? We have half an hour's flight to our spatial equivalent, and another half hour in transposition."

"Give it to me on the way," he said, and turned to Vulthor Tharn. "Our Esaron costumes ready?"

"Yes. Over there in the control tower. We have a temporary conveyer head set up about two hundred miles south of here, which will take you straight through to the plantation."

"Suppose you change now, Dalla," he said. "Subchief, I'd like a word with you privately."

He and Vulthor Tharn excused themselves and walked over to the edge of the landing stage. The SecReg Subchief was outwardly composed, but Vall sensed that he was worried and embarrassed.

"Now, what's been done since you got Agent Skordran's report?" Vall asked.

"Well, sir, it seems that this is more serious than we had anticipated. Field Agent Skordran, who will give you the particulars, says that there is every indication that a large and well-organized gang of paratemporal criminals, our own people, are at work. He says that he's found evidence of activities on Fourth Level Kholghoor that don't agree with any information we have about conditions on that sector."

"Beside transmitting Agent Skordran's report to Dhergabar through the robot report-system, what have you done about it?"

"I confirmed Agent Skordran in charge of the local investigation, and gave him two detectives and a psychist, sir. As soon as we could furnish hypno-mech indoctrination in Kharanda to other psychists, I sent them along. He now has four of them, and eight detectives. By that time, we had a conveyer head right at this Consolidated Outtime Foodstuffs plantation."

"Why didn't you just borrow psychists from SecReg for Kholghoor, Eastern India?" Vall asked. "Subchief Ranthar would have loaned you a few."

"Oh, I couldn't call on another SecReg for men without higher-echelon authorization. Especially not from another Sector Organization, even another Level Authority," Vulthor Tharn said. "Beside, it would have taken longer to bring them here than hypno-mech our own personnel."

He was right about the second point. Vall agreed mentally; however, his real reason was procedural.

"Did you alert Ranthar Jard to what was going on in his SecReg?" he asked.

"Gracious, no!" Vulthor Tharn was scandalized. "I have no authority to tell people of equal echelon in other Sector and Level organizations what to do. I put my report through regular channels; it wasn't my place to go outside my own jurisdiction."

And his report had crawled through channels for fourteen hours, Vall thought.

"Well, on my authority, and in the name of Chief Tortha, you message Ranthar Jard at once; send him every scrap of information you have on the subject, and forward additional information as it comes in to you. I doubt he'll find anything on any time-line that's being exploited by any legitimate paratimers. This gang probably work exclusively on unpenetrated time-lines; this business Skordran Kirv came across was a bad blunder on some underling's part." He saw Dalla emerge from the control tower in breeches and boots and a white cloak, buckling on a heavy revolver. "I'll go change, now; you get busy calling Ranthar Jard. I'll see you when I get back."

"Are you taking over, Chief's Assistant?" Skordran Kirv asked, as the aircar lifted from the landing stage.

"Not at all. My wife and I are starting on our vacation, as soon as I find out what's been happening here, and report to Chief Tortha. Did your native troopers catch those slavers?"

"Yes, they got them yesterday afternoon; we've had them ever since. Do you want the whole thing just as it happened, Assistant Verkan, or just a condensation?"

"Give me what you think it indicates, remembering that you're probably trying to analyze a large situation from a very small sample."

"It's big, all right," Skordran Kirv said. "This gang can't number less than a hundred men, maybe several hundred. They must have at least two two-hundred-foot conveyers and several small ones, and bases on what sounds like some Fifth Level Time line, and at least one air freighter of around five thousand tons. They are operating on a number of Kholghoor and Esaron time lines."

Verkan Vall nodded. "I didn't think it was any petty larceny," he said.

"Wait till you hear the rest of it. On the Kholghoor Sector, this gang is known as the Wizard Traders; we've been using that as a convenience label. They pose as sorcerers—black robes and hood-masks covered with luminous symbols, voice-amplifiers, cold-light auras, energy-weapons, mechanical magic tricks, that sort of thing. They have all the Croutha scared witless. Their procedure is to establish camps in the forest near recently conquered Kharanda cities; then they appear to the Croutha, impress them with their magical powers, and trade manufactured goods for Kharanda captives. They mainly trade firearms, apparently some kind of flintlocks, and powder."

Then they were confining their operations to unpenetrated time lines; there had been no reports of firearms in the hands of the Croutha invaders.

"After they buy a batch of slaves," Skordran Kirv continued, "they transpose them to this presumably Fifth Level base, where they have concentration camps. The slaves we questioned had been airlifted to North America, where there's another concentration camp, and from there transposed to this Esaron Sector time line where I found them. They say that there were at least two to three thousand slaves in this North American concentration camp and that they are being transposed out in small batches and replaced by others airlifted in from India. This lot was sold to a Calera named Nebu-hin-Abenoz, the chieftain of a hill town, Careba, about fifty miles southwest of the plantation. There were two hundred and fifty in this batch; this Coru-hin-Irigod only bought the batch he sold at the plantation."

The aircar lost speed and altitude; below, the countryside was dotted with conveyer heads, each spatially coexistent with some outtime police post or operation. There were a great many of them; the western coast of North America was a center of civilization on many paratemporal sectors, and while the conveyer heads of the commercial and passenger companies were scattered over hundreds of Fifth Level time lines, those of the Paratime Police were concentrated upon one.

The anti-grav-car circled around a three-hundred-foot steel tower that supported a conveyer head spatially coexistent with one on a top floor of some outtime tall building, and let down in front of a low prefabricated steel shed. A man in police uniform came out to meet them. There was a fifty-foot conveyer dome inside, and a fifty-foot red-lined circle that marked the transposition point of an outtime conveyer. They all entered the dome, and the operator put on the transposition field.

"You haven't heard the worst of it yet." Skordran Kirv was saying. "On this time line, we have reason to think that the native, Nebu-hin-Abenoz, who bought the slaves, actually saw the slavers' conveyer. Maybe even saw it activated."

"If he did, we'll either have to capture him and give him a memory-obliteration, or kill him," Vall said. "What do you know about him?"

"Well, this Careba, the town he bosses, is a little walled town up in the hills. Everybody there is related to everybody else; this man we have, Coru-hin-Irigod, is the son of a sister of Nebu-hin-Abenoz's wife. They're all bandits and slavers and cattle rustlers and what have you. For the last ten years, Nebu-hin-Abenoz has been buying slaves from some secret source. Before the Kholghoor Sector people began coming in, they were mostly white, with a few brown people who might have been Polynesians. No Negroes—there's no black race on this sector, and I suppose the paratime slavers didn't want too many questions asked. Coru-hin-Irigod, under narco-hypnosis, said that they were all outlanders, speaking strange languages."

"Ten years! And this is the first hint we've had of it," Vall said. "That's not a bright mark for any of us. I'll bet the slave population on some of these Esaron time lines is an anthropologist's nightmare."

"Why, if this has been going on for ten years, there must be millions upon millions of people dragged from their own time lines into slavery!" Dalla said in a shocked voice.

"Ten years may not be all of it," Vall said. "This Nebu-hin-Abenoz looks like the only tangible lead we have, at present. How does he operate?"

"About once every ten days, he'll take ten or fifteen men and go a day's ride—that may be as much as fifty miles; these Caleras have good horses and they're hard riders—into the hills. He'll take a big bag of money, all gold. After dark, when he has made camp, a couple of strangers in Calera dress will come in. He'll go off with them, and after about an hour, he'll come back with eight or ten of these strangers and a couple of hundred slaves, always chained in batches of ten. Nebu-hin-Abenoz pays for them, makes arrangements for the next meeting, and the next morning he and his party start marching the slaves to Careba. I might add that, until now, these slaves have been sold to the mines east of Careba; these are the first that have gotten into the coastal country."

"That's why this hasn't come to light before, then. The conveyer comes in every ten days, at about the same place?"

"Yes. I've been thinking of a way we might trap them," Skordran Kirv said. "I'll need more men, and equipment."

"Order them from Regional or General Reserve." Vall told him. "This thing's going to have overtop priority till it's cleared up."

He was mentally cursing Vulthor Tharn's procedure-bound timidity as the conveyer flickered and solidified around them and the overhead red light turned green.

They emerged into the interior of a long shed, adobe-walled and thatch-roofed, with small barred windows set high above the earth floor. It was cool and shadowy, and the air was heavy with the fragrance of citrus fruits. There were bins along the walls, some partly full of oranges, and piles of wicker baskets. Another conveyer dome stood beside the one in which they had arrived; two men in white cloaks and riding boots sat on the edge of one of the bins, smoking and talking.

Skordran Kirv introduced them—Gathon Dard and

Krador Arv, special detectives—and asked if anything new had come up. Krador Arv shook his head.

"We still have about forty to go," he said. "Nothing new in their stories; still the same two time lines."

"These people," Skordran Kirv explained, "were all peons on the estate of a Kharanda noble just above the big bend of the Ganges. The Croutha hit their master's estate about a ten-days ago, elapsed time. In telling about their capture, most of them say that their master's wife killed herself with a dagger after the Croutha killed her husband, but about one out of ten say that she was kidnaped by the Croutha. Two different time lines, of course. The ones who tell the suicide story saw no firearms among the Croutha; the ones who tell the kidnap story say that they all had some kind of muskets and pistols. We're making synthetic summaries of the two stories."

"We're having trouble with the locals about all these strangers coming in," Gathon Dard added. "They're getting curious."

"We'll have to take a chance on that," Vall said. "Are the interrogations still going on? Then let's have a look-in at them."

The big double doors at the end of the shed were barred on the inside. Krador Arv unlocked a small side door, letting Vall, Dalla and Gathon Dard out. In the yard outside, a gang of slaves were unloading a big wagon of oranges and packing them into hampers; they were guarded by a couple of native riflemen who seemed mostly concerned with keeping them away from the shed, and a man in a white cloak was watching the guards for the same purpose. He walked over and introduced himself to Vall.

"Golzan Doth, local alias Dosu Golan. I'm Consolidated Outtime Foodstuffs' manager here."

"Nasty business for you people," Vall sympathized. "If it's any consolation, it's a bigger headache for us."

"Have you any idea what's going to be done about these slaves?" Golzan Doth asked. "I have to remember that the Company has forty thousand Paratemporal Exchange Units invested in them. The top office was very specific in requesting information about that."

Vall shook his head. "That's over my echelon," he said. "Have to be decided by the Paratime Commission. I doubt if your company'll suffer. You bought them innocently, in conformity with local custom. Ever buy slaves from this Coru-hin-Irigod before?"

"I'm new, here. The man I'm replacing broke his neck when his horse put a foot in a gopher hole about two ten-days ago."

Beside him, Vall could see Dalla nod as though making a mental note. When she got back to Home Time Line, she'd put a crew of mediums to work trying to contact the discarnate former plantation manager; at Rhogom Institute, she had been working on the problem of return of a discarnate personality from outtime.

"A few times," Skordran Kirv said. "Nothing suspicious; all local stuff. We questioned Coru-hin-Irigod pretty closely on that point, and he says that this is the first time he ever brought a batch of Nebu-hin-Abenoz's outlanders this far west."

★ ★ ★

The interrogations were being conducted inside the plantation house, in the secret central rooms where the paratimers lived. Skordran Kirv used a door-activator to slide open a hidden door.

"I suppose I don't have to warn either of you that any positive statement made in the hearing of a narco-hypnotized subject—" he began.

"...Has the effect of hypnotic suggestion—" Vall picked up after him.

"...And should be avoided unless such suggestion is intended," Dalla finished.

Skordran Kirv laughed, opening another, inner door, and stood aside. In what had been the paratimers' recreation room, most of the furniture had been shoved into the corners. Four small tables had been set up, widely spaced and with screens between; across each of them, with an electric recorder between, an almost naked Kharanda slave faced a Paratime Police psychist. At a long table at the far side of the room, four men and two girls were working over stacks of cards and two big charts.

"Phrakor Vuln," the man who was working on the charts introduced himself. "Synthesist." He introduced the others.

Vall made a point of the fact that Dalla was his wife, in case any of the cops began to get ideas, and mentioned that she spoke Kharanda, had spent some time on the Fourth Level Kholghoor, and was a qualified psychist.

"What have you got, so far?" he asked.

"Two different time lines, and two different gangs of Wizard Traders," Phrakor Vuln said. "We've established the latter from physical descriptions and because both batches were sold by the Croutha at equivalent periods of elapsed time."

Vall picked up one of the kidnap-story cards and glanced at it.

"I notice there's a fair verbal description of these firearms, and mention of electric whips," he said. "I'm curious about where they came from."

"Well, this is how we reconstructed them, Chief's Assistant," one of the girls said, handing him a couple of sheets of white drawing paper.

The sketches had been done with soft pencil; they bore repeated erasures and corrections. That of the whip showed a cylindrical handle, indicated as twelve inches in length and one in diameter, fitted with a thumb-switch.

"That's definitely Second Level Khiftan," Vall said, handing it back. "Made of braided copper or silver wire and powered with a little nuclear-conversion battery in the grip. They heat up to about two hundred centigrade; produce really painful burns."

"Why, that's beastly!" Dalla exclaimed.

"Anything on the Khiftan Sector is." Skordran Kirv looked at the four slaves at the tables. "We don't have a really bad case here, now. A few of these people were lash-burned horribly, though."

Vall was looking at the other sketches. One was a musket, with a wide butt and a band-fastened stock; the lock-mechanism, vaguely flintlock, had been dotted in tentatively. The other was a long pistol, similarly definite in outline and vague in mechanical detail; it was merely a knob-butted miniature of the musket.

"I've seen firearms like these; have a lot of them in my

collection," he said, handing back the sketches. "Low-order mechanical or high-order pre-mechanical cultures. Fact is, things like those could have been made on the Kholghoor Sector, if the Kharandas had learned to combine sulfur, carbon and nitrates to make powder."

The interrogator at one of the tables had evidently heard all his subject could tell him. He rose, motioning the slave to stand.

"Now, go with that man," he said in Kharanda, motioning to one of the detectives in native guard uniform. "You will trust him; he is your friend and will not harm you. When you have left this room, you will forget everything that has happened here, except that you were kindly treated and that you were given wine to drink and your hurts were anointed. You will tell the others that we are their friends and that they have nothing to fear from us. And you will not try to remove the mark from the back of your left hand."

As the detective led the slave out a door at the other side of the room, the psychist came over to the long table, handing over a card and lighting a cigarette.

"Suicide story," he said to one of the girls, who took the card.

"Anything new?"

"Some minor details about the sale to the Caleras on this time line. I think we've about scraped bottom."

"You can't say that," Phrakor Vuln objected. "The very last one may give us something nobody else had noticed."

Another subject was sent out. The interrogator came over to the table.

"One of the kidnap-story crowd," he said. "This one

was right beside that Croutha who took the shot at the wild pig or whatever it was on the way to the Wizard Traders' camp. Best description of the guns we've gotten so far. No question that they're flintlocks." He saw Verkan Vall. "Oh, hello, Assistant Verkan. What do you make of them? You're an authority on outtime weapons, I understand."

"I'd have to see them. These people simply don't think mechanically enough to give a good description. A lot of peoples make flintlock firearms."

He started running over, in his mind, the paratemporal areas in which gunpowder but not the percussion-cap was known. Expanding cultures, which had progressed as far as the former but not the latter. Static cultures, in which an accidental discovery of gunpowder had never been followed up by further research. Post-debacle cultures, in which a few stray bits of ancient knowledge had survived.

Another interrogator came over, and then the fourth. For a while they sat and talked and drank coffee, and then the next quartet of slaves, two men and two women, were brought in. One of the women had been badly blistered by the electric whips of the Wizard Traders; in spite of reassurances, all were visibly apprehensive.

"We will not harm you," one of the psychists told them. "Here; here is medicine for your hurts. At first, it will sting, as good medicines will, but soon it will take away all pain. And here is wine for you to drink."

A couple of detectives approached, making a great show of pouring wine and applying ointment; under cover of the medication, they jabbed each slave with a hypodermic needle, and then guided them to seats at the four tables. Vall and Dalla went over and stood behind one of the psychists, who had a small flashlight in his hand.

"Now, rest for a while," the psychist was saying. "Rest and let the good medicine do its work. You are tired and sleepy. Look at this magic light, which brings comfort to the troubled. Look at the light. Look . . . at . . . the . . . light."

They moved to the next table.

"Did you have hand in the fighting?"

"No, lord. We were peasant folk, not fighting people. We had no weapons, nor weapon-skill. Those who fought were all killed; we held up empty hands, and were spared to be captives of the Croutha."

"What happened to your master, the Lord Ghromdour, and to his lady?"

"One of the Croutha threw a hatchet and killed our master, and then his lady drew a dagger and killed herself."

The psychist made a red mark on the card in front of him, and circled the number on the back of the slave's hand with red indelible crayon. Vall and Dalla went to the third table.

"They had the common weapons of the Croutha, lord, and they also had the weapons of the Wizard Traders. Of these, they carried the long weapons slung across their backs, and the short weapons thrust through their belts."

A blue mark on the card; a blue circle on the back of the slave's hand.

They listened to both versions of what had happened at the sack of the Lord Ghromdour's estate, and the march into the captured city of Jhirda, and the second march into the forest to the camp of the Wizard Traders.

"The servants of the Wizard Traders did not appear

until after the Croutha had gone away; they wore different garb. They wore short jackets, and trousers, and short boots, and they carried small weapons on their belts—"

"They had whips of great cruelty that burned like fire; we were all lashed with these whips, as you may see, lord—"

"The Croutha had bound us two and two, with neck-yokes; these the servants of the Wizard Traders took off from us, and they chained us together by tens, with the chains we still wore when we came to this place—"

"They killed my child, my little Zhouzha!" the woman with the horribly blistered back was wailing. "They tore her out of my arms, and one of the servants of the Wizard Traders—may Khokhaat devour his soul forever!—dashed out her brains. And when I struggled to save her. I was thrown on the ground, and beaten with the fire-whips until I fainted. Then I was dragged into the forest, along with the others who were chained with me." She buried her head in her arms, sobbing bitterly.

Dalla stepped forward, taking the flashlight from the interrogator with one hand and lifting the woman's head with the other. She flashed the light quickly in the woman's eyes.

"You will grieve no more for your child," she said. "Already, you are forgetting what happened at the Wizard Traders' camp, and remembering only that your child is safe from harm. Soon you will remember her only as a dream of the child you hope to have, some day." She flashed the light again, then handed it back to the psychist. "Now, tell us what happened when you were taken into the forest; what did you see there?"

The psychist nodded approvingly, made a note on the card, and listened while the woman spoke. She had stopped sobbing, now, and her voice was clear and cheerful.

Vall went over to the long table.

"Those slaves were still chained with the Wizard Traders' chains when they were delivered here. Where are the chains?" he asked Skordran Kirv.

"In the permanent conveyer room," Skordran Kirv said. "You can look at them there; we didn't want to bring them in here, for fear these poor devils would think we were going to chain them again. They're very light, very strong; some kind of alloy steel. Files and power saws only polish them; it takes fifteen seconds to cut a link with an atomic torch. One long chain, and short lengths, fifteen inches long, staggered, every three feet, with a single hinge-shackle for the ankle. The shackles were riveted with soft wrought-iron rivets, evidently made with some sort of a power riveting-machine. We cut them easily with a cold chisel."

"They ought to be sent to Dhergabar Equivalent, Police Terminal, for study of material and workmanship. Now, you mentioned some scheme you had for capturing this conveyer that brings in the slaves for Nebu-hin-Abenoz. What have you in mind?"

"We still have Coru-hin-Irigod and all his gang, under hypno. I'd thought of giving them hypnotic conditioning, and sending them back to Careba with orders to put out some kind of signal the next time Nebu-hin-Abenoz starts out on a buying trip. We could have a couple of men posted in the hills overlooking Careba, and they could send a message-ball through to Police Terminal. Then, a party could be sent with a mobile conveyer to ambush Nebu-hin-Abenoz on the way, and wipe out his party. Our people could take their horses and clothing and go on to take the conveyer by surprise."

"I'd suggest one change. Instead of relying on visual signals by the hypno-conditioned Coru-hin-Irigod, send a couple of our men to Careba with midget radios."

Skordran Kirv nodded. "Sure. We can condition Coru-hin-Irigod to accept them as friends and vouch for them at Careba. Our boys can be traders and slave buyers. Careba's a market town; traders are always welcome. They can have firearms to sell—revolvers and repeating rifles. Any Calera'll buy any firearm that's better than the one he's carrying; they'll always buy revolvers and repeaters. We can get what we want from Commercial Four-Oh-Seven; we can get riding and pack horses here."

Vall nodded. "And the post overlooking or in radio range of Careba on this time line, and another on PolTerm. For the ambush of Nebu-hin-Abenoz's gang and the capture of the conveyer, use anything you want to— sleep-gas, paralyzers, energy-weapons, antigrav-equipment, anything. As far as regulations about using only equipment appropriate to local culture-levels, forget them entirely. But take that conveyer intact. You can locate the base time line from the settings of the instrument panel, and that's what we want most of all."

Dalla and the police psychist, having finished with and dismissed their subject, came over to the long table.

"... That poor creature," Dalla was saying. "What sort of fiends are they?"

"If that made you sick, remember we've been listening to things like that for the last eight hours. Some of the stories were even worse than that one."

"Well, I'd like to use a heat-gun on the whole lot of them, turned down to where it'd just fry them medium-rare," Dalla said. "And for whoever's back of this, take him to Second Level Khiftan and sell him to the priests of Fasif."

"Too bad you're not coming back from your vacation, instead of starting out, Chief's Assistant Verkan," Skordran Kirv said. "This is too big for me to handle alone, and I'd sooner work under you than anybody else Chief Tortha sends in."

"Vall!" Dalla cried in indignation. "You're not going to just report on this and then walk away from it, are you?"

"But, darling," Vall replied, in what he hoped was a convincing show of surprise. "You don't want our vacation postponed again, do you? If I get mixed up in this, there's no telling when I can get away, and by the time I'm free, something may come up at Rhogom Institute that you won't want to drop—"

"Vall, you know perfectly well that I wouldn't be happy for an instant on the Dwarma Sector, thinking about this—"

"All right, then; let's forget about the vacation. You want to stay on for a while and help me with this? It'll be a lot of hard work, but we'll be together."

"Yes, of course. I want to do something to smash those devils. Vall, if you'd heard some of the things they did to those poor people—"

"Well, I'll have to go back to PolTerm, as soon as I'm

reasonably well filled in on this, and report to Tortha Karf
and tell him I've taken charge. You can stay here and help
with these interrogations; I'll be back in about ten hours.
Then, we can go to Kholghoor East India SecReg HQ to
talk to Ranthar Jard. We may be able to get something
that'll help us on that end—"

"You may be able to have your vacation before too long,
Dr. Hadron," Skordran Kirv told her. "Once we capture
one of their conveyers, the instrument panel'll tell us what
time line they're working from, and then we'll have them."

"There's an Indo-Turanian Sector parable about a
snake charmer who thought he was picking up his snake
and found that he had hold of an elephant's tail," Vall said.
"That might be a good thing to bear in mind, till we find
out just what we have picked up."

Coming down a hallway on the hundred and seventh
floor of the Management wing of the Paratime Building,
Yandar Yadd paused to admire, in the green mirror of the
glassoid wall, the jaunty angle of his silver-feathered cap,
the fit of his short jacket, and the way his weapon hung at
his side. This last was not instantly recognizable as a
weapon; it looked more like a portable radio, which
indeed it was. It was, none the less, a potent weapon. One
flick of his finger could connect that radio with one at Tri-
Planet News Service, and within the hour anything he said
into it would be heard by all Terra, Mars and Venus. In
consequence, there existed around the Paratime Building
a marked and understandable reluctance to antagonize
Yandar Yadd.

He glanced at his watch. It was twenty minutes short

of 1000, when he had an appointment with Baltan Vrath, the comptroller general. Glancing about, he saw that he was directly in front of the doorway of the Outtime Claims Bureau, and he strolled in, walking through the waiting room and into the claims-presentation office. At once, he stiffened like a bird dog at point.

Sphabron Larv, one of his young legmen, was in altercation across the counter-desk with Varkar Klav, the Deputy Claims Agent on duty at the time. Varkar was trying to be icily dignified; Sphabron Larv's black hair was in disarray and his face was suffused with anger. He was pounding with his fist on the plastic counter-top.

"You have to!" he was yelling in the older man's face. "That's a public document, and I have a right to see it. You want me to go into Tribunes' Court and get an order? If I do, there'll be a Question in Council about why I had to, before the day's out!"

"What's the matter, Larv?" Yandar Yadd asked lazily. "He trying to hold something out on you?"

Sphabron Larv turned; his eyes lit happily when he saw his boss, and then his anger returned.

"I want to see a copy of an indemnity claim that was filed this morning," he said. "Varkar, here, won't show it to me. What does he think this is, a Fourth Level dictatorship?"

"What kind of a claim, now?" Yandar Yadd addressed Larv, ignoring Varkar Klav.

"Consolidated Outtime Foodstuffs—one of the Thalvan Interests companies—just claimed forty thousand P.E.U. for a hundred slaves bought by one of their plantation managers on Third Level Esaron from a local slave dealer. The Paratime Police impounded the slaves for narco-hypnotic interrogation, and then transposed the lot of them to Police Terminal."

Yandar Yadd still held his affectation of sleepy indolence.

"Now why would the Paracops do that, I wonder? Slavery's an established local practice on Esaron Sector; our people have to buy slaves if they want to run a plantation."

"I know that." Sphabron Larv replied. "That's what I want to find out. There must be something wrong, either with the slaves, or the treatment our people were giving them, or the Paratime Police, and I want to find out which."

"To tell the truth, Larv, so do I." Yandar Yadd said. He turned to the man behind the counter. "Varkar, do we see that claim, or do I make a story out of your refusal to show it?" he asked.

"The Paratime Police asked me to keep this confidential," Varkar Klav said. "Publicity would seriously hamper an important police investigation."

Yandar Yadd made an impolite noise. "How do I know that all it would do would be to reveal police incompetence?" he retorted. "Look, Varkar; you and the Paratime Police and the Paratime Commission and the Home Time Line Management are all hired employees of the Home Time Line public. The public has a right to know what its employees are doing, and it's my business to see that they're informed. Now, for the last time—will you show us a copy of that claim?"

"Well, let me explain, off the record—" the official begged.

"Huh-uh! Huh-uh! I had that off-the-record gag worked on me when I was about Larv's age, fifty years ago. Anything I get, I put on the air or not at my own discretion."

"All right," Varkar Klav surrendered, pointing to a reading screen and twiddling a knob. "But when you read it, I hope you have enough discretion to keep quiet about it."

The screen lit, and Yandar Yadd automatically pressed a button for a photo-copy. The two newsmen stared for a moment, and then even Yandar Yadd's shell of drowsy negligence cracked and fell from him. His hand brushed the switch as he snatched the hand-phone from his belt.

"Marva!" he barked, before the girl at the news office could more than acknowledge. "Get this recorded for immediate telecast! . . . Ready? Beginning: The existence of a huge paratemporal slave trade came to light on the afternoon of One-Five-Nine Day, on a time line of the Third Level Esaron Sector, when Field Agent Skordran Kirv, Paratime Police, discovered, at an orange plantation of Consolidated Outtime Foodstuffs—"

Salgath Trod sat alone in his private office, his half-finished lunch growing cold on the desk in front of him as he watched the teleview screen across the room, tuned to a pickup behind the Speaker's chair in the Executive Council Chamber ten stories below. The two thousand seats had been almost all empty at 1000, when Council had convened. Fifteen minutes later, the news had broken; now, at 1430, a good three quarters of the seats were occupied. He could see, in the aisles, the gold-plated robot pages gliding back and forth, receiving and delivering messages. One had just slid up to the seat of Councilman Hasthor Flan, and Hasthor was speaking urgently into the recorder mouthpiece. Another message for him, he supposed; he'd gotten at least a score such calls since the crisis had developed.

People were going to start wondering, he thought. This situation should have been perfect for his purposes; as leader of the Opposition he could easily make himself the next General Manager, if he exploited this scandal properly. He listened for a while to the Centrist-Management member who was speaking; he could rip that fellow's arguments to shreds in a hundred words— but he didn't dare. The Management was taking exactly the line Salgath Trod wanted the whole Council to take: treat this affair as an isolated and extraordinary occurrence, find a couple of convenient scapegoats, cobble up some explanation acceptable to the public, and forget it. He wondered what had happened to the imbecile who had transposed those Kholghoor Sector slaves onto an exploited time line. Ought to be shanghaied to the Khiftan Sector and sold to the priests of Fasif!

A buzzer sounded, and for an instant he thought it would be the message he had seen Hasthor Fan recording. Then he realized that it was the buzzer for the private door, which could only be operated by someone with a special identity sign. He pressed a button and unlocked the door.

The young man in the loose wrap-around tunic who entered was a stranger. At least, his face and his voice were strange, but voices could be mechanically altered, and a skilled cosmetician could render any face unrecognizable. He looked like a student, or a minor commercial executive, or an engineer, or something like that. Of course, his tunic bulged slightly under the left armpit, but even the most respectable tunics showed occasional weapon-bulges.

"Good afternoon, councilman," the newcomer said, sitting down across the desk from Salgath Trod. "I was just talking to . . . somebody we both know."

Salgath Trod offered cigarettes, lighted his visitor's and then his own.

"What does Our Mutual Friend think about all this?" he asked, gesturing toward the screen.

"Our Mutual Friend isn't at all happy about it."

"You think, perhaps, that I'm bursting into wild huzzas?" Salgath Trod asked. "If I were to act as everybody expects me to, I'd be down there on the floor, now, clawing into the Management tooth and nail. All my adherents are wondering why I'm not. So are all my opponents, and before long one of them is going to guess the reason."

"Well, why not go down?" the stranger asked. "Our Mutual Friend thinks it would be an excellent idea. The leak couldn't be stopped, and it's gone so far already that the Management will never be able to play it down. So the next best thing is to try to exploit it."

Salgath Trod smiled mirthlessly. "So I am to get in front of it, and lead it in the right direction? Fine . . . as long as I don't stumble over something. If I do, it'll go over me like a Fifth Level bison-herd."

"Don't worry about that," the stranger laughed reassuringly. "There are others on the floor who are also friends of Our Mutual Friend. Here: what you'd better do is attack the Paratime Police, especially Tortha Karf and Verkan Vall. Accuse them of negligence and incompetence, and, by implication, of collusion, and demand a special committee to investigate. And try to get a motion for a confidence vote passed. A motion to censure the Management, say—"

Salgath Trod nodded. "It would delay things, at least. And if Our Mutual Friend can keep properly covered, I might be able to overturn the Management." He looked at the screen again. "That old fool of a Nanthav is just getting started; it'll be an hour before I could get recognized. Plenty of time to get a speech together. Something short and vicious—"

"You'll have to be careful. It won't do, with your political record, to try to play down these stories of a gigantic criminal conspiracy. That's too close to the Management line. And at the same time, you want to avoid saying anything that would get Verkan Vall and Tortha Karf started off on any new lines of investigation."

Salgath Trod nodded. "Just depend on me; I'll handle it."

After the stranger had gone, he shut off the sound reception, relying on visual dumb-show to keep him informed of what was going on on the Council floor. He didn't like the situation. It was too easy to say the wrong thing. If only he knew more about the shadowy figures whose messengers used his private door—

Coru-hin-Irigod held his aching head in both hands, as though he were afraid it would fall apart, and blinked in the sunlight from the window. Lord Safar, how much of that sweet brandy had he drunk, last night? He sat on the edge of the bed for a moment, trying to think. Then, suddenly apprehensive, he thrust his hand under his pillow. The heavy four-barreled pistols were there, all right, but—*The money!*

He rummaged frantically among the bedding, and among his clothes, piled on the floor, but the leather bag was nowhere to be found. Two thousand gold *obus*, the price of a hundred slaves. He snatched up one of the pistols, his headache forgotten. Then he laughed and tossed the pistol down again. Of course! He'd given the bag to the plantation manager, what was his outlandish name, Dosu Golan, to keep for him before the drinking bout had begun. It was safely waiting for him in the plantation strong box. Well, nothing like a good scare to make a man forget a brandy head, anyhow. And there was something else, something very nice—

Oh, yes, there it was, beside the bed. He picked up the beautiful gleaming repeater, pulled down the lever far enough to draw the cartridge halfway out of the chamber, and closed it again, lowering the hammer. Those two Jeseru traders from the North, what were their names? Ganadara and Atarazola. That was a stroke of luck, meeting them here. They'd given him this lovely rifle, and they were going to accompany him and his men back to Careba; they had a hundred such rifles, and two hundred six-shot revolvers, and they wanted to trade for slaves. The Lord Safar bless them both, wouldn't they be welcome at Careba!

He looked at the sunlight falling through the window

on the still recumbent form of his companion, Faru-hin-Obaran. Outside, he could hear the sounds of the plantation coming to life—an ax thudding on wood, the clatter of pans from the kitchens. Crossing to Faru-hin-Obaran's bed, he grasped the sleeper by the ankle, tugging.

"Waken, Faru!" he shouted. "Get up and clear the fumes from your head! We start back to Careba today!"

Faru swore groggily and pushed himself into a sitting position, fumbling on the floor for his trousers.

"What day's this?" he asked.

"The day after we went to bed, ninny!" Then Coru-hin-Irigod wrinkled his brow. He could remember, clearly enough, the sale of the slaves, but after that—Oh, well, he'd been drinking; it would all come back to him, after a while.

Verkan Vall rubbed his hand over his face wearily, started to light another cigarette, and threw it across the room in disgust. What he needed was a drink—a long drink of cool, tart white wine, laced with brandy—and then he needed to sleep.

"We're absolutely nowhere!" Ranthar Jard said. "Of course they're operating on time lines we've never penetrated. The fact that they're supplying the Croutha with guns proves that; there isn't a firearm on any of the time lines our people are legitimately exploiting. And there are only about three billion time lines on this belt of the Croutha invasion—"

"If we could think of a way to reduce it to some specific area of paratime—" one of Ranthar Jard's deputies began.

"That's precisely what we've been trying to do, Klav," Vall said. "We haven't done it."

Dalla, who had withdrawn from the discussion and was on a couch at the side of the room, surrounded by reports and abstracts and summaries, looked up.

"I took hours and hours of hypno-mech on Kholghoor Sector religions, before I went out on that wild-goose chase for psychokinesis and precognition data," she said. "About six or eight hundred years ago, there were religious wars and heresies and religious schisms all over the Kharanda country. No matter how uniform the Kholghoor Sector may be otherwise, there are dozens and dozens of small belts and sub-sectors of different religions or sects or god-cults."

"That's right," Ranthar Jard agreed, brightening. "We have hagiologists who know all that stuff; we'll have a couple of them interrogate those slaves. I don't know how much they can get out of them—lot of peasants, won't be up on the theological niceties—but a synthesis of what we get from the lot of them—"

"That's an idea," Vall agreed. "About the first idea we've had, here—Oh, how about politics, too? Check on who's the king, what the stories about the royal family are, that sort of thing."

Ranthar Jard looked at the map on the wall. "The Croutha have only gotten halfway to Nharkan, here. Say we transpose detectives in at night on some of these time lines we think are promising, and check up at the tax-collection offices on a big landowner north of Jhirda named Ghromdour? That might get us something."

"Well, I don't want you to think we're trying to get out

of work, Chief's Assistant," one of the deputies said, "but is there any real necessity for our trying to locate the Wizard Trader time lines? If you can get them from the Esaron Sector, it'll be the same, won't it?"

"Marv, in this business you never depend on just one lead," Ranthar Jard told him. "And beside, when Skordran Kirv's gang hits the base of operations in North America, there's no guarantee that they may not have time to send off a radio warning to the crowd at the base here in India. We have to hit both places at once."

"Well, that, too," Vall said. "But the main thing is to get these Wizard Trader camps on the Kholghoor Sector cleaned out. How are you fixed for men and equipment, for a big raid, Jard?"

Ranthar Jard shrugged. "I can get about five hundred men with conveyers, including a couple of two-hundred-footers to carry airboats," he said.

"Not enough. Skordran Kirv has one complete armored brigade, one airborne infantry brigade, and an air cavalry regiment, with Ghaldron-Hesthor equipment for a simultaneous transposition," Vall said.

"Where in blazes did he get them all?" Ranthar Jard demanded.

"They're guard troops, from Service Sector and Industrial Sector. We'll get you the same sort of a force. I only hope we don't have another Prole insurrection while they're away—"

"Well, don't think I'm trying to argue policy with you," Ranthar Jard said, "but that could raise a dreadful stink on Home Time Line. Especially on top of this news-break about the slave trade."

"We'll have to take a chance on that," Vall said. "If you're worried about what the book says, forget it. We're throwing the book away, on this operation. Do you realize that this thing is a threat to the whole Paratime Civilization?"

"Of course I do," Ranthar Jard said. "I know the doctrine of Paratime Security as well as you or anybody else. The question is, does the public realize it?"

A buzzer sounded. Ranthar Jard pressed a switch on the intercom-box in front of him and said: "Ranthar here. Well?"

"Visiphone call, top urgency, just came in for Chief's Assistant Verkan, from Novilan Equivalent. Where can I put it through, sir?"

"Here; booth seven." Ranthar Jard pointed across the room, nodding to Vall. "In just a moment."

Gathon Dard and Antrath Alv—temporary local aliases, Ganadara and Atarazola—sat relaxed in their saddles, swaying to the motion of their horses. They wore the rust-brown hooded cloaks of the northern Jeseru people, in sober contrast to the red and yellow and blue striped robes and sun-bonnets of the Caleras in whose company they rode. They carried short repeating carbines in saddle scabbards, and heavy revolvers and long knives on their belts, and each led six heavily-laden pack-horses.

Coru-hin-Irigod, riding beside Ganadara, pointed up the trail ahead.

"From up there," he said, speaking in Acalan, the lingua franca of the North American West Coast on that sector, "we can see across the valley to Careba. It will be an hour, as we ride, with the pack-horses. Then we will rest, and drink wine, and feast."

Ganadara nodded. "It was the guidance of our gods—and yours, Coru-hin-Irigod—that we met. Such slaves as you sold at the outlanders' plantation would bring a fine price in the North. The men are strong, and have the look of good field-workers; the women are comely and well-formed. Though I fear that my wife would little relish it did I bring home such handmaidens."

Coru-hin-Irigod laughed. "For your wife, I will give you one of our riding whips." He leaned to the side, slashing at a cactus with his quirt. "We in Careba have no trouble with our wives, about handmaidens or anything else."

"By Safar, if you doubt your welcome at Careba, wait till you show your wares," another Calera said. "Rifles and revolvers like those come to our country seldom, and then old and battered, sold or stolen many times before we see them. Rifles that fire seven times without taking butt from shoulder!" He invoked the name of the Great Lord Safar again.

The trail widened and leveled; they all came up abreast, with the pack-horses strung out behind, and sat looking across the valley to the adobe walls of the town that perched on the opposite ridge. After a while, riders began dismounting and checking and tightening saddle-girths; a couple of Caleras helped Ganadara and Atarazola inspect their pack-horses. When they remounted, Atarazola bowed his head, lifting his left sleeve to cover his mouth, and muttered into it at some length. The Caleras looked at him curiously, and Coru-hin-Irigod inquired of Ganadara what he did.

"He prays," Ganadara said. "He thanks our gods that we have lived to see your town, and asks that we be spared to bring many more trains of rifles and ammunition up this trail."

The slaver nodded understandingly. The Caleras were a pious people, too, who believed in keeping on friendly terms with the gods.

"May Safar's hand work with the hands of your gods for it," he said, making what, to a non-Calera, would have been an extremely ribald sign.

"The gods watch over us," Atarazola said, lifting his head. "They are near us even now; they have spoken words of comfort in my ear."

Ganadara nodded. The gods to whom his partner prayed were a couple of paratime policemen, crouching over a radio a mile or so down the ridge.

"My brother," he told Coru-hin-Irigod, "is much favored by our gods. Many people come to him to pray for them."

"Yes. So you told me, now that I think on it." That detail had been included in the pseudo-memories he had been given under hypnosis. "I serve Safar, as do all Caleras, but I have heard that the Jeserus' gods are good gods, dealing honestly with their servants."

An hour later, under the walls of the town, Coru-hin-Irigod drew one of his pistols and fired all four barrels in rapid succession into the air, shouting, "Open! Open for Coru-hin-Irigod, and for the Jeseru traders, Ganadara and Atarazola, who are with him!"

A head, black-bearded and sun-bonneted, appeared

between the brick merlons of the wall above the gate, shouted down a welcome, and then turned away to bawl orders. The gate slid aside, and, after the caravan had passed through, naked slaves pushed the massive thing shut again. Although they were familiar with the interior of the town, from photographs taken with boomerang-balls—automatic-return transposition spheres like message-balls—they looked around curiously. The central square was thronged—Caleras in striped robes, people from the south and east in baggy trousers and embroidered shirts, mountaineers in deerskins. A slave market was in progress, and some hundred-odd items of human merchandise were assembled in little groups, guarded by their owners and inspected by prospective buyers. They seemed to be all natives of that geographic and paratemporal area.

"Don't even look at those," Coru-hin-Irigod advised. "They are but culls; the market is almost over. We'll go to the house of Nebu-hin-Abenoz, where all the considerable men gather, and you will find those who will be able to trade slaves worthy of the goods you have with you. Meanwhile, let my people take your horses and packs to my house; you shall be my guests while you stay in Careba."

It was perfectly safe to trust Coru-hin-Irigod. He was a murderer and a brigand and a slaver, but he would never incur the scorn of men and the curse of the gods by dealing foully with a guest. The horses and packs were led away by his retainers; Ganadara and Atarazola pushed their horses after his and Faru-hin-Obaran's through the crowd.

The house of Nebu-hin-Abenoz, like every other building in Careba, was flat-roofed, adobe-walled and window-less except for narrow rifle-slits. The wide double-gate stood open, and five or six heavily armed Caleras lounged just inside. They greeted Coru and Faru by name, and the strangers by their assumed nationality. The four rode through, into what appeared to be the stables, turning their horses over to slaves, who took them away. There were between fifty and sixty other horses in the place.

Divesting themselves of their weapons in an anteroom at the head of a flight of steps, they passed under an arch and into a wide, shady patio, where thirty or forty men stood about or squatted on piles of cushions, smoking cheroots, drinking from silver cups, talking in a continuous babel. Most of them were in Calera dress, though there were men of other communities and nations, in other garb. As they moved across the patio, Gathon Dard caught snatches of conversations about deals in slaves, and horse trades, about bandit raids and blood feuds, about women and horses and weapons.

An old man with a white beard and an unusually clean robe came over to intercept them.

"Ha, lord of my daughter, you're back at last. We had begun to fear for you," he said.

"Nothing to fear, father of my wife," Coru-hin-Irigod replied. "We sold the slaves for a good price, and tarried the night feasting in good company. Such good company that we brought some of it with us—Atarazola and Ganadara, men of the Jeseru; Cavu-hin-Avoran, whose daughter mothered my sons." He took his father-in-law by the sleeve and pulled him aside, motioning Gathon Dard and Antrath Alv to follow.

"They brought weapons; they want outland slaves, of the sort I took to sell in the Big Valley country," he whispered. "The weapons are repeating rifles from across the ocean, and six-shot revolvers. They also have much ammunition."

"Oh, Safar bless you!" the white-beard cried, his eyes brightening. "Name your own price; satisfy yourselves that we have dealt fairly with you; go, and return often again! Come, lord of my daughter; let us make them known to Nebu-hin-Abenoz. But not a word about the kind of weapons you have, strangers, until we can speak privately. Say only that you have rifles to trade."

Gathon Dard nodded. Evidently there was some sort of power-struggle going on in Careba; Coru-hin-Irigod and his wife's father were of the party of Nebu-hin-Abenoz, and wanted the repeaters and six-shooters for themselves.

Nebu-hin-Abenoz, swarthy, hook-nosed, with a square-cut graying beard, lounged in a low chair across the patio; near him four or five other Caleras sat or squatted or reclined, all smoking the rank black tobacco of the country and drinking wine or brandy. Their conversation ceased as Cavu-hin-Avoran and the others approached. The chief of Careba listened to the introduction, then heaved himself to his feet and clapped the newcomers on the shoulders.

"Good, good!" he said. "We know you Jeseru people; you're honest traders. You come this far into our mountains too seldom. We can trade with you. We need weapons. As for the sort of slaves you want, we have none too many now, but in eight days we will have plenty. If you stay with us that long—"

"Careba is a pleasant place to be," Ganadara said. "We can wait."

"What sort of weapons have you?" the chief asked.

"Pistols and rifles, lord of my father's sister," Coru-hin-Irigod answered for them. "The packs have been taken to my house, where our friends will stay. We can bring a few to show you, the hour after evening prayers."

Nebu-hin-Abenoz shot a keen glance at his brother-in-law's son and nodded. "Or, better, I will come to your house then; thus I can see the whole load. How will that be?"

"Better; I will be there, too," Cavu-hin-Avoran said, then turned to Gathon Dard and Antrath Alv. "You have been long on the road; come, let us drink cool wine, and then we will eat," he said. "Until this evening, Nebu-hin-Abenoz."

He led his son-in-law and the traders to one side, where several kegs stood on trestles with cups and flagons beside them. They filled a flagon, took a cup apiece, and went over to a pile of cushions at one side.

As they did, three men came pushing through the crowd toward Nebu-hin-Abenoz's seat. They wore a costume unfamiliar to Gathon Dard—little round caps with red and green streamers behind, and long, wide-sleeved white gowns—and one of them had gold rings in his ears.

"Nebu-hin-Abenoz?" one of them said, bowing. "We are

three men of the Usasu cities. We have gold *obus* to spend; we seek a beautiful girl, to be first concubine to our king's son, who is now come to the estate of manhood."

Nebu-hin-Abenoz picked up the silver-mounted pipe he had laid aside, and re-lighted it, frowning.

"Men of the Usasu, you have a heavy responsibility," he said. "You have the responsibility for the future of your kingdom, for a boy's character is more shaped by his first concubine than by his teachers. How old is the boy?"

"Sixteen, Nebu-hin-Abenoz; the age of manhood among us."

"Then you want a girl older, but not much older. She should be versed in the arts of love, but innocent of heart. She should be wise, but teachable; gentle and loving, but with a will of her own—"

The three men in white gowns were fidgeting. Then, suddenly, like three marionettes on a single string, they put their right hands to their mouths and then plunged them into the left sleeves of their gowns, whipping out knives and then sprang as one upon Nebu-hin-Abenoz, slashing and stabbing.

Gathon Dard was on his feet at once; he hurled the wine flagon at the three murderers and leaped across the room. Antrath Alv went bounding after him, and by this time three or four of the group around Nebu-hin-Abenoz's chair had recovered their wits and jumped to their feet. One of the three assailants turned and slashed with his knife, almost disemboweling a Calera who had tried to grapple with him. Before he could free the blade, another Calera brought a brandy bottle down on his head. Gathon Dard sprang upon the back of a second assassin, hooking his left elbow under the fellow's chin and grabbing the wrist of his knife-hand with his right; the man struggled for an instant, then went limp and fell forward. The third of the trio of murderers was still slashing at the fallen chieftain when Antrath Alv chopped him along the side of the neck with the edge of his hand; he simply dropped and lay still.

Nebu-hin-Abenoz was dead. He had been slashed and cut and stabbed in twenty places; his throat had been cut at least three times, and he had almost been decapitated. The wounded Calera wasn't dead yet; however, even if he had been at the moment on the operating table of a First Level Home Time Line hospital, it was doubtful if he could have been saved, and under the circumstances, his life-expectancy could be measured in seconds. Some cushions were placed under his head, and women called to attend him, but he died before they arrived.

The three assassins were also dead. Except for a few cuts on the scalp of the one who had been felled with the bottle, there was not a mark on any of them. Cavu-hin-Avoran kicked one of them in the face and cursed.

"We killed the skunks too quickly!" he cried. "We should have overcome them alive, and then taken our time about dealing with them as they deserved." He went on to specify the nature of their deserts. "Such infamy!"

"Well, I'll swear I didn't think a little tap like I gave that one would kill him," the bottle-wielder excused himself. "Of course, I was thinking only of Nebu-hin-Abenoz, Safar receive him—"

Antrath Alv bent over the one he had hand-chopped.

"I didn't kill this one," he said. "The way I hit him, if I

had, his neck would be broken, and it's not. See?" He twisted at the dead man's neck. "I think they took poison before they drew their knives."

"I saw all of them put their hands to their mouths!" a Calera exclaimed. "And look; see how their jaws are clenched." He picked up one of the knives and used it to pry the dead man's jaws apart, sniffing at his lips and looking into his mouth. "Look, his teeth and his tongue are discolored; there is a strange smell, too."

Antrath Alv sniffed, then turned to his partner. "Halatane," he whispered. Gathon Dard nodded. That was a First Level poison; paratimers often carried halatane capsules on the more barbaric time-lines, as a last insurance against torture.

"But, Holy Name of Safar, what manner of men were these?" Coru-hin-Irigod demanded. "There are those I would risk my life to kill, but I would not throw it away thus."

"They came knowing that we would kill them, and took the poison that they might die quickly and without pain," a Calera said.

"Or that your tortures would not wring from them the names and nation of those who sent them," an elderly man in the dress of a rancher from the southeast added. "If I were you, I would try to find out who these enemies are, and the sooner the better."

Gathon Dard was examining one of the knives—a folding knife with a broad single-edged blade, locked open with a spring; the handle was of tortoise shell, bolstered with brass.

"In all my travels," he said, "I never saw a knife of this

workmanship before. Tell me, Coru-hin-Irigod, do you know from what country these outland slaves of Nebu-hin-Abenoz's come?"

"You think that might have something to do with it?" the Calera asked.

"It could. I think that these people might not have been born slaves, but people taken captive. Suppose, at some time, there had been sold to Nebu-hin-Abenoz, and sold elsewhere by him, one who was a person of consequence— the son of a king, or the priest of some god," Gathon Dard suggested.

"By Safar, yes! And now that nation, wherever it is, is at blood-feud with us," Cavu-hin-Avoran said. "This must be thought about; it is an ill thing to have unknown enemies."

"Look!" a Calera who had begun to strip the three dead men cried. "These are not of the Usasu cities, or any other people of this land. See, they are uncircumcised!"

"Many of the slaves whom Nebu-hin-Abenoz brought to Careba from the hills have been uncircumcised," Coru-hin-Irigod said. "Jeseru, I think you have your sights on the heart of it." He frowned. "Now, think you, will those who had this done be satisfied, or will they carry on their hatred against all of us?"

"A hard question," Antrath Alv said. "You Caleras do not serve our gods, but you are our friends. Suffer me to go apart and pray; I would take counsel with the gods, that they may aid us all in this."

It was full daylight, but the sun was hidden; a thin rain fell on the landing around at Police Terminal Dhergabar

Equivalent when Vall and Dalla left the rocket. Across the black lavalike pavement, they could see the bulky form of Tortha Karf, hunched under a long cloak, with his flat cap pulled down over his brow. He shook hands with Vall and kissed cheeks with Dalla when they joined him.

"Car's over here," he said, nodding toward the waiting vehicle. "Yesterday wasn't one of our better days, was it?"

"No. It wasn't." Vall agreed. They climbed into the car, and the driver lifted straight up to two thousand feet and turned, soaring down to land on the Chief's Headquarters Building, a mile away. "We're not completely stopped, sir. Ranthar Jard is working on a few ideas that may lead him to the Kholghoor time lines where the Wizard Traders are operating. If we can't get them through their output, we may nail them at the intake."

"Unless they've gotten the wind up and closed down all their operations," Tortha Karf said.

"I doubt if they've done that, Chief," Vall replied. "We don't know who these people are, of course, and it's hard to judge their reactions, but they're willing to take chances for big gains. I believe they think they're safe, now that they've closed out the compromised time line and killed the only witness against them."

"Well, what's Ranthar Jard doing?"

"Trying to locate the sub-sector and probability belt from what the slaves can tell him about their religious beliefs, about the local king, and the prince of Jhirda, and the noble families of the neighborhood," Vall said. "When he has it localized as closely as he can, he's going to start pelting the whole paratemporal area with photographic auto-return balls dropped from aircars on Police Terminal over the spatial equivalents of a couple of Croutha-conquered cities. As soon as he gets a photo that shows Croutha with firearms, he'll have a Wizard Trader time line."

"Sounds simple," the Chief said. The car landed, and he helped Dalla out. "I suppose both you and he know how many chances against one he has of finding anything." They went over to an antigrav-shaft and floated down to the floor on which Tortha Karf had a duplicate of the office in the Paratime Building on Home Time Line. "It's the only chance we have, though."

"There's one thing that bothers me," Dalla said, as they entered the office and went back behind the horseshoe-shaped desk. "I understand that the news about this didn't break on Home Time Line till the late morning of One-Six-One Day. Nebu-hin-Abenoz was murdered at about 1700 local time, which would be 0100 this morning Dhergabar time. That would give this gang fourteen hours to hear the news, transmit it to their base, and get these three men hypno-conditioned, disguised, transposed to this Esaron Sector time line, and into Careba." She shook her head. "That's pretty fast work."

Tortha Karf looked sidewise at Verkan Vall. "Your girl has the makings of a cop, Vall," he commented.

"She's been a big help, on Esaron and Kholghoor Sectors," Vall said. "She wants to stay with it and help me; I'll be very glad to have her with me."

Tortha Karf nodded. He knew, too, that Dalla wouldn't want to have to go back to Home Time Line and wait the long investigation out.

"Of course; we can use all the help we can get. I think

we can get a lot from Dalla. Fix her up with some kind of a title and police status—technical-expert, assistant, or something like that." He clasped hands, man-fashion, with her. "Glad to have you on the cops with us, Dalla," he said. Then he turned to Vall. "There was almost twenty-four hours between the time I heard about this and when this blasted Yandar Yadd got hold of the story. Of all the infernal, irresponsible—" He almost choked with indignation. "And it was another fourteen hours between the time Skordran sent in his report and I heard about it."

"Golzan Doth sent in a report to his company about the same time Skordran Kirv made his first report to his Sector-Regional Subchief." Vall mentioned.

"That might be it," Tortha Karf considered. "I wish there were another explanation, because that implies a very extensive intelligence network, which means a big organization. But I'm afraid that's it. I wish I could pull in everybody in Consolidated Outtime Foodstuffs who handled that report, and narco-hypnotize them. Of course, we can't do things like that on Home Time Line, and with the political situation what it is now—"

"Why, what's been happening, Chief?"

Tortha Karf swore with weary bitterness. "Salgath Trod's what's been happening. At first, after Yandar Yadd broke the story on the air, there was just a lot of unorganized Opposition sniping in Council; Salgath waited till the middle of the afternoon, when the Management members were beginning to rally, and took the floor. The Centrists and Right Moderates were trying the appeal-to-reason approach; that did as much good as trying to put out a Fifth Level forest fire with a hand-extinguisher. Finally. Salgath got a motion of censure against the Management recognized. That means a confidence vote in ten days. Salgath has a rabble of Leftists and dissident Centrists with him; I doubt if he can muster enough votes to overturn the Management, but it's going to make things rough for us."

"Which may be just the reason Salgath started this uproar," Vall suggested.

"That," Tortha Karf said, "is being considered; there is a discreet inquiry being made into Salgath Trod's associates, his sources of income, and so on. Nothing has turned up as yet, but we have hopes."

"I believe," Vall said, "that we have a better chance right on Home Time Line than outtime."

Tortha Karf looked up sharply. "So?" he asked.

Vall was stuffing tobacco into a pipe. "Yes. Chief. We have a big criminal organization—let's call it the Slave Trust, for a convenience-label. The people who run it aren't stupid. The fact that they've been shipping slaves to the Esaron Sector for ten years before we found out about it proves that. So does the speed with which they got rid of this Nebu-hin-Abenoz, right in front of a pair of our detectives. For that matter, so does the speed with which they moved in to exploit this Croutha invasion of Kholghoor Sector India.

"Well, I've studied illegal and subversive organizations all over paratime, and among the really successful ones, there are a few uniform principles. One is cellular organization—small groups, acting in isolation from one another, coöperating with other cells but ignorant of their composition. Another is the principle of no upward contact—leaders contacting their subordinates through contact-blocks and ignorant intermediaries. And another is a willingness to kill off anybody who looks like a potential betrayer or forced witness. The late Nebu-hin-Abenoz, for instance.

"I'll be willing to bet that if we pick up some of these Wizard Traders, say, or a gang that's selling slaves to some Nebu-hin-Abenoz personality on some other time line, and narco-hypnotize them, all they'll be able to do will be name a few immediate associates, and the group leader will know that he's contacted from time to time by some stranger with orders, and that he can make emergency contacts only through some blind accommodation-address. The men who are running this are right on Home Time Line, many of them in positions of prominence, and if we can catch one of them and narco-hyp him, we can start a chain-reaction of disclosures all through this Slave Trust."

"How are we going to get at these top men?" Tortha Karf wanted to know. "Advertise for them on telecast?"

"They'll leave traces; they won't be able to avoid it. I think, right now, that Salgath Trod is one of them. I think there are other prominent politicians, and business people. Look for irregularities and peculiarities in outtime currency-exchange transactions. For instance, to sections in Esaron Sector *obus*. Or big gold bullion transactions."

"Yes. And if they have any really elaborate outtime bases, they'll need equipment that can only be gotten on Home Time Line," Tortha Karf added. "Paratemporal conveyer parts, and field-conductor mesh. You can't just walk into a hardware store and buy that sort of thing."

Dalla leaned forward to drop her cigarette ash into a tray.

"Try looking into the Bureau of Psychological Hygiene," she suggested. "That's where you'll really strike it rich."

Vall and Tortha Karf both turned abruptly and looked at her for an instant.

"Go on," Tortha Karf encouraged. "This sounds interesting."

"The people back of this," Dalla said, "are definitely classifiable as criminals. They may never perform a criminal act themselves, but they give orders for and profit from such acts, and they must possess the motivation and psychology of criminals. We define people as criminals when they suffer from psychological aberrations of an antisocial character, usually paranoid—excessive egoism, disregard for the rights of others, inability to recognize the social necessity for mutual coöperation and confidence. On Home Time Line, we have universal psychological testing, for the purpose of detecting and eliminating such characteristics."

"It seems to have failed in this case," Tortha Karf began, then snapped his fingers. "Of course! How blasted silly can I get, when I'm not trying?"

"Yes, of course," Verkan Vall agreed. "Find out how these people missed being spotted by psychotesting; that'll lead us to *who* missed being tested adequately, and also who got into the Bureau of Psychological Hygiene who didn't belong there."

"I think you ought to give an investigation of the whole BuPsychHyg setup very high priority," Dalla said. "A psychotest is only as good as the people who give it, and if we have criminals administering these tests—"

"We have our friends on Executive Council," Tortha Karf said. "I'll see that that point is raised when Council re-convenes." He looked at the clock. "That'll be in three hours, by the way. If it doesn't accomplish another thing, it'll put Salgath Trod in the middle. He can't demand an investigation of the Paratime Police out of one side of his mouth and oppose an investigation of Psychological Hygiene out of the other. Now what else have we to talk about?"

"Those hundred slaves we got off the Esaron Sector," Vall said. "What are we going to do with them? And if we locate the time line the slavers have their bases on, we'll have hundreds, probably thousands, more."

"We can't sort them out and send them back to their own time lines, even if that would be desirable," Tortha Karf decided. "Why, settle them somewhere on the Service Sector. I know, the Paratime Transposition Code limits the Service Sector to natives of time lines below second-order barbarism, but the Paratime Transposition Code has been so badly battered by this business that a few more minor literal infractions here and there won't make any difference. Where are they now?"

"Police Terminal, Nharkan Equivalent."

"Better hold them there, for the time being. We may have to open a new ServSec time line to take care of all the slaves we find, if we can locate the outtime base line these people are using—Vall, this thing's too big to handle as a routine operation, along with our other work. You take charge of it. Set up your headquarters here, and help yourself to anything in the way of personnel and equipment you need. And bear in mind that this confidence vote is coming up in ten days—on the morning of One-Seven-Two Day. I'm not asking for any miracles, but if we don't get this thing cleared up by then, we're in for trouble."

"I realize that, sir. Dalla, you'd better go back to Home Time Line, with the Chief," he said. "There's nothing you can do to help me, here, at present. Get some rest, and then try to wangle an invitation for the two of us to dinner at Thalvan Dras' apartments this evening." He turned back to Tortha Karf. "Even if he never pays any attention to business, Dras still owns Consolidated Outtime Foodstuffs," he said. "He might be able to find out, or help us find out, how the story about those slaves leaked out of his company."

"Well, that won't take much doing," Dalla said. "If there's as much excitement on Home Time Line as I think, Dras would turn somersaults and jump through hoops to get us to one of his dinners, right now."

Salgath Trod pushed the litter of papers and record-tape spools to one side impatiently.

"Well, what else did you expect?" he demanded. "This was the logical next move. BuPsychHyg is supposed to detect anybody who believes in looking out for his own interests first, and condition him into a pious law-abiding sucker. Well, the sacred Bureau of Sucker-Makers slipped up on a lot of us. It's a natural alibi for Tortha Karf."

"It's also a lot of grief for all of us," the young man in the wrap-around tunic added. "I don't want my psychotests reviewed by some duty-struck bigot who can't be reasoned with, and neither do you."

"I'm getting something organized to counter that," Salgath Trod said. "I'm going to attack the whole scientific basis of psychotesting. There's Dr. Frasthor Klav; he's always contended that what are called criminal tendencies are the result of the individual's total environment, and that psychotesting and personality-analysis are valueless, because the total environment changes from day to day, even from hour to hour—"

"That won't do," the nameless young man who was the messenger of somebody equally nameless retorted. "Frasthor's a crackpot; no reputable psychologist or psychist gives his opinions a moment's consideration. And besides, we don't want to attack Psychological Hygiene. The people in it with whom we can do business are our safeguard; they've given all of us a clean bill of mental health, and we have papers to prove it. What we have to do is to make it appear that that incident on the Esaron Sector is all there is to this, and also involve the Paratime Police themselves. The slavers are all paracops. It isn't the fault of BuPsychHyg, because the Paratime Police have their own psychotesting staff. That's where the trouble is; the paracops haven't been adequately testing their own personnel."

"Now how are you going to do that?" Salgath Trod asked disdainfully.

"You'll take the floor, the first thing tomorrow, and utilize these new revelations about the Wizard Traders. You'll accuse the Paratime Police of being the Wizard Traders themselves. Why not? They have their own paratemporal transposition equipment shops on Police Terminal, they have facilities for manufacturing duplicates of any kind of outtime items, like the firearms, for instance, and they know which time lines on which sectors are being exploited by legitimate paratime traders and which aren't. What's to prevent a gang of unscrupulous paracops from moving in on a few unexploited Kholghoor time lines, buying captives from the Croutha, and shipping them to the Esaron Sector?"

"Then why would they let a thing like this get out?" Salgath Trod inquired.

"Somebody slipped up and moved a lot of slaves onto an exploited Esaron time line. Or, rather, Consolidated Outtime Foodstuffs established a plantation on a time line they were shipping slaves to. Parenthetically, that's what really did happen; the mistake our people made was in not closing out that time line as soon as Consolidated Foodstuffs moved in," the young man said.

"So, this Skordran Kirv, who is a dumb boy who doesn't know what the score is, found these slaves and blatted about it to this Golzan Doth, and Golzan reported it to his company, and it couldn't be hushed up, so now Tortha Karf is trying to scare the public with ghost stories about a gigantic paratemporal conspiracy, to get more appropriations and more power."

"How long do you think I'd get away with that?" Salgath Trod demanded. "I can only stretch parliamentary immunity so far. Sooner or later, I'd have to make formal charges to a special judicial committee, and that would mean narco-hypnosis, and then it would all come out."

"You'll have proof," the young man said. "We'll produce

a couple of these Kharandas whom Verkan Vall didn't get hold of. Under narco-hypnosis, they'll testify that they saw a couple of Wizard Traders take their robes off. Under the robes were Paratime Police uniforms. Do you follow me?"

Salgath Trod made a noise of angry disgust.

"That's ridiculous! I suppose these Kharandas will be given what is deludedly known as memory obliteration, and a set of pseudo-memories; how long do you think that would last? About three ten-days. There is no such thing as memory obliteration; there's memory-suppression, and pseudo-memory overlay. You can't get behind that with any quickie narco-hypnosis in the back room of any police post, I'll admit that," he said. "But a skilled psychist can discover, inside of five minutes, when a narco-hypnotized subject is carrying a load of false memories, and in time, and not too much time, all that top layer of false memories and blockages can be peeled off. And then where would we be?"

"Now wait a minute, Councilman. This isn't just something I dreamed up," the visitor said. "This was decided upon at the top. At the very top."

"I don't care whose idea it was," Salgath Trod snapped. "The whole thing is idiotic, and I won't have anything to do with it."

The visitor's face froze. All the respect vanished from his manner and tone; his voice was like ice cakes grating together in a winter river.

"Look, Salgath; this is an Organization order," he said. "You don't refuse to obey Organization orders, and you don't quit the Organization. Now get smart, big boy; do what you're told to." He took a spool of record tape from his pocket and laid it on the desk. "Outline for your speech; put it in your own words, but follow it exactly." He stood watching Salgath Trod for a moment. "I won't bother telling you what'll happen to you if you don't," he added. "You can figure that out for yourself."

With that, he turned and went out the private door. For a while, Salgath Trod sat staring after him. Once he put his hand out toward the spool, then jerked it back as though the thing were radioactive. Once he looked at the clock; it was just 1600.

The green aircar settled onto the landing stage; Verkan Vall, on the front seat beside the driver, opened the door.

"Want me to call for you later, Assistant Verkan?" the driver asked.

"No thank you, Drenth. My wife and I are going to a dinner-party, and we'll probably go night-clubbing afterward. Tomorrow morning, all the anti-Management commentators will be yakking about my carousing around when I ought to be battling the Slave Trust. No use advertising myself with an official car, and giving them a chance to add, 'at public expense.'"

"Well, have some fun while you can," the driver advised, reaching for the car-radio phone. "Want me to check you in here, sir?"

"Yes, if you will. Thank you. Drenth."

Kandagro, his human servant, admitted him to the apartment six floors down.

"Mistress Dalla is dressing," he said. "She asked me to tell you that you are invited to dinner, this evening, with Thalvan Dras at his apartment."

Vall nodded. "I'll talk to her about it now," he said. "Lay out my dress uniform: short jacket, boots and breeches, and needler."

"Yes, master: I'll go lay out your things and get your bath ready."

The servant turned and went into the alcove which gave access to the dressing rooms, turning right into Vall's. Vall followed him, turning left into his wife's.

"Oh, Dalla!" he called.

"In here!" her voice came out of her bathroom.

He passed through the dressing room, to find her stretched on a plastic-sheeted couch, while her maid, Rendarra, was rubbing her body vigorously with some pungent-smelling stuff about the consistency of machine-grease. Her face was masked in the stuff, and her hair was covered with an elastic cap. He had always suspected that beauty was the real feminine religion, from the willingness of its devotees to submit to martyrdom for it. She wiggled a hand at him in greeting.

"How did it go?" she asked.

"So-so. I organized myself a sort of miniature police force within a police force and I have liaison officers in every organization down to Sector Regional so that I can be informed promptly in case anything new turns up anywhere. What's been happening on Home Time Line? I picked up a news-summary at Paratime Police Headquarters; it seems that a lot more stuff has leaked out. Kholghoor Sector, Wizard Traders and all. How'd it happen?"

Dalla rolled over to allow Rendarra to rub the blue-green grease on her back.

"Consolidated Outtime Foodstuffs let a gang of reporters in, today. I think they're afraid somebody will accuse them of complicity, and they want to get their side of it before the public. All our crowd are off that time line except a couple of detectives at the plantation."

"I know." He smiled; Dalla was thinking of the Paratime Police as "our crowd" now. "How about this dinner at Dras' place?"

"Oh, that was easy." She shifted position again. "I just called Dras up and told him that our vacation was off, and he invited us before I could begin hinting. What are you going to wear?"

"Short-jacket greens; I can carry a needler with that uniform, even wear it at the table. I don't think it's smart for me to run around unarmed, even on Home Time Line. Especially on Home Time Line," he amended. "When's this affair going to start, and how long will Rendarra take to get that goo off you?"

Salgath Trod left his aircar at the top landing stage of his apartment building and sent it away to the hangars under robot control; he glanced about him as he went toward the antigrav shaft. There were a dozen vehicles in the air above; any of them might have followed him from the Paratime Building. He had no doubt that he had been under constant surveillance from the moment the nameless messenger had delivered the Organization's ultimatum. Until he delivered that speech, the next morning, or manifested an intention of refusing to do so, however, he would be safe. After that—

Alone in his office, he had reviewed the situation point

by point, and then gone back and reviewed it again; the conclusion was inescapable. The Organization had ordered him to make an accusation which he himself knew to be false; that was the first premise. The conclusion was that he would be killed as soon as he had made it. That was the trouble with being mixed up with that kind of people—you were expendable, and sooner or later, they would decide that they would have to expend you. And what could you do?

To begin with, an accusation of criminal malfeasance made against a Management or Paratime Commission agency on the floor of Executive Council was tantamount to an accusation made in court; automatically, the accuser became a criminal prosecutor, and would have to repeat his accusation under narco-hypnosis. Then the whole story would come out, bit by bit, back to its beginning in that first illegal deal in Indo-Turanian opium, diverted from trade with the Khiftan Sector and sold on Second Level Luvarian Empire Sector, and the deals in radioactive poisons, and the slave trade. He would be able to name few names—the Organization kept its activities too well compartmented for that—but he could talk of things that had happened, and when, and where, and on what paratemporal areas.

No. The Organization wouldn't let that happen, and the only way it could be prevented would be by the death of Salgath Trod, as soon as he had made his speech. All the talk of providing him with corroborative evidence was silly; it had been intended to lead him more trustingly to the slaughter. They'd kill him, of course, in some way that would be calculated to substantiate the story he would no longer be able to repudiate. The killer, who would be promptly rayed dead by somebody else, would wear a Paratime Police uniform, or something like that. That was of no importance, however; by then, he'd be beyond caring.

One of his three ServSec Prole servants—the slim brown girl who was his housekeeper and hostess, and also his mistress—admitted him to the apartment. He kissed her perfunctorily and closed the door behind him.

"You're tired," she said. "Let me call Nindrandigro and have him bring you chilled wine; lie down and rest until dinner."

"No, no; I want brandy." He went to a cellaret and got out a decanter and goblet, pouring himself a drink. "How soon will dinner be ready?"

The brown girl squeezed a little golden globe that hung on a chain around her neck; a tiny voice, inside it, repeated: "Eighteen twenty-three ten, eighteen twenty-three eleven, eighteen twenty-three twelve—"

"In half an hour. It's still in the robo-chef," she told him.

He downed half the goblet-full, set it down, and went to a painting, a brutal scarlet and apple-green abstraction, that hung on the wall. Swinging it aside and revealing the safe behind it, he used his identity-sigil, took out a wad of Paratemporal Exchange Bank notes and gave them to the girl.

"Here, Zinganna; take these, and take Nindrandigro and Calilla out for the evening. Go where you can all have a good time, and don't come back till after midnight. There will be some business transacted here, and I want them out of this. Get them out of here as soon as you can; I'll see to the dinner myself. Spend all of that you want to."

The girl riffled through the wad of banknotes. "Why, *thank* you, Trod!" She threw her arms around his neck and kissed him enthusiastically. "I'll go tell them at once."

"And have a good time, Zinganna; have the best time you possibly can," he told her, embracing and kissing her. "Now, get out of here; I have to keep my mind on business."

When she had gone, he finished his drink and poured another. He drew and checked his needler. Then, after checking the window-shielding and activating the outside viewscreens, he lit a cheroot and sat down at the desk, his goblet and his needler in front of him, to wait until the servants were gone.

There was only one way out alive. He knew that, and yet he needed brandy, and a great deal of mental effort, to steel himself for it. Psycho-rehabilitation was a dreadful thing to face. There would be almost a year of unremitting agony, physical and mental, worse than a Khiftan torture rack. There would be the shame of having his innermost secrets poured out of him by the psychotherapists, and, at the end, there would emerge someone who would not be Salgath Trod, or anybody like Salgath Trod, and he would have to learn to know this stranger, and build a new life for him.

In one of the viewscreens, he saw the door to the service hallway open. Zinganna, in a black evening gown and a black velvet cloak, and Calilla, the housemaid, in what she believed to be a reasonable facsimile of fashionable First Level dress, and Nindrandigro, in one of his master's evening suits, emerged. Salgath Trod waited until they had gone down the hall to the antigrav shaft, and then he turned on the visiphone, checked the security, set it for sealed beam communication, and punched out a combination.

A girl in a green tunic looked out of the screen.

"Paratime Police," she said. "Office of Chief Tortha."

"I am Executive Councilman Salgath Trod," he told her. "I am, and for the past fifteen years have been, criminally involved with the organization responsible for the slave trade which recently came to light on Third Level Esaron. I give myself up unconditionally; I am willing to make full confession under narco-hypnosis, and will accept whatever disposition of my case is lawfully judged fit. You'll have to send an escort for me; I might start from my apartment alone, but I'd be killed before I got to your headquarters—"

The girl, who had begun to listen in the bored manner of public servant phone girls, was staring wide-eyed.

"Just a moment, Councilman Salgath; I'll put you through to Chief Tortha."

The dinner lacked a half hour of being served; Thalvan Dras' guests loitered about the drawing room, sampling appetizers and chilled drinks and chatting in groups. It wasn't the artistic crowd usual at Thalvan Dras' dinners; most of the guests seemed to be business or political people. Thalvan Dras had gotten Vall and Dalla into the small group around him, along with pudgy, infantile-faced Brogoth Zaln, his confidential secretary, and Javrath Brend, his financial attorney.

"I don't see why they're making such a fuss about it," one of the Banking Cartel people was saying. "Causing a lot of public excitement all out of proportion to the importance of the affair. After all, those people were slaves on their own time line, and if anything, they're much better off on the Esaron Sector than they would be as captives of the Croutha. As far as that goes, what's the difference between that and the way we drag these Fourth Level Primitive Sector-Complex people off to Fifth Level Service Sector to work for us?"

"Oh, there's a big difference, Farn," Javrath Brend said. "We recruit those Fourth Level Primitives out of probability worlds of Stone Age savagery, and transpose them to our own Fifth Level time lines, practically outtime extensions of the Home Time Line. There's absolutely no question of the Paratime Secret being compromised."

"Beside, we need a certain amount of human labor, for tasks requiring original thought and decision that are beyond the ability of robots, and most of it is work our Citizens simply wouldn't perform," Thalvan Dras added.

"Well, from a moral standpoint, wouldn't these Esaron Sector people who buy the slaves justify slavery in the same terms?" a woman whom Vall had identified as a Left Moderate Council Member asked.

"There's still a big difference," Dalla told her. "The ServSec Proles aren't beaten or tortured or chained; we don't break up families or separate friends. When we recruit Fourth Level Primitives, we take whole tribes, and they come willingly. And—"

One of Thalvan Dras' black-liveried human servants, of the class under discussion, approached Vall.

"A visiphone call for your lordship," he whispered. "Chief Tortha Karf calling. If your lordship will come this way—"

In a screen-booth outside, Vall found Tortha Karf looking out of the screen; he was seated at his desk, fiddling with a gold multicolor pen.

"Oh, Vall; something interesting has just come up." He spoke in a voice of forced calmness. "I can't go into it now, but you'll want to hear about it. I'm sending a car for you. Better bring Dalla along; she'll want in on it, too."

"Right; we'll be on the top southwest landing stage in a few minutes."

Dalla was still heatedly repudiating any resemblance between the normal First Level methods of labor-recruitment and the activities of the Wizard Traders; she had just finished the story of the woman whose child had been brained when Vall rejoined the group.

"Dras, I'm awfully sorry," he said. "This is the second time in succession that Dalla and I have had to bolt away from here, but policemen are like doctors—always on call, and consequently unreliable guests. While you're feasting, think commiseratingly of Dalla and me; we'll probably be having a sandwich and a cup of coffee somewhere."

"I'm terribly sorry." Thalvan Dras replied. "We had all been looking forward—Well! Brogoth, have a car called for Vall and Dalla."

"Police car coming for us; it's probably on the landing stage now," Vall said. "Well, good-by, everybody. Coming, Dalla?"

★ ★ ★

They had a few minutes to wait, under the marquee, before the green police aircar landed and came rolling across the rain-wet surface of the landing stage. Crossing to it and opening the rear door, he put Dalla in and climbed in after her, slamming the door. It was only then that he saw Tortha Karf hunched down in the rear seat. He motioned them to silence, and did not speak until the car was rising above the building.

"I wanted to fill you in on this, as soon as possible," he said. "Your hunch about Salgath Trod was good; just a few minutes before I called you, he called me. He says this slave trade is the work of something he calls the Organization; says he's been taking orders from them for years. His attack on the Management and motion for a censure-vote were dictated from Organization top echelon. Now he's convinced that they're going to force him to make false accusations against the Paratime Police and then kill him before he's compelled to repeat his charges under narco-hypnosis. So he's offered to surrender and trade information for protection."

"How much does he know?" Vall asked.

Tortha Karf shook his head. "Not as much as he claims to, I suppose; he wouldn't want to reduce his own trade-in value. But he's been involved in this thing for the last fifteen years, and with his political prominence, he'd know quite a lot."

"We can protect him from his own gang; can we protect him from psycho-rehabilitation?"

"No, and he knows it. He's willing to accept that. He seems to think that death at the hands of his own associates is the only other alternative. Probably right, too."

The floodlighted green towers of the Paratime Building were wheeling under them as they circled down.

"Why would they sacrifice a valuable accomplice like Salgath Trod, in order to make a transparently false accusation against us?" Vall wondered.

"Ha, that's our new rookie cop's idea!" Tortha Karf chuckled, nodding toward Dalla. "We got Zortan Harn to introduce an urgent-business motion to appoint a committee to investigate BuPsychHyg, this morning. The motion passed, and this is the reaction to it. The Organization's scared. Just as Dalla predicted, they don't want us finding out how people with potentially criminal characteristics missed being spotted by psychotesting. Salgath Trod is being sacrificed to block or delay that."

Vall nodded as the wheels bumped on the landing stage and the antigrav field went off. That was the sort of thing that happened when you started on a really fruitful line of investigation. They got out and hurried over under the marquee, the car lifting and moving off toward the hangars. This was the real break; no matter how this Organization might be compartmented, a man like Salgath Trod would know a great deal. He would name names, and the bearers of those names, arrested and narco-hypnotized, would name other names, in a perfect chain reaction of confessions and betrayals.

Another police car had landed just ahead of them, and three men were climbing out; two were in Paratime Police green, and the third, handcuffed, was in Service Sector Proletarian garb. At first, Vall though that Salgath Trod had been brought in disguised as a Prole prisoner, and then he saw that the prisoner was short and stocky, not at all like the slender and elegant politician. The two officers who had brought him in were talking to a lieutenant, Sothran Barth, outside the antigrav shaft kiosk. As Vall and Tortha Karf and Dalla walked over, the car which had brought them lifted out.

"Something that just came in from Industrial Twenty-four, Chief," Lieutenant Sothran said in answer to Tortha Karf's question. "May be for Assistant Verkan's desk."

"He's a Prole named Yandragno, sir," one of the policemen said. "Industrial Sector Constabulary grabbed him peddling Martian hellweed cigarettes to the girls in a textile mill at Kangabar Equivalent. Captain Jamzar thinks he may have gotten them from somebody in the Organization."

A little warning bell began ringing in the back of Verkan Vall's mind, but at first he could not consciously identify the cause of his suspicions. He looked the two policemen and their prisoner over carefully, but could see nothing visibly wrong with them. Then another car came in for a landing and rolled over under the marquee; the door opened, and a police officer got out, followed by an elegantly dressed civilian whom he recognized at once as Salgath Trod. A second policeman was emerging from the car when Vall suddenly realized what it was that had disturbed him.

It had been Salgath Trod, himself, less than half an hour ago, who had introduced the term, "the Organization," to the Paratime Police. At that time, if these people were what they claimed to be, they would have been in transposition from Industrial Twenty-four, on the Fifth Level. Immediately, he reached for his needler. He was clearing it of the holster when things began happening.

The handcuffs fell from the "prisoner's" wrists; he jerked a neutron-disruption blaster from under his jacket. Vall, his needler already drawn, rayed the fellow dead before he could aim it, then saw that the two pseudo-policemen had drawn their needlers and were aiming in the direction of Salgath Trod. There were no flashes or reports; only the spot of light that had winked on and off under Vall's rear sight had told him that his weapon had been activated. He saw it appear again as the sights centered on one of the "policemen." Then he saw the other imposter's needler aimed at himself. That was the last thing he expected ever to see, in that life; he tried to shift his own weapon, and time seemed frozen, with his arm barely moving. Then there was a white blur as Dalla's cloak moved in front of him, and the needler dropped from the fingers of the disguised murderer. Time went back to normal for him; he safetied his own weapon and dropped it, jumping forward.

He grabbed the fellow in the green uniform by the nose with his left hand, and punched him hard in the pit of the stomach with his right fist. The man's mouth flew open, and a green capsule, the size and shape of a small bean, flew out. Pushing Dalla aside before she would step on it, he kicked the murderer in the stomach, doubling him over, and chopped him on the base of the skull with the edge of his hand. The pseudo-policeman dropped senseless.

With a handful of handkerchief-tissue from his pocket,

he picked up the disgorged capsule, wrapping it carefully after making sure that it was unbroken. Then he looked around. The other two assassins were dead. Tortha Karf, who had been looking at the man in Proletarian dress whom Vall had killed first, turned, looked in another direction, and then cursed. Vall followed his eyes, and cursed also. One of the two policemen who had gotten out of the aircar was dead, too, and so was the all-important witness, Salgath Trod—as dead as Nebu-hin-Abenoz, a hundred thousand parayears away.

The whole thing had ended within thirty seconds; for about half as long, everybody waited, poised in a sort of action-vacuum, for something else to happen. Dalla had dropped the shoulder-bag with which she had clubbed the prisoner's needler out of his hand, and caught up the fallen weapon. When she saw that the man was down and motionless, she laid it aside and began picking up the glittering or silken trifles that had spilled from the burst bag. Vall retrieved his own weapon, glanced over it, and holstered it. Sothran Barth, the lieutenant in charge of the landing stage, was bawling orders, and men were coming out of the ready-room and piling into vehicles to pursue the aircar which had brought the assassins.

"Barth!" Vall called. "Have you a hypodermic and a sleep-drug ampoule? Well, give this boy a shot; he's only impact-stunned. Be careful of him; he's important." He glanced around the landing stage. "Fact is, he's all we have to show for this business."

Then he stooped to help Dalla gather her things, picking up a few of them—a lighter, a tiny crystal perfume flask, miraculously unbroken, a face-powder box which had sprung open and spilled half its contents. He handed them to her, while Sothran Barth bent over the prisoner and gave him an injection, then went to the body of the other pseudo-policeman, forcing open his mouth. In his cheek, still unbroken, was a second capsule, which he added to the first. Tortha Karf was watching him.

"Same gang that killed that Carera slaver on Esaron Sector?" he asked. "Of course, exactly the same general procedure. Let's have a look at the other one."

The man in Proletarian dress must have had his capsule between his molars when he had been killed; it was broken, and there was a brownish discoloration and chemical odor in his mouth.

"Second time we've had a witness killed off under our noses," Tortha Karf said. "We're going to have to smarten up in a hurry."

"Here's one of us who doesn't have to, much," Vall said, nodding toward Dalla. "She knocked a needler out of one man's hand, and we took him alive. The Force owes her a new shoulder-bag: she spoiled that one using it for a club."

"Best shoulder-bag we can find you, Dalla," Tortha Karf promised. "You're promoted, herewith, to Special Chief's Assistant's Special Assistant— You know, this Organization murder-section is good; they could kill anybody. It won't be long before they assign a squad to us. Blast it, I don't want to have to go around bodyguarded like a Fourth Level dictator, but—"

A detective came out of the control room and approached.

"Screen call for you, sir," he told Tortha Karf. "One of

the news services wants a comment on a story they've just picked up that we've illegally arrested Councilman Salgath and are holding him incommunicado and searching his apartment."

"That's the Organization," Vall said. "They don't know how their boys made out; they're hoping we'll tell them."

"No comment," Tortha Karf said. "Call the girl on my switchboard and tell her to answer any other news-service calls. We have nothing to say at this time, but there will be a public statement at . . . at 2330," he decided after a glance at his watch. "That'll give us time to agree on a publicity line to adopt. Lieutenant Sothran! Take charge up here. Get all these bodies out of sight somewhere, including those of Councilman Salgath and Detective Malthor. Don't let anybody talk about this; put a blackout on the whole story. Vall, you and Dalla and . . . oh, you, over there; take the prisoner down to my office. Sothran, any reports from any of the cars that were chasing that fake police car?"

Verkan Vall and Dalla were sitting behind Tortha Karf's desk; Vall was issuing orders over the intercom and talking to the detectives who had remained at Salgath Trod's apartment by visiscreen; Dalla was sorting over the things she had spilled when her bag had burst. They both looked up as Tortha Karf came in and joined them.

"The prisoner's still under the drug," the Chief said. "He'll be out for a couple of hours; the psych-techs want to let him come out of it naturally and sleep naturally for a while before they give him a hypno. He's not a ServSec Prole; uncircumcised, never had any syntho-enzyme shots or immunizations, and none of the longevity operations or grafts. Same thing for the two stiffs. And no identity records on any of the three."

"The men at Salgath's apartment say that his housekeeper and his two servants checked out through the house conveyer for ServSec One-Six-Five, at about 1830," Vall said. "There's a Prole entertainment center on that time line. I suppose Salgath gave them the evening off before he called you."

Tortha Karf nodded. "I suppose you ordered them picked up. The news services are going wild about this. I had to make a preliminary statement, to the effect that Salgath Trod was not arrested, came to Headquarters of his own volition, and is under no restraint whatever."

"Except, of course, a slight case of rigor mortis," Dalla added. "Did you mention that, Chief?"

"No, I didn't." Tortha Karf looked as though he had quinine in his mouth. "Vall, how in blazes are we going to handle this?"

"We ought to keep Salgath's death hushed up, as long as we can," Vall said. "The Organization doesn't know positively what happened here; that's why they're handing out tips to the news services. Let's try to make them believe he's still alive and talking."

"How can we do it?"

"There ought to be somebody on the Force close enough to Salgath Trod's anthropometric specifications that our cosmeticians could work him over into a passable impersonation. Our story is that Salgath is on PolTerm, undergoing narco-hypnosis. We will produce an audio-visual of him as soon as he is out of narco-hyp.

That will give us time to fix up an impersonator. We'll need a lot of sound-recordings of Salgath Trod's voice, of course—"

"I'll take care of the Home Time Line end of it; as soon as we get you an impersonator, you go to work with him. Now, let's see whom we can depend on to help us with this. Lovranth Rolk, of course; Home Time Line section of the Paratime Code Enforcement Division. And—"

Verkan Vall and Dalla and Tortha Karf and four or five others looked across the desk and to the end of the room as the telecast screen broke into a shifting light-pattern and then cleared. The face of the announcer appeared; a young woman.

"And now, we bring you the statement which Chief Tortha of the Paratime Police has promised for this time. This portion of the program was audio-visually recorded at Paratime Police Headquarters earlier this evening."

Tortha Karf's face appeared on the screen. His voice began an announcement of how Executive Councilman Salgath Trod had called him by visiphone, admitting to complicity in the recently-discovered paratemporal slave-trade.

"Here is a recording of Councilman Salgath's call to me from his apartment to my office at 1945 this evening."

The screen-image shattered into light-shards and rebuilt itself: Salgath Trod, at his desk in the library of his apartment, the brandy-goblet and the needler within reach, appeared. He began to speak: from time to time the voice of Tortha Karf interrupted, questioning or prompting him.

"You understand that this confession renders you liable to psycho-rehabilitation?" Tortha Karf asked.

Yes, Councilman Salgath understood that.

"And you agree to come voluntarily to Paratime Police Headquarters, and you will voluntarily undergo narcohypnotic interrogation?"

Yes, Salgath Trod agreed to that.

"I am now terminating the playback of Councilman Salgath's call to me," Tortha Karf said, re-appearing on the screen. "At this point Councilman Salgath began making a statement about his criminal activities, which we have on record. Because he named a number of his criminal associates, whom we have no intention of warning, this portion of Councilman Salgath's call cannot at this time be made public. We have no intention of having any of these suspects escape, or of giving their associates an opportunity to murder them to prevent their furnishing us with additional information. Incidentally, there was an attempt, made on the landing stage of Paratime Police Headquarters, to murder Councilman Salgath, when he was brought here guarded by Paratime Police officers—"

He went on to give a colorful and, as far as possible, truthful, account of the attack by the two pseudo-policemen and their pseudo-prisoner. As he told it, however, all three had been killed before they could accomplish their purpose, one of them by Salgath Trod himself.

The image of Tortha Karf was replaced by a view of the three assassins lying on the landing stage. They all looked dead, even the one who wasn't; there was nothing to indicate that he was merely drugged. Then, one after

another, their faces were shown in closeup, while Tortha
Karf asked for close attention and memorization.

"We believe that these men were Fifth Level Proles;
we think that they were under hypnotic influence or
obeying posthypnotic commands when they made their
suicidal attack. If any of you have ever seen any of these
men before, it is your duty to inform the Paratime Police."

That ended it. Tortha Karf pressed a button in front of
him and the screen went dark. The spectators relaxed.

"Well! Nothing like being sincere with the public, is
there?" Dalla commented. "I'll remember this the next
time I tune in a Management public statement."

"In about five minutes," one of the bureau-chiefs, said,
"all hell is going to break loose. I think the whole thing is
crazy!"

"I hope you have somebody who can give a convincing
impersonation," Lovranth Rolk said.

"Yes. A field agent named Kostran Galth," Tortha Karf
said. "We ran the personal description cards for the whole
Force through the machine; Kostran checked to within
one-twentieth of one per cent; he's on Police Terminal,
now, coming by rocket from Ravvanan Equivalent. We
ought to have the whole thing ready for telecast by 1730
tomorrow."

"He can't learn to imitate Salgath's voice convincingly
in that time, with all the work the cosmeticians'll have to
be doing on him," Dalla said.

"Make up a tape of Salgath's own voice, out of that pile
of recordings we got at his apartment, and what we can
get out of the news file." Vall said. "We have phoneticists

who can split syllables and splice them together. Kostran will deliver his speech in dumb-show, and we'll dub the sound in and telecast them as one. I've messaged PolTerm to get to work on that; they can start as soon as we have the speech written."

"The more it succeeds now, the worse the blow-up will be when we finally have to admit that Salgath was killed here tonight," the Chief Inter-officer Coördinator, Zostha Olv said. "We'd better have something to show the public to justify that."

"Yes, we had," Tortha Karf agreed. "Vall, how about the Kholghoor Sector operation. How far's Ranthar Jard gotten toward locating one of those Wizard Trader time lines?"

"Not very far," Vall admitted. "He has it pinned down to the sub-sector, but the belt seems to be one we haven't any information at all for. Never been any legitimate penetration by paratimers. He has his own hagiologists, and a couple borrowed from Outtime Religious Institute; they've gotten everything the slaves can give them on that. About the only thing to do is start random observation with boomerang-balls."

"Over about a hundred thousand time lines," Zostha Olv scoffed. He was an old man, even for his long-lived race; he had a thin nose and a narrow, bitter, mouth. "And what will he look for?"

"Croutha with guns." Tortha Karf told him, then turned to Vall. "Can't he narrow it more than that? What have his experts been getting out of those slaves?"

"That I don't know, to date." Vall looked at the clock. "I'll find out, though; I'll transpose to Police Terminal and call him up. And Skordran Kirv. No. Vulthor Tharn; it'd hurt the old fellow's feelings if I by-passed him and went to one of his subordinates. Half an hour each way, and at most another hour talking to Ranthar and Vulthor; there won't be anything doing here for two hours." He rose. "See you when I get back."

Dalla had turned on the telescreen again; after tuning out a dance orchestra and a comedy show, she got the image of an angry-faced man in evening clothes.

"...And I'm going to demand a full investigation, as soon as Council convenes tomorrow morning!" he was shouting. "This whole story is a preposterous insult to the integrity of the entire Executive Council, your elected representatives, and it shows the criminal lengths to which this would-be dictator, Tortha Karf, and his jackal Verkan Vall will go—"

"So long, jackal." Dalla called to him as he went out.

He spent the half-hour transposition to Police Terminal sleeping. Paratime-transpositions and rocket-flights seemed to be his only chance to get any sleep. He was still sleepy when he sat down in front of the radio telescreen behind his duplicate of Tortha Karf's desk and put through a call to Nharkan Equivalent. It was 0600 in India; the Sector Regional Deputy Subchief who was holding down Ranthar Jard's desk looked equally sleepy; he had a mug of coffee in front of him, and a brown-paper cigarette in his mouth.

"Oh, hello, Assistant Verkan. Want me to call Subchief Ranthar?"

"Is he sleeping? Then for mercy's sake don't. What's the present status of the investigation?"

"Well, we were dropping boomerang balls yesterday, while we had sun to mask the return-flashes. Nothing. The Croutha have taken the city of Sohram, just below the big bend of the river. Tomorrow, when we have sunlight, we're going to start boomerang-balling the central square. We may get something."

"The Wizard Traders'll be moving in near there, about now," Vall said. "The Croutha ought to have plenty of merchandise for them. Have you gotten anything more done on narrowing down the possible area?"

The deputy bit back a yawn and reached for his coffee mug.

"The experts have just about pumped these slaves empty," he said. "The local religion is a mess. Seems to have started out as a Great Mother cult; then it picked up a lot of gods borrowed from other peoples; then it turned into a dualistic monotheism; then it picked up a lot of minor gods and devils—new devils usually gods of the older pantheon. And we got a lot of gossip about the feudal wars and faction-fights among the nobility, and so on, all garbled, because these people are peasants who only knew what went on on the estate of their own lord."

"What did go on there?" Vall asked. "Ask them about recent improvements, new buildings, new fields cleared, new paddies flooded, that sort of thing. And pick out a few of the highest IQ's from both time lines, and have them locate this estate on a large-scale map, and draw plans showing the location of buildings, fields and other visible features. If you have to, teach them mapping and sketching by hypno-mech. And then drop about five

hundred to a thousand boomerang balls, at regular
intervals, over the whole paratemporal area. When you
locate a time line that gives you a picture to correspond
to their description, boomerang the main square in
Sohram over the whole belt around it, to find Croutha
with firearms."

The deputy looked at him for a moment then gulped
more coffee.

"Can do, Assistant Verkan. I think I'll send somebody
to wake up Subchief Ranthar, right now. Want to talk to
him."

"Won't be necessary. You're recording this call, of
course? Then play it back to him. And get cracking with
the slaves; you want enough information out of them to
enable you to start boomerang balling as soon as the sun's
high enough."

He broke off the connection and sent out for coffee for
himself. Then he put through a call to Novilan Equivalent,
in western North America.

It was 1530, there, when he got Vulthor Tharn on the
screen.

"Good afternoon. Assistant Verkan. I suppose you're
calling about the slave business. I've turned the entire
matter over to Field Agent Skordran; gave him a
temporary rank of Deputy Subchief. That's subject to your
approval and Chief Tortha's, of course—"

"Make the appointment permanent," Vall said. "I'll
have a confirmation along from Chief Tortha directly. And
let me talk to him now, if you please, Subchief Vulthor."

"Yes, sir. Switching you over now." The screen went

into a beautiful burst of abstract art, and cleared, after a while, with Skordran Kirv looking out of it.

"Hello, Deputy Skordran, and congratulations. What's come up since we had Nebu-hin-Abenoz cut out from under us?"

"We went in on that time line, that same night, with an airboat and made a recon in the hills back of Careba. Scared the fear of Safar into a party of Caleras while we were working at low altitude, by the way. We found the conveyer-head site: hundred-foot circle with all the grass and loose dirt transposed off it and a pole pen, very unsanitary where about two-three hundred slaves would be kept at a time. No indications of use in the last ten days. We did some pretty thorough boomeranging on that spatial equivalent over a couple of thousand time lines and found thirty more of them. I believe the slavers have closed out the whole Esaron Sector operation, at least temporarily."

That was what he'd been afraid of; he hoped they wouldn't do the same thing on the Kholghoor Sector.

"Let me have the designations of the time lines on which you found conveyer heads," he said.

"Just a moment, Chief's Assistant; I'll photoprint them to you. Set for reception?"

Vall opened a slide under the screen and saw that the photoprint film was in place, then closed it again, nodding. Skordran Kirv fed a sheet of paper into his screen cabinet and his arm moved forward out of the picture.

"On, sir," he said. He and Vall counted ten seconds together, and then Skordran Kirv said: "Through to you." Vall pressed a lever under his screen, and a rectangle of microcopy print popped out.

"That's about all I have, sir. Want me to keep my troops ready here, or shall I send them somewhere else?"

"Keep them ready, Kirv," Vall told him. "You may need them before long. Call you later."

He put the microcopy in an enlarger, and carried the enlarged print with him to the conveyer room. There was something odd about the list of time line designations. They were expressed numerically, in First Level notation; extremely short groups of symbols capable of exact expression of almost inconceivably enormous numbers. Vall had only a general-education smattering of mathematics—enough to qualify him for the chair of Higher Mathematics at any university on, say, the Fourth Level Europo-American Sector—and he could not identify the peculiarity, but he could recognize that there existed some sort of pattern. Shoving in the starting lever, he relaxed in one of the chairs, waiting for the transposition field to build up around him, and fell asleep before the mesh dome of the conveyer had vanished. He woke, the list of time line designations in his hand, when the conveyor rematerialized on Home Time Line. Putting it in his pocket, he hurried to an antigrav shaft and floated up to the floor on which Tortha Karf's office was.

Tortha Karf was asleep in his chair; Dalla was eating a dinner that had been brought in to her—something better than the sandwich and mug of coffee Vall had mentioned to Thalvan Dras. Several of the bureau chiefs who had been there when he had gone out had left, and the psychist who had taken charge of the prisoner was there.

"I think he's coming out of the drug, now," he reported.

"Still asleep, though. We want him to waken naturally before we start on him. They'll call me as soon as he shows signs of stirring."

"The Opposition's claiming, now, that we drugged and hypnotized Salgath into making that visiscreen confession," Dalla said. "Can you think of any way you could do that without making the subject incapable of lying?"

"Pseudo-memories," the psychist said. "It would take about three times as long as the time between Salgath Trod's departure from his apartment and the time of the telecast, though—"

"You know much higher math?" Vall asked the psychist.

"Well, enough to handle my job. Neuron-synapse inter-relations, memory-and-association patterns, that kind of thing, all have to be expressed mathematically."

Vall nodded and handed him the time-line designation list.

"See any kind of a pattern there?" he asked.

The psychist looked at the paper and blanked his face as he drew on hypnotically-acquired information.

"Yes. I'd say that all the numbers are related in some kind of a series to some other number. Simplified down to kindergarten level, say the difference between A and B is, maybe, one-decillionth of the difference between X and A, and the difference between B and C is one-decillionth of the difference between X and B, and so on—"

A voice came out of one of the communication boxes:

"Dr. Nentrov; the patient's out of the drug, and he's beginning to stir about."

"That's it," the psychist said. "I have to run." He handed the sheet back to Vall, took a last drink from his coffee cup, and bolted out of the room.

Dalla picked up the sheet of paper and looked at it. Vall told her what it was.

"If those time lines are in regular series, they relate to the base line of operations," she said. "Maybe you can have that worked out. I can see how it would be; a stated interval between the Esaron Sector lines, to simplify transposition control settings."

"That was what I was thinking. It's not quite as simple as Dr. Nentrov expressed it, but that could be the general idea. We might be able to work out the location of the base line from that. There seems to be a break in the number sequence in here; that would be the time line Skordran Kirv found those slaves on." He reached for the pipe he had left on the desk when he had gone to Police Terminal and began filling it.

A little later, a buzzer sounded and a light came on on one of the communication boxes. He flipped the switch and said, "Verkan Vall here." Sothran Barth's voice came out of the box.

"They've just brought in Salgath Trod's servants. Picked them up as they came out of the house conveyer at the apartment building. I don't believe they know what's happened."

Vall flipped a switch and twiddled a dial; a viewscreen lit up, showing the landing stage. The police car had just landed: one detective had gotten out, and was helping the girl, Zinganna, who had been Salgath Trod's housekeeper and mistress, to descend. She was really beautiful, Vall thought: rather tall, slender, with dark eyes and a creamy light-brown skin. She wore a black cloak, and, under it, a black and silver evening gown. A single jewel twinkled in her black hair. She could have very easily passed for a woman of his own race.

The housemaid and the butler were a couple of entirely different articles. Both were about four or five generations from Fourth Level Primitive savagery. The maid, in garishly cheap finery, was big-boned and heavy-bodied, with red-brown hair; she looked like a member of one of the northern European reindeer-herding peoples who had barely managed to progress as far as the bow and arrow. The butler was probably a mixture of half a dozen primitive races; he was wearing one of his late master's evening suits, a bright mellow-pink, which was distinctly unflattering to his complexion.

The sound-pickup was too far away to give him what they were saying, but the butler and maid were waving their arms and protesting vehemently. One of the detectives took the woman by the arm; she jerked it loose and aimed a backhand slap at him. He blocked it on his forearm. Immediately, the girl in black turned and said something to her, and she subsided. Vall said, into the box:

"Barth, have the girl in the black cloak brought down to Number Four Interview Room. Put the other two in separate detention cubicles; we'll talk to them later." He broke the connection and got to his feet. "Come on, Dalla. I want you to help me with the girl."

"Just try and stop me," Dalla told him. "Any interviews you have with that little item, I want to sit in on."

* * *

The Proletarian girl, still guarded by a detective, had already been placed in the interview room. The detective nodded to Vall, tried to suppress a grin when he saw Dalla behind him, and went out. Vall saw his wife and the prisoner seated, and produced his cigarette case, handing it around.

"You're Zinganna; you're of the household of Councilman Salgath Trod, aren't you?" he asked.

"Housekeeper and hostess," the girl replied. "I am also his mistress."

Vall nodded, smiling. "Which confirms my long-standing respect for Councilman Salgath's exquisite taste."

"Why, thank you," she said. "But I doubt if I was brought here to receive compliments. Or was I?"

"No, I'm afraid not. Have you heard the newscasts of the past few hours concerning Councilman Salgath?"

She straightened in her seat, looking at him seriously.

"No. I and Nindrandigro and Calilla spent the evening on ServSec One-Six-Five. Councilman Salgath told me that he had some business and wanted them out of the apartment, and wanted me to keep an eye on them. We didn't hear any news at all." She hesitated. "Has anything . . . serious . . . happened?"

Vall studied her for a moment, then glanced at Dalla. There existed between himself and his wife a sort of vague, semitelepathic, rapport; they had never been able to transmit definite and exact thoughts, but they could clearly prehend one another's feelings and emotions. He was conscious, now, of Dalla's sympathy for the Proletarian girl.

"Zinganna, I'm going to tell you something that is being

kept from the public," he said. "By doing so, I will make it necessary for us to detain you, at least for a few days. I hope you will forgive me, but I think you would forgive me less if I didn't tell you."

"Something's happened to him," she said, her eyes widening and her body tensing.

"Yes, Zinganna. At about 2010, this evening," he said, "Councilman Salgath was murdered."

"Oh!" She leaned back in the chair, closing her eyes. "He's dead?" Then, again, statement instead of question: "He's dead!"

For a long moment, she lay back in the chair, as though trying to reorient her mind to the fact of Salgath Trod's death, while Vall and Dalla sat watching her. Then she stirred, opened her eyes, looked at the cigarette in her fingers as though she had never seen it before, and leaned forward to stuff it into an ash receiver.

"Who did it?" she asked, the Stone Age savage who had been her ancestor not ten generations ago peeping out of her eyes.

"The men who actually used the needlers are dead," Vall told her. "I killed a couple of them myself. We still have to find the men who planned it. I'd hoped you'd want to help us do that, Zinganna."

He side-glanced to Dalla again; she nodded. The relationship between Zinganna and Salgath Trod hadn't been purely business with her; there had been some real affection. He told her what had happened, and when he reached the point at which Salgath Trod had called Tortha Karf to confess complicity in the slave trade, her lips tightened and she nodded.

"I was afraid it was something like that," she said. "For the last few days, well, ever since the news about the slave trade got out, he's been worried about something. I've always thought somebody had some kind of a hold over him. Different times in the past, he's done things so far against his own political best interests that I've had to believe he was being forced into them. Well, this time they tried to force him too far. What then?"

Vall continued the story. "So we're keeping this hushed up, for a while. The way we're letting it out, Salgath Trod is still alive, on Police Terminal, talking under narco-hypnosis."

She smiled savagely. "And they'll get frightened, and frightened men do foolish things," she finished. She hadn't been a politician's mistress for nothing. "What can I do to help?"

"Tell us everything you can," he said. "Maybe we can be able to take such actions as we would have taken if Salgath Trod had lived to talk to us."

"Yes, of course." She got another cigarette from the case Vall had laid on the table. "I think, though, that you'd better give me a narco-hypnosis. You want to be able to depend on what I'm going to tell you, and I want to be able to remember things exactly."

Vall nodded approvingly and turned to Dalla.

"Can you handle this, yourself?" he asked. "There's an audio-visual recorder on now; here's everything you need." He opened the drawers in the table to show her the narco-hypnotic equipment. "And the phone has a whisper mouthpiece; you can call out without worrying about your message getting into Zinganna's subconscious.

Well, I'll see you when you're through; you bring Zinganna to Police Terminal; I'll probably be there."

He went out, closing the door behind him, and went down the hall, meeting the officer who had taken charge of the butler and housemaid.

"We're having trouble with them, sir," he said. "Hostile. Yelling about their rights, and demanding to see a representative of Proletarian Protective League."

Vall mentioned the Proletarian Protective League with unflattering vulgarity.

"If they don't coöperate, drag them out and inject them and question them anyhow," he said.

The detective-lieutenant looked worried. "We've been taking a pretty high hand with them as it is," he protested. "It's safer to kill a Citizen than bloody a Prole's nose; they have all sorts of laws to protect them."

"There are all sorts of laws to protect the Paratime Secret," Vall replied. "And I think there are one or two laws against murdering members of the Executive Council. In case P.P.L. makes any trouble, they aren't here; they have faithfully joined their beloved master in his refuge on PolTerm. But one or both of them work for the Organization."

"You're sure of that?"

"The Organization is too thorough not to have had a spy in Salgath's household. It wasn't Zinganna, because she's volunteered to talk to us under narco-hyp. So who does that leave?"

"Well, that's different; that makes them suspects." The lieutenant seemed relieved. "We'll pump that pair out right away."

When he got back to Tortha Karf's office, the Chief was awake, and doodling on his notepad with his multicolor pen. Vall looked at the pad and winced; the Chief was doodling bugs again—red ants with black legs, and blue-and-green beetles. Then he saw that the psychist, Nentrov Dard, was drinking straight 150-proof palm-rum.

"Well, tell me the worst," he said.

"Our boy's memory-obliterated," Nentrov Dard said, draining his glass and filling it again. "And he's plastered with pseudo-memories a foot thick. It'll be five or six ten-days before we can get all that stuff peeled off and get him unblocked. I put him to sleep and had him transposed to Police Terminal. I'm going there, myself, tomorrow morning, after I've had some sleep, and get to work on him. If you're hoping to get anything useful out of him in time to head off this Council crisis that's building up, just forget it."

"And that leaves us right back with our old friends, the Wizard Traders," Tortha Karf added. "And if they've decided to suspend activities on the Kholghoor Sector, too—" He began drawing a big blue and black spider in the middle of the pad.

Nentrov Dard crushed out his cigar, drank his rum, and got to his feet.

"Well, good night, Chief; Vall. If you decide to wake me up before 1000, send somebody you want to get rid of in a hurry." He walked around the desk and out the side door.

"I hope they don't," Vall said to Tortha Karf. "Really, though, I doubt if they do. This is their chance to pick up a lot of slaves cheaply; the Croutha are too busy to bother haggling. I'm going through to PolTerm, now; when Dalla and Zinganna get through, tell them to join me there."

On Police Terminal, he found Kostran Galth, the agent who had been selected to impersonate Salgath Trod. After calling Zulthran Torv, the mathematician in charge of the Computer Office and giving him the Esaron time-line designations and Nentrov Dard's ideas about them, he spent about an hour briefing Kostran Galth on the role he was to play. Finally, he undressed and went to bed on a couch in the rest room behind the office.

It was noon when he woke. After showering, shaving and dressing hastily, he went out to the desk for breakfast, which arrived while he was putting a call through to Ranthar Jard, at Nharkan Equivalent.

"Your idea paid off, Chief's Assistant," the Kholghoor SecReg Subchief told him. "The slaves gave us a lot of physical description data on the estate, and told us about new fields that had been cleared, and a dam this Lord Ghromdour was building to flood some new rice-paddies. We located a belt of about five parayears where these improvements had been made: we started boomeranging the whole belt, time line by time line. So far, we have ten or fifteen pictures of the main square at Sohram showing Croutha with firearms, and pictures of Wizard Trader camps and conveyer heads on the same time lines. Here, let me show you; this is from an airboat over the forest outside the equivalent of Sohram."

There was no jungle visible when the view changed; nothing but clusters of steel towers and platforms and

buildings that marked conveyer heads, and a large
rectangle of red-and-white antigrav-buoys moored to
warn air traffic out of the area being boomeranged. The
pickup seemed to be pointed downward from the bow of
an airboat circling at about ten thousand feet.

"Balls ready to go," a voice called, and then repeated a
string of time-line designations. "Estimated return, 1820,
give or take four minutes."

"Varth," Ranthar Jard said, evidently out of the boat's
radio. "Your telecast is being beamed on Dhergabar
Equivalent; Chief's Assistant Verkan is watching. When
do you estimate your next return?"

"Any moment, now, sir; we're holding this drop till they
rematerialize."

Vall watched unblinkingly, his fork poised halfway to
his mouth. Suddenly, about a thousand feet below the eye
of the pickup, there was a series of blue flashes, and, an
instant later, a blossoming of red-and-white parachutes,
ejected from the photo-reconnaissance balls that had
returned from the Kholghoor Sector.

"All right; drop away," the boat captain called. There
was a gush, from underneath, of eight-inch spheres, their
conductor-mesh twinkling golden-bright in the sunlight.
They dropped in a tight cluster for a thousand or so feet
and then flashed and vanished. From the ground, six or
eight aircars rose to meet the descending parachutes and
catch them.

The screen went cubist for a moment, and then
Ranthar Jard's swarthy, wide-jawed face looked out of it
again. He took his pipe from his mouth.

"We'll probably get a positive out of the batch you just

saw coming in," he said. "We get one out of about every two drops."

"Message a list of the time-line designations you've gotten so far to Zulthran Torv, at Computer Office here," Vall said. "He's working on the Esaron Sector dope; we think a pattern can be established. I'll be seeing you in about five hours; I'm rocketing out of here as soon as I get a few more things cleared up here."

Zulthran Torv, normally cautious to the degree of pessimism, was jubilant when Vall called him.

"We have something, Vall," he said. "It is, roughly, what Dr. Nentrov suggested—each of the intervals between the designations is a very minute but very exact fraction of the difference between lesser designation and the base-line designation."

"You have the base-line designation?" Vall demanded.

"Oh, yes. That's what I was telling you. We worked that out from the designations you gave me." He recited it. "All the designations you gave me are—"

Vall wasn't listening to him. He frowned in puzzlement.

"That's not a Fifth Level designation," he said. "That's First Level!"

"That's correct. First Level Abzar Sector."

"Now why in blazes didn't anybody think of that before?" he marveled, and as he did, he knew the answer. Nobody ever thought of the Abzar sector.

Twelve millennia ago, the world of the First Level had been exhausted; having used up the resources of their home planet, Mars, a hundred thousand years before, the descendants of the population that had migrated across space had repeated on the third planet the devastation of

the fourth. The ancestors of Verkan Vall's people had
discovered the principle of paratime transposition and had
begun to exploit an infinity of worlds on other lines of
probability. The people of the First Level Dwarma Sector,
reduced by sheer starvation to a tiny handful, had
abandoned their cities and renounced their technologies
and created for themselves a farm-and-village culture
without progress or change or curiosity or struggle or
ambition, and a way of life in which every day was like
every other day that had been or that would come.

The Abzar people had done neither. They had wasted
their resources to the last, fighting bitterly over the
ultimate crumbs, with fission bombs, and with muskets,
and with swords, and with spears and clubs, and finally
they had died out, leaving a planet of almost uniform
desert dotted with vast empty cities which even twelve
thousand years had hardly begun to obliterate.

So nobody on the Paratime Sector went to the Abzar
Sector. There was nothing there—except a hiding-place.

"Well, message that to Subchief Ranthar Jard,
Kholghoor Sector at Nharkan Equivalent, and to Subchief
Vulthor, Esaron Sector, Novilan Equivalent," Vall said.
"And be sure to mark what you send Vulthor, 'Immediate
attention Deputy Subchief Skordran.'"

That reminded him of something; as soon as he was
through with Zulthran, he got out an order in the name
of Tortha Karf authorizing Skordran Kirv's promotion on
a permanent basis and messaged it out. Something was
going to have to be done with Vulthor Tharn, too. A
promotion of course—say Deputy Bureau Chief. Hypno-
Mech Tape Library at Dhergabar Home Time Line; there

Vulthor's passion for procedure and his caution would be assets instead of liabilities. He called Vlasthor Arph, the Chief's Deputy assigned to him as adjutant.

"I want more troops from ServSec and IndSec," he said. "Go over the TO's and see what can be spared from where; don't strip any time line, but get a force of the order of about three divisions. And locate all the big antigrav-equipped ship transposition docks on Commercial and Passenger Sectors, and a list of freighters and passenger ships that can be commandeered in a hurry. We think we've spotted the time line the Organization's using as a base. As soon as we raid a couple of places near Nharkan and Novilan Equivalents, we're going to move in for a planet-wide cleanup."

"I get it, Chief's Assistant. I do everything I can to get ready for a big move, without letting anything leak out. After you strike the first blow, there won't be any security problem, and the lid will be off. In the meantime, I make up a general plan, and alert all our own people. Right?"

"Right. And for your information, the base isn't Fifth Level; it's First Level Abzar." He gave the designation.

Vlasthor Arph chuckled. "Well, think of that! I'd even forgotten there was an Abzar Sector. Shall I tell the reporters that?"

"Fangs of Fasif, no!" Vall fairly howled. Then, curiously: "What reporters? How'd they get onto PolTerm?"

"About fifty or sixty news-service people Chief Tortha sent down here, this morning, with orders to prevent them from filing any stories from here but to let them cover the raids, when they come off. We were instructed to furnish them weapons and audio-visual equipment and vocowriters and anything else they needed, and—"

Vall grinned. "That was one I'd never thought of," he admitted. "The old fox is still the old fox. No, tell them nothing; we'll just take them along and show them. Oh, and where are Dr. Hadron Dalla and that girl of Salgath Trod's?"

"They're sleeping, now. Rest Room Eighteen."

Dalla and Zinganna were asleep on a big mound of silk cushions in one corner, their glossy black heads close together and Zinganna's brown arm around Dalla's white shoulder. Their faces were calmly beautiful in repose, and they smiled slightly, as though they were wandering through a happy dream. For a little while, Vall stood looking at them, then he began whistling softly. On the third or fourth bar, Dalla woke and sat up, waking Zinganna, and blinked at him perplexedly.

"What time is it?" she asked.

"About 1245," he told her.

"Ohhh! We just got to sleep," she said. "We're both bushed!"

"You had a hard time. Feel all right after your narco-hyp, Zinganna?"

"It wasn't so bad, and I had a nice sleep. And Dalla . . . Dr. Hadron, I mean—"

"Dalla," Vall's wife corrected. "Remember what I told you?"

"Dalla, then," Zinganna smiled. "Dalla gave me some hypno-treatment, too. I don't feel so badly about Trod, any more."

"Well, look, Zinganna. We're going to have a man impersonate Councilman Salgath on a telecast. The cosmeticians are making him over now. Would you find it too painful to meet him, and talk to him?"

"No, I wouldn't mind. I can criticize the impersonation; remember, I knew Trod very well. You know, I was his hostess, too. I met many of the people with whom he was associated, and they know me. Would things look more convincing if I appeared on the telecast with your man?"

"It certainly would; it would be a great help!" he told her enthusiastically. "Maybe you girls ought to get up, now. The telecast isn't till 1930, but there's a lot to be done getting ready."

Dalla yawned. "What I get, trying to be a cop," she said, then caught the other girl's hands and rose, pulling her up. "Come on, Zinna; we have to get to work!"

Vall rose from behind the reading-screen in Ranthar Jard's office, stretching his arms over his head. For almost an hour, he had sat there pushing buttons and twiddling selector and magnification-adjustment knobs, looking at the pictures the Kholghoor-Nharkan cops had taken with auto-return balls dropped over the spatial equivalent of Sohram. One set of pictures, taken at two thousand feet, showed the central square of the city. The effects of the Croutha sack were plainly visible; so were the captives herded together under guard like cattle. By increasing magnification, he looked at groups of the barbarian conquerors, big men with blond or reddish-brown hair, in loose shirts and baggy trousers and rough cowhide

buskins. Many of them wore bowl-shaped helmets, some
had shirts of ring-mail, all of them carried long straight
swords with cross-hilts, and about half of them had pistols
thrust through their belts or muskets slung from their
shoulders.

The other set of pictures showed the Wizard Trader
camps and conveyer heads. In each case, a wide oval had
been burned out in the jungle, probably with heavy-duty
heat guns. The camps were surrounded with stout wire-
mesh fence: in each there were a number of metal
prefab-huts, and an inner fenced slave-pen. A trail had
been cut from each to a similarly cleared circle farther back
in the forest, and in the centers of one or two of these
circles he saw the actual conveyer domes. There was a great
deal of activity in all of them, and he screwed the
magnification-adjustment to the limit to scrutinize each
human figure in turn. A few of the men, he was sure, were
First Level Citizens; more were either Proles or outtimers.
Quite a few of them were of a dark, heavy-featured, black-
bearded type.

"Some of these fellows look like Second Level
Khiftans," he said. "Rush an individual picture of each
one, maximum magnification consistent with clarity, to
Dhergabar Equivalent to be transposed to Home Time
Line. You get all the dope from Zulthran Torv?"

"Yes; Abzar Sector," Ranthar Jard said. "I'd never have
thought of that. Wonder why they used that series system,
though. I'd have tried to spot my operations as completely
at random as possible."

"Only thing they could have done," Vall said. "When
we get hold of one of their conveyers, we're going to find

the control panel's just a mess of arbitrary symbols, and there'll be something like a computer-machine built into the control cabinet, to select the right time line whenever a dial's set or a button pushed, and the only way that could be done would be by establishing some kind of a numerical series. And we were trustingly expecting to locate their base from one of their conveyers! Why, if we give all those people in the pictures narco-hyps, we won't learn the base-line designation; none of them will know it. They just go where the conveyers take them."

"Well, we're all set now," Ranthar Jard said. "I have a plan of attack worked out; subject to your approval, I'm ready to start implementing it now." He glanced at his watch. "The Salgath telecast is over, on Home Time Line, and in a little while, a transcript will be on this time line. Want to watch it here, sir?"

The telecast screen in the living room of Tortha Karf's town apartment was still on; in it, a girl with bright red hair danced slowly to soft music against a background of shifting color. The four men who sat in a semicircle facing it sipped their drinks and watched idly.

"Ought to be getting some sort of public reaction soon," Tortha Karf said, glancing at his watch.

"Well, I'll have to admit, it was done convincingly," Zostha Olv, the Chief Interoffice Coördinator, admitted grudgingly. "I'd have believed it, if I hadn't known the real facts."

"Shooting it against the background of those wide windows was smart," Lovranth Rolk said. "Every schoolchild would recognize that view of the rocketport as being on Police Terminal. And including that girl Zinganna; that was a real masterpiece!"

"I've met her, a few times," Elbraz Vark, the Political Liaison Assistant, said. "Isn't she lovely!"

"Good actress, too," Tortha Karf said. "It's not easy to impersonate yourself."

"Well, Kostran Galth did a fine job of acting, too," Lovranth Rolk said. "That was done to perfection—the distinguished politician, supported by his loyal mistress, bravely facing the disgraceful end of his public career."

"You know, I believe I could get that girl a booking with one of the big theatrical companies. Now that Salgath's dead, she'll need somebody to look after her."

"What sharp, furry ears you have, Mr. Elbraz!" Zostha Olv grunted.

The music stopped as though cut off with a knife, and the slim girl with the red hair vanished in a shatter of many colors. When the screen cleared, one of the announcers was looking out of it.

"We interrupt the program for an important newscast of a sensational development in the Salgath affair," he said. "Your next speaker will be Yandar Yadd—"

"I thought you'd managed to get that blabbermouth transposed to PolTerm," Zostha said.

"He wouldn't go." Tortha Karf replied. "Said it was just a trick to get him off Home Time Line during the Council crisis."

Yandar Yadd had appeared on the screen as the pickup swung about.

"... Recording ostensibly made by Councilman Salgath on Police Terminal Time Line, and telecast on Home

Time Line an hour ago. Well, I don't know who he was, but I now have positive proof that he definitely was not Salgath Trod!"

"We're sunk!" Zostha Olv grunted. "He'd never make a statement like that unless he could prove it."

"...Something suspicious about the whole thing, from the beginning," the newsman was saying. "So I checked. If you recall, the actor impersonating Salgath gestured rather freely with his hands, in imitation of a well-known mannerism of the real Salgath Trod; at one point, the ball of his right thumb was presented directly to the pickup. Here's a still of that scene."

He stepped aside, revealing a viewscreen behind him; when he pressed a button, the screen lighted; on it was a stationary picture of Kostran Galth as Salgath Trod, his right hand raised in front of him.

"Now watch this. I'm going to step up the magnification, slowly, so that you can be sure there's no substitution. Camera a little closer, Trath!"

The screen in the background seemed to advance, until it filled the entire screen. Yandar Yadd was still talking, out of the picture; a metal-tipped pointer came into the picture, touching the right thumb, which grew larger and larger until it was the only thing visible.

"Now here," Yandar Yadd's voice continued. "Any of you who are familiar with the ancient science of dactyloscopy will recognize this thumb as having the ridge-pattern known as a 'twin loop.' Even with the high degree of magnification possible with the microgrid screen, we can't bring out the individual ridges, but the pattern is unmistakable. I ask you to memorize that image, while I show you another right thumb print, this time a certified photo-copy of the thumb print of the real Salgath Trod." The magnification was reduced a little, a card was moved into the picture, and it was stepped up again. "See, this thumb print is of the type known as a 'tented arch.' Observe the difference."

"That does it!" Zostha Olv cried. "Karf, for the first and last time, let me remind you that I opposed this lunacy from the beginning. Now, what are we going to do next?"

"I suggest that we get to Headquarters as soon as we can," Tortha Karf said. "If we wait too long, we may not be able to get in."

Yandar Yadd was back on the screen, denouncing Tortha Karf passionately. Tortha went over and snapped it off.

"I suggest we transpose to PolTerm," Lovranth Rolk said. "It won't be so easy for them to serve a summons on us there."

"You can go to PolTerm if you want to," Tortha Karf retorted. "I'm going to stay here and fight back, and if they try to serve me with a summons, they'd better send a robot for a process server."

"Fight back!" Zostha Olv echoed. "You can't fight the Council and the whole Management! They'll tear you into inch bits!"

"I can hold them off till Vall's able to raid those Abzar Sector bases," Tortha Karf said. He thought for a moment. "Maybe this is all for the best, after all. If it distracts the Organization's attention—"

★ ★ ★

"I wish we could have made a boomerang-ball reconnaissance," Ranthar Jard was saying, watching one of the viewscreens, in which a film, taken from an airboat transposed to an adjoining Abzar sector time line, was being shown. The boat had circled over the Ganges, a mere trickle between wide, deeply cut banks, and was crossing a gullied plain, sparsely grown with thornbush. "The base ought to be about there, but we have no idea what sort of changes this gang has made."

"Well, we couldn't: we didn't dare take the chance of it being spotted. This has to be a complete surprise. It'll be about like the other place, the one the slaves described. There won't be any permanent buildings. This operation only started a few months ago, with the Croutha invasion; it may go on for four or five months, till the Croutha have all their surplus captives sold off. That country," he added, gesturing at the screen, "will be flooded out when the rains come. See how it's suffered from flood-erosion. There won't be a thing there that can't be knocked down and transposed out in a day or so."

"I wish you'd let me go along," Ranthar Jard worried.

"We can't do that, either," Vall said. "Somebody's got to be in charge here, and you know your own people better than I do. Beside, this won't be the last operation like this. Next time, I'll have to stay on Police Terminal and command from a desk; I want first-hand experience with the outtime end of the job, and this is the only way I can get it."

He watched the four police-girls who were working at the big terrain board showing the area of the Police Terminal time line around them. They had covered the miniature buildings and platforms and towers with a fine mesh, at a scale-equivalent of fifty feet; each intersection marked the location of a three-foot conveyer ball, loaded with a sleep-gas bomb and rigged with an automatic detonator which would explode it and release the gas as soon as it rematerialized on the Abzar Sector. Higher, on stiff wires that raised them to what represented three thousand feet, were the disks that stood for ten hundred-foot conveyers; they would carry squads of Paratime Police in aircars and thirty-foot air boats. There was a ring of big two-hundred-foot conveyers a mile out; they would carry the armor and the airborne infantry and the little two-man scooters of the air-cavalry, from the Service and Industrial Sectors. Directly over the spatial equivalent of the Kholghoor Sector Wizard Traders' conveyers was the single disk of Verkan Vall's command conveyer, at a represented five thousand feet, and in a half-mile circle around it were the five news service conveyers.

"Where's the ship-conveyer?" he asked.

"Actually it's on antigrav about five miles north of here," one of the girls said. "Representationally, about where Subchief Ranthar's standing."

Another girl added a few more bits to the network that represented the sleep-gas bombs and stepped back, taking off her earphones.

"Everything's in place, now, Assistant Verkan," she told him.

"Good. I'm going aboard, now," he said. "You can have it, Jard."

He shook hands with Ranthar Jard, who moved to the switch which would activate all the conveyers simultaneously, and accepted the good wishes of the girls at the terrain board. Then he walked to the mesh-covered dome of the hundred-foot conveyer, with the five news service conveyers surrounding it in as regular a circle as the buildings and towers of the regular conveyer heads would permit. The members of his own detail, smoking and chatting outside, saw him and started moving inside; so did the news people. A public-address speaker began yelping, in a hundred voices all over the area, warning those who were going with the conveyers to get aboard. He went in through a door, between two aircars, and on to the central control-desks, going up to a visiscreen over which somebody had crayoned "Novilan EQ." It gave him a view, over the shoulder of a man in the uniform of a field agent third class, of the interior of a conveyer like his own.

"Hello, Assistant Verkan," a voice came out of the speaker under the screen, as the man moved his lips. "Deputy Skordran! Here's Chief's Assistant Verkan, now!"

Skordran Kirv moved in front of the screen as the operator got up from his stool.

"Hello, Vall; we're all set to move out as soon as you give the word," he said. "We're all in position on antigrav."

"That's smart work. We've just finished our gas-bomb net," Vall said. "Going on antigrav now," he added, as he felt the dome lift. "I hope you won't be too disappointed if you draw a blank on your end."

"We realize that they've closed out the whole Esaron Sector," Skordran Kirv, eight-thousand-odd miles away, replied. "We're taking in a couple of ships; we're going to make a survey all up the coast. There are a lot of other sectors where slaves can be sold in this area."

In the outside viewscreen, tuned to a slowly rotating pickup on the top of a tower spatially equivalent with a room in a tall building on Second Level Triplanetary Empire Sector, he could see his own conveyer rising vertically, with the news conveyers following, and the troop conveyers, several miles away, coming into position. Finally, they were all placed; he reported the fact to Skordran Kirv and then picked up a hand-phone.

"Everybody ready for transposition?" he called. "On my count. Thirty seconds . . . Twenty seconds . . . Fifteen seconds . . . Five   seconds . . . Four   seconds . . . Three seconds . . . Two seconds . . . One second, *out!*"

All the screens went gray. The inside of the dome passed into another space-time continuum, even into another kind of space-time. The transposition would take half an hour; that seemed to be the time needed to build up and collapse the transposition field, regardless of the paratemporal distance covered. The dome above and around them vanished; the bare, tower-forested, building-dotted world of Police Terminal vanished, too, into the uniform green of the uninhabited Fifth Level. A planet could take pretty good care of itself, he thought, if people would only leave it alone. Then he began to see the fields and villages of Fourth Level. Cities appeared and vanished, growing higher and vaster as they went across the more civilized Third Level. One was under air attack—there was almost never a paratemporal transposition which did not run through some scene of battle.

He unbuckled his belt and took off his boots and tunic; all around him, the others were doing the same. Sleep-gas didn't have to be breathed; it could enter the nervous system by any orifice or lesion, even a pore or a scratch. A spacesuit was the only protection. One of the detectives helped him on with his metal and plastic armor; before sealing his gauntlets, he reciprocated the assistance, then checked the needler and blaster and the long batonlike ultrasonic paralyzer on his belt and made sure that the radio and sound-phones in his helmet were working. He hoped that the frantic efforts to gather several thousand spacesuits onto Police Terminal from the Industrial and Commercial and Interplanetary Sectors hadn't started rumors which had gotten to the ears of some of the Organization's ubiquitous agents.

The country below was already turning to the parched browns and yellows of the Abzar Sector. There was not another of the conveyers in sight, but electronic and mechanical lag in the individual controls and even the distance-difference between them and the central radio control would have prevented them from going into transposition at the same fractional microsecond. The recon-details began piling into their cars. Then the red light overhead winked to green, and the dome flickered and solidified into cold, inert metal. The screens lighted up again, and Vall could see Skordran Kirv, across Asia and the Pacific, getting into his helmet. A dot of light in the center of the underview screen widened as the mesh under the conveyer irised open around the pickup.

Below, the Organization base—big rectangles of

fenced slave pens, with metal barracks inside; the huge circle of the Kholghoor Sector conveyer-head building, and a smaller structure that must house conveyers to other Abzar Sector time lines; the work-shops and living quarters and hangars and warehouses and docks—was wreathed in white-green mist. The ring of conveyers at three thousand feet were opening and spewing out aircars and airboats, farther away, the greater ring of heavy conveyers were unloading armored and shielded combat-craft. An aircar which must have been above the reach of the gas was streaking away toward the west, with three police cars after it. As he watched, the air around it fairly sizzled blue with the rays of neutron disruption blasters, and then it blew apart. The three police cars turned and came back more slowly. The three-thousand-ton passenger ship which had been hastily fitted with armament was circling about; the great dock conveyer which had brought it was gone, transposed back to Police Terminal to pick up another ship.

He recorded a message announcing the arrival of the task-force, pulled out the tape and sealed it in a capsule, and put the capsule in a mesh message ball, attaching it to a couple of wires and flipping a switch. The ball flashed and vanished, leaving the wires cleanly sheared off. When it got back to Police Terminal, half an hour later, it would rematerialize, eject a parachute, and turn on a whistle to call attention to itself. Then he sealed on his helmet, climbed into an aircar, and turned on his helmet-radio to speak to the driver. The car lifted a few inches, floated out an open port, and dived downward.

★ ★ ★

He landed at the big conveyer-head building. There were spaces for fifty conveyers around it, and all but eight of them were in place. One must have arrived since the gas bombs burst; it was crammed with senseless Kharanda slaves. A couple of Paratime Police officers were towing a tank of sleep-gas around on an antigrav-lifter, maintaining the proper concentration in case any more came in. At the smaller conveyer building, there were no conveyers, only a number of red-lined fifty-foot circles around a central two-hundred-foot circle. The Organization personnel there had been dragged outside, and a group of paracops were sealing it up, installing robot watchmen, and preparing to flood it with gas. At the slave pens, a string of two-hundred-foot conveyers, having unloaded soldiers and fighting-gear, were coming in to take on unconscious slaves for transposition to Police Terminal. Aircars and airboats were bringing in gassed slavers; they were being shackled and dumped into the slave barracks; as soon as the gas cleared and they could be brought back to consciousness, they would be narco-hypnotized and questioned.

He had finished a tour of the warehouses, looking at the kegs of gunpowder and the casks of brandy, the piles of pig lead, the stacks of cases containing muskets. These must have all come from some low-order handcraft time line. Then there were swords and hatchets and knives that had been made on Industrial Sector—the Organization must be getting them through some legitimate trading company—and mirrors and perfumes and synthetic fiber textiles and cheap jewelry, of similar provenance. It looked as though this stuff had been brought in by ship from somewhere else on this time line; the warehouses were too far from the conveyers and right beside the ship dock—

There was a tremendous explosion somewhere. Vall and the men with him ran outside, looking about, the sound-phones of their helmets giving them no idea of the source of the sound. One of the policemen pointed, and Vall's eyes followed his arm. The ship that had been transposed in in the big conveyer was falling, blown in half; as he looked, both sections hit the ground several miles away. A strange ship, a freighter, was coming in fast, and as he watched, a blue spark winked from her bow as a heavy-duty blaster was activated. There was another explosion, overhead; they all ran for shelter as Vall's command-conveyer disintegrated into falling scrap-metal. At once, all the other conveyers which were on antigrav began flashing and vanishing. That was the right, the only, thing to do, he knew. But it was leaving him and his men isolated and under attack.

"So that was it," Dalgroth Sorn, the Paratime Commissioner for Security said, relieved when Tortha Karf had finished.

"Yes, and I'll repeat it under narco-hyp, too," Tortha Karf added.

"Oh, don't talk that way, Karf," Dalgroth Sorn scolded. He was at least a century Tortha Karf's senior; he had the face of an elderly and sore-toothed lion. "You wanted to keep this prisoner under wraps till you could mind-pump him, and you wanted the Organization to think Salgath was alive and talking. I approve both. But—"

He gestured to the viewscreen across the room, tuned

to a pickup back of the Speaker's chair in the Council Chamber. Tortha Karf turned a knob to bring the sound volume up.

"Well. I'm raising this point," a member from the Management seats in the center was saying, "because these earlier charges of illegal arrest and illegal detention are part and parcel with the charges growing out of the telecast last evening."

"Well, that telecast was a fake; that's been established," somebody on the left heckled.

"Councilman Salgath's confession on the evening of One-Six-Two Day wasn't a fake," the Management supporter, Nanthav Skov, retorted.

"Well, then why was it necessary to fake the second one?"

A light began winking on the big panel in front of the Speaker, Asthar Varn.

"I recognize Councilman Hasthor Flan," Asthar said.

"I believe I can construct a theory that will explain that," Hasthor Flan said. "I suggest that when the Paratime Police were questioning Councilman Salgath under narco-hypnosis, he made statements incriminating either the Paratime Police as a whole or some member of the Paratime Police whom Tortha Karf had to protect—say somebody like Assistant Verkan. So they just killed him, and made up this impostor—"

Tortha Karf began, alphabetically, to blaspheme every god he had ever heard of. He had only gotten as far as a Fourth Level deity named Allah when a red light began flashing in front of Asthar Varn, and the voice of a page-robot, amplified, roared:

"Point of special urgency! Point of special urgency! It has been requested that the news telecast screen be activated at once, with playback to 1107. An important bulletin has just come in from Nagorabar, Home Time Line, on the Indian subcontinent—"

"You can stop swearing, now, Karf," Dalgroth Sorn grinned. "I think this is it."

Kostran Galth sat on the edge of the couch, with one arm around Zinganna's waist; on the other side of him, Hadron Dalla lay at full length, her elbows propped and her chin in her hands. The screen in front of them showed a fading sunset, although it was only a little past noon at Dhergabar Equivalent. A dark ship was coming slowly in against the red sky; in the center of a wire-fenced compound a hundred-foot conveyer hung on antigrav twenty feet from the ground, and beyond, a long metal prefab-shed was spilling light from open doors and windows.

"That crowd that was just taken in won't be finished for a couple of hours," a voice was saying. "I don't know how much they'll be able to tell; the psychists say they're all telling about the same stories. What those stories are, of course, I'm not able to repeat. After the trouble caused by a certain news commentator who shall be nameless—he's not connected with this news service, I'm happy to say—we're all leaning over backward to keep from breaking Paratime Police security.

"One thing; shortly after the arrival of the second ship from Police Terminal—and believe me, that ship came in just in the nick of time!—the dead Abzar city which the criminals were using as their main base for this time line, and from which they launched the air attack against us, was located, and now word has come in that it is entirely in the hands of the Paratime Police. Personally, I doubt if a great deal of information has been gotten from any prisoners taken there. The lengths to which this Organization went to keep their own people in ignorance is simply unbelievable."

A man appeared for a moment in the lighted doorway of the shed, then stepped outside.

"Look!" Dalla cried. "There's Vall!"

"There's Assistant Verkan, now," the commentator agreed. "Chief's Assistant, would you mind saying a few words, here? I know you're a busy man, sir, but you are also the public hero of Home Time Line, and everybody will be glad if you say something to them—"

Tortha Karf sealed the door of the apartment behind them, then activated one of the robot servants and sent it gliding out of the room for drinks. Verkan Vall took off his belt and holster and laid them aside, then dropped into a deep chair with a sigh of relief. Dalla advanced to the middle of the room and stood looking about in surprised delight.

"Didn't expect this, from the mess outside?" Vall asked. "You know, you really are on the paracops, now. Nobody off the Force knows about this hideout of the Chief's."

"You'd better find a place like this, too," Tortha Karf advised. "From now on, you'll have about as much privacy at that apartment in Turquoise Towers as you'd enjoy on the stage of Dhergabar Opera House."

"Just what is my new position?" Vall asked, hunting his cigarette case out of his tunic. "Duplicate Chief of Paratime Police?"

The robot came back with three tall glasses and a refrigerated decanter on its top. It stopped in front of Tortha Karf and slewed around on its treads; he filled a glass and sent it to the chair where Dalla had seated herself; when she got a drink, she sent it to Vall. Vall sent if back to Tortha Karf, who turned it off.

"No; you have the modifier in the wrong place. You're Chief of Duplicate Paratime Police. You take the setup you have now, and expand it; continue the present lines of investigation, and be ready to exploit anything new that comes up. You won't bother with any of this routine flying-saucer-scare stuff; just handle the Organization business. That'll keep you busy for a long time, I'm afraid."

"I notice you slammed down on the first Council member who began shouting about how you'd wiped out the Great Paratemporal Crime-Ring," Vall said.

"Yes. It isn't wiped out, and it won't be wiped out for a long time. I shall be unspeakably delighted if, when I turn my job over to you, you have it wiped out. And even then, there'll be a loose end to pick up every now and then till you retire."

"We have Council and the Management with us, now," Vall said. "This was the first secret session of Executive Council in over two thousand years. And I thought I'd drop dead when they passed that motion to submit themselves to narco-hypnosis."

"A few Councilmen are going to drop dead before they

can be narco-hypped," Dalla prophesied over the rim of her glass.

"A few have already. I have a list of about a dozen of them who have had fatal accidents or committed suicide, or just died or vanished since the news of your raid broke. Four of them I saw, in the screen, jump up and run out as soon as the news came in, on One-Six-Five Day. And a lot of other people; our friend Yandar Yadd's dropped out of sight, for one. You heard what we got out of those servants of Salgath Trod's?"

"I didn't," Dalla said. "What?"

"Both spies for the Organization. They reported to a woman named Farilla, who ran a fortune-telling parlor in the Prole district. Her occult powers didn't warn her before we sent a squad of plain-clothes men for her. That was an entirely illegal arrest, by the way, but it netted us a list of about three hundred prominent political, business and social persons whose servants have been reporting to her. She thought she was working for a telecast gossipist."

"That's why we have a new butler, darling," Vall interrupted. "Kandagro was reporting on us."

"Who did she pass the reports on to?" Dalla asked.

Tortha Karf beamed. "She thinks more like a cop every time I talk to her," he told Vall. "You better appoint her your Special Assistant.

"Why, about 1800 every day, some Prole would come in, give the recognition sign, and get the day's accumulation. We only got one of them, a fourteen-year-old girl. We're having some trouble getting her deconditioned to a point where she can be hypnotized into talking; by the time we do, they'll have everything closed out, I suppose. What's the latest from Abzar Sector? I missed the last report in the rush to get to this Council session."

"All stalled. We're still boomeranging the sector, but it's about five billion time-lines deep, and the pattern for the Kholghoor and Esaron Sectors doesn't seem to apply. I think they have a lot of these Abzar time lines close together, and they get from one to another via some terminal on Fifth Level."

Tortha Karf nodded. It was impossible to make a transposition of less than ten parayears—a hundred thousand time lines. It was impossible that the field could build and collapse that soon.

"We also think that this Abzar time line was only used for the Croutha-Wizard Trader operation. Nothing we found there was more than a couple of months old; nothing since the last rainy season in India, for instance. Everything was cleaned out on Skordran Kirv's end."

"Tell him to try the Mississippi, Missouri and Ohio Valleys," Tortha Karf said. "A lot of those slaves are sure to have been sold to Second Level Khiftan Sector."

"Well, it looks as though our vacation's out the window for a long time," Dalla said resignedly.

"Why don't you and Vall go to my farm, on Fifth Level Sicily," Tortha Karf suggested. "I own the whole island, on that time line, and you can always be reached in a hurry if anything comes up."

"We could have as much fun there as on the Dwarma Sector," Dalla said. "Chief, could we take a couple of friends along?"

"Well, who?"

"Zinganna and Kostran Galth," she replied. "They've gotten interested in one another; they're talking about a tentative marriage."

"It'll have to be mighty tentative," Vall said. "Kostran Galth can't marry a Prole."

"She won't be a Prole very long. I'm going to adopt her as my sister."

Tortha Karf looked at her sharply. "You sure you know what you're doing, Dalla?" he asked.

"Of course I'm sure. I know that girl better than she knows herself. I narco-hypped her, remember. Zinna's the kind of a sister I've always wished I'd had."

"Well, that's all right then. But about this marriage. She was in love with Salgath Trod," Tortha Karf said. "Now, she's identifying Agent Kostran with him—"

"She was in love with the kind of man Salgath could have been if he hadn't gotten into this Organization filth," Dalla replied. "Galth is that kind of a man. They'll get along all right."

"Well, she'll qualify on IQ and general psych rating for Citizenship. I'll say that. And she's the kind of girl I like to see my boys take up with. Like you, Dalla. Yes, of course; take them along with you. Sicily's big enough that two couples won't get in each others' way."

A phone-robot, its slender metal stem topped by a metal globe, slid into the room on its ball-rollers, moving falteringly, like a blind man. It could sense Tortha Karf's electro-encephalic wave-patterns, but it was having trouble locating the source. They all sat motionless, waiting; finally it came over to Tortha Karf's chair and stopped. He unhooked the phone and held a lengthy whispered conversation with somebody before replacing it.

"Now, there," he explained to Dalla. "That's a sample of why we have to set up this duplicate organization. Revolution just broke out at Ftanna, on Third Level Tsorshay Sector; a lot of our people, mostly tourists and students, are cut off from their conveyers by street fighting. Going to be a pretty bloody business getting them out." He finished his drink and got to his feet. "Sit still; I just have to make a few screen-calls. Send the robot for something to eat, Vall. I'll be right back."

ABOUT THE AUTHORS

Poul Anderson (1926–2001) was one of the most prolific and popular writers in science fiction. He won the Hugo Award seven times and the Nebula Award three times, as well as many other awards, notably including the Grand Master Award of the Science Fiction Writers of America for a lifetime of distinguished achievement. With a degree in physics and a wide knowledge of other fields of science, he was noted for building stories on a solid foundation of real science, as well as for being one of the most skilled creators of fast-paced adventure stories. He was author of more than one hundred science fiction and fantasy novels and story collections, and several hundred short stories, as well as historical novels, mysteries, and non-fiction books. He wrote several series, notably the Technic Civilization novels and stories, the Psychotechnic League series, the Harvest of Stars novels, and his Time Patrol series. In my not-all-that-humble opinion, all novels and stories in his gigantic opus are worth seeking out, but then, they were written by Poul Anderson, so that really goes without saying.

Hank Davis (b. 1944) is originally from Kentucky, wasted far too much time in New York, and has been a sometimes-spectral presence at Baen Books for more than three decades. He has never quite shaken off the life-changing event of reading A.E. Van Vogt's *Slan* while in the second grade, leading to his reading every bit of SF he could get his hands on during his portion of the twentieth century, along with watching a lot of TV shows and movies, many of them pretty bad. However, the twenty-first century has mostly been disappointing (even with better movies and TV shows). For example, he sold a story to Harlan Ellison in 1969, shortly before being shipped off to Vietnam to help the 101st Airborne Division lose the war, under LBJ's ineptitude, and recently learned, over half a century later, that it will not be published in *The Last Dangerous Visions*. More successfully, he has had stories published in the magazines *If*, *Analog*, *The Magazine of Fantasy & Science Fiction*, and *Bluegrass Woman*, as well as *Orbit 11* and a few other original anthologies (but not in *TLDV*). He is currently vegetating in North Carolina and, as an advanced glaucoma case, listens to e-texts and wishes that even if the disappointing twenty-first century doesn't have flying cars, it could at the very least have brought forth cars that drive themselves by now.

T.R. Fehrenbach (1925–2013) was a noted historian, and at one time headed the Texas Historical Commission. After his death, the Commission established the T.R. Fehrenbach Award for notable books about Texas. His most popular and enduring work was *Lone Star*, an authoritative history of his native state. Born in San Benito, Texas, he served during

World War II in the U.S. Infantry, and later served in the Korean War. In between, he graduated from Princeton in 1947. He published more than twenty books, including *U.S. Marines in Action*, *The Battle of Anzio*, and *This Kind of War* (about the Korean War). He sold numerous pieces to such publications as *The Saturday Evening Post*, *Esquire*, *The Atlantic*, *The New Republic*, and other magazines, as well as writing a newspaper column. *Analog* editor John W. Campbell obviously thought highly of Fehrenbach's "Remember the Alamo" and reprinted it in *Analog I*, the first of a series of anthologies reprinting stories from that magazine. About thirty years later, when another anthology reprinted the story, a reviewer in *Locus* was outraged and poured scorn on the piece. Its inclusion here will probably again upset the sort of people who deserve to be upset, and I (Hank) look forward to it.

Edmond Hamilton (1904–1977) was one of the most prolific contributors to *Weird Tales*, which published 79 of his stories between 1926 and 1948. Unusually for a *WT* mainstay, most of his work was science fiction (or, as the magazine tagged it initially, "weird-scientific stories") rather than fantasy, dark or otherwise. He was also prolific outside the pages of *WT*, with stories in many other pulps, sometimes under pseudonyms. In the late 1940s, as interest in rip-roaring adventure SF waned, Hamilton developed a more serious style, with deeper characterizations, notably in "What's It Like Out There?" (included in Baen's *Space Pioneers*) and his 1960 novel, *The Haunted Stars*.

During the 1950s, he was also a prolific scripter for such D.C. comic books as *The Legion of Super-Heroes*.

He continued writing into the 1970s, with stories in the SF magazines and new novels in paperback. He was a writer's writer, with a gift for exciting tales of adventure. Some critics may have felt that such tales were insignificant, but that was—and is—their loss. Readers should be grateful for such a good and prolific writer and "Comrades of Time," demonstrates that in spades.

Robert A. Heinlein (1907–1988) began his career with a competently told, but not very striking story, "Lifeline," which gave no clue that it was the first installment of the grandest saga in the history of science fiction, his "Future History" series, but soon, more substantial and vitamin-packed landmark yarns followed in those magical years when new Heinlein stories were regularly appearing in John W. Campbell, Jr.'s *Astounding*, making it known to all what untapped potential the SF field was capable of reaching. Sometimes, there would even be more than one Heinlein story in an issue, though the originator of some of those masterpieces would be concealed under pseudonym such as Anson MacDonald and John Riverside. (True, John Riverside's byline appeared only once, in Campbell's other classic pulp, *Unknown Worlds*, rather than *Astounding*, but as long as Heinlein and Campbell were remaking the shape of science fiction, fantasy had it coming, too.)

Alas, it was much too soon to take a long pause, but, thanks to Hitler, Mussolini, and the Japanese warlords, it was utterly necessary. Heinlein's incandescent writing career had to cool down while Heinlein and several million others around the globe pitched in to put Hitler and his pals out of business. Heinlein's career resumed after the war's end, and the next four decades brought the classic juvenile novels, the sales to high-paying "slick" magazines, the trailblazing movie *Destination Moon*, the *New York Times* bestsellers, and more. This is, of course, an inadequate introduction to a Heinlein yarn; but, then, aren't they all?

Jacob Holo's story, "Doctor Quiet," relates a small episode in the sprawling and far-ranging time war that Holo and co-author David Weber have conceived and depicted in the best-selling novel *The Gordian Protocol*, and its recent best-selling sequel, *The Valkyrie Protocol* (both from Baen). Between novels, Jacob enjoys gaming of all sorts, whether video gaming, card gaming, miniature wargaming, or watching speed runs on YouTube. He is a former-Ohioan, former-Michigander who now lives in sunny South Carolina with his wife/boss H.P. and his cat/boss Nova.

Robert Anson Hoyt grew up in the comforting shadow of the Rocky Mountains with a namesake that—let's be honest—nobody could live up to. Still, he has not been completely idle. A writer since the age of eight, he both completed his first novel and made his first professional short story sale in middle school. Today his short stories can be found in a number of anthologies, and his first novel, *Cat's Paw*, as well as its prequel novella, *Ratskiller*, can be found on Amazon. (He also enjoys utterly shameless plugs.) Despite a demanding professional life, he is continuing to work on both novels and short stories as often as he is able.

Although he's been called far from where he was raised, his roots will always reach back deep into the mountain foothills. But as for home—home is, and always will be, wherever his loving wife is there to greet him when he gets home from a long day; wherever a cat stands ready to grudgingly accept pets after snubbing him properly for leaving; wherever his two thousand, six hundred and fourteen little side projects rest just one crucial step from completion. His fondest hope is that when you read his stories you find them fun—at least as much fun as they are to write.

Sarah A. Hoyt won the Prometheus Award for her novel *Darkship Thieves*, the first in a series of novels which so far includes *Darkship Renegades* (a Prometheus Award finalist), *A Few Good Men*, *Through Fire* and *Darkship Revenge* (the last two being Prometheus Award finalists). Her collaborative novel with Kevin J. Anderson, *Uncharted*, won the Dragon Award for Best Alternate History Novel. Her first novel, *Ill Met by Moonlight*, was a finalist for the Locus and Mythopoeic Awards in its year. Her latest bestseller is *Monster Hunter International: Guardian*, a collaborative novel with Larry Correia set in his *New York Times* best-selling series. In fantasy, her popular shape shifter series so far includes *Draw One in the Dark*, *Gentleman Takes a Chance*, and *Noah's Boy*. Her short fiction has been published—among other places—in *Analog*, *Asimov's*, and *Amazing Stories*. She has written numerous short stories and novels in science fiction, fantasy, mystery, historical fiction and genre-straddling historical mysteries, many under a number of pseudonyms, and once stated, "No genre is safe from me." She has a strong online presence, with an impressive number of novels and story collections available as e-books, and her *According to Hoyt* is one of the most outspoken and fascinating blogs on the internet, as is her Facebook group "Sarah's Diner." Originally from Portugal, she lives the U.S.A. with her husband and "the surfeit of cats necessary to a die-hard Heinlein fan."

Keith Laumer (1925–1993) was born in Syracuse, NY, and raised in Buffalo, NY, and Florida. He served as a captain in the U.S. Air Force, and later as a Foreign Service Officer in the U.S. Foreign Service, in posts all over the world. This gave him a solid background both for his fast-moving adventure stories and his satirical comedies of Retief, the galaxy's only two-fisted diplomat, who deftly and repeatedly saved both the skins of beleaguered human colonists and the careers of his bungling superiors in a popular series that spanned four decades. Almost as popular were his stories of the Bolos, gigantic robot tanks who serve valiantly throughout the galaxy, guarding humans who are often far less noble than their cybernetic defenders. He was renowned as one of the top writers of science fiction adventure and several of his novels and stories were finalists for the Hugo and Nebula awards.

Fritz Leiber (1910–1992) began his writing career in a 1939 issue of the now-legendary fantasy magazine *Unknown*, with "Two Sought Adventure," which introduced his popular and enduring characters, Fafhrd and the Gray Mouser. The pair of itinerant swordsmen and thieves would return in a host of short stories, novellas, and novels, marking a high point in the fantasy subgenre of sword and sorcery, a term that Leiber coined. He may be best remembered for the Mouser and Fafhrd yarns, but he was equally adept at horror fiction, and often appeared in another classic fantasy magazine, *Weird Tales*. And of course, he was a master of science fiction. In 1981, the Science Fiction Writers of America made it official, naming him a SFWA Grand Master. His many other honors include being the guest of honor at the 1951 and 1979 World SF Conventions and a total of six Hugo Awards, two Nebula Awards, and three World Fantasy Awards—one of them for lifetime achievement. The Horror Writers Association also recognized his importance to their field, presenting him in 1988 with their Bram Stoker Award for lifetime achievement. In 2001, he was inducted into the Science Fiction Hall of Fame. More could be cited, but space is limited, unlike Leiber's talent.

Henry Beam Piper (1901–1964) was a prolific writer of science fiction from the late 1940s until the early sixties when he committed suicide. While he apparently had a number of reasons for checking out, one often cited is that he thought he was a failure as a writer. In fact, the reality was that he had an incompetent agent who had not notified Piper of a number of sales, nor sent along the proceeds before he suddenly died. (Note to beginning writers, choose an agent who is both competent and healthy!) The irony here is deafening, since his works proved very popular in the years after his death, with numerous paperback editions, and other writers continuing his series, including his Federation series, of which the "Fuzzy" stories about small but intelligent furry aliens have been a strikingly popular offshoot, and, in particular for this anthology, Piper's "paratime" stories, in which one of a number of parallel timelines has invented the technology to travel between the adjacent universes, and exploits their resources in a benign but secret way. Piper's own short stories in the series have been collected in the book *Paratime*, and the novel *Lord Kalvan of Otherwhen* was posthumously published. Piper was a student of history and a gun collector who put his knowledge to good use in his fiction. And as another person given the unfortunate name of "Henry," I envy him the use of that more striking single initial.

Christopher Ruocchio is the internationally award-winning author of the Sun Eater, a series blending elements of both science fiction and fantasy, as well as more than twenty works of short fiction. A graduate of North Carolina State University, he sold his first novel, *Empire of Silence*, at 22, and his books have appeared in 5 languages. He curated 8 short story anthologies for Baen Books, including *Sword & Planet*, *Time Troopers*, and *Worlds Long Lost*. His work has also appeared in Marvel Comics. Christopher lives in Raleigh, North Carolina with his family.

Robert Silverberg, prolific author not just of SF, but of authoritative nonfiction books, columnist for *Asimov's SF Magazine*, winner of a constellation of awards, and renowned bon vivant surely needs no introduction—but that's never stopped me before. Born in 1935, Robert Silverberg sold his first SF story, "Gorgon Planet," before he was out of his teens, to the British magazine *Nebula*. Two years later, his first SF novel, a juvenile, *Revolt on Alpha C* followed. Decades later, his total SF titles, according to his semi-official website, stands at 82 SF novels and 457 short stories. Early on, he won a Hugo Award for most promising new writer—rarely have the Hugo voters been so perceptive.

Toward the end of the 1960s and continuing into the 1970s, he wrote a string of novels much darker in tone and deeper in characterization than his work of the 1950s, such as the novels *Nightwings*, *Dying Inside*, *The Book of Skulls*, and many other novels. He took occasional sabbaticals from writing to later return with new works, such as the Majipoor series. His most recent novels include *The Alien Years*, *The Longest Way Home*, and a new trilogy of Majipoor novels. In addition the Science Fiction and Fantasy Hall of Fame inducted him in 1999. In 2004, the Science Fiction Writers of America presented him with the Damon Knight Memorial Grand Master Award. For more information see his "quasi-official" website at www.majipoor.com heroically maintained by Jon Davis (no relation).

Alfred Elton Van Vogt (1912–2000) was a roaring success as a science fiction writer, being one of the earliest to have novels and story collections published by major publishers in the postwar era, while Asimov's first books, for example, came from fan presses, such as Gnome Press. His books stayed in print in paperback, and omnibus editions. He was the very model of a successful SF writer, you might say, and that seemed odd since he was one of the most attacked writers by notable SF critics, Damon Knight in particular, but also by such major writer-critics as Algis Budrys and Frederik Pohl (though Pohl's adverse opinion didn't keep him from publishing Van Vogt's stories in the magazines he edited in the 1960s). Van Vogt's targeting by critics might have led him to echo the prize fight promoter's remark, "I cry all the way to the bank," except that he also had his defenders, including such critics as David Hartwell and Leslie Fiedler, and such highly praised writers as Philip K. Dick, Barry Malzberg, and Harlan Ellison. And then there was France, where Van Vogt was even more popular in French than in English, and French critics considered him one of the leading surrealists of the twentieth century. In any case, Van Vogt remained in print, and obviously pleased the only critics who really matter, the readers, and this reader in particular, with such novels as *The Voyage of the Space Beagle*, and *The Weapon Shops of Isher* and its sequel *The Weapon Makers*, *Empire of the Atom* and its sequel, *The Wizard of Linn*, with its unforgettable image of spaceships that barbarian hordes use to transport horse cavalry to other planets, *The Book of Ptath*, *The Mind Cage*, *The War Against the Rull*, *The Pawns of Null-A* (which I much prefer to its predecessor, *The World of Null-A*), and many more novels, plus such shorter works as "Recruiting Station," "The Vault of the Beast," "Asylum," "The Monster," "Dear Pen Pal," "Enchanted Village," "The Search," "Far Centaurus," and I'd better stop there, though I will further note that reading Van Vogt's great novel *Slan* when I was in the second grade made me a permanent SF addict. Thank you, sir, wherever you are.

Gene Wolfe (1931–2019) was one of, if not the most critically praised and award-winningest writers in science fiction and fantasy (if he saw a difference; he was once quoted as saying that "All novels are fantasies. Some are more honest about it."). He received two Nebula Awards, four World Fantasy Awards, a John W. Campbell Memorial Award, an August Derleth Award, a British SF Association Award, a Rhysling Award, seven Locus Awards, and was nominated for a Hugo Award eight times, but with no wins, which is . . . interesting . . . in view of some of the specimens of thin gruel that have won that tarnished rocket lately. And when it comes to lifetime achievement, he has received the World Fantasy Award and the Science Fiction Writers of America's award for just that. In 2007, he was inducted into the Science Fiction Hall of Fame. All that, and, according to Wikipedia, in his other life as an engineer, he contributed to the machine used to make Pringle's potato chips. Of such things is immortality made. Ursula K. LeGuin stated, "Wolfe is our Melville." I don't recall his writing about pursuit of great white whales, or even of stubborn scriveners, but if he had, I'm sure it would have been typically brilliant and typically atypical.

John C. Wright has been an attorney, a newspaperman, a technical writer, and, most important (of course), a notable science fiction and fantasy writer. His first novel, *The Golden Age*, was praised by *Publishers Weekly*, whose reviewer wrote that Wright "may be this fledgling century's most important new SF talent." The novel was followed by *The Phoenix Exultant* and *The Golden Transcendence*, to make up the major space opera trilogy The Golden Oecumene, which reads like a collaboration between A.E. Van Vogt and Jack Vance. Speaking of Van Vogt, Wright wrote a powerful continuation (and possible culmination) of that writer's classic Null-A novels, the *Null-A Continuum*, as well as a companion book to another classic, William Hope Hodgson's *The Night Land*, titled *Awake in the Night Land*. His fantasy novel *Orphans of Chaos* was a Nebula Award finalist, and his novel *Somewhither* won the Dragon Award for the best novel of 2016. In 2015, he was nominated for six Hugo awards in both fiction and nonfiction: one short story, one novelette, three novellas, and one nonfiction related work, setting a historical record for the most Hugo Award nominations in a single year. His short fiction has appeared in *The Magazine of Fantasy & Science Fiction*, *Asimov's Science Fiction magazine*, *Absolute Magnitude*, and other publications. For more details on his work, visit http://www.scifiwright.com/. He lives in Virginia with his wife, fellow writer L. Jagi Lamplighter, and their four children.

ADVENTURES OF SCIENCE AND MAGIC IN THE FANTASTIC WORLDS OF
JAMES L. CAMBIAS

"James Cambias will be one of the century's major names in hard science fiction."
—Robert J. Sawyer, Hugo Award-winning author of *Red Planet Blues*

"Fast-paced, pure quill hard science fiction. . . . Cambias delivers adroit plot pivots that keep the suspense coming."
—Gregory Benford, Nebula Award-winning author of *Timescape*

"Cambias has achieved a feat of world-building: an expansive, believable setting with fascinating aliens, compelling mysteries, and a rich sense of history." —*Bookpage*

"Far-flung adventure . . . Cambias offers up an entertaining coming-of-age novel filled with action and surprises. His aliens are suitably non-human in mannerisms, attitudes, and objectives, and his worldbuilding suggests a vast universe ready for further exploration. Readers . . . will find this hits the spot."
—*Publishers Weekly*

ACTION IN THE
GRAND SCIENCE FICTION TRADITION

A Coming-of-Age Story
in the Mode of Robert A. Heinlein

JOHN VAN STRY
Summer's End

TPB: 978-1-9821-9229-7 • $17.00 US / $22.00 CAN

Sometimes a dark past can haunt you. Other times it just may be the only thing keeping you alive.

Fresh out of college with his Ship Engineer 3rd-Class certificate, Dave Walker's only thought is to try and find a berth on a corporate ship plying the trade routes. Instead, he's forced to take the first job he can find and get out of town quick. He ends up on an old tramp freighter running with a minimal crew, plying the routes that the corporations ignore, visiting the kind of places that the folks on Earth pretend don't exist.

Turns out having a stepfather who's a powerful Earth senator that wants you dead can remind you that there is still a lot to learn. But one lesson is coming back hard and with a vengeance: how to be ruthless.

THE GODEL OPERATION

TPB: 978-1-9821-2556-1 • $16.00 US / $22.00 CAN

Daslakh is an AI with a problem. Its favorite human, a young man named Zee, is in love with a woman who never existed—and he will scour the Solar System to find her. But in the Tenth Millennium a billion worlds circle the Sun—everything from terraformed planets to artificial habitats, home to a quadrillion beings.

And don't miss:

ARKAD'S WORLD

HC: 978-1-4814-8370-4 • $24.00 US / $33.00 CAN

Arkad, a young boy struggling to survive on an inhospitable planet, was the only human in his world. Then three more humans arrived from space, seeking a treasure that might free Earth from alien domination. With both his life and the human race at risk, Arkad guides the visitors across the planet, braving a slew of dangers—and betrayals—while searching for the mysterious artifact.

THE INITIATE

HC: 978-1-9821-2435-9 • $25.00 US / $34.00 CAN
PB: 978-1-9821-2533-2 • $8.99 US / $11.99 CAN

If magic users are so powerful, why don't they rule the world? Answer: They do. And one man is going to take them down.